THE VIEW FROM GANYMEDE

A NOVEL BY

E. M. LEANDER

The View from Ganymede

© 2021 E. M. Leander

ISBN (Print): 978-1-09839-001-3
ISBN (eBook): 978-1-09839-002-0

FOR MY FAMILY,
WHO HAS ALWAYS BELIEVED IN ME.

CHAPTER 1

The immensity of Jupiter loomed before her, swirling with sunset hues, bold and luminous against velvety blackness. The eternal red eye seemed to wink at her, its co-conspirator, its new accomplice in the biggest cover-up in human history.

She fought to keep from fidgeting in her chair, which held her in place with a crisscross of canvas straps across the chest. The ship was cold. *Space* was cold, in her limited experience. Her damp curls trickled little beads of freezing water down the back of her neck, but she barely noticed. Nora—along with five other recruits—was headed straight for that massive planet, in a ship that was nothing like the bulky NASA shuttles she'd seen before on TV.

She looked out through the shuttle's front viewing panel. The secret drummed on repeat through her brain, each pulse bringing a flashback from her hurried preparations. She took a deep breath to steady herself, closing her eyes for a moment, counting to ten. There was comfort in the slowing steadiness of her pulse, now nonplussed by the adrenaline coursing through her body. She let the breath out slowly, opening her eyes and once more taking in the impossible view, the first of many impossible sights on this trip. She craned her neck, looking for the next, her new home.

There was a secret base on Ganymede, one of Jupiter's many moons. And she, Nora Clark, of all people, had been selected for admission to the academy there. There was no application process – after all, no one knew about it. It would have saved her a lot of time on college trips and essays if she'd known she was going to end up here. She scratched her neck, where a cold drop of water had tracked, back behind the collar of her uniform and tore her eyes momentarily from the gas planet to gauge her companion's reactions.

Beside her, mouth open and likewise staring at the scene before them, sat Greg. Greg had really grown on her over the past few days, during the physical and psychological evaluations that had taken place before they were all cleared for travel. Man, she was glad *that* was over. It was like what she imagined Marine Boot Camp was like. Her chest still throbbed from attempting the pushups and she had a blister on one toe from the running. She'd thought she'd be cross-eyed forever after studying the flight manuals and physics texts all night. It did not come naturally to her, any of it. She'd been consistently the worst recruit in the bunch, but she'd passed. They all had. The other boys with them were nice enough, she thought, but Greg was as close to being something like a friend as she had ever known. He caught her gaze, and grinned up at her, his mismatched eyes—one blue, and one brown—gleaming in the fluorescent light. His hands were clutching the black straps at his chest, too, squeezing and releasing, squeezing and releasing, and his right knee bounced up and down as he swiveled his neck to look at the orbiting moons. They glittered like enormous gems strung across the galaxy's biggest necklace, reflecting and refracting the distant sunlight into a hundred thousand shards of color. Nora yearned for a bigger viewing panel, regretting that this was no sight-seeing tour they were on. This ship was on a mission, delivering the last of the new recruits to the station.

"Can you believe it, Clark? We're nearly there! Man oh man. Hey, look at that! Do you see that, there? I didn't know Jupiter had rings, did you?" Greg said, his words coming out in a rush, his knee still bobbing.

Nora looked up, her fingers absently tracing the patterned weave of the straps across her shoulders as her hands clenched them. She was unconsciously straining against the straps, forgetting how cold her fingertips were, trying to absorb as much of the scene as she could. The giant planet took up nearly the entire view panel now. It looked like an old-fashioned clear glass marble, filled with eddies of cream and orange smoke, the red eye of the perpetual maelstrom sitting just at the edge of the horizon. She was as surprised as Greg to see the thin set of rings around the planet. They were startlingly beautiful against the whirling backdrop of Jupiter—thin glittering bands of red and pale blue, stark against the backdrop of space. The other boys looked, too, each locked in silent reverie. Benjamin and Wesley and Ty and Benton, each looking like normal high school seniors, each witnessing something that even their remarkable high school careers could not have prepared them for.

They all stared at the rings until their ship banked right, and the planet faded from view. Now there was a smaller grayish moon to their left and another darker one straight ahead of them.

That *had* to be it. It was a craggy brown globe with frosted poles, like icing on a gingerbread sphere, looming ever larger in the view panel. Jupiter's reflected glow cast jagged black shadows across its surface, and dark sulci ran across it like spider webs. It was an eerie-looking place. Nora's mind – drilled hastily but effectively in their prep session on Earth – now automatically identified the largest craters, and what she thought must be the Galileo Region. She looked out over the rocky moon that would be her home for the next four years, her heart pounding as she tried to absorb every single detail. She felt dizzy, and gulped several deep breaths to clear her head.

Ganymede.

Five weeks ago, she had never even heard of it. The only Ganymede she knew was from her mother's old Greek mythology books. She'd avoided them lately, though once they'd loved to flip through the glossy pictures together, and read the outlandish tales. The memory hurt, like a shard of glass lodged in her throat. She swallowed hard. She was an awfully long way from Louisiana and their rusted old stationwagon.

Instead, she was in a sleek black shuttle, a curved thing like a crescent moon or a boomerang, hurtling toward the moon at a speed no NASA ship could ever hope to match. She was heading towards a facility that reminded her of the military colleges back on earth, an organized, contained campus, except for the bizarre location.

Oh, and the aliens.

Memories of her mother receded like the looming mass of Jupiter behind her. Her mind still ached from the computations she and Greg and the others had been tutored in over the previous hours, since they'd been awakened from the cryo tanks. They were traveling at a velocity many-times faster than the clunky old space shuttles, so fast in fact that the entire crew – recruits included – had had to put themselves in a medically-induced coma and surround themselves with inertia-dampening goo so their eyeballs wouldn't fly out of their heads. She'd laughed at this when she first heard it, but it turned out the stoic crewman who'd said it was completely serious.

Her fingers, she noted, were still pruned from the prolonged submersion in the tanks. The blue stuff was still caked under her fingernails and into her scalp, and she picked at it nervously, flaking off bits to fall to the floor like snowflakes in the cool air. Or like really bad dandruff.

Nora, Greg, and the other recruits sat in chairs that were usually folded up into the wall at the back of the bridge. However, given the twenty-foot section of view screen before them, the scene was still spectacular from all the way back there, nearly a 180-degree panoramic, including a hint at the periphery of the sleek, dark wings of the ship, which was affectionately called a PJ, or Puddle Jumper.

"Captain!" a voice said. Nora craned her head around Greg to take a look at the speaker. It was another recruit - Wesley, the teenage genius. She didn't much mind the excuse to look at him. While she felt like the month she'd spent in that skin-tight neoprene suit submerged in the cryo tank (or "coma couches," as Greg called them) had left her hair stringy and skin gray, Wesley looked as handsome as ever, in spite of the accumulation of dark stubble on his cheeks—or maybe because of it. Her gaze flicked past him to Tylajah; he had to have lost at least twenty pounds of his former linebacker bulk. The other recruits – Greg, the blond giant Benton, and the obnoxious redhead named Benjamin - with their varying states of stubble, seemed otherwise unchanged.

"Yes?" the Captain asked. He was a tall, athletic man, seated at a console near the center of the bridge.

"Is that…?" Wesley's question hung in the air. Captain Hale scrolled through something on his console, then nodded.

4

There was no evidence of habitat on the moon. As far as Nora could tell, it was just a lump of brown rock. Where was the station she'd seen, the sparkling white domes that would give her the new beginning she'd been promised? Where was the school, the training facility where she and the other recruits were to start, like freshmen in college, in the most exceptional circumstances imaginable?

The pilot brought the ship into a smooth, sweeping turn. There were four similar consoles staggered around him for the other deck officers. The console screens and their keyboards were clear, all illuminated with glowing green keys and text. Nora's fingers itched to try one out, but their captain had said there wasn't time for proper training. They'd be given log-in information and passwords at their orientation once they arrived. Would they actually let her fly one of these things someday? The brochure said it was one of the many tracks that cadets followed – for someone who'd never driven anything other than her parents' decrepit old car, the idea of flying a spaceship was so unfathomable, it made her giddy.

What would they find here on Ganymede? A little wave of panic hit her—a nervous, jiggly feeling behind her belly button. She'd seen the pictures of the aliens – or at least, the two races they'd have contact with. It reminded her more of the time she'd gone to the beach with her parents, years ago. The feeling of swimming out into the eternal depth, not knowing what was out there. That panic had seized her and almost made her drown. It was precisely how she felt now.

"Hey, breathe, girl," Greg said, looking over at her. Nora hadn't even realized she'd been holding her breath again. She took in a ragged gulp of recycled air and gave him her best attempt at a smile. He reached for her hand. Her fingers were clammy and cold in his, which were warm and slightly damp.

"It's going to be okay," he said, squeezing her hand gently before letting go. He brushed back a strand of his straight brown hair from his eyes. It had grown long and shaggy during their trip.

"Better than okay, even. I mean, we're in freaking space!" he continued.

Nora let out a choked laugh. The ship continued its sweep around Ganymede, Jupiter receding around the back. There was still no sign of the space station.

As she looked at the moon, desperate for a sign of life, Nora finally thought she could see faint pairs of lines tracking across the moon's surface. There was no way those were natural, she realized, sitting up straighter, brushing hair back from her eyes so she could see clearly. Nothing in nature made straight lines like that.

"Ganymede's tidal locked," Captain Hale said. "The same side always faces Jupiter, just like our moon back home. The station is on the middle of that side, the side that will never see Earth. You do get a spectacular view of Jupiter from there, though," he said. The *Santa Maria* completed its turn, and Jupiter left its field of vision.

And then, there it was, sprawling across the pockmarked landscape. Ganymede Station.

It looked like some toddler had been given a collection of toy white domes and cylindrical halls and connected them in some sort of haphazard pattern. An unfurling fern-like hallway here, a zig-zagging one there. Two larger domes side-by-side in the middle, then another way off on the perimeter, and a few smaller ones sprinkled about. Nora couldn't see any rhyme or reason to it.

But it was gorgeous. Beyond gorgeous, even. It was breathtaking.

The thing was, she knew it shouldn't even exist. Seven billion people on Earth would laugh in her face if she told them there was a space station on one of Jupiter's moons. And if asked, the handful of people on the Ganymede Project Board of Directors would deny ever hearing of it.

And yet, here she was. She, Nora Clark, No One Special of Nowhereville. After meeting the other cadets in her group—five boys, all near her age, which was barely eighteen—she had marveled at their differences. The only common thread seemed to be a lack of attachment. They were all loners from a variety of circumstances, orphans mostly. It was what had made them so appealing to the Ganymede Project, they'd been told. In addition, they were also polyglots, or teenage geniuses, or star athletes. They'd all achieved greatness already—in fact, the insufferable Benjamin had once sailed across the entire Atlantic Ocean by himself. Sometimes, during their Boot Camp, she wondered if he hadn't still wished he was out in the ocean, alone, away from the rest of them. Nora still didn't really know where *she* fit in with this crowd. She was an orphan (so recently though the thought of it still felt like a needle stabbing through her breastbone), just like Wesley and Greg and Benjamin, but other than that, she didn't understand her place there. Her legal guardians had been a part of the Ganymede Project Board, so she assumed they'd just shipped her off to Jupiter when the opportunity presented itself, rather than having to deal with her themselves. She nodded along with the other recruits and tried to say as little as possible so they wouldn't know how out-classed she was.

She'd been told the Board of Directors had researched them each carefully and assigned them a focus—something like a college major, she thought—based on their particular aptitudes. Greg—along with Benjamin, Ty, and Benton (whom they'd nicknamed "Wingman" for his impressive arm-span)—was in something called the Officer Track. Wesley would be pre-medical. Nora was in something nebulous called the Science Track. She'd squirmed a bit when they'd told her this. Had they even *looked* at her abysmal school records? She'd done all right in math classes—but chemistry? She'd wondered briefly if the Board would send her back to Earth immediately once her final chemistry exam was graded. Would Principal Hughes be able to transmit her records over four million miles of vacuum? She rather doubted it. The man had barely been able to remember the name of their school's mascot – outer-space transmissions were probably a bit beyond him. She figured that she'd be OK with the whole science-major thing, though, even OK with cleaning all of the beakers for chemistry labs over and over again, if they still let her fly the spaceships. She watched their pilot's fingers fly deftly over the controls, making small movements of a joystick that correlated to sweeping turns and three-dimensional drops. Now *that* looked like fun.

Her scalp itched. She picked off another flake of dried goo and watched a dozen more snow down to settle on the arm of her sweatshirt, un-melting. She dusted them off. Maybe it was a mistake, she thought. Maybe she didn't belong here. She wasn't a genius like Wesley, didn't have the self-confidence and charisma that the others radiated like sunbeams. She was just Nora. A plain girl with no family and no friends, just her legal guardians who had acted more like prison wardens in the few months she'd been in their custody. She desperately wanted to fit in here. She'd never really felt like she fit in anywhere back home – back on Earth, she corrected herself. Up until recently, she'd been worried about college applications and the homecoming dance (she didn't want to go by herself *again*). But now -- she wanted to belong here, wanted to join this elite club of talented people. Wanted to feel like she fit in somewhere. And more than that, she wanted to find out the secrets that Jupiter was keeping. She chewed on a fingernail, contemplating what would happen to her when everyone discovered the truth -

That she was, in a phrase, exceptionally ordinary.

Except for the fact that she was about to set foot in a space station no one knew existed. That much, at least, she had in common with them.

The station was coming into clearer view now as they approached, and this distracted her from her terrifying introspection. She could see that some of the domes had clear glass panes between the massive metal struts, and she could see people walking around inside, like toys in a snow globe. All of the recruits stared, silent. Greg's knees had even stopped their bouncing. She thought she saw sleek black shapes darting into one of the domes, and as they approached, she saw there were even more PJs, swooping like ravens into the gaped opening of a massive white dome. Their pilot turned the ship into a graceful descent and entered that dome – no, a hangar, Nora realized. A thin, glittering veil covered the opening, passing over them like water in a carwash as they entered.

"Field keeps the air in," Captain Hale explained. The recruits were straining against their seatbelts, their necks twisting to take in the gigantic hangar bay they'd entered, a stark white structure filled with dozens of PJs and men and women scurrying about in navy blue overalls.

They'd arrived. They'd made it, after weeks of tests and a month spent in coma couches. They were finally here. Nora looked around, drinking in the sights and sounds, the *whoosh* of the hydraulic rear bay opening, the scurrying of workers outside, and leaned forward so hard that the harness cut into her shoulders, giving her what would turn out to be a nasty rope burn. She barely noticed.

She couldn't wait. It was right there in front of her, all within her grasp.

Space Camp.

CHAPTER 2

The doors of the Puddle Jumper opened wide, and Nora followed the other recruits out into the abrupt whiteness of the landing bay. It was startlingly bright after a month spent in the soft darkness of space. Her eyes watered and she blinked fiercely for a few moments, until the blurring faded and the shapes approaching them became not amorphous blobs, but people.

They were approached by a team of men and women, who - instead of greeting the new recruits - immediately ushered them out of the way so they could see to the ship. Nora envied them, and glanced back admiringly at the ship that had been her home for the past month - the PJ had one level, and the rear half of the ship consisted entirely of the engine room and xenon-ion drive. It had been her little sanctuary for the past month – even if most of that time she'd spent unconscious – and she felt a little nostalgic leaving it behind. The whole ship was about the size of her old high school gym, and nearly as tall, with wide, sweeping wings that gave it an almost crescent shape. The bridge was situated in the smooth curve at the front, and four dark engine exhausts twice as tall as she was projected from the sleek panels at the back. Mechanics now hustled up the loading ramp, which extended between the sets of engines, carrying heavy bags of equipment and sensors to check the ship.

"Nora, come on!" Greg called in a fierce whisper. Nora spun, and chased after her little group, which was almost on the other side of the hangar. Greg looped his arm through hers once she caught up – though for her comfort or his, she wasn't sure.

She and the boys followed Captain Hale down a short round hallway to an air lock made of a clear plastic cylindrical tunnel. They stepped inside. It was a little cramped with all of them together. The smell of coma couch goo still lingered, acrid, in the air, until it was pumped out of the enclosure by some sort of whirring pressurizer—and then the clear door opened on the other side. Nora raised a hand to her damp curls, to see if the goo smell was coming from her. She didn't want the station's first impression of her to be as the girl who was so inept she couldn't even rinse the cryo goo off right. Despite about forty gallons of conditioner, she hadn't felt she'd been able to completely erase the month's worth of electrolyte gel from her hair. Each ringlet seemed to cling to the stuff like it was glue.

She felt like she'd been marinated.

They emerged from the hall into another one of the large domed structures they'd seen from the air, and as the boys passed her she was somewhat relieved to find that they *all* smelled a little goo-like.

Thoughts of blue goo faded as she looked around. They had entered what seemed to be a common area, like a town square, with benches and paths and Astroturf-covered areas with small rolling hills where some cadets in green jumpsuits, or navy uniforms reminiscent of the US military, were tossing around a football. The paths and the dome were white and smooth, lit brightly from some source she couldn't identify. There was a faint scent of freshly-cut grass in the air, a detail that surprised her. Everywhere she looked there were people—talking in pairs, or poring over tablet computers and picnic tables (grained metal, and not wood, she realized- wood must have been phenomenally impractical to transport so far). It could have been any college campus on Earth. Captain Hale told them to wait for their escort and enjoy Ganymede. Then he left, heading toward the far end of the dome.

"Hey, when do you think we'll get to see our first Qaig?" Greg said, swiveling his head around to look.

"Hopefully not for a long time," Wingman said. "You really think you're up to taking on a Qaig on your own, little man?" He reached for Greg, putting the smaller boy in a headlock. A brief scuffle ensued, but Greg's arms and legs were too short to reach the giant Viking who held him.

"I give up," Greg panted at last. Wingman released him, and Greg laughed, attempting to smooth down his unruly hair.

"What about the J'nai, though?" Ty asked. His voice was deep and quiet, but carried like thunder rolling across a New Orleans' bog. They all scanned the room, but there was no evidence of the other alien race. Only Benjamin seemed disinterested, instead affecting a bored, slouched posture.

"Not until the new year, I think," Wesley said. He stood tall, gazing about the dome with an expression of wonder. His voice was distant, dreamlike. "But Dr. Never told me that one of our professors is one." Nora thought of the eccentric man who'd given them their initial lectures about Ganymede. They'd barely believed him at first, that white-haired and disheveled genius, but as he showed them video after video of the station, and the alien beings that inhabited it, they'd quickly come to hang on his every word.

"*Cool*," Benton (though they mostly called him Wingman, to prevent confusing him with Benjamin) said, whistling and scratching his cleft chin appreciatively. It was a gesture he'd done often, Nora noted. "And he said we'll have them in our classes too, right?"

"It'll be just like having exchange students," Greg said, shoving Nora. She grinned, shaken from her reverie about Benton's chin, and pushed him back.

"Yeah. Exactly the same. Intergalactic alien exchange students."

Her heart soared in spite of her sarcasm. This was going to be a good place. She could tell. Her lungs felt swollen with a new sense of direction. She'd been floating—metaphorically but also physically in the zero-G of space—for months, like a jellyfish drifting with the current, listless. It felt good to be here – and not just because it was warmer than the shuttle had been. She felt suffused with wellbeing as well as warmth. A whole new universe of horizons had just been unveiled. All around her, people moved with purpose – poring over tablets, or engaged in quiet conversation. She would find her purpose here, too, she thought. She would -

"Fresh meat!" a girl's harsh voice called, ringing through the dome like a shot. The speaker screeched to a halt next to their little group of recruits riding something that looked like a motorbike - but with crackling blue electricity, like tamed lightning bolts, for wheels. Nora peered around Ty to get a better look at her.

The girl was cool in a way Nora could never be, with long, dark, wavy hair shot through with streaks of bright teal and cobalt. She wore her flight suit unzipped and peeled to the waist with the arms knotted, a tight tank top under it showing off bare arms covered with strange tattoos. She tossed her hair over one shoulder, looking the boys up and down as they examined her and her sizzling bike.

Otherwise, Nora noted, her stomach lurching, despite the tats and the dyed hair, the girl looked *exactly like her.* Like Nora. Not in a "we could be sisters" kind of way but in a "you are my cooler, older, doppelgänger" way.

She had the same face, the same indeterminately-colored eyes, the same fair skin. If it hadn't been for the age difference, Nora would have sworn she was meeting a long-lost twin. Nora fingered her own wayward curls as she stared at the girl. She was so dumbstruck by the similarities between them that her brain could barely process them. Her neurons had had too many impossible things to think about over these past few weeks— space travel being the least of it—to even begin to understand the apparition before her. Instead, all Nora could think about was this girl's hair—how she'd not only tamed the mane that Nora had long given up on but also managed to make it look *cool.* And Nora would *never* have the guts to dye her hair - especially in those startling shades of blue.

Her hair was her defining feature, she'd always thought. She wasn't particularly tall or short, not fat or thin (though leaning toward flabby, if she had to be honest). Her eyes weren't brown or hazel but an unremarkable in-between. She had to wear sunscreen and a baseball hat almost every day to keep her skin from burning, which only made her hair stick out worse. Once she realized she'd never be a tanned, willowy blonde but instead she'd be that weird pale kid with the wild mane of hair, she'd stopped caring much at all about her appearance.

Standing before this girl, though, she started to wish she'd cared a bit more. She felt shabby—young and naïve and awkward, like a new kid at school all over again. She pulled her sweatshirt sleeves over her hands, the fingertips gone suddenly cold despite the warmth here. The peaceful, optimistic feeling that had been suffusing through her system had evaporated. She could practically see the goo fumes radiating off her body, marking her as a neophyte.

"Well, welcome to Space Camp," the girl purred, looking the cadets over. Ty crossed his arms, acutely disconcerted by the appearance of this "new Nora" but as silent as ever. Greg did a rapid double take, then triple take, stepping back from Nora, his mouth gaping as he was—for once—at a loss for words.

When the girl finally caught sight of her, her eyes widened a little, and her lips curled up in a feline sneer. Nora exchanged a look with Greg; his mismatched eyes were so wide, she could see the whites all the way around them.

"Well, it's about time we got another one around here," the girl grumbled. She dismounted from the bike and flicked a switch near the handlebars. The electric wheels vanished, and the whole thing folded into a compact metal rectangle a little bigger than a textbook. She hefted it on her hip and strode over to them. She was a few inches taller than Nora, and leaner, with a hard sort of edge.

Nora gulped and looked up at her.

"Another what?" she said.

Wingman and Benny crossed their arms behind her, no doubt wondering if they had long-lost twins as well. What was going on?

"I'm Thalia," the girl said, extending a hand. Nora slipped her hands out of the shirt sleeves and took it, hoping Thalia wouldn't feel the sweat that had broken out on her palm. Thalia stepped back, one hand on her hip, appraising Nora with a long look from head to toe—and apparently finding her lacking in some regard. She cocked a perfectly-sculpted eyebrow, clearly waiting for a reply.

"I'm Eleanora. Nora, I mean," Nora said, trying to fight back the embarrassed flush creeping into her cheeks. Why couldn't she even say her name right? The feeling of awe and excitement that had flooded her upon entering the station receded fast, replaced by the sensation of bile in her throat, and sweat on her forehead.

"*Alien*-ora?" Thalia said. She threw her head back and laughed, making everyone in the dome stop what they were doing to stare. "I finally get a Mini Me on this rock and her name is *Alien*-ora?"

What *was* it about her that made everyone she ever met automatically use that nickname? Her name wasn't so hard to pronounce, but the other one had stuck on her like superglue from the time she'd been in kindergarten, following her from Earth into space.

"It's *Nora*," she growled, hitching her bag up higher on her shoulder. "And I'm nothing like you."

"You're exactly like me, darling," Thalia said, in a matter-of-fact manner. When Nora didn't respond, Thalia looked her over again, an incredulous expression emerging on her face.

"You really don't know who you are, do you?"

"I'm Nora Clark, from Louisiana," Nora said, but her voice cracked a bit. Why did that feel so hard to say, as if suddenly she wasn't even sure of *that* fact anymore? She could feel the pulse of blood in her face now, a sure sign she was turning bright red, belying the affected bravado in her words. Her mother had always said she was easy to read. Nora's backpack slid, unnoticed, from her shoulder to the ground.

"Oh, dear, you are a naïve little lamb," Thalia said with a laugh and patted Nora on the head. "Don't you worry, little Hypatia, you'll get caught up soon enough." She flipped her bike out again and mounted it. With a wave and a wink at the boys, she tore off across the dome, her wheels leaving a trail of blue sparks behind her.

"What did she call me?" Nora asked, addressing no one in particular. And no one answered. Had it been some sort of slang, something offensive maybe? Some Space Camp lingo? The boys behind her – so chatty over the previous days – were silent, exchanging awkward glances. Greg looked at her only briefly before averting those mismatched eyes, suddenly finding a scuff mark on the floor exceedingly interesting. Her throat felt tight, and her head was spinning – who *was* that girl? Did she have a relative out in the world she hadn't known about? Thalia was cool, no doubt about it – but something about her manner made Nora feel about an inch tall and as awkward as a preteen again. She doubted she and Thalia could become best friends, even if they *were* related. She wished Greg would look at her. She could use a reassuring smile, or one of his easy jokes. None came.

"Gents, if you'll come with me?" a British voice called, breaking through their thoughtful silence. The voice belonged to a lanky boy dressed in a navy uniform. He gestured for them to follow him from the dome.

"We've a lady with us, too," Greg corrected, and finally gave Nora a little half-smile of encouragement. He seemed to have recovered his composure somewhat. Nora shook her head to likewise clear the tumult of the unexpected encounter with Thalia from her thoughts, and picked up her backpack.

"Oh no, you're to wait here for Nancy. She'll be along in a minute," the boy said, holding up a hand to stop her. "Now come on, you lot. We haven't got all day."

"That was weird, huh?" Greg said, putting a hand on her shoulder.

"Way weird," Nora agreed. She wanted him to stay with her, and realizing that bothered her. Still, she didn't want to be left alone in this strange place. What if Thalia came back? She looked up at Greg, at those strange yet oddly comforting eyes. He opened his mouth to say something once, twice, before clearing his throat and starting again -

"Hey look, if you…"

"Any day now, recruit," the boy called. The others were waiting for Greg to catch up, Benjamin frowning so hard, he looked almost like a cartoon caricature of himself. Wesley was waving at them, gesturing for Greg to hurry.

"Aww, man. Look, I gotta go…," Greg said. He rubbed the back of his neck with one hand, glancing at the other boys and then back to her, an apologetic grin on his face.

"Go," Nora said, pushing him off. She gave him her best reassuring smile, but inside she was still shaking. She'd been alone before. It wasn't like this was any different. Bullies were bullies no matter what planet you were on. She'd just keep her head down and wait until this Nancy person came to get her, and hope it happened before Thalia showed up again.

"Go. Don't want you to be late and make a bad first impression," she said, shooing him with her hand.

"I need all the help I can get," he said, and they both giggled a little at that, a cut-off sort of sound.

"I'll find you later," Greg promised, then shouldered his duffle bag. "And hey, don't let her get to you. You're a million times the girl she is."

"Liar," she said, but she grinned all the same. She watched his retreating figure, watched all the people she knew there—though to be fair, they had all been unconscious for most of their time together—turn into a hall leading from the dome. Greg and Ty looked back once, waved in unison, and then disappeared.

And then she was alone. Again.

A mix of excitement, awe, and more than a little self-pity washed over her. She looked around the dome, at the cadets and older officers strolling and talking and laughing. She wrapped her arms around herself, hugging her elbows, and waited.

▰ ▰ ▰

It was never easy being the new kid in town—and she'd done it enough times now to be an expert. If there was one thing Nora Clark excelled at, it was bland introductions. And soon after, she lost her novelty, and the other kids—hopefully, Thalia this time—would leave her alone. It had happened more times than she could count. This place would be no different, she thought, pacing the area by the hangar bay door. Up until a few weeks ago, she'd expected her next move to be from the swamplands of Louisiana (which she'd developed a certain fondness for over the past year, for the humid wildness of it, for the Spanish moss and the twisted oak trees and even for the havoc the perpetual dampness wreaked on her hair) to Podunk, Minnesota, home of the World's Largest Ear of Corn. She'd audibly groaned when she'd discovered that she'd soon be living in the same town as *that* prestigious artifact. It was also going to be the first move she went through in the company of her legal guardians, the first move since her parents …

All in all, she decided, squaring up her shoulders, Ganymede was already a significant improvement, Thalia or no.

So where *was* this Nancy person, Nora wondered for the thousandth time in the five-or-so minutes that had passed. She glanced around the dome, looking for anyone who might be looking for her. She was largely ignored. A few people glanced up briefly at her - if only to avoid colliding when they passed – but otherwise, they all continued about their own business, as if a lost new recruit was nothing of interest. She was somewhat grateful to be ignored. It beat being taunted.

As if on cue, Thalia came roaring out of one of the halls into the dome like an electrified dervish, nearly running over a couple holding hands by the wall, and then careening off a lamppost.

"Watch it!" she shouted, speeding down the path. As Nora looked on—and it was hard to say exactly what happened—Thalia appeared to veer a little towards a small, pale girl as she passed. The girl toppled, spilling something metallic from a large glass container. Thalia sped on.

Nobody stopped to help. Everyone just kept walking. A few shot glances at the girl, who struggled to pick up the spilled contents of her glass, but no one stopped. Nora wondered if that girl felt as alone as she did right then.

Nora grabbed her backpack, put it on, and walked over to her.

"Uh, hi," she said as she approached. The girl jumped, her wide brown eyes and startled stance reminding Nora of a fawn, or a kitten – an effect of the massive coke-bottle glasses she wore too, no doubt. She pushed a halo of frizzy hair back from her face.

"Must have tripped. Wasn't watching where I was going," she mumbled, eyes once more downcast. The glass container looked like a large Mason jar, the kind you'd pour sweet tea into on a hot summer day.

The items that spilled, however, were not as familiar. They looked like polished steel balls, the size of marbles, but moved about oddly on the floor. They seemed magnetic; some bunched in pairs or clusters, rolling along the pathway, but others repelled one another. The result was like chasing chickens through a yard, Nora thought, as she helped the girl collect the strange objects.

"You didn't trip," Nora said. She frowned and scooped up a couple of the smooth, cool spheres. "Thalia nearly ran you over."

"I'm just such a klutz," the girl continued, as if she hadn't heard Nora at all. "Happens all the time."

"HEY!" a voice shouted. It ricocheted off the walls like a shot. Nora looked up, nearly dropping the spheres and struggling with their magnetic repulsion as she stood. A strikingly pretty girl with narrowed green eyes was storming over to them. Her long black hair billowed around her face like a thundercloud.

"What do you think you're doing?" she barked, hands on hips as she came to a halt a few inches from Nora's face. Nora took a step back and held out the handful of metal.

"Uh, she dropped these," Nora said, glancing down at the pale girl.

"Oh, let me guess. She just happened to 'trip' and drop them all again, right?" the girl said, nearly shouting. "I swear to *God*, Cat, you've got to start standing up for yourself! People like *this* think they can just walk all over you. I swear, your kind are even worse than the Originals…" she said, jabbing her index finger at Nora.

"No, Thalia…" Nora tried, still struggling to hold the spheres.

"Oh, all you Hypatias are the same, aren't you? Just bully people around and—"

"Sophie, she's helping me," the pale girl said. She clutched the Mason jar to her chest with both arms like a shield. The other girl—Sophie—blinked.

"What?"

"*I* dropped the spheres. The Hypatia stopped to help me," she said, her voice trembling. Sophie raised one perfectly arched eyebrow and looked Nora over.

"Really," she said. It wasn't a question. Nora nodded emphatically. She was under the impression that this Sophie was not someone whose bad side she wanted to be on.

"Clark?" a voice called. Nora whipped around. The voice belonged to a girl with blond hair cut short who couldn't have been more than a year or two older than she was. She wore her uniform stiffly, as if it were overly starched, and had a disinterested look on her face.

"You're with me. Can't keep the dean waiting." The girl—was this Nancy, at last?—turned and started walking away, her patent leather shoes clicking against the polished floor. Nora dropped her handful of metal into the pale girl's jar and mumbled an apology. Sophie crossed her arms, apparently still making up her mind as to whether Nora was telling the truth. She was watching thoughtfully Nora as she fled.

Why did Sophie dislike her immediately? Did it have something to do with her resemblance to Thalia? Nora turned, and saw Nancy's blond head going into a side hallway. Terrified the girl would disappear and leave without her, Nora sprinted across the dome, leaving Sophie and Cat behind.

CHAPTER 3

"Hey!" Nora called, jogging after Nancy, her bag thumping against her shoulder blades. She turned once to see Sophie and the other girl talking softly, gathering up the rest of the spilled objects together, before she went into the side hallway and her view was blocked. She nearly ran into Nancy as the girl turned back around, and Nora had to grab the wall to keep from toppling over.

Nora wondered about the girls she'd met in the dome and how Sophie had instantly disliked her, calling her by that strange word again: Hypatia. She'd never heard the term before today; she was certain of it. It sounded exotic, though Sophie had spat it out with a sort of disgust. Thalia, too, had made it sound belittling. So what *did* it mean?

"I know this must all seem real confusing," the girl said with what Nora recognized as a Boston accent, oblivious to Nora's discomfort. "I heard about you. Don't worry, we're taking you right to Dean Prasad. She'll get you all sorted out."

"The dean?"

"Oh, don't worry. You haven't done anything wrong. We just need to get you caught up a bit. Most of *them* had time to prepare, you know."

She walked quickly, and Nora struggled to keep up. She strode down one side hall, and then another.

"Prepare? Prepare for what? And who is 'them'?" Nora panted.

"Yeah, I'm going to leave that for Dr. Prasad. Don't worry, she's got your file, knows all about your aptitude for science, and will get you in the right classes." Her accent dragged the Dean's name out to nearly three syllables – *Prah-sa-ahd.*

"I think someone's been seriously misinformed," Nora said, rubbing the back of her neck. Why did everyone keep thinking she was some kind of science prodigy?

High school was tough for everyone, her mother had said, but it had seemed to be exceptionally hard for *Alien*-ora. Her parents had high expectations of her academic performance; she imagined they hoped she'd be a lawyer or astronaut or executive something someday. She always felt like she let them down. Her report cards were less than stellar. She was often written up or put in detention for reading during class or failing to turn in assignments (mostly because she found them boring). It had earned her a reputation among her teachers, all of whom felt she had this nebulous "hidden potential," that she was a caterpillar waiting to emerge from a cocoon—blah blah blah—if she would just apply herself. Her mother, in particular, had a favorite phrase she repeated so often that Nora could still hear it echoing through her mind.

*Once you find something worth fighting
for, you can change the stars.*

It was her way of telling Nora that if she applied herself, if she could find the motivation and had the right nudge, she could accomplish anything—even pass chemistry. Her eyes burned a little at the thought of her mother. She found her vision suddenly hazy, and blinked several times to clear it so she wouldn't lose sight of her terse companion.

Nancy kept walking at a rapid pace, and the crowds they passed readily parted for her. Then she stopped so abruptly before a metal door that Nora nearly ran into her again. Nancy scowled at her, then rang a button by a plaque that read, "Dean, Doctor Aditi Prasad, Student Relations."

The doors parted after a moment to reveal a cozy office, decorated in warm maroon and gold against the otherwise ubiquitous gray and white metal. A trim Indian woman stood from behind a desk to greet them.

"Aditi Prasad," the woman said, smiling. She shook Nora's hand and ushered her into the room, taking her bag and setting it aside as she did so. Her desk was spotless, with an assortment of eccentric knickknacks – a vase of feathers, a painted rock, a miniature lava lamp. Nora was shown to a cushioned chair, and the woman sat opposite her, a tablet computer in hand. Nora looked back over her shoulder, but the doors were closed and Nancy was gone. She swallowed hard, and looked at the dean, who gazed back at her with bird-bright eyes.

"So, you're Dr. ..."

"Aditi, please. At least in here. When we're out there, you may have to call me Dr. Prasad though," she confided, nodding toward the door. Aditi was a petite woman in a navy uniform jacket over a skirt and heels. She exuded a sense of warmth and calmness, reflected in her office by the soft lights and mellow décor that included a potted orchid, amongst her other odd collections. In space. Nora wondered at the ordinariness of the plant – how had something so terrestrial gotten all the way out here? Although, she thought with another hard swallow, maybe the same could be said about her.

"Okay," Nora said. Being here was a bit like sitting in the principal's office—something she'd done time and time again—even if it resembled a spa this time. Though Aditi's insistence on using her first name reminded Nora of the therapist her school had forced her to see.

"So, Nora. Nickname for Eleanora," Aditi said, opening a file on her tablet. She leaned back, relaxing, her legs crossed at the knee. "Beautiful name. I believe it's Latin, isn't it?"

"I don't know," Nora said. "It was a family name." Her voice faltered at the memory of her parents.

"Yes," Aditi said crisply, though her eyes seemed a little sad, and her lips twitched downwards. She put the tablet down on her desk with a small sigh. "I was ever so sorry to hear of their deaths. We were friends, once. A long time ago…" She stopped, pursed her lips, and straightened her skirt. "Well. Let's just say we have a lot to talk about."

"Yes," Nora said, looking around the room. She struggled not to cry. Nearly three months had passed since that day, and the memory was still fresh as ever. She could still see the faces of those police officers, as clearly as if they were standing before her now. She could still hear the terrible words coming from their mouths.

"You knew my parents?" Nora asked. She shook her head, trying to dispel the memories. She hadn't cried then, and she wouldn't cry now. It was just the stress of the journey making her emotional, she thought. Maybe something to do with the chemicals in the cryo tanks.

"I...yes, though it's been many years since we've seen each other," Aditi said. "But I'm sure you have other questions for me today, don't you?"

Only about a billion, Nora thought. Where to start? Why was I recruited here? What did the board see in me? Why is this place kept a secret? Who are the J'nai, and when can I meet them? How long has this station been here, and why doesn't anyone know? What is a Hypatia and why did everyone call her that?

But she just settled on: "So... this is Space Camp?"

"Our cadets call it that, yes," Aditi said with a gentle smile. "Tea?"

"What? Oh, I mean, yes, thanks," Nora said. She accepted a white ceramic mug that Aditi pulled from a wall panel. The wall, with the touch of a button, had spouted a stream of steaming black tea into the mug. Nora suddenly felt as if she were back at home, pouring a cup of tea from their old red kettle after school, a ritual she and her mother had observed religiously. There was something innately calming in that simple act, and with the memory of it, she felt her nerves unkink by a millimeter or two.

"Sugar?"

"No, thank you," Nora said.

"Milk, then?"

"No, thank you," Nora repeated. She leaned back a bit into her chair, feeling the solid warmth of the mug in her hands. It comforted her, thawing fingers that had become ice cold.

"I'm sure you're wondering why you're here with me rather than with your fellow recruits," Aditi said. Nora nodded and took a sip of her tea. It was delicious, the first thing about this place that was familiar. If this was part of Aditi's plan to get her to relax and open up, it just might work.

"The admiral had heard that your…well, that the Clarks hadn't informed you of much of your talents. Of our plans to bring you here. We decided it would be best for you to hear it from me first, here, rather than in an assembly, or from another student."

"Talents? What plans?" Nora was pretty sure if she had some hidden talent, it would have presented itself by now. She was a decent pianist but nothing extraordinary, especially since her dad had gotten rid of the piano a few years back. She somehow doubted that was the talent Aditi was referring to. She was certainly no genius in school; along with a slew of detentions, her inability to stay focused always brought whispers of an ADD diagnosis from her teachers.

"Oh yes," Aditi continued, nonchalant, sipping her tea. "Plans made since before you were born."

"What plans?" she repeated. Nora could have spit out her tea. Did she mean the kind of plans all parents have for their children – the kinds of ambitions and hopes and dreams that their child would grow up safe and healthy and happy? Something in Aditi's tone made her doubt it – was there something else, then? She had thought that she and her parents were too close for any sort of secrets. Since they'd had to move so much for her father's job, the only friends any of them seemed to have were each other - and her father's boss, Mr. Oscar Flynn. That was probably the reason her parents had listed the Flynn's as her legal guardians. Just in case.

Nora looked up at Aditi, awaiting a response. Please, she pleaded silently – were my parents keeping something from me? Was that why they pushed me so hard in my classwork – did they have something in mind for me? Did they know about Ganymede? Her sudden uncertainties about her upbringing crashed down on her like a tidal wave, another wave of impossible things to add to her growing list. She found it hard to breathe against the momentary panic, and struggled to collect her thoughts. She counted her impossible experiences, and ticked them off in her mind – Being orphaned. Getting selected for the top-secret Ganymede Project – of which her legal guardian was conveniently a member of the governing board. Going to outer space. Arriving at a space station where she'd meet aliens. Meeting a girl who could be her twin. And – finally – learning that maybe her parents had known about all of this all along. Her mind reeled.

"They planned to bring you here, where you could be with students just like you," Aditi said.

"Just like me," Nora whispered. She leaned back in her chair, her eyes unfocused, and her heart hammered in her ears. They had known. Her parents had known about Ganymede, had planned to send her here, and hadn't told her anything. When she'd seen that first brochure given to her by Mr. Flynn, Ganymede had looked more like a boarding school than a space station. She rubbed her temples. She thought of Thalia, of the impossible similarities between them. *Just like me.* The phrase echoed in her skull. She looked up, and met Aditi's kind gaze. She steeled herself to add another impossibility to her tally.

"I ... I met a girl out there—Thalia—before I came in here. She looked just like me. Not kind of like me, but *exactly* like me. And she called me something. I thought at first she was making fun of me, but now I'm not sure," Nora said.

Aditi put down her teacup and leaned forward, her hands clasped over her knee. It was almost as if she could hear the turmoil screaming inside Nora's skull, and was waiting for it to settle before stirring it up again with her response. The slight tenseness around her eyes faded a little.

"She called you Hypatia?"

"Yes," Nora breathed out, almost pleadingly. "What does it mean?"

"Well, it's certainly not an insult," Aditi said. Her mouth twisted in an odd expression, something between pain and fear, like she was going to break bad news. Nora had seen that expression before.

"Hypatia was a Greek philosopher," Aditi said. "She taught in the city of Alexandria in the early AD 400s. She was, according to some, one of the most brilliant minds the world has ever known."

"So why would Thalia call me that? And why do I look like *her*?"

"Nora, there are so many things your handlers...I'm sorry, your parents..."

"My *what*?" The words stuck in her throat, the muscles around her vocal cords suddenly constricting.

"There are so many things they should have told you. They...did tell you they're not your *real* parents, didn't they?" Aditi looked moderately horrified at the prospect of being the one to tell Nora that particular bit of news. Nora bit her lip. She'd been doing a pretty good job these past few weeks of not thinking about her parents. Why couldn't she get them out of her head now? Why did Aditi have to keep bringing them up?

"I figured it out on my own when I was about five. I know I was adopted."

At this, Aditi let out a sigh. She delivered her next lines with the smoothness and perfect fluidity of a professional newscaster: "Not just adopted, Nora. You were *created.*"

"What does that mean? Like, in a test tube? *In vitro?*" She shook her head. IVF was nothing new, nothing special.

"Nora, look around you. Do you really think a place like Ganymede Station could have been built in just fifteen years with the kind of minds that exist on our planet today?"

Nora's ears caught the subtle emphasis on that last word.

"The kind of minds *today?* Aditi—what are you saying?"

"I'm saying...well, let's try it this way. Do you remember Dolly? The sheep?"

"The clone?" she asked, bewildered at the leap their conversation had taken. "Yeah, why? What's that got to do with anything? Wasn't that like ten years ago?"

"More than fifteen," Aditi said with a wry smile. "Although our project was underway long before that. Let's put it this way: you look like Thalia, enough to be twins, and yet you're years younger. If we ran your DNA, it would be identical to hers. Why do you think that is?"

"Because...we're...well, not twins, but clones - like Dolly? Me and Thalia?"

"Yes, brilliant, Nora. Exactly right. You and Thalia are clones." Aditi appeared pleased with her response. Nora wondered if this was the first time the dean had had to explain this to one of the new cadets. It certainly felt like it.

"So you cloned someone related to this…Hypatia person and hoped we inherited her brains or something?"

"No, Nora. Hypatia never married, never had any children."

"Aditi, what are you saying?" She was confused and starting to get a little frustrated with the circular conversation. Aditi was trying to get Nora's mind to open up and grasp some elusive fact, to come to the conclusion on her own, but Nora's brain was still in shock. Only hours ago she'd been submerged in blue goo; only weeks ago, she'd been back in Louisiana, totally unaware there was a space station with hundreds of people circling Jupiter. At this moment in time, the synapses of Nora's brain were having a hard enough time coping with these facts without completely overloading.

But Aditi just beamed. She leaned forward, her voice in a whisper, as if concerned they might be overheard.

"You and Thalia don't just share DNA. You are *both* Hypatia—you are her exact genetic replica."

"I'm *what?*" Nora squeaked, nearly dropping her teacup. A splash of hot liquid ran over the edge and onto her leg, leaving a stinging damp spot. She swiped at it automatically. Her mouth opened, but no sound came out. She licked her lips, took a deep breath, and tried again.

"You cloned Hypatia? You cloned a woman who lived a thousand years ago?" her voice squeaked again on those last words. Nora felt she'd done remarkably well accepting some far-flung ideas lately—from the deaths of her parents to the moment she was told she was selected as a recruit for an elite academy on Ganymede. She'd managed to accept it all. But now it felt like a part of her brain was splintering off and shattering like glass on a tiled floor.

"Yes, Nora. We cloned a lot of people, as a matter of fact."

"*What?* Like who?"

She felt dizzy. She was going to faint. She was a clone? That was why the Board wanted her here—not for her particular talents, but for her DNA. It was sobering. Her mind whirled like a tornado – her balance felt off, like she would collapse if she tried to stand. She couldn't help but wish she was special after all, that she had some hidden potential like her mother had always told her — that she was a butterfly inside, waiting to be unleashed.

That the Board of Directors for Ganymede Station had seen something inside of her worth taking a risk on.

But that wasn't true.

She was a clone. She wasn't even Eleanora Clark. She was far more alien than she'd ever have been able to guess, a girl out of time and place. She felt like she was having an out-of-body experience, looking down on herself from the outside. Her breathing quickened, and she could barely hear Aditi's words over her own rapid pulse.

"We have cloned the greatest minds who ever lived," Aditi said, in the kind of voice you'd use to soothe a scared animal, like her calm tone and her words could slow Nora's thoughts. "Well, the ones whose DNA was uncorrupted, anyway. You'll be meeting lots of them around the station. Clones make up about a third of the population here."

There was a long pause.

"That's impossible," Nora breathed. No way. There was no way. Thalia was a long-lost cousin or something, maybe. That was all.

"Is it? Is it, Nora? What is truly impossible? You're standing on a space station on a moon four hundred million miles from Earth. You will step out that door and meet a race of beings that, until last week, you didn't have a clue existed. Last month, you might have called all of those things impossible. And you think technology we publicly announced fifteen years ago couldn't have advanced to human cloning?"

"That's...unethical, then. Aren't there laws against this kind of thing?"

"Nora," Aditi said patiently. "You have been granted the most amazing gift. You get to be part of history here, and not just because of what you'll do here, but because of *who you are*. What's unethical about that? Is it unethical to bring back the Mother Teresa's and Gandhi's of the world if it means peace? Or the Edison's or Tesla's if it means ushering humanity into the brightest chapter of its existence? We have such high hopes for you—for you and your peers. You will bring humanity a peace they could never have dreamed of when we're done here."

"Why doesn't the rest of Earth know about this? About Ganymede and cloning? This could change everything!"

"Because that would *ruin* everything, Nora, at least right now. Can you imagine the politicians up here with their red tape, throwing flags down on Ganymede, claiming it for the United States or China or wherever? Can you imagine the warlords on Earth cloning a hundred Hitlers if they had our technology? This is a place for *science,* not flags—and when the world is ready, we'll show it to them. Show them what humanity can be when its fullest potential is realized—when we work together, in peace. When we unite the greatest minds of our world. Once we can get them to recognize the scope of this galaxy and how petty our little conflicts on Earth truly are."

"Unbelievable," Nora murmured. Her tea mug sat, still full, in her hands, little ripples in the dark liquid stirred up from her trembling hands.

"Nora," Aditi said. "You were created out of sincere goodwill, to give Earth a chance to spring ahead, thousands of years ahead, in science and space exploration. There was a prevailing theory that nature, your genes, your DNA, would be better equipped for a place and time and situation like this than any other person we could find. You are special. It's the old 'nature versus nurture' argument where you are concerned. A number of very promising researchers on Earth have published extensively on the importance of genes in education and development."

"So you are counting on my nature," Nora said, her mind suddenly blank, overloaded with too much information. Was this shock, she thought? Was she going crazy?

"And planning to nurture it," Aditi said with a smile, and Nora felt slammed back into her own consciousness, a headache forming behind her eyebrows. She felt suddenly like a part of her was foreign, like her consciousness was now inhabiting a body not fully her own. She was a conscious mind in an alien body. She wasn't Nora. She was Hypatia. She was Thalia. They were all one.

She was going to black out.

"I think that's enough for today, don't you?" Aditi said, her voice soft, reaching her ears as if from a great distance. Nora nodded and took a deep breath. "I know this is a lot to take in all at once. That's why we wished your han...parents...had gotten a start on it earlier. It's easier when it's broken up a bit. Gives your brain time to digest it properly."

Nora said nothing. She stared into the mug grasped in her fingers, at the dark ripples. Her mind was blank, overloaded. All she could think of was how little control she had over her own body – was it even her own? – if she couldn't stop the shaking of her own two hands.

"Nora, it will be okay," Aditi said. She reached out and put a warm hand on Nora's arm.

"When you've had some time to think about it, when you want to talk, you come find me, all right? Come on then, I'll show you to your room. You get settled, meet your roommates, and we'll talk again when you're ready." Her voice was soothing, the rhythm of her words a steadying tempo.

Nora couldn't have breathed a response even if her brain had been able to keep up. Aditi ushered her out of the office, an arm around her shoulders, and led her into the corridor.

CHAPTER 4

Nora tried to keep track of the twists and turns, but all of the halls looked exactly the same—stark white, slightly rounded, with blue printed signs at each juncture. Her brain was in a daze as Aditi led her to her room. It was like walking through fog, no distinct shapes anywhere, everything abstract.

Thalia. Hypatia. Clones. *Clones.* Her parents had known. They had known and not told her. Now they were gone, and she'd never be able to hear the truth from their lips, the truth about where she came from: *you were created.* She used to wonder about her heritage, and if she'd ever get the chance to meet the rest of her family. It had only been her and her parents – her *handlers* – for as long as she could remember.

It turns out she'd been wanting to meet a family who'd been gone for more than 1500 years, living in a city half-way across the world. Nora wondered about Alexandria, about what life must have been like there. Could Hypatia have ever have conceived of a place like Ganymede Station, in her wildest dreams?

Through one of the wide windows, Nora glimpsed a series of rooms coming off this main corridor. It was something like a barracks, maybe, or a dormitory. And then they arrived at Room 10013. Her foggy brain was slammed back into present day.

"You'll have roommates for now. After graduation, you'll get your own space," Aditi said, stopping in front of a metal door that reminded Nora of something she'd seen on a naval ship, one she'd toured with her parents – *handlers* - years ago. Aditi told Nora the code for the keypad and warned her not to give the code to anyone, *especially* boys. She made her repeat the code back several times before actually letting her try it.

The room looked like what you'd find in an old-fashioned train car, but bigger. Stacked in three pairs, the beds were recessed into the wall on the right and had gray curtains that could be drawn for privacy. Tall lockers stood between the pairs. Nora tossed her backpack on an upper bunk at the far end of the room that Aditi pointed to. She wanted to climb the little recessed ladder and have a look around at her space—there seemed to be a tablet on the pillow, waiting for her—but the view outside caught her attention.

While one wall was occupied by the six bunks, the opposite wall was almost entirely windows, large floor-to-ceiling things ten feet wide. From there, Nora could see Ganymede's dark, craggy surface curving away to the black horizon. She could see the back side of another room next to theirs and the curve of the hall where more rooms sprouted off like leaves on a fern.

The window had a wide base, and Nora sat on it, peering up at the massive, gleaming surface of Jupiter. The reds and oranges and creams were layered in stunning bands of color, all wrapped with a thin, glittering ring. This was all real, she thought, resting her hand on the window. On the other side of this glass was the vacuum of the moon's surface, now dimly lit by Jupiter's reflected glow. No sunlight here, she thought. How long would be it be before she saw the sun again? If she held up her fist, she could just about block out Jupiter's gleaming face from the sky, could imagine the sun there, in its place. When she pulled her hand back, though, the red planet was back. It loomed like a half-full moon back home, split between light and shadow.

"You may as well try and get settled. I imagine your roommates are out exploring. There's a washing unit at the back there; just drop your clothes in at the end of the day, and they should be ready by morning. The tablet," she said, picking up the device from Nora's bunk, "will let you access anything you want to know about Ganymede Station, the J'nai, or anything, really. It won't connect to Earth's Internet—for security reasons, you understand. Can't have a disgruntled cadet blabbing to Facebook or tweeting the station's location. But we've tried to make as much information as possible available to you. Okay?"

"Okay," Nora said, accepting the tablet. It was a large black rectangle, of a manufacture she didn't recognize, but the interface seemed easy enough to understand, and the picture was very sharp.

"We've also included a series of pictures and videos from Earth," Aditi said, "in case you start feeling homesick."

"Will I ever go back there?" Nora asked. The question felt like it had a stranglehold on her vocal cords. She'd never thought she'd miss the swamps of Louisiana so much—the Spanish moss waving in the breeze, the sounds of the birds and frogs. Hell, she'd even settle for a glimpse of the corn fields of Wisconsin. Aditi gave her a soft smile.

"Perhaps," she said, and then left.

Nora stayed seated on the ledge, too numb to stand. She realized she felt nauseated and pressed her head to the window. The glass—or whatever it was—felt cool against her clammy skin. She closed her eyes. During her struggle to adapt to high school life back on Earth, why hadn't her parents told her she was destined for this life – whatever *it* was – since she'd been born? Or created?

Who *was* she? A week ago, the answer would have been easy. Now, it was almost unfathomably complicated. Was she Hypatia? Was she a brilliant scientist, dragged one thousand years out of her time? Or was she Thalia, her cooler, tougher doppelgänger?

No, she decided, opening her eyes. She was nothing like Thalia, of that much she was sure. She wiped her eyes, surprised at the dampness she found there. It must have been condensation from her breath against the glass.

She looked around the room and was just about to get up and unpack when a *beep* sounded and the door swung back into the room.

"I'm telling you, Cat, it's going to be fine. Really, you'll see – no one is going to pick on you anymore after they find out what Raina can do to them. I bet—oh, hello there," the girl said, stopping short when she saw

Nora. "You've got to be kidding me. You're our last roommate? Are we *all* Faxes, then?"

It was Sophie. And peeking out from behind her was the small, nervous-looking girl with frizzy hair who had spilled the metal spheres after Thalia nearly ran her over. Nora's heart flip-flopped heavily in her chest.

"Hi," Nora said. Silence loomed between them.

"You and Thalia then, huh?" Sophie said. She put one hand on her hip.

"Yeah, I guess we're both Hypatias," Nora said, pulling absently on a stray curl. "Please don't hold that against me."

At this, Sophie cracked a smile.

"Well, welcome to Space Camp then, Hypatia."

"I'm Eleanora. Nora," she said, putting out her hand.

"Sophie Bauer, officially pleased to meet you, and thanks for helping Cat earlier," she said. The nervous-looking girl mumbled and extended her hand to Nora, then quickly let go as if she were afraid Nora would burn her. She pushed her thick glasses back up on her small nose and scrambled towards one of the bunks.

"So why did you call me a fax? What does that mean?" Nora asked.

"Like back on Earth—you know, like a facsimile? We're all copies," Sophie said, with a megawatt grin.

"So...wait, who are you a copy of, then?" Neither girl looked familiar.

"Well, Cat's a Curie," Sophie said. "And I'm a Hedwig Eva Maria Kesler."

"A what?"

"Her screen name was Hedy Lamarr. You know, from the old movies?"

"You lost me. I don't mean to be rude, but why..."

"Clone a movie star?" Sophie asked, tossing her glossy hair over her shoulder with a smile. "Because Hedy Lamarr also happened to be a genius. She practically invented Bluetooth technology, like decades before it actually got put into use." She was clearly proud of this fact—or of herself? It was all very confusing.

"And…you're a Marie Curie?" Nora asked Cat. The girl nodded, then darted past them to her bunk. She put down her backpack and started taking out notebooks.

"She's a little shy, but she'll warm up to you, you'll see," Sophie said, linking arms with Nora. "We've all been here for days at *least*- I've been here almost two weeks. You must have come on the very last shuttle. It's a real relief, you being a Fax and all. I think they try to bunk us together so we have someone to share the experiences with, you know? An Original wouldn't understand you like we will."

"An orig…"

Again, Sophie answered the question before Nora completed it.

"A non-clone. You know. 'Normal' people, made the old-fashioned way." She used her fingers to make quotations in the air. She grinned. "So, were there any cute guys on your shuttle?"

"I guess…." Nora said, suddenly missing Greg. The thought of him warmed her, taking the edge off of the chill in the air. Was all of space so cold, she wondered?

Sophie pulled her along to her bunk, breaking her reverie. It was the one right below Nora's, and she sat her down, still talking a thousand miles a minute.

"So, Eleanora—that's a cool name," she said.

"Yeah, family name," Nora mumbled. She'd always hated it, but at least it was better than her middle name.

"Well, I like it," Sophie proclaimed. She curled her legs under her and started braiding her hair, her fingers flying faster than Nora's ever had over ivory keys, and in more intricate movements, too.

"So, when did you find out you were a Hypatia? I've known I was a clone for years, of course. The resemblance, you know, since she's such a star. Strangers have been calling me Hedy Lamarr *forever*. Even got offered a modeling contract when I turned fifteen."

"Um, I found out like an hour ago."

"What? You mean, you didn't know?" Her fingers stopped moving. The unfinished braid began to unravel as Sophie's hands fell into her lap.

"My parents didn't tell me anything," Nora said. She felt the moisture trickling back into her eyes and fixed her gaze on the fluorescent lights overhead, willing it to stop. The conversation in Aditi's office was starting to sink in, her parent's betrayal of her trust percolating through her.

"Oh. My. God. You really don't have any idea what's going on here, do you? And your handlers. You called them your parents? What—did they tell you that you were adopted or something? Nora, that is the most adorable thing I've ever heard!" Sophie pursed her lips as she considered this bit of news, then frowned. "And maybe also the saddest."

"Tell me about it," Nora said. She'd never felt so confused, so abandoned.

"Well, it'll be fine. Trust me. There's like a ton of us here. You're going to fit right in."

Then, with conviction, Sophie got up from the bunk, her gaze determined.

"Come on. I'm going to show you around," she said. "Give your brain something other than this cloning business to think about. The self-pity will get you if you let it. Now this locker is yours; you'll want to change into uniform. They get kinda snippy if you walk around in jeans here."

Sophie flung the locker door open and grandly swept her hand before the contents. It was full of clothes—neat navy uniforms with pants and skirts and jackets, a pair of sage green one-piece things with a bazillion pockets that Sophie called "flight suits," shiny black shoes, workout gear, T-shirts and shorts for pajamas, even underthings.

"They really think of everything, don't they?" Nora murmured, grabbing the pieces of uniform.

"Seriously," Sophie said, opening her own locker. It held the same pieces as Nora's, but there was also a short black dress and a pair of sky-high heels. "Just in case," she said with a wink. She primped her hair in the locker door mirror as Nora changed before helping Nora with the small buttons and nametag and—finally—nodding her approval. Sophie wore her uniform with the same air one would wear an evening gown on the red carpet – Nora just felt stuffy.

"You're a real cadet, now, Clark," Sophie said, saluting her. Nora tried to smile – maybe she'd get used to the feeling of all of the layers and buttons and zippers. She fidgeted, trying to get the shoulders of her jacket to settle.

The rest of their roommates arrived soon after, and Sophie warmly introduced Nora to each of them. First was Lara, a tall blond girl who was an Eleanor Roosevelt clone. She had a loud laugh and large front teeth, and Nora liked her instantly. She seemed nice and had a thick Australian accent. She greeted Nora with a hearty slap on the shoulder and a cheery, "Good onya, mate," which Sophie explained meant something like 'nice to meet you.'

Raina, a fiercely pretty Indian girl, was a fax of someone called Rani Lakshmibai, who apparently was a rebellious Indian queen in the 1800's. Her last roommate was Zoe, a clone of a warrior empress called Zenobia who had ruled northern Africa long before even Hypatia had been born. Nora hadn't heard of her, either, but she sounded like a total badass.

Meeting clones meant meeting two separate people. It was hard enough to remember their names, much less their *other* names, Nora thought, but she realized it didn't really matter. She wasn't meeting a First Lady, or an Empress, or a warrior queen– she was meeting three more teenage girls who were new here, just like her. This recognition made her feel a little better. Her roommates weren't meeting Hypatia. They were meeting Eleanora Clark. She felt an instant connection with them, her heart rate slowing as Sophie continued her introductions.

It seemed that while Cat and Sophie were in the science program like her, Raina, Zoe, and Lara were on the Officer Track, which meant they could be running the station someday. Clones weren't often let off station for some reason, but opportunities on the station—and, rumor had it, someday in colonies, or on Terra Prime—were said to be plentiful.

"Well, we've got to show you around the station, Nora," Lara said, taking her hand and offering a broad, toothy grin. "You're going to love it here. I know it's overwhelming, but think about it. We're all just like you!"

Nora looked around at the other girls and realized Lara was right. It was overwhelming, but they were all in exactly the same situation. They'd been created for this place, specifically chosen for their particular genes.

This was the home they'd never realized they'd missed—with sisters they never knew they had. It was a place where she might not be *Alien*-ora, but just Nora—herself, yet not herself - a clone, true, but someone destined to be here. *Made* to be here. She belonged.

"Are there many more clones here?" Nora asked.

"Tons!" Sophie gushed. "We've got three or four Leos down in engineering and a few more of 'em in command. There are two Teslas who run engineering, too. Twins. An a Copernicus is in charge of the telescope dome. Medical's mostly run by a Galen and a few Hippocrates. A Curie like Cat here runs the lab. The officers are mostly Washingtons. There are literally hundreds of us! And they're getting new one every day. Following me so far?"

"Not at all. What's a Leo?"

"Leonardo da Vinci."

"God, I was hoping you meant DiCaprio."

"Sorry," Sophie said with a smile. "The boys have been requesting a Cleopatra or Gisele Bündchen, but I don't think that's gonna fly. There's a strict process for choosing clones, after all."

"Is there?"

"Sure. I mean, Hitler was brilliant, but can you imagine anyone authorizing a Hitler clone? Or like a Genghis Khan? Ugh."

"Not to mention, it's wicked expensive," Lara said.

"This is all so crazy," Nora said. She shook her head, and rubbed the spot between her eyebrows.

"Yeah," Lara agreed. "But once they get the clone program really up to speed, there'll be no need to import all those orphaned originals from Earth to keep the station running. It'll just be Faxes like us, ruling the galaxy."

"Personally, I can't wait," Raina said, pursing her lips. "I'm sick of Originals looking at us like we're test tube experiments."

"We *are* test tube experiments," Zoe said, grinning. Raina turned red and pursed her lips – Nora sensed a temper in her – so before she could explode in a tirade, Nora jumped in.

"So, who else is here? I mean, who else have they cloned?" She wound a curl around her finger, tugging on it as her brain spun.

"Oh yeah. We've also got a Charlemagne, an Elizabeth I, Xerxes, Churchill, Einsteins by the dozens of course, Darwin...and I hear that in a few years, we may get a Galileo! Who else? God, I can't remember them all... Ooh, I think we've got the first Alexander the Great clone in our year, too!" Sophie said, clapping her hands together.

"You know, last week I was worried about starting my senior year of high school. You know, bullies and pimples and homecoming dances. Normal stuff. This is kind of a lot to take in," Nora said.

"I know. That's why we're going exploring. Even *your* fax brain can overload if you think about it too much," Sophie said, poking Nora's forehead with her finger. "Let's go down to the Rec. You can introduce me to those guys you came here with."

"Sophie, they're Originals," Raina said, rolling her eyes.

"So what?"

"So, they can't keep up with you. You'll be bored of them after a week."

"I'm not looking for anything serious," Sophie said, tossing her hair. "Just some fun. Come on, Nora, let's go pick up your schedule for class, and I'll give you the grand tour!"

CHAPTER 5

As they walked out for the tour, Nora kept running Raina's phrase over in her mind.

"Sophie, what did Raina mean when she said the Originals can't keep up with you?"

"Oh, that?" Sophie said, and waved a hand in the air as if brushing the comment away. "Some people just think that since Faxes are genetically created to be superior, that it's basically impossible for Originals and Faxes to be…you know, 'involved'." Again with the air quotes. "They think the Originals will always feel inferior."

"Do you believe that?" Nora couldn't quite imagine feeling superior to anyone.

"Hey, I'm all for equality. If there's a hot guy who happens to be an Original, you think that would stop me?"

Nora realized it wouldn't and couldn't help but grin.

"That's the spirit. Now, this corridor will take you to the academic wing. It actually goes quite a ways underground, too. Apparently some of the more delicate research equipment gets buggy if it's in one of these surface areas. The radiation, you know. No ozone layer on Ganymede. And we can get your class schedule here," she said.

"Uh, radiation? Should we be worried?" Nora's skin prickled. She'd worn SPF 50 her entire life because of her fair skin – could she even get sunburn out here, hundreds of millions of miles away from the sun? Or was there something worse?

"No worries," Sophie said, shaking her head. "Everything above-ground is shielded, but even a single stray quark can make those things go hay-wire, apparently. I talked to this guy in the Astrolab last week and he said the amount of radiation we'll get here in our lifetime is less than a single xray back on Earth."

A lifetime here. Nora shivered despite the warm air around her, and another thought occurred to her.

"So it's not warm here because of solar radiation or anything, right?" Nora asked. "I mean, the ships were pretty cold."

"Nope. That's thanks to the fusion reactor this whole place is built on top of," Sophie said, with a wicked grin. Nora rolled her eyes. Of course. Let's add nuclear fusion to the list of impossible things around here.

"Fusion? Is that... safe?"

"Probably not," Sophie said, shrugging. She stopped before an auto-mated device that looked like an ATM.

"Ok, look, you punch in your name, here." Sophie showed her, and the machine spit out a short rolling piece of paper with a list of classes:

Driver's Ed
Science 101
Math 101
Break
Physical Education
Intergalactic Politics and History 101
Volunteering

"Well, we've got a few classes together, anyway. I've got more politics and history, of course, and you don't have communications at all," Sophie said. "I've heard they like to get us focused early, like picking a major in college."

"Don't you get a choice?" Nora asked. She'd thought about college, back on Earth. She'd thought maybe she'd take some music classes in college. Now she'd never get the chance.

"Why would you?" Sophie asked, blinking. "We already know you have one of the most brilliant minds for science and philosophy that the world ever saw. Why waste your time with the other stuff?"

"I guess," Nora said, frowning down at her schedule. She hoped there wouldn't be too much chemistry in her Science 101 class. As for the others, she had her doubts, too.

"PE? Driver's Ed?" They seemed awfully mundane after everything she'd just been through. Were they going to do those rope climbs like back home? See how many sit-ups you could do in a minute? Watch those 1970's videos about turn signals and street signs?

"Yeah, I can't wait for *that*," Sophie said, her voice flat with sarcasm. "You think my girl Hedy ever broke a nail playing dodge ball? *So* not my style. And I don't know about the driving stuff – I heard its more station safety than anything else. Look, classes start tomorrow. Let's show you the basics so you don't get lost, ok? Not a good first impression."

"No," Nora agreed, and followed Sophie. Like Greg had said – she'd need all the help she could get.

As they headed out of the academic wing, Nora caught sight of Ty and Wingman. They were a solid head taller than most of the people milling around the Rec Dome, for which she was immediately grateful. Seeing a few familiar faces—even if she barely knew them—was reassuring. Sophie had been chatting nonstop about their roommates for a few minutes—how Zoe was a genius but tried to hide it by acting tough, and how Lara knew girl knew the capital of every single country and state and rock and iceberg in the world—and Nora's brain felt like Play-Doh after all of the information crammed into it today. She grinned, grateful, when Greg's smiling face (or, more likely, Ty's biceps) put a quick stop to Sophie's soliloquy.

"Hey, ladies," Greg said, coming up to them. Ty and Wingman were close behind.

"Hey yourself," Sophie said, looking them over.

"So Nora. We were going to check out the Zero-G dome. You want to come?" Greg said. Nora looked to Sophie; she was already nodding.

"Sure. Haven't been there myself, actually," Sophie said. She let Greg and Nora lead the way and hung back a bit to talk with Ty and Wingman.

Nora could hear her giggle intermittently at something or another that Ty had said.

"So, Nora, I heard they took you to see one of the deans. Everything okay?" he asked, returning her attention.

"Yeah. My parents—*handlers*—never told me about any of this stuff growing up. You know about…all this? The cloning and stuff?" she asked, gesturing at herself. He nodded, and Nora sighed. "Seems like everyone else did, too. Aditi…er, I mean Dean Prasad…just wanted to make sure I got caught up. She's nice, I think."

"They told us about that stuff once we got to our bunks. So it's true? You and that Thalia girl—you're clones? You're some kind of science prodigy, too?" His eyes were wide, but he kept his tone light. Nora shrugged.

"I'm not sure. I've never been that good at science, or any classes really. I was pretty good at piano, but my dad got rid of it a few years back. I guess," Nora said, a twisting thought stabbing at her insides, "he was trying to make me focus more on school and less on music. You know, make me more like Hypatia."

"How are you…dealing with it all? With having a clone?"

"I don't know. I think it's like having a long-lost twin sister, you know?" she said, side stepping to avoid getting trampled by some cadets coming the other direction.

"An evil twin, maybe," Greg said. "She gives me the creeps. No offense."

"None taken. She is kind of intimidating, isn't she?"

"Totally. Not like you at all," he said, glancing at her sideways. His tone was mocking, and there was a smirk on his face.

"I am not intimidating!"

"Oh? Have you *met* yourself lately? Oh wait, you have!" he said, smacking his forehead with his hand. She shoved his shoulder, and he grinned.

They made it to the Zero-G room, a large white dome with a sort of air lock like the one that led from the PJ landing area to the main complex. Inside, she could see two cadets floating in midair, trying—and failing—to swim through it. They weren't going *anywhere*. They were completely suspended.

"Aw, let's go help them out, shall we?" Greg said, and they all stepped through the air lock.

Once inside, Nora felt the utter disorientation of weightlessness. Sophie shrieked and grabbed onto Ty, who willingly let her latch on, flexing his biceps as her hands wrapped around his arm. Nora felt the ends of her hair rise off her back and grinned, grabbing for a bar on the wall to steady herself. Greg pushed off the ground and sailed toward the two stranded cadets. He crashed into them, and the combined momentum drove them into the ceiling, where they collided awkwardly in a pile of arms and legs. They all took a second to reorient themselves, then dove back toward the floor with big smiles on their faces. Greg came careening into Nora and wrapped himself around her to keep her from falling. She could swear the collision was intentional.

The two cadets—a handsome, lanky boy and a girl with strawberry blond hair—thanked Greg for the rescue and introduced themselves.

"You must be new here! We're second years. I'm Xander. I'm a Tesla. And this is Christina. She's an Elizabeth I."

"No way," Sophie gawked. The girl grinned.

"Yes way. And nice to meet you guys!"

"Wow. This whole clone thing goes way deeper than I ever imagined," Greg said.

"Hey, if they can clone a philosopher whose been dead for two thousand years, why not a queen?" Nora said, trying to wrap her head around it herself.

"A queen who is currently late for a class," Christina said. "We were stuck up there a while. Xander, are you coming?"

"Yeah," he said, pushing off toward the door. "Have fun in here. We can pretty much use it whenever. It's supposed to be for EVA practice, but no one minds if you hang out."

"What we really need is zero-gravity football," Ty said. He hung on to one of the bars on the side to keep himself—and Sophie, who was still clinging to him—on the ground.

"We tried to turn it into a Quidditch pitch once, but management got peeved with the bludgers. They kept getting loose and…well, after the balls cracked a dome panel, they put the kibosh on it. No more Quidditch," the boy said. He looked genuinely crestfallen before remembering something and perking up.

"But we do have some amazing Iron Man suits. A Leo in the R&D lab made them."

"Oh man, Iron Man? For real?" Greg said, then whooped as he pushed off the floor and went sailing toward the ceiling again.

"Yeah. You should try to find him. He's a fanatic when it comes to that stuff. See ya!" Xander called, then he and Christina exited through the air lock.

For a while, they took turns zooming around the room. Wingman was the most awkward—his long arms and legs kept getting in his way—while Greg was by far the most acrobatic, turning somersaults and fearless cartwheels and bashing into Nora and Sophie whenever he got the chance.

After a while, they tired and made their way from the dome, wandering until they found a sign for the cafeteria.

"*Finally*," Greg said. "I'm starving! Think they'll have that astronaut ice cream? The freeze-dried stuff?"

"Ugh, I hope not," Sophie said, and stuck out her tongue. Nora's stomach growled – she couldn't remember the last time she'd actually eaten anything. The thought of food made her mouth water. Funny how something so mundane could even register on her brain after today's experiences.

The cafeteria dome proved to be remarkably like any other high school cafeteria Nora had ever seen—if cleaner. The standard assortment of long tables and round tables were sprinkled around the room, with groups of cadets, graduates, and officers all chatting as if it were the most normal thing in the world to be eating a meal together four hundred million miles from home. And there was no astronaut ice cream—to Greg's immense disappointment. In fact, the food was as unremarkable as the cafeteria itself, with plenty of fruits and vegetables that Sophie said were supplied by the

Greenhouse, though Nora couldn't remember if she'd seen that particular dome on her arrival.

"I mean, I was hoping for some like blue bananas or exotic tentacled goo, at least," Greg said, sighing as he twirled a fish stick through plain red ketchup. Nora, for one, was profoundly grateful for the familiarity of the food, even if the others were a bit let down – she didn't think she could stomach tentacled goo after the excitement of the past day.

"Hey, you girls want to go check out the Rec Dome?" Wingman asked, polishing off his fourth—or fifth?—sandwich. Nora and Sophie exchanged a glance. Sophie yawned dramatically.

"Maybe another time," Nora said.

"First day of school tomorrow, boys. We need our beauty sleep." Sophie tossed her curls.

"Hey Ty, that means you, too, buddy," Greg said, punching him on the arm. They said goodnight, and Sophie linked her arm through Nora's as they made their way back to their dorm.

"See?" Sophie whispered as they left the cafeteria. "I know it's a lot to take in, but it's not so bad, right? It's going to be fine."

It felt a little bit like Sophie was trying to reassure herself as much as Nora.

"Yeah," Nora said, realizing the shock and heart-clenching dread brought on by Thalia and the whole Aditi thing had melted away. Even the sting of her parent's betrayal had faded to a dull ache. "I really think it is."

That night, Nora huddled in her bunk and turned on the tablet Aditi had given her. The glow illuminated the little space, and shrouded as she was by the drawn curtain on the side, she felt intensely isolated. Her gaze flicked from the tablet to the picture she'd put on the little shelf at the side of the bunk, her fingers tracing the crease in one corner. Her dad had taken it last Christmas, in their cheesy annual tradition of wearing ugly Christmas sweaters. She'd teased him about the giant fake ornaments on his sweater, and he had told her she looked like a reindeer. She did, too. He'd laughingly forced her to wear a Rudolph nose. She was embarrassed at the time but now glad she did it. He had cherished the picture and hung it in his office so he could see their smiling faces every time he sat down for one of his innumerable conference calls. Calls which she now realized were probably related to the Ganymede Project, and not his 'consulting firm.'

Nora sniffled once and returned her attention to the tablet. There was an icon for e-mail and another for the Ganymede network. She opened the latter and typed "HYPATIA" into the search bar.

A lengthy article popped up, preceded by: "Current Hypatia clones: 2."

She let out a shaky breath. At least there were no more surprises coming on that front. Nora was relieved; any more like Thalia and her time here was going to be tough, indeed.

She continued to the article and soaked it all in. She read about plane astrolabes, and conic sections. She read about the brief life and brutal end of this woman, the oldest documented female mathematician, astronomer, and philosopher. She read about the intolerances at the time of pagan and Christian viewpoints, at the nonsensical violence between the two. Then she was a picture of Hypatia near the bottom of the article of the page, a serene-looking woman with the same curly hair as Nora, pulled back in classic Greek style. Nora touched the picture gently, wondering what the philosopher would have thought if she knew she'd have two clones more than a thousand years after her death who sailed through the stars she'd only dreamed of.

She read on until she was stopped cold by a quote from Socrates:

"There was a woman at Alexandria named Hypatia, daughter of the philosopher Theon, who made such attainments in literature and science, as to far surpass all the philosophers of her own time. Having succeeded to the school of Plato and Plotinus, she explained the principles of philosophy to her auditors, many of whom came from a distance to receive her instructions. On account of the self-possession and ease of manner which she had

acquired in consequence of the cultivation of her mind, she not infrequently appeared in public in the presence of the magistrates."

Nora put down the tablet. Self-possession? Good at public speaking? Surpassing all contemporaries in the field of science? Clearly there'd been a mistake. Nora was none of these things. She powered the tablet down, and in the dim light of the bunk, she caught her reflection in the shining surface of the tablet. She tilted it slightly. No, she thought. There was no mistaking it. She *looked* exactly like Hypatia, who looked exactly like Thalia.

She put the tablet on the shelf, turned off the reading lamp, and settled onto her pillow. When she closed her eyes, the picture of Hypatia danced behind her eyelids, a knowing half-smile on the carved marble lips. Nora tossed and turned before pulling the blanket over her head. She might look like Hypatia, but whether the cloning process also passed down the woman's intellect and poise was yet to be seen.

CHAPTER 6

The next morning, all the cadets gathered in an amphitheater buried a few stories underground. Apparently, or at least according to Sophie, Ganymede's lack of atmosphere meant all the cosmic radiation Earth's ozone layer protected you from came streaming through here unimpeded. Turns out, it was easier to bury most of the compound underground than shield it all with two inches of lead. It was possible to coat the glass upstairs—but expensive. So most of the labs, the classes, the nuclear reactor—anything that might be affected by radiation or anything that would be too large to shield (like the amphitheater)—were all buried beneath the rock.

Nora was sandwiched between Cat and Sophie, and all around them, wide-eyed cadets in their new navy blue uniforms, along with a few in sage green flight suits, packed into the auditorium. Standing on the platform below, hands clasped behind his back, was a large man with close-cropped gray hair and an impeccably pressed uniform.

"Is that the admiral?" Cat squeaked. Nora shrugged.

"Yes," Sophie said, slouching a bit so she could whisper. "And that guy behind him is the XO. That's Arthur McGregor."

The executive officer looked to be at least six and a half feet tall, with snow white hair that belied his age, which didn't look to be more than forty. He had a dignified presence, whereas the admiral was outright terrifying, a pent-up wild animal pacing the stage.

"I heard he's a Charlemagne," Zoe whispered, looking back at the XO.

"No way," Nora said. "The guy's way too old to be a clone."

"That's just what I heard," Zoe said, shrugging. "They say *he* should really be in charge here, but the corporate higher-ups don't trust clones with that kind of power."

"What are they worried about?" Nora said "That he might go crazy and jettison us all out an airlock?"

"Who knows?" Raina said. "But the admiral's an Original. Go figure. Those bastards always get the best jobs. And we're women, besides. It's going to be a tough gig for us here, ladies."

"His call sign when he was a pilot was Paladin," Lara said, looking at McGregor. "Doesn't seem like the kind of nickname you give to a person you don't trust."

A boy a few rows below turned as he heard Lara's voice and called up.

"Hey, Lara! How about the capital of Tuvalu?"

"Funafuti," she called back. Sophie rolled her eyes. The boy nudged another boy sitting next to him, who shrugged.

"You are totally just making things up now," Sophie complained. "Tutti-frutti?"

"Oh *will* you shut up?" another voice called. The hair on Nora's arms stood up before she even saw who it was: Thalia. She looked to find her fellow clone glaring at them over her shoulder a few rows up. "You're giving me a migraine."

"Your *face* is giving me a migraine," Sophie muttered, then looked at Nora. "Not, um, because she looks like you or anything. God, you know what I mean."

"Sure," Nora said, trying to hide a giggle.

The admiral stepped to the front of the platform.

"Good morning," he boomed. His voice needed no artificial amplification, and the rumblings of chatter immediately ceased.

"For those of you who are new here, welcome to Ganymede Station," he said in a clipped manner. "Welcome, and congratulations. You have been enrolled in our four-year training program, colloquially known as Space Camp. Your focus, like a major in college, will be geared toward those jobs that best fit your aptitude. After four years, you join our ranks of distinguished graduates. Your time here will be a time of growth and challenges. I expect you all to give your best efforts, and you will, in turn, be rewarded accordingly.

"Now more than fifty years old, the Ganymede Project was, at its outset, to be a scientific utopia. After we were contacted, a group of scientists—mostly from America and a few European nations—set out to help the stranded J'nai after their unprovoked genocide by the Qaig, and to further human understanding of our own place in this universe. The board of directors maintains that directive to this day and is charged with protecting the secrecy of our mission.

"Classes will begin this morning. I would like to remind each of you of the seriousness and extreme privilege of being here. Your work here will echo through eternity in a way that has never before been possible.

"And I would like to remind all cadets, and some of our graduates as well"—Nora could have sworn he was looking right at Thalia—"that the eclipse time, the dark time, is *not* a time for…shenanigans."

"Did he *really* just say 'shenanigans'?" Lara whispered. Nora snorted, covering her mouth with her hand and faking a cough to hide it. Her mind was spinning – not just over the Admiral's word choice, but over his comment about the J'nai – genocide? By the Qaig? When was she going to get the full story?

"So, what, it gets really dark?" Sophie said, interrupting Nora's contemplation and nodding toward Thalia. "I wonder what she's been up to."

"It happens about once a week—every 7.15 days," Cat whispered. "Jupiter eclipses the light of the sun. The surface of Ganymede goes completely dark for just over two hours."

"Well isn't that interesting," Sophie purred, and tapped a finger against her lips as she considered this bit of news.

"Sophie, he said *no shenanigans*," Zoe whispered. Sophie laughed out loud and waved sheepishly when people nearby turned to look.

"Okay, that's enough. Go to class," the admiral said and turned his back, heading for the stairs.

"Man of few words, isn't he?" Raina said, gathering her book bag.

⬦ ⬦ ⬦

As they walked to class, there was a moment when Nora realized there was *gravity* in the station. Of course there was gravity, she thought; she'd been walking around comfortably for over a day now. The only place that didn't have the usual forces was the Zero-G dome, and come to think of it, the surface of Ganymede had *some* gravity, if only a little. How did that dome have none at all? She stopped in her tracks. The thought hit her like a lightning bolt, momentarily paralyzing her limbs.

"What's wrong?" Greg asked.

"There's gravity here," she said, confused. "But not in the Zero-G room."

"Yeah, obviously."

"But how?"

"Gravitons. They placed emitters all over the place, and an anti-emitter in the Zero-G room to counteract Ganymede's gravity. Wesley told me all about it from some article he found on the tablets. The Newtons and Einsteins figured it out the first year the station was built. Now, supraluminal travel—that one's still giving them headaches."

⬦ ⬦ ⬦

Classes were exhilarating and left her head spinning. Driver's Ed turned out to be a crash course in operating all of the station's equipment, from the Rovers that made long escapades across the surface of Ganymede to basic flight of the more rudimentary shuttles in case of emergency. It would be weeks before they'd actually let her try to drive anything, but the thought made her giddy. Greg was in that class, too, which helped her mood even more.

Her science and math classes were pretty much what she expected, with an emphasis on astronomy and such, while PE had proved rather less enjoyable than she'd anticipated. It was a class designated to help the students keep their fitness up in space. There weren't soccer fields or anything up here, so they had to improvise. Most of their physical education would involve building up a tolerance for the EVA suits—those bulky (and heavy) apparatuses that would allow them to walk over Ganymede's surface. Technically, Nora learned, EVA, for Extra-Vehicular Activities, was an outdated term from the time of the very first moon walk decades ago – when astronauts had had to leave vehicles, not stations. Still, the name stuck, despite Greg's attempts to get people to start calling them Extra-Stationary Devices or even Super Suits.

Politics Class provided her first opportunity to see a J'nai – it was taught by one, and the cadets surged into the classroom to see her. They rushed into their seats and stared unabashedly at their instructor. She was tall with dark pink skin and a graceful voice that sounded British to Nora.

"Welcome," she said, smiling as the flustered cadets took their seats. They were in a small room, below the surface, with terraced rows of desks and a large, flat screen at the front displaying a blue and green planet that was definitely *not* Earth.

"I am J'hara'niet," she said, "but you may call me J'hara. I imagine I am the first of the J'nai you have seen, yes?" Her smile didn't dim. There was a mutter of agreement.

J'hara wore the station officer's navy blue uniform with the gold star on the lapel that Greg said was the mark of a diplomat. Their instructor was someone important to the J'nai race.

"I have so very much to teach you and so little time," she said, clasping her hands together—three fingers and a thumb per hand, Nora noted. Otherwise, she was startlingly human in appearance; that is, if you discounted her pink skin and long white hair, worn in an intricate braid. Her features were a little more taut, a little more linear, but it was the resemblance rather than the differences that really struck Nora.

"So. Let us start with the basics."

There was a flurry of activity as the cadets hastily got out their tablets and notepads, intent on not missing a word from their new instructor.

"We'll start with biology," she said, and with the wave of her hand, she changed the picture on the screen to one of a younger J'nai, maybe herself, about two or three years old, with shell-pink skin and a shock of white hair.

"The prevailing theory of our existence—and yours and even the Qaig," she said, making a face at the word, "is called Convergence Evolution. The theory says that, given similar circumstances, beings will develop in similar ways."

The screen changed again, this time to a picture of a shark and another of a dolphin. Nora was confused, and based on the audible "hmm?"s from her classmates, she wasn't the only one.

"Take, for example, the shark and the dolphin, on Earth," J'hara continued. "One is a fish. One is a mammal. But both were exposed to water, both to the same minerals, and they evolved similarly—a dorsal fin, a strong tail to propel them at speed, sharp teeth for catching their meals."

The image flicked back to the first one, the blue and green planet gleaming like a marble in a black sky.

"This is our current home planet. It is much like yours, or so I am told, as was our original home world. Plenty of water. Plenty of oxygen, though our planet is older than your Earth. Oxygen meant we evolved respiration. Water and air meant we developed not so differently from humans, since we were exposed to a similar chemical environment. Oxygen also meant that we, like you,"—she looked around the room at her captivated audience—"were able to gather and smelt metals, a few thousand years ahead of you, of course. We could build starships. Soon after, relatively speaking, there were J'nai on dozens of planets, all around the galaxy. We built our star port system—no, I don't have time to talk about it today, maybe next time—and as time passed, each J'nai colony evolved a little differently based on the mixture of gases and elements on their particular planet. For example, my people have pink skin because in our diet we consume many fish-like creatures with a chemical in them that accumulates in our skin as we age."

"Like flamingoes," Greg whispered. There was a trickle of quickly hushed laughter. J'hara heard it and smiled.

"Exactly like flamingoes," she agreed. Greg flushed. Apparently, the J'nai had evolved good hearing, as well.

She went on to discuss the subtle—and not so subtle—differences between the J'nai and humans. In the not-so-subtle category, the J'nai had evolved two hearts, one of which resided near their stomach. They also aged much slower, for the most part; the light pink child in the picture she'd shown was, in fact, nearly twenty years old by standard Earth years. By the end of the lesson, Nora's mind buzzed with pictures of brightly colored J'nai and the impossible-to-wrap-your-head-around proof that they truly *were not alone* in the galaxy. The idea boggled her mind.

And not only were they not alone, J'hara said, but there were literally *hundreds* of other races—though not as technologically advanced, not by far, and the J'nai had strict laws to not interfere with any of them, if possible. Nora and her fellow cadets were in a daze by the time the class ended.

And still, there was no further mention of the Qaig.

The term "volunteering" on her schedule turned out to be a euphemism for boring grunt work. For an hour a day, cadets would be responsible for various parts of station maintenance, to better acquaint them with the way the station was run and to keep it in working order. Nora found herself cataloging spare parts in a dusty storage room with Zoe for an interminable hour that first day.

"Is it really 'volunteering' if you're forced to do it?" Zoe asked, sneezing as a cloud of dust fell on her as she pulled down another box.

"It sounds so much nicer than 'indentured servitude,'" Nora said, checking off parts on her clipboard as Zoe called them out.

"On the plus side, if you ever need ten thousand light bulbs, now you know where to find them," Zoe said, sneezing again.

By the time they were done, it was late afternoon, and they found themselves starving. They drifted into the cafeteria with the rest of the cadets and swapped stories with their roommates.

"Food's good, at least," Zoe said.

"Yeah, the chefs here are geniuses. Like literally. I think one of them's a Leo," Sophie said, nibbling at her salad and watching the other cadets.

"Are we the only female Faxes in our year?" Nora realized, looking around.

"I think so," Raina said in a huff. "There are just more men in general here, actually. I guess they don't think we're as good as them."

"Please," Sophie said, eyeing a group of first-year boys at the next table. "It just means *we* have more options on who we spend our time with."

"I guess that's why they wanted us all rooming together," Zoe said. "Cat's less likely to get picked on if she's hanging around us, you know?"

Cat blushed but didn't disagree. Zoe had a point. Cat *had* attracted a lot of unwanted attention from cadets who wanted her to "help" them with their homework.

"So we have to stick together," Sophie announced, waving her fork - which trailed lettuce like a banner.

"Faxes forever!"

<hr />

The next day during PE, Nora got her first instructions with the EVA suits. The suits were large, complicated things that smelled unpleasantly like the inside of a shoe, or maybe a boy's locker room. She didn't get to do much more than put it on and have her instructor point out all the things she'd done wrong and how many ways she would have died if she'd walked outside with her suit like that. It would be weeks before they were given their first chance to walk outside on Ganymede, and there would be hours of lecture before then. And, their instructor was quick to say, the station would not tolerate any *shenanigans* on their walks outside.

It was almost impossible not to burst out laughing when they heard the word again.

"Shenanigans," Raina grumbled.

Sophie said it, too, though with glee, though their instructor glared daggers at her.

Nora wished she had a big space helmet over her head so she could roar with the laughter that was fighting to bubble up. Instead, she coughed, trying to hide her smile with her hand.

"They keep using that word. I do not think it means what they think it means," Greg said in an affected Spanish accent, grinning. They all looked at him.

"What? *The Princess Bride*? Anyone? You can't tell me nobody's seen that."

CHAPTER 7

Nora heard the faint sounds of something familiar drifting from down the hall.

It took her a second to realize exactly what she was hearing; it barely reached her ears over the din of the hallway traffic, but her brain soaked it up like a wilting plant drinking in a drop of rain. She stopped dead in her tracks when she recognized it and apologized absently to the guy who nearly tripped over her.

Music.

She realized with a jolt that it was the first music she'd heard since she'd left home. God, was it only a few weeks ago? It felt like years, but she realized it was only barely September. Something ached deep in her chest, and she found herself moving out of the main corridor toward a smaller one near a sign that read, "Crew Quarters."

Music used to be her life. She'd spent endless hours practicing on her piano, and eventually, even though it was hard for her to admit, she got pretty good. She and her mother would play duets; her mother was a real magician with the keys, better than Nora could ever imagine becoming. But one day, she came home from school, and the little old upright she'd become so attached to was gone. Her father said it had gone to the shop for tuning, but when she asked when it was coming back, he just shrugged. He suggested she turn her energy back to her schoolwork. Her mother—no, her *handler*—had disapproved of this but had let it happen.

It had never come back from the shop.

Now Nora realized it was just another one of their tricks to get her Hypatia-brain to realize its potential in academia and focus on things that "mattered," things she had been created for.

These thoughts swirled through her head like the colors of Jupiter as she floated down the hallways, trying to find the source of the music. She couldn't remember having gone more than a few hours back home without turning on the radio. She hadn't realized how much she missed the sounds. Space—other than the sounds of voices and machinery—was eerily quiet.

The sounds drifted through the air softly, like fog just before dawn. The smooth sound of a saxophone wafted gently down - from where? She took a left turn. Definitely louder here. There were fewer people down this hall, less traffic. She couldn't remember if she'd been down here before. There were no more signs to help, either. The doors were closed, except for one at the end that was partially ajar.

She moved toward it, almost hypnotized. The sound grew louder. It was jazz, the classic stuff, and as she reached the door, she paused, closing her eyes to relish it. It was the singularly most beautiful thing she'd ever heard. She didn't realize how accustomed she'd already become to the sounds of the station—mechanical noises, the whoosh of vents, and the far-off rumbles of PJs. She let out a deep breath, feeling herself relax.

"Are you lost?"

She tensed. She opened her eyes and peeked her head around the door. She was at the entrance of a private room, she realized. It was one of the crew's quarters that Aditi had said the graduates occupied. It was a large-ish rectangular structure, with a wide window that overlooked the craggy surface of Ganymede.

The room had a neatly made bed, although only minimal attempts had been made at making the area feel cozy. There was a small desk with an oriental-looking lamp that gave off a harsh white glow. The small couch looked stiff and uncomfortable, but the man sprawled across it didn't seem to notice. He was a few years older than her, probably, with dark blond hair and intensely furrowed eyebrows. He wore his flight suit like Thalia, unzipped with the arms tied loosely at his waist. His dog tags jingled against a white undershirt as he moved to sit up, still holding his tablet. He looked as if he'd been in the middle of something important and was irritated at having been disturbed.

"Did you need something?" he asked. Nora swallowed hard. He didn't look familiar – and she *definitely* would have remembered him.

"What?" she asked. "No, I mean—sorry. I didn't mean to interrupt your…reading?"

She glanced at the tablet, and he put it aside with a sigh.

"You're new here."

She could feel the rush of heat to her face and knew she was blushing. What would Sophie say?

"That obvious?" she asked, trying to smile.

"Yes," he said, looking her up and down in a matter-of-fact sort of way. "I would have remembered seeing *you*. You are a Hypatia."

There was the hint of an accent in his voice—French, if she had to guess. He drew out the I's in his words like taffy.

"Good guess," she grumbled, tucking a loose strand of hair behind her ear. She looked at the desk, where a small speaker was still playing the jazz she'd heard down the hall. She watched the device a moment, catching another phrase in the song, before glancing back. He was still watching her, with an expression that was a cross between annoyance and curiosity— those eyebrows still tightly drawn.

"Not really a guess. You look just like Thalia."

"I'm nothing like Thalia," she said. The words were out of her mouth before she knew it, and she instantly regretted them. She didn't know Thalia that well, after all. And wasn't saying she didn't like her like saying she didn't like herself, or a part of herself? She wasn't sure. She shot him a glance; one side of his mouth was bent up in a sort of wry smile. It vanished as soon as he saw her looking.

"I'm Nora," she said. "And yeah. I'm a Hypatia. Who are you?"

"Sebastian," he said, then sighed, knowing she was waiting for the rest of it, the rest of his identity. "Just Sebastian."

"You're an Original," she said, the words still sounding strange on her tongue. What a weird way to describe someone. He shrugged when she used that term, his face once more expressing his annoyance, and lay back down on the couch, turning his attention back to his tablet.

"Classrooms are down that way," he said, pointedly not looking at her but nodding toward the open door.

"Yeah," she said and turned to go. But when she was halfway out, her hand caught the metal doorframe as if it wouldn't let her go until she told him why she'd come there.

"I didn't mean to disturb you. I just…liked your music. It's the first I've heard since leaving home. I didn't realize how much I missed it until—" He was looking at her so intently, that flicker of annoyance ever present in his blue eyes, that she momentarily faltered.

"Well, I guess I was feeling a little homesick," she finished. What she wouldn't give to hear her mother's old piano, hear the sounds of the classics rolling down the hallway.

"You know you are literally hundreds of millions of miles from home."

"Yeah," she said, looking at the floor. "Thanks for reminding me."

And she left.

CHAPTER 8

Half their Driver's Ed class gathered in the landing dome. The station's five Rovers were waiting for them, looking like souped-up Batmobiles on monster-truck chasses. Their instructors, including the inscrutable Sebastian, were waiting, too. Nora cringed when she saw him and tried not to make eye contact. Each instructor would take five cadets, and to her dismay, everyone wanted to go with Sebastian. Sophie and Greg rushed toward his Rover, but a group of star-struck future pilots made it there before them.

"Seriously? They can't even appreciate his genius," Greg said, stuffing his hands into the pockets of his uniform.

"Just his dreamy cheekbones," Sophie sighed.

Nora rolled her eyes and pulled Sophie and a slouching Greg along to the next Rover, where a graduate named Oliver met them. Ty and Cat followed along, too, not seeming to care much about which Rover they ended up in. Cat's nose was buried in her tablet, and more than once she stumbled into Ty as they walked.

"Dreamy or not, he's the youngest pilot in the history of the station. He graduated just last year," Greg said, scrambling up the ladder.

"You've *got* to introduce me," Sophie said. She squeezed in beside Greg, batting her eyelashes up at him and pleading. It was a move she'd claimed no man could resist. She'd tried to teach Nora on more than one occasion, with hilarious results. Nora couldn't help but grin.

"Uh, no," Greg said, shaking his head, apparently unmoved by Sophie's doe-eyes. "I want him to be my flight instructor. Can't go filling his head with nonsense and things that might distract him."

"Oh, we girls are *nonsense* now?"

Sophie crossed her arms and harrumphed. She crossed her legs and pointedly looked out the window, sighing as she watched Sebastian climb into the adjacent Rover. Greg looked to Nora for help, but she just laughed and shook her head. She thought of those furrowed brows, how Sebastian had mocked her homesickness, and decided against bringing up her run-in with this paragon of theirs.

"You'll never win against Sophie," she said instead. "It's better to just give in."

Oliver, like Sebastian, was grounded and stuck with Driver's Ed duties until his PJ returned from Terra Prime with the next batch of J'nai recruits. He was nice enough, even if he was a bit tyrannical about their harnesses. He adamantly refused to let them touch anything and told them that if they did, they'd be walking back to the station. Without an EVA suit.

Nora couldn't quite figure out if he was joking.

Their assignment was to use their tablets to track their location using the Rover's GPS, which was based on the station. No satellites orbited Ganymede, which could make navigation tricky. Oliver's task was to take them on a winding course away from the station and their job was to plot it. He seemed to take pride in making the course as tortuous as possible, turning them first one way and then another.

Ganymede Station was positioned at the edge of the Nabu Crater, at almost exactly 0° longitude. This longitude was not arbitrarily assigned, as it turned out; rather, it marked the exact line down the middle of the moon's side that faced Jupiter. Since the moon was tidal locked, the same side faced Jupiter at all times. That meant anyone pointing a telescope at Ganymede would not be able to see them, which was important.

"But if someone was pointing a really powerful telescope at us from Earth, at just the right time when Ganymede came around Jupiter, couldn't they, theoretically, see us? Or at least see our shuttles landing?" Greg said. He smacked the side of his tablet, which kept sending incorrect data streams

THE VIEW FROM GANYMEDE

to his screen, leaving his calculations millions of miles from accurate. Then he shook it, holding it high in the air, and frowned again at it. Cat snatched it from him and started to fiddle with it, her head bent so her face was hidden beneath her bushy hair.

"It would be pretty hard for them to see a PJ from Earth," Oliver deadpanned. He couldn't have sounded more bored. "They can barely see this crater—and it's forty kilometers across—let alone our base. Besides, we've got pretty powerful people in place to make sure that doesn't happen."

"Why did they pick this crater?" Greg asked. Cat handed his tablet back to him, and Nora glanced down at it. It seems that whatever glitch had been bugging his tablet was now fixed, and his screen showed their exact location tracing a fine green line away from the station.

Greg leaned forward in his seat next to Nora, soaking it in with boyish glee. The view was pretty spectacular: brown, craggy rocks as far as the eye could see, with an infinite black sky blotted out by Jupiter. Currently the planet was a wide crescent of red and rust and cream, the great storm partially obscured by the dark side.

"Easy to conceal the station from Earth, basically. And less chance of being hit by a meteor..."

"A *meteor*?" Sophie squeaked.

"How do you think the Nabu Crater formed?" Oliver said.

"But aren't you worried about the station getting hit?"

"We're facing Jupiter. All the time. It'd be pretty hard for something to hit us here."

"Says the guy who *lives in a crater*," Sophie muttered.

"The Nabu crater is like a billion years old. It probably formed before Ganymede was even captured by Jupiter's gravity. Chill," Oliver snapped. Sophie frowned and looked out the window, chewing on her bottom lip.

The Rover rumbled over the hard-packed surface of the moon in a lurching, bouncing manner. Nora was starting to regret having eaten breakfast that morning. The taste of powdered eggs lingered on the back of her throat while Oliver rattled off the specs, including the radiation shielding (as Ganymede had no atmosphere). There were also no graviton emitters in the Rovers, which meant that unless they'd been buckled down, Oliver's driving would have had them flying all over the place. As it was, their hair just floated in the air while they mostly remained seated.

"I think I'm going to throw up," Sophie said, putting a hand over her mouth.

"If you throw up in this thing, it's going everywhere," Oliver said. "Low grav, remember?"

"Then if you don't want regurgitated coffee all over your precious vehicle I suggest you slow down," Sophie growled. Oliver shrugged, but the course of the Rover noticeably slowed and smoothed out.

Rovers frequently traveled all over the planet, mostly picking up containers dropped off by the J'nai or sometimes to access and retrieve fresh water from the southern pole. Apparently, the Rover crews broke off huge glaciers and dragged them all the way back to the station. Nora tried not to think too much about the water recycling system and what it meant. She realized this was her first time off-station since her arrival. Leaving the station behind made her feel somehow more alone – it was just the six of them and the Rover on the surface of the moon. The station had vanished from view, and Nora's stomach clenched with the recognition.

All in all, they drove out for only about an hour, turned, and came back. The view was extraordinary but fairly monotonous – brown sand and rocks, black sky punctuated by Jupiter's bulk and a million brilliant stars. The real trick was trying to keep track of their GPS coordinates on the tablets while Oliver bounced them up and down the small hills and ravines. Nora's stomach was starting to feel a little less queasy by the time he finally turned them around, though Sophie had turned a rather pasty shade of green. Cat seemed oblivious to their discomfort, muttering something about the curvature of the moon and something about an oblate spheroid while dutifully plugging away at the programs on her monitor. Once the Rovers were back in the dome and through the waterfall-like shield, they could exit, and did so gratefully. Sophie accepted Ty's help down the Rover's steps with a trembling but radiant smile; Nora gulped the recycled air of the station like she'd been drowning. She never thought she'd be so glad to be back at Ganymede Station and out of the rank, claustrophobic little Rover, though the ride had been exhilarating.

"God, I could just kiss the ground," Greg said, kneeling on the plastic-coated floor. Oliver was less than amused.

"Don't forget, your pairings for next week's Rover training sessions will be uploaded to your tablets tonight," Oliver called as they made their way from the dome.

"Nora, can you believe it? They're going to let us *drive* one of those monsters!" Greg said, pushing up against her playfully.

"Can't wait," Nora said, putting one hand against her stomach. Rover driving was *nothing* like being in one of the sleek PJ's she'd arrived on – it was like a carnival ride from Hell. Her equilibrium felt off, and Greg put a hand on her arm.

"Hey, you ok? You're looking a little white…"

"Fine," she said, swallowing hard. "Ten bucks says I'm the first to puke on a Rover this year though."

"Not if I beat you to it," Sophie said, fanning herself dramatically.

CHAPTER 9

J'hara's next lecture was a presentation of the hierarchy and history of the J'nai people. She explained that Terra Prime was not the true J'nai homeworld; no, that planet had been decimated years ago by Qaig invaders – but that was as much as she said about the genocide that the Admiral had alluded to. Nora's skull itched – there wasn't even anything on the tablets to indicate what had really happened to the J'nai, or how bad it had been. Over the past ten years though, thousands of stranded J'nai had made their way to Terra Prime, to their new outpost, and established colonies all over the planet, effectively intermingling different subgroups of J'nai from all over the galaxy. At least, that's what J'hara told them.

"The Star Ports were our only connection to each other," J'hara said, continuing her lecture. A spinning picture of the Milky Way flashed across the screen at the front of the class, and a thin highlighted structure, vaguely ring-like with bright spots every so often, ran through it like thousands of beads on a chain.

"Now. Back when the universe was younger, light moved faster than it does today."

Wesley immediately shot his hand into the air. It looked like he'd burst if he didn't say something.

"No, I'm not going to get into the details," J'hara continued, now pacing in front of the room. Wesley reluctantly lowered his hand. "Ask your astronomy professor. But basically, as the universe expanded, the energy of the universe also stretched, and light slowed. I had a human explain it to me once like this: Imagine you were rolling out a piece of clay, thinner and thinner and thinner, until it was as thin as it could be. And then you kept stretching it. Eventually, you'd see cracks, splits, between the bits of clay. You could see through it then, see what the clay had been covering up. You might say something similar happened to our universe. The J'nai call these cracks the Current, a place where light—and matter—moves at the speed it once used to, millions of years ago. Humans might call them wormholes, or hyperspace routes. Over thousands of years, J'nai worked to create the Star Ports along this pathway. You can jump onto the Current anywhere you like, but getting out is much trickier. J'nai ships can only leave the Current at Star Ports, making the outposts at those locations ideal places for our colonies.

"When the Qaig attacked, they began by blowing up the Star Ports. Each one is linked, you see. When one went out, it became a stopping place in the Current. No one could pass; as more Ports were destroyed, the chain of the Current became disjointed, like a loop of string cut into bits."

The beads on the chain illuminated on the screen blinked out slowly, until only a few fragments of connected light remained, on far ends of the galaxy.

"We don't really know how many other ports are still functioning. The only two we can access at this time are the one here at Jupiter and the one near Terra Prime, our new home world. It would take thousands of years—even using our xenon engines—to reach them all. So for now, it seems, we are stranded. This is why we contacted your Earth for help."

The room was silent. J'hara sighed, then she straightened her shoulders and continued with her lecture.

"Despite the atrocities of our past, the various nations of the J'nai—all that's left—are now united as never before. Our traditions were strengthened. Family means more now than ever. The familial unit of the J'nai is a little different from that of humans; the structure I'm told is analogous to a wolf pack back on your Earth." She showed a picture of a smiling, pink-skinned J'nai family. Their clothing was some sort of shimmery silver material, but other than that (and the pink skin), it could have been any family portrait at first glance.

"Can't you tell us more about the Qaig?" Nora asked. J'hara's head whipped around, and she met her gaze for several interminable seconds. Nora swallowed hard. She could feel the eyes of the class upon her, like lasers. She didn't know why she'd felt compelled to ask that question, but now that it was out, she wished she could take it back. She wasn't the kind to speak up in class, especially not about something that was clearly taboo. She could hear someone giggle in the back of the room, and her face flushed. She wished she could shrink into oblivion.

And then, J'hara completely ignored her question, and continued her lecture.

"There are the leaders," she said, pointing to the male and female pair in the center. "They make decisions for the rest of the family unit. They are the only ones who form a bonded pair and reproduce."

Since this *was* a class full of teenagers, there was a ripple of barely suppressed snickering – Nora's question, for the moment, forgotten. Nora's heart rate began to return to normal, though she could still feel cold sweat trickling down her back, making her uniform stick to her skin.

"The rest of the unit is made up of their offspring," J'hara said, pointing to some of the slightly smaller J'nai, who were facing the lead pair. "They are the workers of the family. They may, if their lead pair allows it and if they show considerable talent, one day leave to form their own pair.

"We operate on something akin to your human caste systems," she continued. "This family you see here is my family unit. Humans refer to our caste as the Gammas. They are the family units that tend to maintenance work and manual labor."

She switched to a picture of another family unit, this one with skin in shades of green. They were standing before a white tower with massive window panes. J'nai in sleek white robes were moving about behind them.

"These are our Betas. They handle scientific research and engineering."

The slide flicked again, this time to a bowl-shaped room full of J'nai dressed in colorful robes seated before something that looked like an empty throne. J'nai of all shades—and shapes—filled it to the brim. Nora was astonished to see that some of them didn't have the lithe, athletic lines of J'hara but were built on blockier, almost reptilian lines. One or two even had feathers streaking down their arms. They were a beautiful, exotic bunch. The room itself reminded Nora a bit of the pictures she used to see of Congress back home, except in a sleeker, starker building. She also doubted that any congressman ever had the kind of gold and white tattoos that covered these J'nai. They swirled in dots and arrows and lines across all of their faces, down their cheeks and necks, and across their exposed arms and hands.

"These are the Alphas. They are the ruling class. They make the decisions for our people and enforce the laws."

"What's with the tats?" someone asked. J'hara frowned back at the picture.

"The Alphas are marked at infancy. The patterns displayed are inherited, a family crest if you will, passed on from generation to generation. It's an Alpha class tradition."

"Do the rest of the J'nai have tattoos, too?" Sophie asked.

"The only other class that has marks on their skin is the Omega class, in black."

"What's an Omega class?" someone asked, but before J'hara could answer, Sophie added-

"Do you have pictures of them, too?"

J'hara paused.

"No," she said slowly. The class was waiting for her to elaborate, but she seemed unwilling to say anything more on the topic. Nora frowned. J'hara clearly had a very set number of things she felt were appropriate to discuss with her class, and several other things that she would not talk about.

"Who gets to decide?" Wesley asked. His question rang through the silent room like a shot. Unlike Nora had been, he seemed unaware of the attention of the class, their eyes now focused on him like lasers. He raised his eyebrows in question as he awaited a response. It came, finally, slowly, as if drawn out from J'hara by force.

"Decide what?" J'hara asked, each syllable hesitant, her head tilted slightly to one side. Her shell-pink skin was flushed a slightly dark shade, Nora noted.

"Who is an Alpha and who is an Omega. Is it based on your skin color? Are all Gammas pink, like you? Who gets to pick?"

"No one," J'hara said. "You are what you are, whether your skin is pink or green or any color."

"Seems harsh," Greg whispered.

"Efficient," J'hara corrected, then straightened her back. She turned back to her screen, and – ignoring several hands that had gone up in the room – continued her lecture.

"Each district has a leadership council comprising the Alphas from the area. Each district then elects a representative to send to the Queen's Council, which meets in the room I showed you."

She flipped now to a picture of a beautiful J'nai woman with ice-blue skin and shimmering white hair falling to her waist. The woman was standing on a balcony overlooking a harbor with a crown of clear, tall crystals on her head. More crystals draped from it in glittering strands to mingle with her layered blue outfit. She seemed serene, aloof, untouchable. Glittering gold tattoos swirled down the sides of her face and across her hands like imprints of elaborate lace.

"This is our Queen Iyle, the ruler of all J'nai," J'hara explained. "She is the Supreme Alpha, just as her sire was, and so forth, back for one hundred generations. Her family unit has been the ruling body of the J'nai and always will be."

"Are the J'nai here Alphas?" Wingman asked. He was so tall, he made their seats look like they were meant for little children. J'hara frowned again.

"We are referred to as Deltas, a new class" she said. "Most of us were once Gammas, but now that we're adrift from our family units and the rules that define us through them, we are no longer truly Gammas. On Terra Prime, that caste no longer...accepts what we have become. So we have chosen a new designation for ourselves."

This also bothered Nora. The J'nai valued their relationship with humans and needed their help, yet ostracized those they sent to work with them? Did they value humankind so little? Although, to be fair, the humans on Earth had decided to send teenagers into space, not full-fledged scientists and warriors. Maybe it was a similar decision-making process.

By the time they adjourned, the class was subdued. Everyone was in a daze as they gathered their things and moved on, and Nora wondered if their minds were whirring as frantically as hers. Even the usually rambunctious Sophie was quiet as she walked with Nora back to their room. The more she learned about the J'nai, she thought, the more puzzling they became.

CHAPTER 10

The first term passed in a blur. Nora found herself too busy and too tired to think most days. The sheer magnitude of the experience had her questioning everything, and each answer she got just inspired a thousand more questions, some of which were easier to answer than others.

"Wait a second," she said one morning while sipping her coffee at breakfast. She sniffed at the steam coming out of her thick ceramic mug – it sure *smelled* like coffee. She sipped it again, more cautiously – it tasted like coffee. Like the most deliciously brewed coffee she'd ever had. And she knew it had plenty of caffeine – she could already hear her blood buzzing from it.

"How do we even *have* coffee here? Is this another one of the chemical tricks from the mad scientists downstairs? There's no way *this* came from the greenhouse."

She'd been told the chemistry students were particularly proud of their secret plans. They'd concocted things like Thalia's hair dye, and rumor had it, they'd even made moonshine using a spare copper coil from engineering.

"Please," Sophie responded. "You think this kind of place could function without coffee, with the amount of work everyone has to do? The J'nai grow it for us. On Terra Prime. It's a kind of peace offering."

"So, they grow us coffee, and we fix their Star Ports? Seems fair," Nora said.

"I mean, have you *tasted* it?" Raina said, grinning.

"Yeah. No, really, I get it. Not being sarcastic this time. It's a totally fair trade," Nora said, and took another gulp. She felt somehow better knowing that it came from real, honest-to-goodness beans from trees that grew in the ground, rather than from chemicals in the lab.

"I heard the station gets its funding back home from the stuff we mine from the asteroids. You know, rare earth metals," Zoe said, closing her eyes in bliss as she took a sip. They were all enjoying their coffee this morning (except for Cat, who drank water), as the caffeine helped banish the dark circles under their eyes. Nora wasn't the only one with a heavy workload, she realized.

"So?" Raina asked. "Who cares about a few tons of space dust?"

"So they should sell this stuff instead. Put Starbucks out of business," Zoe said with a wicked grin.

"I know, right?" Sophie said. "I hear they keep the best Terra Prime espresso beans in a locker down by the water tanks—to keep cadets from raiding it."

"Don't even think about it, Soph," Nora warned, unable to suppress a hint of grin.

Sophie just shrugged, nonchalant. Overhead, the buzzer that marked the start of the academic day rang, and they left for class, gulping the dregs of their coffee and hurrying from the cafeteria.

▰ ▰ ▰

Later that day, Nora and Sophie sat at one of the rectangular tables in the dining hall, eating their fish sticks and kale and trying not to think too much about what was in the grayish goo they had for dessert – they both agreed, that *definitely* had come from the lab and not Terra Prime like the coffee.

The cafeteria was divided into cliques, just like at any high school. There were the nerdy tables (entirely Faxes), the jocks (Originals), and—according Sophie—the popular table, which was them, of course.

"So I think I found a way to hack the security cameras," Sophie started. "Did you know they have cameras like practically everywhere?

Obviously the cleaning bots have them. Otherwise how would they know where they were going? But…Ohmygod, Nora, look!" Her voice dropped several decibels, but still managed to carry a fearsome urgency.

"What?" Nora asked, turning her head. No alarms were going off; no lights were flashing overhead.

Sophie grabbed her hand, and Nora startled, nearly jumping from her seat.

"No, get down! He might see!" Sophie said, then relaxed. She dropped Nora's hand, brushed a long curling black lock from her face, and smiled incandescently as a small group of older boys walked by wearing green flight suits.

Sebastian was with them. He did a double take when he saw Nora, and when he realized she was looking at him, he gave her the slightest nod of acknowledgement before continuing to make his way across the cafeteria with the rest of the group. Nora turned back to her plate, moderately mortified, and stirred the goo with her fork, while Sophie sighed and rested her chin in her hands.

"Nora, when did you meet Sebastian Benoit?" she asked, her voice still dreamy and her gaze distant as she watched the door he and his friends had walked through. Nora winced at the memory.

"A few weeks ago, I think? I kind of interrupted him…working or reading or something in his room. I don't know what I did, actually," Nora confessed. "But I'm pretty sure I ticked him off."

"WAIT – you were in *Sebastian Benoit's BEDROOM?* How am I just now finding out about this? What's he like? What did you do? Can you show me where it is? Did you charm him with your wit? Seduce him with your… brain?" Sophie said. Nora winced again, this time at the shrill pitch of her friend's voice – so close to being the level of a dog-whistle that several people at tables all across the cafeteria turned to stare at them. She felt her cheeks growing warm.

"It wasn't like *that,* Soph – I heard some music and went to check it out. I swear, I never even heard of the guy before that."

"But he nodded at you! God, I'm so jealous!"

"Oh, come on," Nora said, rolling her eyes. What was there for Sophie to be jealous of? During her single interaction with him she'd only managed to irritate him.

"He's gorgeous, admit it. God, I just want to drown in those eyes. Do you think they're more of a blue-green or maybe like a teal? Or turquoise?"

"More like a gray-blue," Nora said, rubbing the back of her neck. It wasn't hard to conjure up the image of those eyes. Sure, he was cute, if you liked tall, broody men with that certain *je ne sais quoi*. The smile-less greeting he'd just offered, however, felt a lot like the cold shoulder he'd given her when she found him listening to jazz. It wasn't a handsome look on anyone, even one with such sharply chiseled cheekbones.

"I heard Thalia and Sebastian were like a thing last year," Sophie said with a sigh. "It got pretty serious, but then they broke up. I hear it was a bad breakup, too."

Nora thought of the way Sebastian seemed to instantly dislike her and that hidden smile when she said she was nothing like Thalia. His reaction was starting to make a little more sense. She shook her head. No wonder.

"How on earth do you get your information?"

Sophie grinned.

"Isn't that a silly phrase? 'How on earth'? Shouldn't it be 'how on Ganymede?'" Sophie said, twirling a strand of hair and looking in the direction that Sebastian had gone.

"You're changing the subject, Soph," Nora said, but grinned in return.

"Yes," Sophie said. Looking away from them with a sigh, she reluctantly returned to her lunch and to her rant on the cleaning bot's cameras.

If socializing on the station was hard (at least Nora had her room-mates), classes were infinitely harder. She spent hours at night going over her physics homework with Cat, who took to it like a duck to water, but it was no use. Just when she thought she had it figured out, her professor would throw a curve ball. She studied and studied until her eyesight went wiggly. She woke up in a panic most nights, dreaming of the Coma Cluster and Dark Energy and the Planck Era and whatever other subjects she'd been reading about. She'd started feeling panicky just *thinking* about the next exams.

What made it worse was that Thalia—perfect, brilliant Thalia, who had graduated at the top of her class, who was the best at everything she did—was the teacher's assistant. Rumor had it that her lab was working on a project so top-secret that only the Admiral and MacGregor really knew what was going on in there. Thalia certainly touted the fact every chance she got.

Today, though, sitting in her science class, Nora thought for sure she'd nailed it this time. She'd been able to answer every single homework question. But as she sat at her desk checking her answers, her confidence dwindled rapidly into extinction.

"Wrong again, Ms. Clark," the professor said, shaking her head as she looked over Nora's shoulder, reviewing the work and letting out an exasperated sigh. The woman seemed to be nearing the edge of her patience with her – this was a professor who was literally used to working with Einsteins, Nora thought, and cringed. She bet they never missed a single question, ever.

She looked back at her numbers. She didn't understand how the calculation could possibly be wrong. Thalia grinned viciously from the corner of the room, where she sat scrolling through something on her tablet. Nora flushed.

"But I thought …"

"If we built a wiring system based on your numbers, we'd all be blown to heaven the moment we switched it on. Try again."

Nora sighed.

"What was that, Ms. Clark?" the professor said.

Nora shook her head.

"I didn't say anything."

"It sounded like this." Professor Harden mimicked the sigh, then pinched the bridge of her nose and closed her eyes for a moment. She took a deep breath, and Nora prepared herself for a verbal onslaught on the exhale.

"Ms. Clark, are you familiar with the term 'the wisdom of crowds'?"

"No," Nora said, shrinking a little in her seat.

"It means that if I have a jar of pennies and I ask everyone in the station how many pennies are in that jar, some people will guess too high, and some will guess too low. Some might be close, but no one will be able to guess the exact number."

"I could do it," Sophie muttered. Professor Harden ignored her.

"But if I average all those guesses, you know what I'd find?"

"No," Nora said, uneasy with the sudden sugary tone in Professor Harden's voice.

"The average of all of those guesses would likely be within 1 percent of the real answer. So you see, dear, you don't have to have the right answer all of the time. We are none of us truly alone. That's why we work as a team, as a unit, all of Ganymede together."

Nora was dumbfounded. This was as close to a pep talk as anyone had given her, despite her failing almost every single class. Her heart leapt in her chest.

"To cancel out those like you, who would drag the Gaussian curve down!" Thalia called. The cackling in her tone told Nora that she'd planned that line and had been waiting to use it, biding her time like a lioness stalking her prey. Dr. Harden glared at Thalia, and her lips pursed into a thin white line. She readjusted her glasses, but she didn't contradict Thalia's remark.

Nora sank into her chair, her cheeks burning, and wondered if Hypatia had ever felt as embarrassed as she did right now.

━━ ━━ ━━

"Hey, Nora. Want to do my politics assignment for me?" Sophie asked. Her roommates were all back in their room, finishing up homework for the next day. Only Cat seemed to be enjoying it.

"If you'll do this chemistry problem for me," Nora moaned. Chemistry. She *hated* chemistry. It was only marginally better than physics, though a large part of that was due to the fact that Professor Harden and Thalia were not in charge of it.

"That is so not a fair trade," Sophie protested. "How about I do part of your astronomy homework, and you introduce me to Sebastian Benoit?"

"No way," Nora said, shaking her head. "He's scarier than the admiral."

"Eleanora Clementine Clark!" Sophie spurted.

"Oh, you did *not* just use my middle name!"

"Wait, like the fruit?" Raina asked.

"My mom had a thing for citrus," Nora mumbled, her cheeks burning. "Or it's an old family name. Her explanations varied."

"Awwwww!" Lara said. Her wide mouth made an 'o' shape, and her voice mimicked baby-talk. "That's just so adorable! Yes it is!"

Nora tried to ignore the heckling.

"How did you even find that out?" she protested, eyeing Sophie.

"I'm a genetically engineered super spy, remember?" Sophie said, grinning wickedly.

"Sophie, what did you do..." Nora started.

"Nothing they can prove. And you wouldn't *believe* what I found out about Zoe..."

"Oh no you don't!" Zoe said. With the lightning speed *she'd* been genetically gifted, she leaned her chair back and seized a pillow, hurtling it across the length of the table. Sophie shrieked, barely dodging it.

"Oh yes," Sophie teased, hiding behind Nora. "*All* the juicy secrets!"

She was interrupted by another barrage of pillows as Raina and Zoe teamed up against her.

Which is how, ten minutes later, Nora and Sophie came to be huddled in the little bathroom, holding pillows like shields and straining to hold the door shut against the other girls while Lara, Zoe, and Raina mocked them from outside.

"Oh, come out, girls. We *promise* we won't throw these pillows at you!" Raina said.

"And we *certainly* wouldn't *dare* let Zoe sit on you while Raina tickles you," Lara added.

"Oh, that's a good one!" Raina said. "I learned this hold from Olivia yesterday that will keep you completely immobilized, at my mercy..."

"Yes, yes, Raina, we know – we're not trying to torture them," Zoe said.

"Not too much, anyway," Lara cackled. Someone – Zoe or Lara based on the size of the impact – had thrown her shoulder against the door, and cracked it open ever so slightly. Sophie shrieked and yanked it shut again.

Sophie and Nora exchanged a glance, their faces as serious as if they were about to do battle. Outside, the other girls hammered on the bathroom door.

"On the count of three, we let go," Sophie whispered. Her lips were a tight line, her mood, somber. Nora nodded. She doubted any military commander ever in history had taken a battle decision so seriously.

"One, two," Sophie said. Nora tensed.

"THREE!" Sophie shouted, letting go of the door. They'd expected the other girls to fall, tumbling, into the bathroom. Instead, they were immediately bombarded with the rest of the pillows from the entire room, wielded by three girls shouting victoriously as they attacked.

This is also how the girls of room 10013 were introduced to the Night Guards, that pair of unfortunate lower-level officers whose job was to prowl the station on the hunt for "shenanigans."

Apparently, the boys in the room next door had called in a complaint.

"They said it sounded like someone was being murdered in here," one guard said, frowning as he surveyed the state of their room, now with furniture overturned and bedding strewn. Sophie hid her pillow behind her back.

"No murdering here, officers," she said with a bright smile. "So sorry for the disturbance."

So appeased (but barely), the guards left.

"You're going to get us in trouble," Cat called from behind the curtain of her bunk. She'd drawn it when the pillow fight started.

"Those Original spoilsports," Raina muttered, cursing their neighbors under her breath and gathering her blankets from the corner where they'd fallen.

CHAPTER 11

It really wasn't surprising, given how busy she was, that Nora had reached the end of the term before having another minute to think about how homesick she really was. They got weekends here off just like at traditional schools back home, although it was expected that she'd spend the time doing research or reading rather than rooting for local sports teams. She used to spend weekends baking with her mom, or maybe going down to the bayou with her dad and keep a lookout for alligators. It still seemed like yesterday, though it had been – she stopped for a moment as she tried to remember exactly how long it had been – five months? Six? A pang of guilt shot through her. She shook her head, a lump forming in her throat. She tried to refocus on her previous train of thought, but her mind had been de-railed.

She wondered if she'd ever see another movie, ever sit in a dark theater and eat buttered popcorn and laugh at the cheesy storylines like a normal teenager, the kind who worried about what college she was going to, not some clone-girl millions of miles away from home in a giant hamster ball taking classes on alien history.

She found herself in a long corridor off the academic section, just outside the amphitheater with the domed ceiling where she had her politics classes. She stopped at the window at the far end of the hall. From here, she'd discovered, she could see the shuttles in their little dome at the far side of the station. Every so often, if she was lucky, she'd see one of them land or take off. She wondered how long it would take one of them to make it to Louisiana. How long had it taken her to get here? A few weeks, then?

"It's late," a drawling voice said. "Shouldn't you be out celebrating the end of term with the rest of the first years?"

She turned and saw Sebastian coming out of the amphitheater, his tablet tucked under one arm. He locked the door with his thumbprint and then stood watching her, cocking his head to the side, waiting for her to move or respond.

"What are you doing here?" she said, sighing. Facing Sebastian was the last thing she needed right now.

"Are you crying?"

"No," she said, but when she touched her face, she found her cheeks were wet. She turned back to the window.

"It looks like you are."

"Well I'm not."

He walked up and stood there, looking down at her. She'd been right—his eyes were more of a gray-blue than the teal Sophie had imagined, like a calm sea after a storm. Not that she'd ever see the ocean again. She sniffed and stood taller, refusing to be intimidated by him. She'd been intimidated by everyone lately, it felt like – by her teachers, by Thalia, by her own past. How could she possibly ever live up to the expectations everyone put on her? She frowned, and changed the subject.

"Don't you ever sleep? What are you even doing down here this late?" she said.

"I don't go back out for another month or so until my captain comes back with my ship. I use the after-hours time to catch up on some extra studies."

"Your ship?"

"The *Rapscallion*."

"Nice name."

"I always thought so," he conceded. Nora nodded. Silence loomed between them.

She fidgeted, glancing back out the window. She wanted to keep watching the shuttles, but Sebastian's presence made her antsy. She felt like a child who'd been caught doing something she shouldn't.

"Well, see you around then," she said. Ducking her head, she made her way past him and back into the corridor. She didn't want to tell him she'd been watching the shuttles and dreaming of home, not after the way he'd rebuked her the last time she admitted to being homesick.

"Wait," he said. He caught up to her in a few swift strides. "Come with me. I want to show you something."

"No thanks, I've seen all the things," Nora said, but she knew her tone betrayed a desire to go with him. He gave her another one of those half smiles, like the one he'd given her when he didn't think she was looking the first time they met. She assumed it was an expression he didn't use very often, but it looked nice on him.

"Just come on," he said. "You won't regret it. I promise."

"Well, okay," she said, drawing the word as she pretended reluctance. Truthfully, she was being drawn in by the enigmatic—almost gravitational—force that was Sebastian Benoit. She could see why Sophie always made such a fuss about him. He had a presence, a bearing, that she'd only ever seen before exuded by the XO, MacGregor. She'd thought maybe the XO had an air of command, or natural charisma. Sebastian seemed to have a similar aura, she thought.

Or maybe Sebastian was just insanely hot. It was tough to say. Was she really going to turn him down? Sophie would never forgive her if she did.

She followed behind him through the academic corridors, past the crowded rec room (where she could hear raucous, celebratory cheering inside), and beyond the storage rooms she'd been working in lately during her "volunteer" sessions. She was grateful he had his back to her, so she could hide the blush she knew was making her face heat up. What dark corner of the station was he heading to, and why? Why was he suddenly trying to be friendly, if you could even call it that?

"Where are we going?" she asked, frowning. He didn't reply, just motioned for her to keep following. He was infuriating.

After a few more turns, once she was thoroughly lost, he stopped before an air lock made of clear plastic, like the one she'd passed to get into the main hub from the shuttle bay.

"Come on," he said and held the door for her. "I know you feel home-sick. We all do, at first. Earth is so far away, but some parts of it are closer than you can imagine." The area pressurized, and he opened the far door into a large clear dome—so large it must have spanned acres.

Nora drew in a sharp breath.

She was in a greenhouse, or something better than a greenhouse, really. Beyond the clear walls, she could see the blackness of space, the curve of the barren brown surface of Ganymede. In here, however, were rows of tall aluminum A-frames with plants of all kinds—from tomatoes to beans to strawberries—coiling up their sides. Huge heads of kale and cabbage ran along the wooden trays at their bases. The tinkling of automatic waterers dripped all around her, swaddling her in warm humidity that felt like a rainforest—or even, she realized with a grin, the balmy air of the swamps back home. It was a massive place—an orderly, extraterrestrial farm. She knew plants were grown here—she'd been eating them since she'd arrived—but it never occurred to her that they were growing in a place like this. It was somehow both mundane and magical at the same time.

"Sebastian, this is wonderful," she said, trailing her fingers down a row of climbing cucumbers. These plants were the first thing that reminded her of home, the first thing that wasn't entirely alien or cold metal or white-coated plastic. Sebastian trailed behind her as she explored, a silent shadow. She could feel his eyes on her, and flushed again, and tried not to look back. It was easier than she thought – there were so many things to look at in the greenhouse, to distract her.

"What are these?" She asked, running her hand across a tall glass cylinder. It was one of dozens, maybe hundreds, in little pods across the greenhouse. They were more than three times her height, maybe four or five feet wide, and filled with brilliant green algae floating in clear water. They were nearly luminescent, like being underwater in a kelp forest with sunlight filtering down through the tangle, or so she imagined. She laid a hand on the glass, surprised to find it warm, and turned to look at Sebastian.

"Algae tanks," he said, hands in his pockets. He didn't offer more.

"What are they for?" she prompted.

"Oxygen. And protein."

"So, you're saying…"

"Yes. You've been eating the stuff since you got here," he said, and quirked a little corner of his mouth in a smile.

"Gross," she said, but she smiled, too. Her gaze flicked down the row of tanks.

"Are those fish?" Nora blurted and ran over to a pond, elevated and surrounded by a concrete barrier. In a foot or so of clear water, a school of flat green fish the size of her hands swam lazily in circles. When she trailed her fingers in the water, they swam up and nibbled at her fingertips. She couldn't help but giggle.

"What an amazing place. It almost does feel like I'm back home," she said, sighing with contentment. She took in the warmth and humidity and green-ness of this place. If she closed her eyes, she almost imagined she could feel a breeze stirring her hair, feel the sun shining against her skin, smell the damp earth. It brought back memories of the muggy, salty, sulfuric scent of the marsh back home. She could almost hear the buzzing of mosquitos, and her arms prickled at the thought.

Then her eyes popped back open.

She *was* hearing buzzing. She looked at Sebastian, who cocked his head to the side.

"I think I hear …" she started to say. No, she *definitely* heard – was it coming from over … yes, she saw, and jumped up. There was a row of squat cream-colored boxes behind the pond area, and in-and-out of them zipped tiny, velvety bees, industrious and focused on their job.

"They really thought of everything here," she murmured, watching the insects. No wonder there was a double-seal on the greenhouse. She imagined the little bees getting sucked up into the decontamination chamber like in a vacuum cleaner and being spat back out inside.

"There are amazing things here on Ganymede, Nora," Sebastian said, breaking her reverie. She turned, and he nodded for her to follow him. She left the bees reluctantly, wiping her hands dry on her uniform, trying not to think about all the fish sticks she'd eaten as she passed the pond. She followed him to the edge of the greenhouse, where condensation fogged the clear glass of the enclosure. He wiped at it with his hand and looked out over the surface of the moon.

"It's incredible here," she said, putting her fingers to the glass. "Isn't it strange how you can get used to even the most unbelievable things? Ganymede doesn't even look so foreign anymore."

"She will always have a surprise or two waiting for you," Sebastian said. When she looked up at him, waiting for an explanation, he just nodded towards the glass. She was suddenly and acutely aware of their proximity, the sleeve of his jumpsuit nearly brushing her jacket, and took a step back before following his gaze.

"Look."

He pointed to a spot near the horizon, the part of the sky that luminous Jupiter wasn't covering anymore. As she watched, a red glow emerged, like a swarm of fireflies, trailing their light in a hazy wave of color.

"What is that?" she said. She watched it, entranced, as the dim lights danced and swirled and grew.

"The aurora," he said. "On Earth we call it Aurora Borealis or Aurora Australis. Here, it's red because the elements in the air are different, so we call it Aurora Igneus. That means- "

"Flame-colored," Nora breathed, her memory flicking back to nearly-forgotten Latin classes in middle school, and caught the faintest chuckle from Sebastian. She didn't dare look at him, didn't want to tear her eyes from the scene and miss a single heartbeat of it. "It's so beautiful."

"Yes, it is," he said. They watched the faint light show for a while, until it faded into the blackness of space. "Sometimes I watch the eclipses from here. You can see the shadows of Io and the others trace their way all across Jupiter's surface. It is clearer from the observatory, of course, but it's nice to watch it from here. Fewer people come here."

"Thank you for showing me this," she said, her eyes still fixed on the horizon, her breath fogging the glass, wishing for the red lights to reappear. They didn't.

"You're welcome," he said.

"I mean...I know I'm not in Louisiana anymore. I realize this is an unprecedented opportunity, and I'm grateful for it. Really." She turned to him. "Thank you. You – this place – has made me feel better than I have in a long time."

He studied her for a moment.

"*Lorsqu'il fait somber, cherche les ètoiles*," he said after a pause, but offered no explanation.

"Sounds pretty. What's it mean?" Nora said.

"When it's dark, look for stars," he said, and sighed, looking back out at the horizon. Nora thought about this for a moment.

"You were homesick when you got here, weren't you?" Nora asked. He looked back at her briefly, but he didn't say anything. Nora thought he was hoping the aurora would come back, too.

"It's okay, you don't have to tell me," she said. "Did you live in France? Was it nice there?"

He looked at her sideways. His eyes, which had just been as clear and warm as the sky on a summer day, had become darker, stormier. A muscle flickered along his jawline as he clenched his teeth. Aside from the tension there, he was motionless. Nora hadn't meant to upset him. Was there something in his past, then, that he didn't want to discuss?

"We should probably go," he said. "No one's supposed to be here this time of night."

"Right. Yeah, of course," she said and followed him back out of the greenhouse and through the airlock. He was silent. He'd become impenetrable Sebastian again, with his dark brows drawn low over his eyes.

"I'm sorry," she said, trying to break the silence, once they were back in the outside corridor. He hadn't spoken in several minutes. "I didn't mean to pry."

He glanced at her but still said nothing. He just stuffed his hands into the pockets of his flight suit and hunched his shoulders. They walked in silence the rest of the way, until Nora found the corridor that would lead her back to the rec room and the raucous party within. Just when she thought he might not hate her, she'd gone and ruined it by being nosy.

"Go enjoy yourself," he said, nodding towards the room. "The real work will begin soon enough."

"Okay. Thanks again, Sebastian," she said, accepting his dismissal and black humor glumly. He looked at her for a moment, his head slightly cocked to the side.

"My friends just call me Bastian," he said after a moment. Then he left, brushing past her.

"Bastian," she repeated. A friend. He counted her as a friend. He, the Ace himself, Mr. Perfect Cheekbones. She felt a flush run to her face, a little giddy feeling in the bottom of her stomach. She turned and headed into the rec room, brushing a curl back from her face.

CHAPTER 12

Over lunch, as Sophie went on—*again*—about the youthfulness of the station and of the Halloween party she planned on throwing with some of the chemists this weekend (she wouldn't say *why* she was planning it with the chemists, a crowd she usually avoided for their social leprosy), Cat awkwardly blurted in with an admission that made her flush rather red.

She said being with her roommates made her feel like she had sisters, something she'd always longed for. She'd been lonely, growing up.

"Come to think of it," Nora said slowly, "we were all only children, huh?"

Nods all around.

"So why wait until we're sixteen to bring us here?" she mused. "Why not earlier, start up our training and education sooner?"

"You're kidding, right?" Zoe asked, an eyebrow raised. "Can you imagine a space station full of toddlers? You know that saying, 'In space no one can hear you scream'? Let me tell you, sound carries in a tin can like this."

Raina elbowed her, scattering Zoe's spoonful of peas across the table. Zoe shoved her back, knocking the smaller girl off the bench.

"Look, it's not *my* fault the Night Guard heard that guy squealing like a little girl," Zoe whispered to Raina.

"Anyway, they had to make sure you weren't a dud," Raina said, brushing off her uniform and sliding back into place, glaring at Zoe.

"A dud?" Cat asked. Nora had already opened her mouth to ask about Raina's encounter with the Night Guard, but she hesitated, wanting to hear the response to Cat's question, too.

"Since you're here, you know you turned out as expected. It would be a real waste of resources to transport you all the way out here and train you up if you weren't going to perform up to expectations. Like maybe your egg got scrambled during the IVF process, you know? There could be all kinds of glitches in your DNA. Happened a lot in the old days," Zoe said. She shrugged and flicked a pea across the table, bouncing it off Sophie's arm. Sophie brushed it off, a look of disgust on her face.

"So what happens to the duds?" Cat asked, horrified.

"I'm sure they keep on being duds on Earth. That's why the handlers aren't supposed to tell you anything until you're a teenager. You just keep on being a failed Einstein clone or whatever and just live out your totally normal life with your handlers posing as parents," Raina said.

"What's it take to be considered a dud?" Nora asked with wonderment. She was failing – or close to failing – the majority of her classes at the moment, after all. "I'm surprised I didn't qualify."

"Maybe the station was desperate for another Thalia," Lara said, grinning her wide grin. Zoe flicked a pea at her, and Nora stuck out her tongue.

"But if you turned out to be a dud, your handlers, instead of having a sixteen-year-long job, are just stuck with you forever? And you're stuck with *them* forever?" Sophie asked, in an uncharacteristically quiet tone. The rest of the girls paused.

"That wouldn't be so bad," Nora said, thinking back on her upbringing. Other than the constant moving around, it had been a rather pleasant time. She might have liked like a normal life with the Clark's. They certainly had seemed to like her – no, she thought, they loved her, like any parents would have, clone DNA and all.

"Speak for yourself," Sophie said, pushing around the mashed potatoes on her plate.

She met with Aditi again the next week. Aditi had sent her a message on her tablet, asking her to stop by after class.

"Nora, hey," she said, turning off her computer as Nora walked in. "How are you? How are your classes going?"

"Good," Nora said, forcing a smile. "Really good. We're getting to go out on a Rover next week." That much, at least, was true. She was looking forward to it. There was literally no way she could screw that up; all she had to do was climb into the Rover in the landing dome and drive it in a circle. She wouldn't even have to wear a pressurized EVA suit since she'd be inside the Rover the entire time.

"Ah, I remember my first Rover experience," Aditi said. "Ganymede's a beautiful place. Did you know the poles are ice, like on Earth?"

"I heard that," Nora said. "But I don't think we're going to go that far our first trip out."

"No, I don't imagine so," Aditi said. "And I'll bet you probably have a lot more questions for me now that you've settled in and had some time to adjust."

"Did my par…handlers…think I was a dud?" she blurted. "Is that why they didn't tell me about all this?" She waved her hand around, gesturing to the whole of the station, to all of Ganymede. The thought had been worrying her since Raina first brought up the idea last week. Nora knew there was a Board of Directors for the Ganymede Project – she'd been told a sentence or two about them before she agreed to go to Ganymede in the first place – but about the actual process for creating clones she'd heard precious little. And no one seemed to know anything more than she did. Aditi put a hand on her shoulder.

"No," she said, pursing her lips. "You're not a dud, Nora, and nobody ever thought you were. You are an exceptional young woman, and your parents thought so, too. They were so very proud of you. And in their own way, I think they felt they were protecting you."

That comment stayed with Nora for hours.

The next day, Nora was paired with Oliver for her first attempt at Rover driving. She'd had to read the manuals and pass a simulated experience, so other than for her nerves, she was ready to go. The plan was just to go outside the dome, drive in a circle, and come back.

If only it was that easy.

"Jesus, cadet - what lunatic at the DMV passed you when you learned to drive?" Oliver said, hanging tightly to the side of the Rover. It pitched to the side violently as Nora corrected her course. The screen in front of her where a car's pedometer would be showed a zigzag green line of her path from the station.

"Um," Nora said, returning her gaze to the terrain ahead. "I never really got my license…"

"Well, that makes sense," Oliver said, his teeth clenched.

The Rover moved at a sedate ten miles per hour, but there were many rocks, and each felt like a giant pothole. Handling the surface of Ganymede in a Rover wasn't as easy as driving her parents' old sedan in an empty parking lot—or maybe it would be if the parking lot had been filled with invisible quicksand pits and patches of slick ice and craters within craters within craters.

Nora cringed. Her parents kept promising her that someday she'd be able to take the test for her learner's permit, but since they had just the one car and she didn't really want to drive anyway (she had nowhere to go), it had never been an issue.

The low rim of the Nabu crater loomed in the distance, like the crest of a far-off wave. Nabu was just a shadow of a crater, really—a palimpsest, a ghost of its former self. Years of erosion from the moon's water had shaved it down until just the low wall remained, cradling the station in a low, flat bowl. It was like how you could shake one of those old Etch-a-Sketch toys a little, she thought, so just a shadow remained of the picture you'd drawn. She'd found one once in a thrift store and had been so fascinated by the retro gadget that her parents bought it for her. They'd spent hours together giggling over their drawings. None of them was a Da Vinci clone—that was obvious. She smiled at the memory.

"ROCK! Cadet, are you trying to hit every single…Jesus, look out!"

And that's how Nora managed to crash her Rover into the only boulder within a kilometer of the station.

━━ ━━ ━━

Nora was lost in thought on her way back to her room – still playing Oliver's scolding and the mechanics' bewildered sputterings in her head - when she heard, "Hey, watch where you're walking!"

She looked up and realized she'd trod right across a smooth floor that was being waxed by little automated bots. The man who shouted at her was controlling them with a remote, which he was waving at her with one hand.

"Oh, I am so sorry!" she said, backpedaling over her steps. Ten perfectly outlined shoe prints tracked across the otherwise perfectly shiny and clean surface. The man sighed, and ran a hand over his face, rubbing his eyes. Under his eyes were dark bags, and his wild hair was shot through with white.

"It's okay. It's not like they cloned Rembrandts to do this sort of thing," he said, giving her a tired smile.

"No, they didn't," Nora said, frowning. "I mean, you're doing a great job, though. Nice... waxing," she said, cringing at the lameness of her comment. The man nodded, waved her on impatiently, and sent his bots scurrying over to fix the damage.

Nora thought about the man and his robots as she walked. There was something in their brief interaction that tickled in the back of her brain, and it wasn't until she was almost at her door that she realized what that tickle was.

The Board hadn't cloned *any* artists.

Sure, they had their da Vincis, but he was only an artist incidentally. Most of the Leos were down in the lab, inventing things. There were no pure artists, no writers. The notion stuck with her all day, lingering like the scent of floor wax in her nostrils, niggling at her. No Shakespeares. No Van Goghs. And no Ghandis or Mother Teresas, despite what Aditi had told her upon her arrival.

CHAPTER 13

The party Sophie planned for Halloween—or schemed might be a better word—turned out better than even she could have anticipated. It was the kind of epic scene that would live on in infamy on Ganymede Station.

After dinner one night a few days beforehand, she'd sent out a message to all the cadets' tablets (and even a few of the graduates she thought she could count on not to rat them out), inviting them to the First Annual Ganymede Toga Party.

Coming up with the theme was simple, she told Nora. They didn't have access to a lot of things to make costumes out of—and their allotted 3D printing budgets would only take them so far—but one thing they had in abundance was sheets. After all, there were more than five hundred people on this space station, and there had to be sheets enough for all of them. Simple and elegant.

And, at least in Sophie's case, scandalously revealing.

"I'm pretty sure that's not how it's supposed to go," Cat protested as Sophie tied hers up. "It's not really Greek, you know, or even Roman."

Cat had the modesty to wear jeans and a T-shirt under her toga. Sophie did not.

"You look great, Cat, and…ooh, helloooo, Zoe!" Sophie said. Zoe had used what looked like a pillowcase to create a sort of crop-topped toga, with a high slit revealing her muscular legs.

"Rawr," Sophie said. Zoe beamed and turned to help Raina with her costume. Raina kept protesting. Really, did it need to be *so* short?

"You've got great legs. Flaunt them," Zoe said firmly. Raina glared daggers at her.

"That's the spirit!" Sophie said. Nora rolled her eyes. She'd let Sophie get her into a toga, but she'd at least managed to keep the legginess to a minimum. After hours of makeup and hair-dos—Lara had brought a curling iron to the station, to their mutual delight—they were ready. Lara was long gone, though, on a mysterious date with someone she wouldn't reveal. Nora was sure Sophie would get the information before the night was over. She always did.

Sophie and her minions had transformed the chemistry lab into a raucous Greek(ish)-themed party room, with paper columns and a peaked cornice over the doors. White and gold streamers hung from the ceiling, and someone—the engineers, if Nora had to guess—had constructed an actual working aqueduct out of painted Styrofoam and tubing that spanned the lab tables. They'd hooked up some sort of pump, and down the aqueduct flowed...

"Is that *vodka?*" Zoe said, watching a pair of cadets push cups under the spout at the end.

"God, I love the chemistry department," Sophie said, sighing in contentment.

"You know aqueducts were Roman, not Greek," Cat said. "And mixing Doric and Ionic columns? They're only a few *hundred years* apart."

"Come on, Cat." Sophie rolled her eyes. "Here. Have something to drink."

She'd somehow convinced the chemists to make a rather potent vodka out of pilfered potatoes from the aquaponics garden. They'd spent weeks on it, apparently, sneaking the spuds a few at a time, and to their knowledge, nobody had caught on. The students were quite proud of themselves, and bragged to a few of the Originals in the room about it.

"I mean, I'm no Emperor Octavian, but I think we did ok, wouldn't you say?" one of them – Nora thought his name was Ned, an Archimedes clone - said. The group of Original girls he was talking to looked unimpressed.

Nora glanced back to Sophie, who was handing her a glass beaker. She hesitated. She'd never had any alcohol before.

"Oh, come on, girl. What are they going to do, ground you? Give you detention sorting dirty laundry? Send you back to Earth?" Sophie giggled, pressing the confiscated lab beaker into her hand.

"Fair enough," Nora said, sniffing the drink. It seemed to be mixed with something sweet and carbonated. It looked harmless enough. She dipped the tip of her tongue into it and then scowled at the taste- acrid, with a faint odor of something like gasoline emanating from it.

Sophie beamed, and threw back a shot of the stuff herself in one swift gesture. She motioned for Nora to do the same, and then waved to the students setting up speakers. Momentarily, music was booming through the room, rattling the lab cabinets and their glassware. Sophie started dancing.

"Nora," she said, dancing close and throwing an arm around her. She handed her another beaker of fuming liquid, this time slightly purple in color. It didn't smell quite as bad as the first one did.

"Drink. It's been a helluva semester. Besides, maybe it'll give you the courage to dance with Greg."

Sophie arched her sculpted eyebrows. Nora flushed.

"I hit a nerve. I knew it! I'm never wrong about things like that," Sophie crowed. "Now, cheers!" She clinked her beaker against Nora's and chugged. Nora hesitated a split second, then managed to gulp a little down. It burned in her throat like fire.

"God, that's even more awful as the last one!"

"I know!" Sophie grinned. "Come on, you've got to help me get this dance party started."

"Why do we even celebrate Halloween up here? Don't tell me you want to have Alien Prom, too," Nora groaned.

"Well, let's see...half the school is made up of child soldiers, and the other half is basically the kind of nerds who'd end up stuffed in lockers back home. Something like prom is everyone's worst nightmare. Nearly everyone, anyway. Maybe everyone but me. Not to mention, you should never, *ever* ask a J'nai to dance. Just trust me on that one."

"Wait, why, did you...?"

"*Trust me.* Now go mingle!"

Greg showed up just at that moment, wearing a sleeveless white shirt and a sheet draped from shoulder to shoulder. Above his quirky, mismatched eyes, perched awkwardly on his head, was an olive-leaf crown of cutout green paper. He stopped her when she tried to fix it so it sat straight.

"Hey, it's a part of the costume! You know, toga! Toga! Toga!"

"What are you talking about?"

"Belushi? *Animal House?* Dear God, tell me you nerds have seen it..."

"We're playing *Clash of the Titans* later, if you're interested," Nora teased. He rolled his eyes.

"Just as well. I'm too skinny to play a good Belushi."

After a while – and another drink, she and Greg felt comfortable enough to get that dance Sophie predicted, a fast one to a booming song with tons of bass. The lights were dimmed, now, and spinning lasers sent fractured shards of color all over the walls. She was really starting to have fun, even though she'd never really danced like this before. She grinned up at Greg, who was showing off for her. She laughed – the lights, the song, the music, it was all pulsing through her, moving her to its own rhythm. Greg caught her hand – his own palm sticky with heat – and spun her around. The sensation was instantly dizzying. She couldn't remember ever having had such a good time.

Some of the other boys from her initial shuttle—Ty, Wingman, and Wesley—eventually trickled in, all looking acutely uncomfortable with white sheets draped around their sweats. Those boys—and most of the Originals, come to think of it—hung back, talking among themselves, occasionally shooting glances at Greg.

"Greg, why are they all looking at us?" Nora said, as they refreshed their drinks at the aqueduct. Greg shrugged.

"Probably just jealous that I'm dancing with the prettiest girl in the room," he said gallantly, putting a hand on her arm.

Nora frowned.

"That's not it," she said. Greg shook his head.

"Didn't you hear me? I was trying to give you a compliment," he said. The room was so loud, he'd had to lean in to her ear to make sure she heard him. Nora reflexively gave him a smile, and scanned the room. Something seemed wrong.

Every group was sectioned off. Her roommates were mostly socializing with themselves, though a crowd of male Faxes were huddled around Sophie, who ate up the attention like Queen Cleopatra receiving supplicants. The Originals were all hanging by the aqueduct, drinking little and saying less. Her feeling of fun disappeared in an instant, replaced by an increase in her dizziness – what was going on?

"Greg," she whispered. "No one's…you know, mingling."

"We are," he said and slipped an arm around her waist. The scent of mouthwash hit her nostrils, and it made her suddenly nauseated. She brushed him off, swallowing hard.

"Seriously. What's wrong with everyone?"

"Not everyone is comfortable with each other yet, you know. There's some old resentment here at the base between Originals and Faxes. Neither side really trusts the other. I don't even think they like the fact that I'm dancing with you," he said, glaring at the Originals in the corner.

"Why not?"

"Oh, because Faxes have big brains and bigger egos, and Originals think Faxes get special treatment because of their DNA." He shrugged. "Some sort of segregation is inevitable, I guess. Half of the PJs won't let Faxes on board, or so I heard. Even the Ace himself won't fly with a Fax."

"Is that what you think? That I've got a big ego?" Nora said. Her head buzzed. The overhead lights began to hurt her eyes. The Ace? Was that Bastian? She couldn't remember.

"What do you think?" he said, reaching for her hand. His own was damp and warm, his mismatched eyes slightly glazed. "Because I think you've dazzled me since day one."

"Before you knew what—who—I was, you mean?" Nora said. Overhead, the lights pulsed and gleamed, shining off of the frown on Greg's face.

"What? No, don't be ridiculous. I can overlook something like you being a clone if…"

"Hey, you know what, I'm sorry," she said, shaking her head. "I think…you know, the drink and the…things. I didn't mean to make it sound like you were prejudiced like the rest of them. I'm just going to go. Got a headache, you know."

She waved a hand through the air and turned to leave. Suddenly she felt like she needed to vomit.

"Okay…" he said, drawing the word out several syllables. "You want me to walk you back to your room?"

"No," she said, shaking her head. She headed out of the lab, stumbling a bit as she moved. Where had that counter top come from? Her hip ached from the impact. That was going to leave a bruise.

Sophie hurried to her, moving faster than Nora's slightly-blurred vision could follow, and grabbed her arm.

"You know he was *trying* to hook up with you," she scolded. "'Walk you back to your room' is code for 'Let's go to your room and make out.' God, Nora, don't play so innocent. Isn't this what you wanted?"

"What, are you everywhere? How'd you hear that? I just had a little too much…you know, want to clear my head. I'll catch you later."

Sophie protested, but Nora didn't seem to hear (or care). She slipped from the lab and felt even more sick to her stomach as she left. Her vision was tilting wildly. Was this what it felt like to be drunk? She wasn't sure she liked it at all. She gulped in air, moving away from the pounding music, which was driving daggers into the back of her eyes with each bass-heavy beat.

Faxes. Originals. The words rolled around in her head like marbles on that spinning thingy they used for gambling in Las Vegas. That game with the numbers—what was it called?

At least the air was cooler in the dim hallway. She took a deep breath, and the fog in her head seemed to dissipate a little. She rubbed her temples as she started back, thinking about how the students had self-segregated at the party, how she and Greg were stared at, about his comment on the two factions not trusting each other entirely—that kind of division sounded so…Earthlike. She couldn't believe they'd brought it four million miles. And what *was* that stupid game called? She saw her thoughts like marbles rolling along the wheel, stopping over red and black squares, over Faxes and Originals.

She was so focused on her thoughts that she didn't keep track of where she was going and ended up deep in the academic section, at a dead end. She turned around slowly, her head swimming. Academic section. End of the hall. She knew this corridor. She used to watch the shuttles land and take off from this window. All she had to do was follow it back and turn left at the…

Damn. She ran a hand through her hair, the crown of ringlets now hanging in limp strands down her back, and turned around again.

And when she did, she turned right into Bastian Benoit. She stumbled a little, and his hand shot out instinctively to grab her elbow. The top of her head barely reached his chin, her foggy brain registered, as close as they were - and then she wobbled as he pulled her upright.

His face flickered from a moment of brief amusement to one of complete exasperation. His cool gray-blue eyes assessed her costume, and he shook his head. Of course, he was wearing his perfectly pressed flight suit, like always. Maybe he'd decided to dress up like a snobby pilot for Halloween. Boring. She giggled at the thought.

"Oh come on," she said, throwing her hands up. "Seriously? Why do I keep running into you?"

"It is a small station. And you are lost."

"No."

"Fine. Where are you?" He crossed his arms.

"I'm here. And I'm going there," she said, wobbling a bit as she pointed down the hall. Bastian came closer, dark brows furrowed, and sniffed at the air.

"Is that…? You have been drinking."

"Maybe," Nora said. She didn't feel drunk anymore, if that's what she'd been feeling before. She felt great! A few moments ago, her stomach had been ready to hurl itself up, but right now, she felt like she could take on the whole world—the whole galaxy! She certainly wasn't about to be intimidated by 'The Ace' Bastian Benoit, no matter how dreamy he looked. She giggled again.

"Bed. That way," Bastian said, turning her by the shoulder and pointing down the long hall. His lips were turned down in a hard line. "Now."

"Yessir," Nora said, and saluted him, more or less. The words had felt mushy in her mouth, like her tongue couldn't wrap itself around them properly. She went to walk but had to reach for the wall. The floor wavered before her eyes like a mirage in a desert.

"*C'est dommage*," Bastian said, rolling his eyes. He grabbed her elbow—tightly, almost painfully—and propelled her down the hall. It was all she could to stay standing and stagger along behind him.

"If anyone sees you, you'll be in detention for a month," he hissed into her ear.

"Why do you care?" she said.

"I care because you have potential, and you seem intent on wasting it."

"Because I'm a Hypatia, like your precious Thalia?" she said. "I thought you didn't care about Faxes."

He stopped, his eyes searching her face.

"No, you were right before. You are nothing like her. Like either of them," he said. He sounded so disappointed. His death grip on her elbow tightened like a blood pressure cuff.

"It was just a party," she mumbled. She wasn't really sure why she felt the need to explain. "It's Halloween, in case you didn't notice. Just trying to unwind. You should try it."

"Fine. Forget it. Let's just get you back to your room before someone sees you, and you can sleep it off," he said, shaking his head. She could barely keep up with his long strides. He ignored her protests as he pulled her along.

"You know what? I think you're jealous." She said. He stopped, and she would have fallen if he hadn't been holding onto her.

She didn't know where that comment came from. She was just tired- *so* tired, and he was walking so fast. She would have said anything to get him to slow down. She tried to wrench her arm from his grip—to no avail. The room still spun, the taste of bile thick in the back of her throat. Somewhere, a station generator was humming. It sounded like a herd of elephants stomping a staccato cadence on her eardrums.

"Jealous? Of what?" His voice was soft, dangerous. It should have been a warning to her, a sign for her to stop talking. She went on, unheeding the caution in his tone.

"Of me. Of us. Of the Faxes. Because you're just an Original. You'll never have the brains or raw talent that we do. No one will ever write history books about you. It's why all of you hate us."

"I do not hate you," he said. His voice was tight, spoken through clenched teeth.

"Then why won't you fly with Faxes?"

"Who told you that?"

"You know...someone," she said, fluttering her hand in the air to brush off the comment. Had it been Greg? Sophie? Well, she wasn't lying at least – it *had* been 'someone.' Tonight, she thought. They had told her tonight.

"I will not fly with Faxes because you all feel entitled, and that makes you dangerous. What have you done with your life? Not Hypatia. You. *She* was one of the greatest minds of the ancient world; she revolutionized theories on planetary orbits. And what do you do? You use that big brain of yours," he said, poking her square in the forehead with his index finger, "to make moonshine, and get drunk. You do not get to claim her actions as yours. Now if you show me someone worthy of respecting, I will fly with that person any day, Fax or not. Because the girl I see in front of me now..."

The scorn hit her harder than any physical blow. She stumbled a bit as he released her arm. He was so angry, he'd been practically shouting at her, his face so close that her ears were ringing. She felt sick to her stomach, dirty even, humiliated and ashamed. It was not a feeling Nora was familiar with. She really, really didn't like it.

"I can get back to my room on my own from here, thanks," she said. She'd meant it to sound dignified, but her slur ruined the effect. She turned and headed down what she hoped was the right hallway, and when she turned back to look, he was gone.

━━ ━━ ━━

The following morning, most of Room 10013 woke up with terrific headaches. The only one who didn't was Cat, but at least she was kind enough to be quiet. Lara was nowhere to be seen.

There wasn't enough coffee on Ganymede to undo the aftermath wrought by the chemistry nerd's illicit alcohol. Cadets all over the station had dark circles under their eyes—and a vaguely green tint to their skin, too. Nora swore she was never drinking again. She couldn't even remember making it back to her room. She'd just sort of woken up in a puddle of drool in her bunk, her hip aching from where she'd bashed it against the countertop in the lab. She was right- it *had* left a bruise.

There wasn't enough alcohol on Ganymede, though, to block out the memory of Bastian's stinging rebuke. It haunted her all day. When the throbbing fog of the hangover started to dissipate in the early afternoon, Nora was startled to realize something.

Bastian was right.

She was homesick. She was struggling in her classes. She was worried about what everyone else thought about her – but she was a Hypatia! She was one of the most brilliant women in history. Would Hypatia have let other people's opinions dictate her actions? No. She kept going. She kept working until everyone in the ancient world knew who she was and what she was capable of.

Nora vowed, as she downed another cup of Terra Prime coffee, that she would do whatever it took to make sure no one - not Dr. Harden, not Thalia, and certainly not Sebastian Benoit - was going to make her feel inferior ever again.

Late that night—though she really, really just wanted to go to bed— Nora joined the other science-focused Faxes at the Astronomy Lab for their mandatory night viewing session with a renewed vigor, even if it was somewhat dampened by the lingering effects of the night before.

The Astronomy Lab was one of those domes way out in the crater, connected to the rest of the station by long, winding tunnels. The lab, run by a strict Filipino woman who reminded Nora of a stereotypical old-school librarian with her thick glasses and severe hairstyle, had telescopes the size of pickup trucks. They were capable of seeing Jupiter and its groups of satellites in sharper detail than NASA could have ever imagined, picking out rock formations the size of grapefruits on the dozens of moons. They mapped orbits and discussed resonances, and compared the Amalthea group to the Galilean moons, of which Ganymede was one. Jupiter had sixty-seven moons that NASA knew about, but Ganymede Station had identified an additional sixteen, mostly small moons barely large enough to bear the name. Cat dreamed of discovering one herself and naming it for Marie Curie. Her enthusiasm at the Astronomy Lab was unparalleled.

"God, I have the *worst* headache," Sophie said, rubbing her temples. She was wearing her giant tortoiseshell sunglasses, and had been all day. "Ran out of mascara" was her excuse when people asked, but Nora knew the light hurt her eyes. She'd seen enough of the other cadets flinching in the bright white illumination of the station to recognize it.

Nora nodded in sympathy and stepped up to take her turn at the telescope. It was a marvelous instrument—how it had been 3D printed and assembled with precision here on Ganymede was a testament to the ingenuity and dedication of the station scientists and technicians. The breathtaking view almost—*almost*—made her forget about her deplorable physical state. She could see each swirling eddy of red within the great eye of Jupiter, each of the moons in such stark relief, it was like they were mere feet away instead of hundreds of thousands of miles.

What interested her most of all was the glittering halo surrounding the Jovian planet. She'd first seen them on her approach on the *Santa Maria* – it seemed so long ago now. When she was younger, she'd never much thought about Jupiter—or space at all, really. She *did* remember from her elementary days that Saturn was the planet with rings.

Jupiter's rings, though, were diaphanous things, ethereal and delicate. It was in such sharp contrast to the stark colors of the gaseous orb that it struck Nora as particularly beautiful. She liked to use her telescope time picking out each of the ring's four parts—the aptly named Halo ring, the Main ring, and the two Gossamer rings named for the moons that moved through them, the Thebe and Amalthea. Thebe and Amalthea reminded her of insects making ripples on a still pool; as they orbited, their motion stirred the particles of the rings and sent them into glittering crystal swarms.

"Time's up, cadet. I'll expect your write-up—with specific references to the orbital resonances of the Galilean moons—by tomorrow," Dr. Fernandes reminded her. Nora sighed and stepped back to let Orphic, an Edison clone, take his turn.

Cat and Sophie were sitting on a bench at the back of the lab. Their window faced away from Jupiter, and the reflected light from the gas giant lit up the outer moons like bright stars. Cat held her index finger just in front of her nose and was pointing them out as Nora approached.

"I think that one's Pasiphae...and that's Carpo," she said.

"That's great, Cat," Sophie said, sighing. "I wonder what everyone else is up to tonight."

"Probably still recovering from your party," Nora said, squeezing onto the bench with her roommates. "I swear, I'm never, ever drinking again."

"I'm tempted to agree with you on that one," Sophie said, pinching the bridge of her nose.

"Shhh!" Dr. Fernandes reprimanded. "Some students are still trying to learn!"

Nora glanced around the lab. Most of the cadets were using their tablets to draw caricatures of their strict professor, though two were sleeping in the corner, propped against each other. Nora remembered them vaguely from the party last night.

"Sorry, professor," Sophie said. After a stern look, Dr. Fernandes turned around, and Sophie continued her conversation.

"After you *didn't* let Greg walk you back to the room last night, I saw him talking to this Original girl, I think her name is Chloe or Zoe or something. She's got *nothing* on you, of course, not half as pretty, but all the same. You don't want to let him get away."

"I wasn't in any shape to flirt," Nora said, rolling her eyes. "I ran into Bastian Benoit on my way back and am pretty sure I managed to insult him in less than two sentences."

"Oh, so he's 'Bastian' now?" Sophie sighed. "Why can't *I* ever run into him?"

"Girls!" Dr. Fernandes shouted—though somehow it was still a whisper. Like a really fierce whisper. "Am I going to have to separate you?"

"No, professor, sorry," Sophie said, giving Dr. Fernandes her most charming smile. The woman didn't seem the least bit charmed or convinced.

Again, Sophie waited a moment for the woman to turn back to the telescope, then continued.

"Why didn't you ask Bastian to walk you back, then?" Sophie said, wiggling her eyebrows. Nora flushed.

"Right, like that would ever happen. He practically tore my arm off trying to drag me back to my room before anyone could see me stumbling around the corridors," Nora said. The memory made her squirmy and uncomfortable. She wasn't used to being embarrassed. She really didn't like it.

"So he wanted to get you back to the room?" Sophie said, archly. "Very interesting,"

"It wasn't like that," Nora said quickly. "And then I said something about him being jealous of Faxes, and he just yelled at me and left."

"Originals can be so touchy," Sophie said, nodding her head in agreement. "It's not our fault we are who we are."

"Sophie, look!" Cat squealed. "I think that's S/2003 J2!"

"That's nice, Cat. Look, all I'm saying is that you may have missed an opportunity to hook up with Bastian Benoit. You *really* blew it last night."

"A second ago you were berating me for not kissing Greg. Will you make up your mind?" Nora said, exasperated. She wasn't sure she wanted to "hook up" with either of them. She liked Greg, she thought. And he seemed to like her. But Bastian? Every time she ran into him, she felt like they both swung to a different emotional extreme. Disappointment. Wonder. Gratitude. Disdain. "Besides, Bastian is the most arrogant, intolerable, uptight...I mean, he's just impossible to talk to, and...it's like talking to a wall sometimes. And he *always* thinks he's right, just because..."

"GIRLS!" This time it really was a shout. "One more time and you'll be in detention for a month!"

"Sorry, professor," Sophie and Nora chimed. Cat was still sitting in rapt attention, gazing out at the moons of Jupiter, her tablet forgotten in her hands.

CHAPTER 14

Sophie stood in front of Nora in short cotton shorts and a sports bra, a pair of sneakers in hand. "Come on, Nora," she said. "You're coming with me."

"Uh, no. Absolutely not," Nora said, returning her gaze to her tablet, where she was trying to memorize the formulas for the next day's physics quiz.

"All this studying is going to fry your brain. You need a break. Besides, we start self-defense class in PE soon. Don't you want to have some muscles so you can throw Thalia on her ass?"

Nora considered that, and minutes later, she'd tugged on her T-shirt and shorts, wishing the latter were longer—like sweatpants, maybe—and they were headed toward the gym. This was a part of the station Nora usually avoided at all costs. She wasn't a gym rat like Sophie.

"You're a terrible influence, you know that?" Nora said.

"Yes, I know." Sophie grinned as she pushed open the doors. "And you keep me from making too many rash decisions. It's why we're besties."

Nora flinched at the slew of machinery and weights before them. Everything in there looked like it could crush her if she screwed it up.

"Let's just start with these, okay?" Sophie said, nodding toward a pair of stationary bikes. "No coordination required. And they're stationary, so you can't run them into anything."

"Am I ever going to live down that Rover mess?"

"Nope," Sophie said and climbed on. Sophie was getting more than a few stares from the male component of the room, which wasn't surprising. Her workout gear didn't cover much.

"They're staring at you. How can you focus if they're staring at you?" Nora grumbled.

"Well, it keeps the attention off you. I thought it would make you more comfortable," Sophie said. Nora rolled her eyes. Sophie didn't have any jiggly bits at all. If Nora had had to be a clone, why not someone like Helen of Troy? Or a silver-screen movie star like Sophie—maybe Elizabeth Taylor or Grace Kelly?

"Thanks, that's so noble of you," Nora groaned and started pedaling. At least Sophie was right about one thing: there was no way for her to screw this up too badly. She flipped through a few programs on the bike, finally settling on one whose screen ran her through a simulated countryside. Her legs burned with the effort after a few minutes, and she struggled to keep up the pace that Sophie so effortlessly maintained. Sweat started trickling down her back, and her face felt hot. Her wild curls were already starting to stick to her forehead. How had she let Sophie talk her into this?

After a while, Ty came in, waved at them, and headed to the weights with some of the other boys.

"He's pretty strong," Nora panted, watching him lift a bar with a series of weights on it.

"Is he?" Sophie said, like she hadn't noticed. But she was watching him from the corner of her eye.

As they left the cardio section of the dome—Nora, red-faced and sweating; Sophie "glistening," as she called it—they came across Zoe and Raina, who were headed to a sort of makeshift boxing ring in the far corner.

They heard cheers go up from the small crowd as two cadets took turns throwing punches at each other. And when they got closer, they heard someone holler, "Nora!"

It was Greg. He raised up from a fighter's crouch and waved at her with a boxing glove–clad fist. Taking advantage of his distraction, his opponent promptly knocked him on his behind.

"Ouch," Greg muttered as the other boy helped him up. He limped out of the ring and threw a towel around his neck.

"That didn't hurt. Not at all," he said. He took a swig from a water bottle and then came over to where the girls were standing.

"What are you doing here?" he asked. Nora shrugged.

"Just wanted to see what was going on."

"Girls, you know the first rule of Fight Club," Greg said, looking at Raina and Zoe in mock admonition. They rolled their eyes.

"Fight Club?" Sophie said.

"Yeah. Can't talk about it. Sorry," he said with a smile, then left them to go get some more water.

"Okay, girls," Zoe said, turning to her friends. "For those of us on officer track—like me and Raina and Lara—the station wants us to learn self-defense, weapons, and hand-to-hand combat. It keeps us fit and our bodies disciplined. Healthy body, healthy mind."

She dropped her towel, rolled her head around on her neck, and stepped into the ring, where Greg's partner was looking for someone new to spar with. The boy sized up Zoe, who was several inches taller than him, and eyed her biceps. He didn't look confident about his odds.

"Want me to show you guys a few moves?" Raina asked Nora and Sophie, seeing their gazes wander across the group. "Right now, we're just learning a lot of basic stuff. I did more than this in my elementary school RAD class." Raina had pulled her long black hair into a tight bun, and cracked her knuckles as she watched the fights.

"And risk breaking a nail? I don't think so," Sophie said.

Nora looked up. She'd been tempted to take Raina up on the offer, but then she spotted Bastian facing off against the biggest J'nai she'd ever seen. She followed Sophie over, and they watched from behind a group of Fight Club cadets.

There was nothing 'basic' about this. It was in a different realm from the way the cadets were bludgeoning one another. This was something else entirely—almost like ballet. A choreographed display.

With punches.

Bastian was squaring off against a green-skinned J'nai who looked like he was half crocodile, half Hulk. He had sharp canines and dark scales down his bare back and across his forearms. Bastian, for once, was not in his flight suit but was dressed similar to the other cadets in loose sweats and a white tank that gave his arms their full range of motion. Looking at the J'nai, Nora imagined he'd need every bit of it.

Bastian was crouched, his center of gravity low, his long blond hair swept back from his eyes. He held his hands in front of him as the J'nai struck out with a lightning-fast punch. They exchanged a sequence of blows, each faster and harder than the last. Any one of the big J'nai's punches looked capable of knocking Bastian over, but Bastian was faster, and none of the blows landed. A ring of observers had formed to watch them, but the fighters were oblivious, locked in the moment, their gazes fixed on each other. The J'nai feinted again, and Bastian ducked back. This time he knocked the strike aside with his right hand and seized the J'nai's wrist. Bastian stepped behind him, grabbing the man's shoulder with his left hand and pulled the arm up. Bastian now held the man's arm in a painful reverse extension, and as he applied pressure to his shoulder, the big J'nai was forced to kneel in front of him.

They held this pose for a second or two, the J'nai trying to force him off, swatting at Bastian with his free hand - but each time he did, Bastian increased the pressure on the joint. Nora was seriously concerned it would pop out of place. After a long minute, the J'nai gave in, and to her surprise he laughed, throwing up his free hand in surrender. Bastian released him, and they shook hands. The big J'nai rolled his shoulder and rubbed it with his other hand, but other than appearing sore, he seemed unhurt. Both of them were gleaming with sweat, and breathing hard. The J'nai slapped Bastian on the back, sending him stumbling.

"One of these days, my friend," the J'nai rumbled.

"Looking forward to it, Dalton," Bastian said. Someone in the surrounding circle—a girl, tall and blond—tossed him a towel.

"Who's *that?*" Sophie hissed. Nora shrugged. The girl looked like some sort of Nordic warrior goddess, with the kind of beauty that made everyone stare – even Sophie.

"That's Olivia. She's a total badass. She teaches the women; Bastian and Dalton teach the boys. Different strengths for us, you know," Raina said. "I'm sure she'll welcome two more for lessons."

"Not a chance," Sophie and Nora said, almost simultaneously – though probably for different reasons, Nora thought - as they watched Bastian and Olivia exchange quiet words.

"Toodles," Sophie added, waving her fingers at their roommates. Then she grabbed Nora's arm, and they left the gym.

"Fight Club?" Nora said. "They're really dividing us up even more—the brains and the brawn, aren't they? Not just Faxes and Originals anymore?"

"I like to think of it as the beauties and the beasts, myself," Sophie said. Nora wondered if she included Olivia in the "beast" category and decided she probably did. While Sophie had plenty of good qualities—loyalty, curiosity, tenacity—she was more than a little jealous of anyone she thought was prettier than her.

Nights in Room 10013 were usually one of the best parts of Space Camp. As the girls became accustomed to their grueling schedules, they liked to reconvene for a while before sleep, to blow off a little steam. They had set up a long table in the room and would finish their homework and talk at night—sometimes for hours.

On this particular evening, Sophie was fed up with homework. She shut off her tablet, and pulled a small bottle from her backpack.

"Wait, where did you get nail polish?" Zoe said, grabbing for Sophie's hand.

"Well, the chemistry department, of course," she said, admiring the little bottle. "Those guys are really starting to grow on me. I used part of my 3D printing allowance this month for the bottle and brush."

She opened the bottle and brandished the brush, then started applying the cherry-colored liquid to her fingernails.

"Those boys really are geniuses. I even got them to make Nora shampoo to keep her hair under control. That other stuff is just *murder* on curls. Didn't you notice?" Sophie said, nodding her head towards Nora. Nora put a hand to her relatively-tamed hair self-consciously – it *had* been nice of her. The curls hung in more-or-less proper ringlets now, not a frizzy mane like it had before. Plus it smelled better than the station-rationed stuff, which was the same color and scent as the coma-couch goo.

"It does look nice, Nor," Raina said.

"Yeah, before you looked like you'd stuck your finger in an electrical socket," Zoe said. Raina elbowed her hard.

"Ow!" Zoe said, rubbing her ribcage. "I just meant that it's a significant improvement! What'd you do that for?"

Raina rolled her eyes, but she was smiling.

"Well, I used my allowance on headphones," Lara said with a grin, digging them from her backpack. She was especially proud of the noise-cancelling feature she'd programmed into them.

"Well that's a good idea," Raina said. "

"Can't hear you," Lara mouthed with a grin, headphones in place, and went back to her studies. Raina rolled her eyes.

"What did you use your allowance on?" Sophie asked. Raina flushed, her golden skin taking on a rather fuchsia hue.

"Nothing."

"Oh, come on. It can't be *that* embarrassing. Zoe, what about you?"

"I didn't spend it on anything," Zoe said, leaning back in her chair. The front two legs were dangerously high, and she balanced on the brink of toppling over. "I gave mine to Raina."

"Oh?" Nora asked.

"She needed a pair of gloves. Her hands keep getting torn up in Fight Club. Our allowance is barely enough for one glove, so I gave her mine."

Raina looked at Zoe but said nothing. Her mouth was a tight, hard line.

"Boring. Cat? What about you?" Sophie asked, paying meticulous attention to her nails.

"What about me?" Cat asked. She was focused on reading something on her tablet.

"What did you print?"

"Needed some new parts for the lab. Connectors keep breaking," she said, not breaking eye contact with whatever she was looking at.

"Seriously? Boxing gloves and lab equipment? Nora, help me out here. Tell me you printed something fun."

"Not really," Nora said, looking over at her bunk. Sophie followed her gaze.

"C'mon, Nora. Tell us," Zoe prompted. Nora hesitated.

"Tell us, or I'll go through your things and find it, whatever it is," Sophie said. Raina nodded.

"Come on – you know Sophie'll find out one way or another," Raina said.

"I … made a picture frame," Nora said. Zoe sat forward, her chair slamming against the metal floor. Cat jumped with a squeak. The sound even penetrated Lara's headphones, and she looked up, startled, her big blue eyes wide.

"You brought a picture from home? A secret boyfriend, maybe?" Zoe said. Nora shook her head and went to get it.

The picture had made it all the way from Louisiana to Ganymede in one piece, suffering just one little wrinkle in the corner, and now she wanted to preserve it as best as she could. Their meager monthly printing allowance was just enough for a thin frame and a clear plastic film to protect the photo. She kept it on the little shelf next to her pillow so her parents—and those silly Christmas sweaters—smiled up at her when she faced the wall to sleep.

"You were really close to your handlers, weren't you?" Raina whispered. Nora nodded.

"Yeah," Nora said. "What about you?" The girls were quiet a moment.

"Well," Cat said, "my handlers died, so they brought me here early. It was easier, I guess. The Board said I was too old to be placed into another home. That's why I'm the youngest here. Not because I'm special or anything, just because they died. Car accident."

"God, Cat, I'm so sorry," Nora said, reaching for her. Cat shrugged her off.

"For some reason, I always think about how they hated parent-teacher meetings. Made them real uncomfortable," Cat said softly. "I guess because we all knew they weren't really my parents. But they took good care of me."

"Well, mine *hated* me," Sophie said, closing her nail polish bottle.

"Go on, please," Zoe said, and leaned her elbows on the table. Sophie shrugged.

"I figured out this whole Ganymede mess before I turned four. You know how hard it is for a four-year-old to keep a secret? Especially with something like this? I had five different sets of handlers before I turned ten. The Board told them to keep me under control," she said, blowing on her nails. "They tried."

The other girls were silent for a moment. Sophie critically looked over her nails, holding them at an arm's length. All of them, even Cat, were watching her.

"What?" she said, finally acknowledging the stares. "Not all of our handlers could have been as warm and fuzzy as the Clarks." She looked to Nora, one perfectly-sculpted eyebrow arched.

"Mine died, you know," Nora reminded her, looking down at the picture. Sophie cleared her throat, and picked at an invisible piece of something on her nails.

"They never told me anything, not about cloning or Ganymede or … any of it. Aditi said they were waiting until I was old enough to understand. She said it wasn't a popular decision with the Board of Directors."

"How'd they die?" Lara asked, her earphones momentarily pushed back into her blond hair.

"Car crash," Nora said. A lump welled up in her throat, constricting her vocal cords. Suddenly it was hard to breath. She coughed once, twice, and looked at the picture in her hands. The room was quiet. Even Zoe's usual antics were – for the moment – subdued.

Raina looked at her, then at Cat, then back again. She pursed her lips, considering, before saying- "There seems to be a high percentage of handlers who conveniently died that way."

"Conveniently?" Nora said, taken aback. There was nothing "convenient" about the way her handlers had died, nothing "convenient" about the gaping hole their loss had left in her life.

"Sorry, bad choice of words- but think about it. Cat's the best in our year, and—and no offense, Cat—maybe she could have used the extra year to, you know, grow up a bit more. I bet her handlers wanted to keep her back, give her more time to get used to the idea of this whole thing, and the directors took action."

The room was silent as they considered Raina's words.

"And Nora," Lara said, eyes wide. "You said Dr. Prasad told you that your handlers' decision wasn't a popular one. You think…"

"You think the Board of Directors for Ganymede would kill our handlers to…?"

"Protect a *very* expensive investment in their clones? Absolutely," Sophie said. "Did you know it costs more than $5 million to clone us? And that's not even counting the surrogacy fees, handler's salaries, and all that."

"Where *do* you get your information?" Lara wanted to know, chin in hand. Sophie shrugged.

"Well that's all moderately terrifying," Zoe said, slumping forward on her elbows. Her usually smiling, joking face now somber.

"No," Cat said, in a voice barely above a whisper. They all turned to her like she'd just shouted at them. She was as white as a sheet. "It actually makes sense."

Nora got up from the table and paced the room. She ran a hand through her hair.

"But why would they do that? My handlers were just waiting for the right time. There was no need to…"

"Unless they never planned on telling you," Sophie said. Lara nodded, and jumped in.

"They treated you like a daughter. What if they didn't want to give you up? What if they tried to play you off as a dud? You said it yourself, your grades were nothing flashy back home."

"That's just crazy," Zoe said. "They thought they could get away with fooling the Board?"

"People do crazy things for those they love," Raina said, uncharacteristically sentimental. Sophie raised an eyebrow, but Raina did not elaborate.

Nora barely heard the conversation around her. She felt numb, the voices of her roommates reaching her as though she had cotton in her ears, or as if she was underwater – distorted, and far-away. Had her handlers wanted her, after all? Had not telling her about her heritage not been a lie for her sake, but a ruse, a way to manipulate the Board into letting her stay with them? Had they come to love her, the Clarks, even knowing that one day she'd be taken away from them? She would never know. She had no way of ever finding out. Somehow, the idea that they *had* actually cared for her, these people assigned to raise her, hurt even more than thinking they had lied to her.

"So either I *am* just a dud, or my handlers loved me so much that they died for me. Those are the options," Nora said. Her roommates were silent, exchanging worried glances.

"I…I just can't…God, I'm going for a walk." She slammed her chair back from the table and ran from the room before her roommates could see the tears starting in her eyes. She didn't know where she was going, but she went out anyway.

CHAPTER 15

Greg was irrepressible. He had been sitting at the edge of her table in the cafeteria for ten minutes, pestering her to put the books down. Despite her awkward and abrupt departure at the party, he'd remained remarkably persistent. Nora found herself alternately annoyed and impressed.

"Come on Nora," he said. "You've been so down lately. Just come hang out with us for a bit."

"For the millionth time, I'm not 'down.' I'm studying," she said. Tablets and notepads lay sprawled out before her. The cafeteria was mostly empty this late, and with the easy access to coffee, it made a nearly ideal study spot—though unfortunately it was not secluded.

"What's with the sudden dedication to studying? Decided to become Ganymede's first hermit? The first Fax Admiral?"

"Just have a lot on my mind," she said, gathering up her papers. Between Thalia's continued mocking, the concern that maybe the Ganymede Board was something more sinister than she'd realized, Bastian's scorn, the fact that still no one could tell her anything about the Qaig War, and basically her concern that any day now she'd be sent back to Earth for being a dud, she was burnt out. She'd found that throwing herself more into her classwork blocked out her internal diatribe for a while, and so she'd done so with all of the spare seconds of her day. As a result, she hadn't spent much time with Greg – or with anyone, really. She got up in the morning before her roommates, and often came back to the room long after most of them were asleep. If she wasn't in class, she was studying, or going to tutoring sessions, or doing extra practice questions. She had to do it – she had to show them all that she, Nora Clark, was just as good as Thalia – no, better, that she was as good as Hypatia.

But if Greg was going to keep pestering, she'd never get anything done here. Better to go back to her room, cramped as it was. At least she could draw the curtain on her bunk for some semblance of peace. She took a sip of her coffee, shooting what she hoped was a glare at Greg. He just grinned, meeting her stare.

"I told you she wouldn't come, Greg," Ty said, coming over. He spoke in soft tones, as if he'd been expecting that answer from her but hoped for the opposite. Greg threw his hands up.

"Oh come *on*, Nor. If I don't have a sidekick, they won't let me into the simulators."

"You want *me* to be your wingman in that sim thing?" Nora asked, voice stretched with disbelief. "You know I crashed the Rover on my first trip out, right?" Like anyone was likely to ever forget that disaster.

"Yeah, but it doesn't matter, it's space!" Greg said, throwing his arms wide. "There's literally nothing for you to run into! All you have to do is stay alive long enough for me to take out Ty and Benny." He looked at Nora with narrowed eyes and – seeing that this argument wasn't quite enough to sway her- decided to change tactics. He grabbed her tablet and books and held them hostage.

"Hey, give those back!"

"Come on, Nora. Just one go! You know it's good to clear your head once in a while from these stuffy books, get some blood flowing. Then I'll leave you alone."

"You promise?" she asked, crossing her arms. Was it worth it – one ten-minute sim to appease him? She *had* been sitting for a very long time. Her lower back was really starting to cramp up from the hard metal benches. Maybe he was right. Maybe it would be a nice break. She'd just about finished tomorrow's assignments, anyway.

"Promise. At least for…oh, another day or so?"

"Fine," Nora grumbled, finally acquiescing. Greg held his hand up for a high-five—which was not enthusiastically received—and steered her toward the far edge of the cafeteria dome, where Benny was waiting for them, tapping one shoe. She hadn't seen him much since their shuttle arrived that first day. Benjamin Lawrence Topper III had such a dour expression on his face, Nora almost wondered if he'd been avoiding her on purpose.

"There's seriously no one else you could have asked to do this?" Nora said, eyeing the redheaded Benny.

"It's late. Everyone else is asleep," Greg said, and then he bumped into her in jest as they walked. "Besides, maybe I want to show off for you."

"It's going to backfire, little man," Ty said, ruffling Greg's hair as he strode past.

"Hey, if you make me look good, I'll set us up on a double date with Sophie," Greg told him. Nora could have sworn a hint of red came into Ty's dark cheeks. It was hard to tell, though, and he'd turned away quickly.

"All three of you are going to be pilots, then?" Nora asked, as they entered the simulation room. Greg nodded.

"Hope so. Benny might make deck officer, though. Maybe navigations. But me and Ty, we're going to be the best pilots the station's ever seen, even better than the Ace. Isn't that right?" Greg said, punching the big man on the bicep.

Nora had only been to the simulator room once before, to practice before her disastrous Rover experience. The Rover simulator was in the far corner, but Greg led her to a series of four large boxy contraptions in the center that had their noses facing one another. Each box was held on an elaborate system of hydraulic lifts and motors to provide that true-life experience. The simulators were in use, and a real-time display with blinking red and green lights (a different color per team) was zooming about a flat screen nearby. Tiny trails of light showed a missile launch, and one by one the ship lights blinked out—the simulators gyrating loudly—until only one remained.

The cadets climbed out of their respective 'shuttles.' Nora was pleased to recognize the giant blond Wingman, although she didn't know the others. Brief introductions were had, and Nora apologized copiously for the rapid defeat she was about to ensure for Greg. Greg just laughed and steered her to the simulators. The systems were rebooting, but in just a few minutes, Greg said, they'd be ready for them to use.

"Ty's been taking lessons from Sebastian Benoit, Ganymede's Ace of Aces," Greg muttered. "Lucky bastard."

"Benoit? Really?" Nora said, surprised. She rubbed the back of her neck absently.

"Yeah, I don't know how Ty got so lucky. Benoit's a total badass. I heard he wants to be a captain, but the station won't let him. Says he's too valuable as a pilot."

"That's not why," Benny said, watching the screen count down the reboot time. "It's because he refuses to fly with Faxes. Says none of them are 'good enough.'"

"That guy's a friggin'…" Nora began but caught herself. Benny actually managed to tear his eyes from the screen at the anger in her voice.

"Nothing personal, Eleanora," he said. "Some people just don't trust your kind."

"My kind," she said, crossing her arms.

"Come on now, Copper Top," Greg said, shaking a finger at Benny like he was a naughty puppy. "Remember what we said about social interactions? Insults are not a very good way to make friends."

"Yeah, you can only insult people *after* you're friends," Ty agreed. "Like if I call Greg a…"

"Hey look, sim's open," Greg interrupted, quickly ushering Nora away from Ty and toward a unit. The doors had swung open after the programming rebooted and were ready to go. Ty took Benny aside and was whispering to him as they left.

"You know he didn't mean that, right?" Greg said, a concerned pucker between his mismatched eyes.

"I know," Nora said with a sigh. "It does seem to be a recurring theme around here though, doesn't it? But it'll just make our victory that much sweeter."

"That's my girl," Greg said, grinning as he showed her into her mock-cockpit (or "mockpit," as he called it).

"Hey Greg!" Ty called. "Benny doesn't think you two will last ten seconds against us. What do you think?"

"Oh, I'm terrified beyond the capacity for rational thought!" Greg said in a high-pitched voice. Nora furrowed her eyebrows – was that another movie quote? He usually did that voice when he was quoting movies. Which he did, a lot.

"What's that from?" she asked. It sounded vaguely familiar.

"What.... What's *that* from?" Greg stuttered. His mouth hung open a moment before he closed it again, shaking his head. "Never you mind. Look, let's just get you strapped in here..."

The controls weren't that different from the Rover, with a joystick-like throttle and a series of switches for the engines, boosters, and front boosters. He helped her buckle into the leather seat, and then—shooting her a beaming smile and a thumbs-up—closed the hatch on her simulator, leaving her momentarily in the dark. And in that instant, her mind flashed to her renewed anger with Bastian and this whole ridiculous thing about Originals not trusting Faxes. She didn't want to think about it, but it just kept turning up, and it was starting to make her feel like an outcast. She may as well have been back on Earth. Something deep inside her chest felt tight, kind of painful, like a coal was burning its way through the bottom of her stomach.

Then, glowing images of three ships—two red, one green—appeared before her, and all thoughts and disappointments momentarily vanished. There was just her and Greg and Ty and Benny in the vastness of simulated space.

Greg's voice came crackling over the shared intercom.

"Okay now, teammate," he said. "No worries, deep breaths, don't cross the streams, and try not to get yourself killed."

Nora groaned. The "try not to get yourself killed" part surely killed the sense of calmness that had, so fleetingly, begun to settle in. She didn't quite get the rest of his pep talk, but she was sure he'd explain it to her – ad nauseum – later.

Truthfully, her nerves had been jangled since Bastian's verbal thrashing. In retaliation, she'd thrown herself into her studies with a fervor she didn't know she'd possessed. It seemed to make little difference, though, she thought, grabbing the control stick. She'd improved, a little, but it was hard to feel accomplished in your classwork when you were literally taking astronomy with Einstein.

When the simulation began, she didn't last two seconds before one of the others—probably Benny—blasted her into oblivion. The machine shook, and the screen went red, giving her the option to reenter or bail out. She touched reenter and tried again. This time, she did much better.

She lasted four seconds.

Her mood was not improving. There was simply too much, too fast in the small confines of the simulated fighting area. She took a deep breath. Today had sucked. The entire past week had sucked. She was on the verge of failing all her classes, and if she kept it up, it wouldn't be long before everyone knew she was a dud. She thought of what Bastian had said about Faxes feeling entitled and about how she hadn't achieved anything.

She gripped the joystick tighter. She'd had enough losing!

The next time, she lasted five seconds.

Focus, Nora, she told herself. One thing at a time. Let your intuition take over. Don't think, just react. Let your reflexes work for you. She took a deep breath and tried to shut out the thoughts scrambling her brain.

And, incredibly, it worked. She spent a minute or so avoiding the blasts from the remaining red ship—one had already quit—before daring to take a few shots of her own. She wasn't about to get hit again. It seemed her ship could take a few indirect shots before she died, as long as no critical systems went down, so she flew spirals and circles and even managed to send the ship into corkscrews and barrel rolls before taking a perfect shot at the remaining red ship, looking exactly like a PJ, outlined in glowing red. She cut it close, but the pulse from the laser cannon hit the ship dead on, and he blinked out.

She'd thought that was the last red ship, but another blinked onto her screen; either Benny or Ty had picked to rejoin. She wondered if the other pilot was growing frustrated with her because they eventually quit antagonizing her and pursued Greg instead. She imagined it wasn't hard to figure out who was who when she was flying like a drunk pigeon, probably ignoring any semblance of real strategy.

She observed the cat-and-mouse game of the red ship chasing Greg for a moment, then groaned as Greg was obliterated.

"It's up to you now, Nora," he said. "Time's almost up. The sim won't let me rejoin again."

She pulled back hard on the steering, sending the ship into a nauseating backflip. They'd included g-forces in the simulator somehow. She'd have to ask Greg about that later. When she righted, the remaining red ship was headed directly at her. She fired, barely clipping the ship as it dodged hard to the right. Nora had to send her ship into a rapid downturn to avoid a collision.

The ship was on her like white on rice, a favorite expression of Greg's and something that seemed particularly appropriate at the moment. She couldn't shake him, no matter the crazy stunts she pulled, no matter the maneuvers she made up. He didn't fire but once, which was infuriating. She'd decided it *must* be Benny in that ship. He was just herding her, taunting her. He chased her all the way across the virtual grid, matching her spin for spin.

Finally, frustrated, and still fuming over Benny's earlier comments, she dodged hard left and sent the engines into reverse, half the boosters firing at max force, essentially braking, skidding in a semicircle across space like a car in an icy parking lot, which put her guns exactly in line with his engines as he flew past. The cannon *beeped* to let her know that it had locked on, and she fired.

The screen blinked out, leaving her shrouded in darkness.

She'd barely had time to unbuckle her harness before the door to her simulator was thrown open and a whooping Greg yanked her out and wrapped her up in a bear hug.

"I taught her everything she knows about flying!" he proclaimed. A dozen or so people had gathered around the simulator and were applauding, even whistling. Nora blushed, pushing her hair from her face, and saw Ty nudge Benny. Benny nodded toward her and reluctantly applauded as well.

Ty. Benny. Greg.

The fourth simulation unit was still closed.

"Wait, what...?" Nora stammered. Greg grinned, giving her a pat on the back that nearly knocked the wind from her lungs.

"Come on," he said, helping her down. "Man, this is so great!"

"What's going on?" Nora asked as the sim unit door opened and a tall man in a green flight suit emerged.

"Bastian," she said, shocked. His blond hair was flopped messily to one side, his suit partially unzipped, but while he looked casual, his gaze was as hard as ice, as focused as laser beams. She swallowed hard.

"Well done," he said, coming over and extending a hand. She shook it, hoping he didn't feel the clamminess of her palm. "Now that's the kind of Fax I could fly with."

"Uh," she stammered. Why did it have to be *him?*

"Turns out you're a better PJ pilot than a Rover driver," he said quietly, leaning in. His lips quirked to one side in that half grin she realized was something of a characteristic expression. He still held her hand, and she was uncomfortably aware of it.

"You heard about that," she stammered.

"The whole station heard about that." She winced, and he let her hand go.

"You let me win," she said, wiping her palm against her pant leg. "You barely took a single shot."

"Eleanora," he said, her name rolling off his tongue in elongated syllables, his eyes leveled on hers. Whatever their prior disagreements, he seemed somehow—unexpectedly—pleased with her performance. "I didn't *let* you do anything. That was all you."

He held her gaze for another long moment, then he straightened and left without another word, a swarm of green-flight-suited men following him out. Nora let out a long, strangled breath.

As soon as he was out the door, however, the noise erupted again.

"Did you know, no one's beaten him in a simulator since he was a newb? Five years!" "He practically *invented* the new P-765!" She barely caught the phrases over the raucous shouts of the cadets before her.

"Nora, that was awesome!" Greg said, slapping her again on the back. "Of course, took you a while to warm up, but wow! Why didn't you tell us you were hiding a secret talent?"

"I don't know what you're making such a big deal about," she said, blushing. "It's just a video game."

"So, about that double date," Ty said, sidling up to her. Greg laughed. Even Benny seemed to be in a good mood, patting her on the arm awkwardly.

"I'll let Sophie know," Nora said, shrugging him off. "Come on, Greg. You said one flight. Now give my books back."

"Seriously, Nora?" Greg said, rolling his eyes. "You want to study at a time like this? We need to go again, see what you can *really* do! We need to talk to the flight instructors! We need to…"

"We need to drop it," Nora said. "It was fun. Thanks for showing me the simulator."

She pushed past the crowd and picked up her books.

"But…" he stammered, chasing after her. "Nora, you're a natural!"

"No, I'm a Hypatia," she said, pushing her way through a throng of cadets, head low. "I'm going to be a scientist, a way better one than…"

"Thalia," Greg guessed. Nora stopped for a moment and glared at him, then left the dome for the white corridor beyond. Greg still followed.

"Nora," he pleaded. "Nora!" He took her arm, and she finally stopped.

"I always wondered about you Faxes," he said. He was grinning wide. It was Nora's turn to roll her eyes – despite her irritation, his good mood was irresistible. He was proud of her, she realized, and excited. Nora found herself smiling reluctantly in return.

"Wondered what?" she asked.

"What sort of surprises you might have for us in the modern age. Like, what if Newton would have been the best goddamn banjo player in the history of the world, but there were no banjos around when he was alive, so he did math instead?"

"And you think flying is my…banjo?" She cocked her head to one side.

"Sure," he said, putting an arm around her shoulders as he walked her back to her room. "And I bet I'm not the only one."

He was right. Nora tried to return to the cafeteria to continue her studies, but in less than an hour, it seemed like news of the simulation had spread throughout the station. Nora couldn't go ten steps without someone asking her what it was like, had she really not flown before, did she cheat, and could she introduce them to Sebastian Benoit because, honestly, he was *such* a dreamboat.

She wondered if this is what celebrity was like. Whatever it was, she wished it would pass, although the knowledge that—for once—she hadn't totally screwed up or let someone down was a rather nice change of pace. It left a glowing spot in her chest that warmed her, even though everything else was so hard.

It also left her feeling extremely confused. She threw her tablet onto her bunk and climbed up, pulling the curtain closed around her. In the small space, her roommates' voices were muffled. She picked up the picture next to her pillow, tracing her fingers over the smooth new frame, her fingertips lingering on her father's face. She sighed. Everything had become so bizarre. A few months ago, she thought she knew who she was: Eleanora Clark, the weird girl who moved a lot and never fit in.

At least things had been simple enough to digest. That couldn't be further from the truth now. She burrowed under the covers, pulling them over her head and almost completely blocking out the sounds of her room. If she wasn't who she *thought* she was, then who exactly *was* she? Was she Hypatia, brilliant scientist and philosopher? She certainly didn't feel like it. Why wasn't she as smart as Thalia? Why didn't chemistry and astrophysics come as easily to her as they did to her fellow Hypatia clone? Why did she get such a thrill when she sat in that mockpit tonight—something she'd never, *ever* felt while solving formulas or doing experiments in the lab? Was abandoning science, the field she was destined for, designed for, and reaching for something else—something completely *insane*, like becoming a pilot—was that something Hypatia would do? Probably not, she thought, frowning into the darkness of her bunk.

But it might just be something Eleanora Clementine Clark would do.

CHAPTER 16

The next day, Nora was walking to her politics class when a sharply uniformed officer—a short, dark woman—stopped her.

"Eleanora Clark?" the woman asked. Her tone made it more of a statement than a question.

"Yes," Nora said, holding her tablet across her chest. What had she done *now*?

"Come with me, please."

"Uh, she has class," Greg said, putting a hand on Nora's arm to keep her from following.

"Then I'll have to make sure she gets a note for her professor when the admiral's done with her, okay?" The woman gave Greg a tight-lipped smile. He flinched.

"The admiral?"

"Maybe he wants to tell me I'm a dud after all," Nora said, giving him what she hoped was a brave smile. Greg took her hand and squeezed it.

"You're no dud. Are you kidding me? After what you did last night?" he said. He'd gained some notoriety following her performance, as well, and basked in it, joking with the upper-level pilot students who suddenly found him worth their time. "I'm sure it's nothing."

"Right," she said. She was less convinced. "The admiral of Ganymede Station just wanted to invite me over for peach tea. And then we'll braid each other's hair."

"It'll be fine," Greg said firmly and released her hand. "He probably just wants to congratulate you in person for kicking the butt of his superstar Ace in the sim. Go on, Nor. I'll see you later."

He waved as he turned to go to class.

"If you're quite finished." The woman stood with her arms crossed, looking at them. Nora sighed and followed her. She was a very fast walker, and by the time they reached the Bridge—a place Nora had never been—she was almost out of breath from the frantic pace. She'd really have to step up her time in the gym.

Despite the exercise, though, she felt cold. What could Admiral Savaryn want with her? Was this about the time she and Bastian broke into the greenhouse? She hadn't hurt anything. Surely that wouldn't warrant a visit to the admiral himself. Or was this about her last astronomy report? She was close to failing *that* class, too, and would have if it hadn't been for Cat's tutoring. Surely it couldn't be about the sim last night, like Greg had suggested. Why would that possibly warrant a meeting with the Admiral? Her stomach felt like it was literally tying itself in knots. The blunt woman stopped at the entrance to the Bridge and pushed Nora through the steel-framed door.

She'd never seen the inside of the command center before. It was circular, just like all the other domes, but with a lower ceiling, and the walls looked like they were made of plate steel instead of clear plastic or white-painted metal. Several rings of tables and computer stations flowed out from the center, with sharply uniformed men and women hustling around and a few somber J'nai talking into headsets, conferring with one another. There were no casual flight suits here, no pilots or PJ crews. This was the brain of the whole operation.

"Oh, sorry," she muttered as a man buried in his tablet brushed past. He barely looked up and didn't respond. She tucked a strand of hair behind her ear, nearly elbowing another automaton-like officer in the chest. She jerked her hand back from her face and decided the best course of action was to clasp her hands tightly in front of her and to try to stay out of everyone's way.

She spotted the admiral having a conversation with McGregor, the Charlemagne. They glanced in her direction as they spoke, and neither party looked happy to see her.

"Ms. Clark," the admiral called after a few moments. "Over here."

He gestured to a rolling chair near the station where he sat. He was a massive man up close, with hands that looked big enough to crush her skull like a grape. He had a hooked nose and mercury-colored eyes. It was not the face of a man who called her in for positive reinforcement. She swallowed, finding her throat suddenly dry.

"I don't have a lot of time, so I'll be blunt," he said, crossing his hands across his abdomen. "I heard about your little stunt in the simulators the other day."

"Stunt?" Nora said, stunned. He made it sound like she'd done something wrong when, in fact, it seemed like the only thing she'd done right since she'd been at Ganymede. It had felt like an actual accomplishment. She'd thought often of the look on Bastian's face, too—that surprised approval—and it left her feeling warmer inside than she'd felt in ages.

"You're a clone, Ms. Clark," the admiral said in a tone that bordered on exasperation. "A very *expensive* clone of a very *important* woman. It would be a shame to lose you to such a dangerous line of work as piloting when we could make much better use of your particular talents here, in the labs."

"I didn't...I mean..."

"Oh, I'm sure you meant no harm," he said, raising a hand to quiet her protests. "And somehow you even managed to charm our best pilot into vouching for you. Quite a nice touch, if I do say so myself. But not even Benoit can change the rules."

"I wasn't trying to charm anyone or do anything..." Nora said, confused. "Wait, what did he say?"

"To switch you from the Science Track to the Officer Track, to let you be a pilot. He told me – how did he phrase it? Oh yes - that if I let you stay in the labs, I was an idiot."

Nora cringed, but the admiral appeared moderately amused.

"He said," the admiral chuckled, "that if I let you go, I'd be losing someone with the potential to be one of our best pilots. But of course, even Benoit can make mistakes."

That fit perfectly with everything else: nothing made sense. The man who said he'd never fly with a Fax had gone to the admiral himself—granted, insulting the man was probably not a good idea—and told him to switch her focus? What was going on in his crazy head?

"I, um, don't know what to say," she said. Her fingertips felt like ice. She clasped them together tightly. Is that what she wanted?

"Look. Stop messing around with the sims," he said. His massive arms were crossed in front of him, his strange eyes staring at her, unblinking. "You're a scientist, not a pilot, and if Thalia's any measure of your potential, I think you've got a lot of exciting things in your future."

He offered a smile that didn't reach his eyes.

"I'm nothing like Thalia," she muttered, thinking of the last time she heard herself say that.

McGregor coughed into his hand to hide a chuckle. Nora met his eyes and took a chance.

"Is it true that Faxes...clones don't fly, not at all?" she blurted. McGregor shot a glance to Savaryn, but the admiral didn't look back.

"Yes," he said, slowly. "Sometimes they'll go out on a mission or two, but never as part of a crew."

"Why? Is it true you don't trust them?"

The admiral swallowed, his gray eyes so cold she felt chills. She was pushing her luck, and she knew it. She shot a glance towards MacGregor – hadn't *he* been a pilot, once? Hadn't Lara said he'd had a call sign and everything?

"I trust clones as much as I trust anybody," he said, articulating each syllable. "As much as I trust the J'nai, as much as I trust all of the men and women working on this station."

"Then why not let me try to be a pilot?" she asked. She wasn't sure what made her ask; she hadn't even known it was something she wanted until he threatened to take it away. The thought of staying in the labs—with

Thalia, forever—made her gut clench like she'd been punched. But wasn't that what she wanted, what she was made for?

"Look, you're a Hypatia. You're a scientist. An *expensive* investment. The. End."

"But – "

"That'll be all, Ms. Clark," he said. He got up and turned his back to her, driving the point home. She left the Bridge in a daze and stood in the hallway just outside. Her heart was beating a million times a minute, and her face was flushed, yet her hands still felt so cold they were numb.

Was it fear making her stomach quiver so? She *was* afraid—the admiral was a very intimidating man—but was that it?

Or was it that he'd just taken away the one thing she might actually be good at? She'd played the simulations over and over in her mind, feeling the thrill anew each time. Finally, she felt like she had something worth contributing. It was like a hidden compartment inside of her had been unlocked, a place she'd given up on finding.

Surely that was worth fighting for, even if it wasn't something Hypatia or Thalia or anyone else expected of her.

She paced the little hallway, her hands clenching and unclenching at her sides. She wondered what Sophie would do, and then, startlingly, her mother's voice rang out in her mind, as clearly as if she were standing beside her: "Once you find something worth fighting for, love, the whole universe will open up for you." Nora's vision blurred.

She'd always thought her mother meant that if she only applied herself, she could excel in whatever field she chose. But in this instance, she realized she could take the advice literally.

She squared her shoulders and marched back into the Bridge. A thought had occurred to her, another Earth memory, and she wondered if it might just strengthen her argument. It was related to what Greg had told her about Newton and banjos, and she smiled when she realized the inspiration behind her scheme.

"Admiral, can I just say one thing?" she announced. Everyone stopped what they were doing to stare at her. She forced herself to look at the admiral, forced him to meet her eyes. There was a trace of amusement

THE VIEW FROM GANYMEDE

on his face. If she hadn't thought he was laughing at her, he would have terrified her. As it was, there was just enough humiliation in the glance to stiffen her spine a bit.

"Yes, cadet?"

"I heard a quote once, back home. Something that really resonated with me."

Admiral Savaryn and McGregor were looking at her, either bored or perplexed, she couldn't tell. She was bumbling. In about two seconds, everyone would forget about her and go back to their work. She licked her lips and took a deep breath. She couldn't remember if the quote was supposed to be from Einstein, or if she'd just read it on a Snapple cap. Too late now.

"It goes like this- Everybody is a genius. But if you judge a fish by its ability to climb a tree, it will live its whole life believing it is stupid."

"What's your point, cadet?" Savaryn said. His fingers were steepled, his voice was soft.

She paused, her mother's wisdom ringing in her ears, and continued.

"My point is - just because I share the same DNA as Thalia and Hypatia doesn't mean I'm exactly like them. I think my test results probably show that." She swallowed, her throat dry as a desert.

"I want you to give me a chance. I think you'll realize that I can be a more valuable asset to you in a cockpit than in a lab. I won't let you down."

The room went silent, the only sound a slight chirping coming from a green rotating radar light on one of the consoles. McGregor and Savaryn exchanged a glance. The admiral looked like he was about to say something, but McGregor stepped forward, his hands clasped behind his back. He was a clone, too, after all, and one in a very important position. He'd probably had to fight his way up the chain of command tooth and nail to get where he was. Nora looked up at him—he was a very tall man—and saw something twinkling in his blue eyes. Was that empathy? She hoped so.

"An interesting analogy, cadet. I think you've made your point," he said, the corner of his mouth twitching ever so slightly.

"I do not..." Savaryn started to say, but McGregor, astonishingly, cut him off.

"Let's give her a chance," he said, turning to the admiral.

135

She would later swear you could have heard a pin drop in that room. This was the second person to confront the admiral on her behalf. She swallowed hard, watching as the admiral's ruddy face turned a darker shade of red.

She briefly wondered if she was about to be thrown out an air lock.

"Ganymede Day is just around the corner," McGregor said. "We could give her the same expectations and coursework as the others. If she makes up for lost time and passes the classes and sims, she can get a rookie assignment that day like the rest of the pilot recruits. If she fails, well…" He didn't need to finish his thought. If she failed, she'd be relegated back to the labs with Thalia. Permanently. The thought sent an icy trickle of sweat down her spine, strengthening her resolve even more to succeed.

A wicked smirk curled its way onto Admiral Savaryn's face.

"Yes. Yes, we could do that," he sneered. "Cadet, get out of here. The XO and I have some things to discuss." He eyed McGregor with a glare colder than Ganymede's ice caps. The XO calmly returned the gaze. Nora knew this was a man who was not easily intimidated. He had stood up for her, a fellow Fax, and if she got a chance, she wouldn't let him down. She'd do whatever it took, no matter how hard it was, no matter the obstacles they threw in her path. She felt a sense of purpose, and it thrilled her. She was relieved to finally find something she cared this much about. Yes, flying was worth fighting for.

CHAPTER 17

"So? How'd it go?" Sophie asked when she and the other girls caught Nora in the cafeteria between classes. Of course they'd already heard about Nora getting called to see the admiral.

"I think they're going to let me be a pilot," Nora said. She was in shock. It felt like she was swimming instead of walking. Everything still sounded far away.

"Wait, what?" Sophie said.

"McGregor convinced the admiral to let me try. They're going to switch my focus, I think, and give me until Ganymede Day to catch up to the other pilot recruits," Nora said, though even to her own ears her voice sounded distant, dream-like.

"You look like you're gonna pass out," Zoe said and sat her down at one of the tables, pushing her down firmly by the shoulders. Nora nodded.

"Here," Raina said, giving her a glass of water. "It'll help."

"So you'll be the first Fax pilot ever?" Sophie said. Then she whistled. "How about that."

"Not to mention one of what, three female pilots?" Raina said. "You go, girl!"

That night, back in their room, Nora lay in her bunk, staring at the picture of her parents. She could still hear her mother's voice echoing in her head. Would they be proud of her for what she'd done? It was no easy task, what McGregor had helped her achieve. Or start to achieve. She had a long way to go if she was going to catch up to where Ty, Benny, and Greg were already at.

"You miss them, don't you?" Sophie asked. She was coming out of the shower, her hair wrapped in a towel, and had seen Nora starting at the picture frame.

"Yeah," Nora said, sitting up. "I don't miss Louisiana much anymore, though. Isn't that strange?"

"Home can be people or places," Zoe said, scrolling through her tablet. She started whistling, absently, an old tune that Nora recognized instantly. She glared at Zoe, who acknowledged the glance but kept on with the song. Nora thought about throwing something at her, but figured it would only make Zoe starting singing instead.

As it turned out, Sophie picked up on it and starting singing the refrain, loudly-

"Oh my darling, oh my darling, oh my daaaaarling Clementine…."

Nora *did* throw a pillow at Sophie, who laughed, and continued on to her little closet, wringing out her hair, humming along with Zoe's whistling as she went.

"Well, *I* miss home," Raina said. She was sitting at the table, her legs swinging as she wrote out a homework assignment. Zoe stopped her whistling.

"Where's home?" Nora asked, realizing she had no idea. She had little idea about any of her roommates' previous lives, really. It was as if they'd all been born again on Ganymede and, for their own reasons, had decided to leave their Earth lives back on the third planet.

"Hawaii," Raina said, sighing. She closed her eyes. "I miss the waves. And the sun. Do you think we'll ever get to go back?"

"I think so," Nora said. "Or at least, I hope so."

"I didn't know you lived in Hawaii," Sophie said, pouting. "Wish we'd been friends before this. I would totally have come to visit."

"It was great," Raina said, grinning. "I surfed every day. I was so tan it was disgusting. We were kind of out in the rural part of Lanai, away from the crowds. My handlers ran this yoga studio—low key, very mellow. When I turned thirteen, they told me who I really was. Then I figured out that the entire point of our rustic, meditative lifestyle was to help me combat the innate homicidal tendencies of my DNA."

"And...I hope it helped?" Lara asked, one eyebrow raised. Raina shrugged.

"The last Rani was a dud. Not sure what happened, but the board was extra careful with me."

"Are we just going to ignore the 'innate homicidal tendencies' remark?" Nora asked, half-joking. Raina'd always had a fierce temper – maybe Nora should have spent some time researching her roommates' pasts. Eleanor Roosevelt seemed benign enough – but ancient warrior queens? Who knew!

"She's no more a homicidal maniac that you are a brilliant astronomer," Zoe said, throwing a pillow up at her. Nora grinned.

"Ouch," she said. "Touché."

"So, Raina the shark biscuit. Never would have thought it," Lara said, rolling her pen across the back of her fingers.

"God, I miss the sunshine," Sophie said, closing her eyes and leaning back. "I haven't been this pale since *forever*."

"They've introduced UV rays into the domes, you know, to cut down on the incidence of seasonal affective disorder. All kinds of people were getting depressed from lack of Vitamin D," Cat said. Sophie stared at her. Cat blushed and shrugged. "Or so I heard."

"Anyway. Surfing is its own meditation, in a way," Raina said dreamily, her eyes focused on something far away. "There's something really exhilarating about challenging the infinite—and winning."

"Shark biscuit and poet? You are full of surprises," Lara said, grinning.

"Oh come on, Lara, you lived in the Outback!" Raina said. "Are you telling me you never once went scuba diving on the Great Barrier Reef? Never surfed those legendary waves? I thought all Australians surfed."

"Bugger me, no. You do know that *everything* in Australia is trying to kill you, right? When I was just a tot, I saw a guy get his arm chewed off by a shark—haven't been back to a beach since."

Even Zoe's jaw dropped.

"I guess I could see that deterring you," Raina said. Lara shrugged.

"No sharks in space, at least," Lara said, grinning her toothy grin.

"Well, on the topic of things we miss," Zoe said, tossing her pen into the air and catching it between her fingers, "I miss Sparky and No-Nose, my dogs. Used to sleep on my bed every night. Don't miss my handlers, though."

"I miss malls," Sophie said, sighing. "I miss being able to wear something other than uniforms and sweats and flight suits."

"I had a bunny," Cat said softly. Everyone turned to look at her. "Her name was Muffin. I really wanted to bring her with me, but they wouldn't let me."

Nora worried for a moment that Cat was going to cry.

"Didn't they used to have pets here?" Sophie asked. "Some sort of lizard thing?"

"Those flying lizards?" Raina said. "I heard too many cadets got themselves bit, so they outlawed all pets. Forever."

"You think we'll ever learn about the other creatures out there? I mean, besides the J'nai and the Qaig?" Nora asked. Lara nodded.

"Once we graduate, we could get stationed at one of the J'nai colonies," Lara said. "Or maybe even the Qaig home world, if we win."

"Think there are a lot of aliens out there?" Sophie asked. Nora shrugged, but Cat spoke up again.

"J'nai and Qaig are pretty much the dominant species of the galaxy," she said. "But there are plenty of planets with life. Just look at the Drake equation."

"The what?" Zoe asked. Cat punched something into her tablet and pulled up a long equation.

$$N = R^* \; x \; f_p \; x \; n_e \; x \; f_l \; x \; f_i \; x \; f_c \; x \; L$$

"If we say N is the number of planets with intelligent life," Cat said, pointing at the figures, "and we look at the rate of formation of new stars, times the number of star systems in the galaxy, times the percent of them that have planets, times the percent of those that have planets where life can be sustained, times the..."

"Yeah, we get it. Lot of variables," Sophie said, frowning. "But what does it mean?"

"It *means*," Cat said, annoyed, "that there are likely *thousands* of planets, in our galaxy alone, where life has evolved."

"Thousands," Lara said, whistling.

"I don't know," Sophie said, frowning. "Last time I hacked the mainframe, it seemed like the files really just centered around the J'nai and the Qaig, maybe a handful of others. I think the two races have been closely related for a lot longer than they're telling us."

"The *last* time you hacked the mainframe?" Zoe said. "Find out anything else useful?"

Sophie shrugged.

"Not really. J'hara told us that the Qaig attacked for no reason, but I think the two species have had some sort of relationship for hundreds of years. There's a lot of files that even mention the Qaigs working for the J'nai, or something – and a few other mentions of some different species working with the J'nai. It seems like the humans aren't the first species the J'nai have had to assimilate with to survive."

"And we haven't even talked about the odds that those other species are humanoid, but they're pretty good," Cat said. "Hairy apes all over this galaxy are evolving into something much more sophisticated. They're just exposed to a slightly different environment. Turns out the mix of oxygen and carbon and hydrogen on Earth was a recipe for success anywhere. It's the same story, over and over and over again, with only slightly different results each time. The J'nai were just the first."

"I think that's the longest speech I've *ever* heard you make," Nora said, drumming her nails against the table. She was pondering what Sophie had said, about the J'nai and Qaig working together for years and years.

What had caused them to go to war, and why was that part left out of their history class?

"Thousands of planets with life out there? Makes you feel pretty small. Really puts it all into perspective," Raina said.

"Like looking into the infinite," Zoe echoed.

▰ ▰ ▰

December was a glorious month at Ganymede Station. Given that practically every day was a holiday—including December 5, which Greg decided was "Intergalactic Ninja Day"—the station was decorated and festive all month long. Between Hanukah, Christmas, New Years, Kwanzaa, and the rest, it was an entire month of parties; that is, when they weren't cramming for their midterm exams. Nora had tackled her studies with an even more zealous energy. Suddenly, it wasn't a chore to spend hours on equations, not when they were related to flight plans and engine design. She and Greg spent time together after class nearly every day. He was like her own personal tutor, and he'd sent her extra notes and charts that he and Ty had come up with earlier in the semester. Bit by bit, she was catching up. She compressed nearly a semester's worth of online quizzes into just a few weeks, and she was passing. She was studying so hard, some nights found her nearly too tired to climb the ladder to her bed. Room 10013 had pooled their 3D-printing allowances to make a string of brightly colored lights that hung from the room's ceiling, and when she finally did fall asleep at night, it was like falling asleep to a rainbow of stars, sending her into pleasant dreams.

But best of all that month was the Zero-G room. One day, an older Edison cadet dropped the ambient temperature to just below freezing and used a snow machine—made from old Rover parts—to fill the dome up like a snow globe. As the cadets flew through the air, their passing made the snow swirl and billow in great white drifts. More than one cadet ended up with a handful of the icy stuff shoved down the back of his flight suit that day. At last, their faces red and shining, Nora and her roommates made their way to the cafeteria, where they sipped hot chocolate with little star-shaped marshmallows. Despite the hard work she was putting in, it was one of the nicest times Nora could ever remember.

Ganymede Day, celebrated on January 7, was an homage to the discovery of the Jovian moon by Galileo in 1610. The day was an excuse to cut classes and hang out in the rec dome, where, rumor had it, some of the Faxes would be debuting their hoverboard technology, a spin on the blue lightning that powered Thalia's motorcycle. Greg had been talking about it for days beforehand, eager to get his chance to try it out.

But most importantly, it was also the day when assignments for the spring field trip to Terra Prime were announced. At the end of March, cadets with a focus that would potentially put them in a PJ would be paired with a crew for a shadowing experience. They wouldn't have any real responsibilities on board other than keeping up with their copious coursework, but the chance to get off station had the whole school buzzing.

"Man, I hope I aced my midterms," Greg groaned, taking out his tablet.

"Yeah," Nora said. They were sitting side-by-side on a bench in the rec dome, waiting for the digital bulletin board in the center to post the assignments. "You think I'll get to go?"

"You're passing your classes, so yeah, I don't think they'll really have an excuse to keep you grounded," Greg said, flipping through his tablet, looking to see if his scores had been posted yet.

"Even though I'm a Fax?" she said. He looked up at her.

"Well, they can't look past that little fact like I can," Greg said, nudging her playfully. "Fax or not, the admiral said you can try, right? I'd like to see anyone try to tell you otherwise."

"Look past it," Nora echoed. She frowned. Whether she liked it or not, she *was* Hypatia—or at least, one of the Hypatias on this rust bucket—just as much as she was Eleanora Clark. She might not have had the philosopher's scientific mindedness, but she couldn't just ignore the fact that it was, after all, her heritage. Could she?

"List is up!" Greg cried, bounding up from the bench as the screen flashed. He grabbed her hand and dragged her to the screen. Nora's view was blocked by Ty and Lara, who both towered over her.

"Lara, I didn't even know you *wanted* to go out on this trip," Nora said, straining to see around her tall friend.

"I had to pull some strings, but if they're really expecting me to learn race relations, I figure it would be a good idea to actually *see* Terra Prime, you know?" she said. Her blue eyes never left the bulletin. Then they suddenly widened, her mouth an O of surprise. She pumped her fist into the air.

"All right! Going to be on the *Andromeda!*" she said.

"Can you see mine?" Nora asked. She was swarmed by the pushing bodies of her fellow cadets.

"My man!" Greg said, slapping Ty's bicep. "I'm going on the *Clarion!*"

"I've got *Daria's Star.* Looks like we're one step closer to the real deal!" Ty said, his big voice booming.

"Lara, can you see anything?" Nora asked again. Her palms were slick and warm, but her lips were suddenly dry. Lara was searching, trying to keep her focus while being jostled by the crowd. All around them, cadets were screeching and high-fiving, congratulating themselves on getting the posts they wanted.

"I see it!" Lara cried. "I see your name, Nora! Hey, you're on the *Rapscallion!* But there's a star by it…"

"Yes!" Nora exclaimed, initially exulting that she'd gotten a post - but then she moaned, burying her head in her hands.

She and Lara moved to a bench in the rec dome to swap plans for their trip. Benny had gotten a post, too, and Wingman had gotten a prize spot on one of the newest ships. Sophie joined them; she was curious, as she always was, but had no desire to leave the station, especially not on one of the "flying deathtraps," as she referred to the PJs. She—and most of the other Faxes—would be staying behind to continue their studies. The only Faxes who would be leaving the station were Nora, Lara, and an Alexander the Great clone, who was in the race relations department like Lara. Only

Nora would be going as an apprentice pilot. Maybe. If she kept jumping through all the hoops.

"Nor, what's wrong? Didn't you get a spot? Shouldn't you be happy?" Sophie asked.

"The admiral's trying to punish me," Nora said, burying her head in her hands. "I humiliated him in front of his XO, and now he's trying to get me to quit. Or get me killed. Bastian will *definitely* kill me when he finds out he's stuck with me for a week on his ship."

"Don't flatter yourself," Bastian said, appearing from nowhere. His hands were stuffed into his flight suit pockets, his hair perfectly rumpled. "It's not worth the effort it would take to kill you and make it look like an accident." Nora sighed.

"Great. Really great. Thanks," Nora said. "I had no idea you held me in such high regard."

"He's kidding," Greg said. He came over and put an arm around her shoulders, glaring daggers at Bastian. "You...*are* kidding, right?" He looked Bastian over, sizing him up.

"Look, I'm the one who recommended you, and Savaryn also knows I do not fly with Faxes. I can't refuse to fly with someone I recommended, so he has me in a bind. If I refuse, I can kiss any chance at a captaincy goodbye."

"*Diva*," Sophie coughed into her hand. Bastian shot her an icy glare.

"Oh come on," Sophie said. She threw her hands up. "You must have seen this coming. You recommend her, despite knowing Faxes don't fly. And *you* make a fool out of the admiral. I mean, we all knew how this was going to turn out."

"*Incroyable*," Bastian said. "Are you always so..." he began, searching for the right word.

"Insouciant?" She smiled up at him sweetly.

Nora glared at her. She loved Sophie, despite all her quirks. Sometimes, though, she was worse than a bull in a china shop.

"Look," Bastian said, coming to stand in front of Nora. Greg continued to glare at him—the man whom, until this moment, he would have done *anything* to learn from. "If you fly with me and you fail, then the admiral has proved once and for all that Faxes like you belong in the lab and that only Originals belong in the shuttles. No other Fax will ever be allowed to fly as a part of the crew. If you put one toe out of line, he'll have you back in science class before you...well...it won't be pretty."

"No pressure. But why do you care?" Nora said.

He sighed. "Because now it's my reputation on the line as well, little Hypatia. If I recommend you and train you and you flunk out, my reputation is ruined, and that's something I have every intention of keeping intact."

"*Wouldn't that be a shame,*" Sophie muttered. Nora kicked her.

"Plus, I heard about what you said to the admiral," he said, that familiar half grin lighting up his face. Nora flushed.

"What did you hear?"

"Enough to know you have some fire in you. And something about a fish in a tree?" He laughed, just once, and shook his head.

"So what do we do?" Nora asked. Bastian smiled, but it was a hard, determined thing.

"I won't lie to you," Bastian said. "You and I have butted heads before. You're young and undisciplined—and far too emotional."

"Oh, thanks," Nora muttered. She put a hand on Sophie's arm, holding her back. Her roommate looked ready to tear Bastian apart.

"But I'm willing to help you—*if* you promise me that you'll work hard. We won't let the admiral best us. We'll turn you into the best pilot this station has ever seen. Or," he said, his lips quirking to one side, "at least the second best."

The next morning, Nora got up at 4:30am to get to the sim room with Bastian for some pre-class tutoring—and if she wanted to spend a few extra minutes making sure her hair and makeup looked perfect, well, she was just trying to be professional.

As she was sneaking out of the room—she'd tried to be quiet, but the room echoed—Sophie yawned and sat up in bed.

"Morning," she said, taking her hair out of its bun and shaking out her long locks. Zoe was getting up, too, and her hair stuck up at all angles like fluffs of dark cotton. She groaned, stood, and stretched out her tall frame, joints popping and creaking as she did so.

"Ugh," Zoe said, looking at Sophie. "For the sake of us mere mortals and our fragile self-esteem, could you please just wake up looking like a troll, like everyone else, just once? It's not fair."

"I bet you don't even have morning breath," Nora mumbled. She loved Sophie, truly, but how that girl could wake up looking gorgeous when Nora had to spend fifteen extra minutes in the bathroom just to look presentable was grossly unfair.

"Want to smell?" Sophie said, and as she raced to tackle Nora, Zoe grabbed her around the waist.

"Oh no you don't!" Zoe hollered and dumped the struggling girl back onto her bunk. "You let Nora alone. She's got a hot date with the Ace himself this morning, remember?"

"Oh for God's sake, it's not a date!" Nora fumed. Sophie raised an eyebrow.

"Then what's with the mascara?" she accused. Nora flushed and headed for the door.

— — —

"None of this would have happened if you hadn't gotten into that sim unit with me," Nora grumbled. They'd been at it for a week now, day in and day out. After that first day, she'd realized mascara was pointless – after a few hours sweating in the sim, she'd resembled a raccoon.

Bastian sighed. One of the terms of her probationary status, which Thalia had teased her about mercilessly, was that she not only pass her current coursework but also that she catch up in the simulation course and acquire as many hours in the mockpits as the other cadets whose focus was flying. And even then, she'd only be allowed to go on the trip if the higher-ups deemed her an acceptable candidate, which they might not tell her until the day before launch.

She still had a lot of work to do.

"Again, Hypatia," he said and reset the sim unit.

"That's not my name," she muttered and rubbed her neck. It was sore from the hours of practices he'd been putting her through every single day after class, until her eyes were crossed from staring at the screen for so long. He'd gotten a private sim unit, not one linked for the battle simulations, but one off to the side of the room, where he could run trial after trial. They prepared for everything. What if this malfunctions? What if *that* malfunctions? What if you lose power? What if, what if, what if.

Practice the basics until it becomes instinct, he said, until your muscles remember what to do before your brain even recognizes there's a problem. Then practice some more. She wanted to fly in the crazy patterns she saw her classmates trying, but Bastian kept her to the simplest motions— to practice not until she got it right, but until she couldn't get it wrong. It had even soaked into her subconscious mind. Sometimes she woke up at night terrified that she'd misjudged a station landing.

"Are you so hard on me because you really don't like Faxes, or is it that you don't want to fly with *me*?" she asked him one night as they headed to the sim room.

"What are you talking about?" he asked.

"I mean…is the reason you don't like me because of Thalia?"

He looked stunned, like someone had just thrown ice water on him.

"Of course it's not. You are not her. And I do not dislike you. If I'm hard on you, it's only because I want to see you succeed—maybe for selfish reasons," he admitted.

"Okay," Nora said. She crossed her arms and, realizing how stern she looked, tried to soften her demeanor. "Look, I'm sorry. I guess I'm just tired. I really do appreciate the time you're taking with me. I don't mean to be so irritable."

"Part of the reason I don't *trust* Faxes may be Thalia," he admitted, frowning. "But you're not going to change my mind if you keep flunking these sims. Now, let's start where we left off yesterday."

"Yes, boss," she said. She rolled her shoulders, the vertebrae in her neck cracking and popping with the motion, and climbed into the mockpit.

"And I don't need your apologies," he grumbled, restarting the sim program. "I need your attention. I need your focus. I never said it would be easy, but I do know that you'll be successful if you keep going."

"Because of my brilliant Fax mind? My innate reasoning skills and flawless logical brain?"

"Because of your talented and patient teacher," he said. She looked at him from the corner of her eye. He was teasing her. Bastian Benoit was *teasing*. The thought was mind-blowing. She narrowed her eyes. There was no trace of mirth on his face. Maybe he was being serious—it was so hard to tell. It was so hard to be certain about anything when it came to Bastian Benoit.

That night, after a particularly grueling session, one where she'd managed to fail almost every single simulation he threw at her, she exited the sim pod to realize they were the only two left in the room. It must be later than she'd realized. She groaned, stretching stiff muscles as she climbed down the ladder. The forces in the sim were brutal, as authentic as actual flight; she'd feel it for sure in the morning.

"That was awful," she moaned, grabbing her backpack. Bastian closed the pod, and they headed from the room.

"You passed two of the simulations," he said, looking at her sideways. She was starting to enjoy the way he dragged out the *i* in his words. It gave his speech a tempo that most native English speakers lacked.

"Two out of what, one hundred? Two hundred? So much for me being a natural," she said, pushing damp strands of hair from her face. Her sweat was making the curls go crazy. She imagined a fuzzy black halo around her head.

"Better than I did when I was in your position," he said. Nora stopped, forgetting her hair for a second, and it took him a moment to realize she was no longer keeping pace with him. He turned to face her.

"Wait, was that a compliment?" she said, a smile spreading across her face.

"No," he said slowly, as if he hadn't realized the comment could have been interpreted as such. "An observation. You are not as bad as you think."

"That *was* a compliment. Holy cow. I never thought I'd hear one coming from you," she said, grinning, and trotted to catch up with him. He turned, shaking his head, and walked from the room.

"It has been known to happen," he acknowledged with a snort.

They rounded the corridor into the recreation dome. Few people were out this late, but one of them, her cobalt-streaked hair luminescent in the dark, sauntered over as they entered.

"Hi Bastian," Thalia said, crossing her arms and eyeing him up and down. "You look good."

"Thalia," he said. "Long day. Think I'm going to turn in."

"Oh," she pouted, putting a hand on his arm. "Need some company?"

Their eyes locked; a muscle jumped along Bastian's jawline as he clenched his teeth.

"Thalia, give it a rest," Bastian said. He sounded exhausted.

"Um," Nora said, adjusting her bag. "I'll just be going. See you later, then."

Her face was flaming for some reason she couldn't understand. Thalia ran a finger down Bastian's chest while he stood stone-faced.

"*Much* later, little Hypatia. Your instructor will be busy for a while," she purred.

Nora glanced over her shoulder as she left. Bastian had shrugged Thalia off and was whispering to her in a fierce, low tone. Thalia continued to pout, gazing up at him, tossing her hair. Nora wanted to puke and probably would have if she'd seen any more.

She made it back to her room—how, she wasn't sure; she didn't really remember the walk much—and flopped onto her bed.

"How was training?" Sophie whispered. The rest of the girls were asleep, lights out in their bunks.

"Fine," Nora grumbled, then flipped her light off and pulled the curtain shut.

CHAPTER 18

A few nights later, Bastian told her she'd done a good job. Well, what he *actually* said was that she had managed not to screw it up too badly, which was basically a compliment where Bastian Benoit was concerned. She grinned like an idiot all the way to the cafeteria, almost forgetting how tired she was.

"You've been spending a lot of time with Benoit," Greg accused, meeting up with her after dinner. Nora nodded.

"Yeah," she said. "He's just as brilliant as you said he was. And I have a lot to get caught up on."

She tried not to think about Thalia, but that was becoming more and more difficult. Her clone had started hanging out in the rec dome almost every night, waiting for Bastian after their training sessions. Most nights he pushed past her, barely acknowledging her, which only seemed to make her try harder to get his attention. Last night, though, when she'd shown up yet again, Bastian told Nora—to her great dismay—to go on ahead, that he'd catch up with her tomorrow, and he had stayed behind to talk to Thalia. Nora didn't sleep well that night. She tried not to imagine what Bastian and Thalia were up to, but the scenarios ran through her head like a video played on loop for hours.

The next day was a fog of worry. Her mind was ruminating, and she was powerless to stop it. She walked between classes like a zombie, barely recognizing Greg when he trotted up beside her to follow her to their next class.

"So, what's it like?" Greg asked, breaking into her unpleasant daydream. "Is he a tyrant?"

"Yes," she admitted, shaking her head to clear the images of Bastian and Thalia. "Well, no, not really. He's demanding. But he's not unfair."

"You think he's just helping you because you remind him of Thalia?" he blurted. Nora tilted her head, looking at him.

"What?"

"You know. They were a…thing, like, together, for a long time. Then she dumped him. Maybe you're like his rebound…project…thing," he said, for once struggling to find the words. His face was red all the way up to his ears. She shook her head. She was too tired for this sort of thing right now.

"God, Greg, it's not like that," Nora said, adjusting her book bag. "He's totally professional."

"I'll bet," Greg muttered. Nora whirled on him.

"Besides, it's really none of your business, is it? It's not like you and I are dating."

"Maybe we *could* be if you weren't spending all your free time with a guy who wishes you were his ex-girlfriend."

"Maybe we *could* be if you weren't such a jerk. I'm actually *good* at this, Greg. You should be happy for me."

"I am," he sighed. "No really, I am. I had no idea when I put you in that sim that this was how everything would turn out. So I guess, in a way, it's my fault."

"What is?"

"It's okay," he said, turning. "Really. Look, I'll see you around."

And he was gone.

Valentine's Day came and went with minimal disruption. Sophie got a ceramic rose from a secret admirer (some enterprising Leo had designed the flower on the 3D printer and sold them to any Casanova who could pay him with printer credits) and wore it pinned in her hair all day. Nora was half hoping Greg would show up with a flower—or just show himself at all, really—but he was nowhere to be seen. She went by his room to see if he wanted to grab dinner or something, but he wasn't there. Raina and Zoe pretended like they couldn't see the parade of red ribbons and heart-shaped candies in the cafeteria, and Cat probably actually didn't notice them. Lara was conspicuously absent for most of the day. When she finally reappeared, her cheeks were flushed, and she refused to answer any of Sophie's persistent questions.

The following day, Nora got a message on her tablet letting her know that since she was a part of the officer track like Raina, Lara, and Zoe now, she was hereby mandated to report to biweekly PT sessions.

Or, as Greg had called it, "Fight Club."

Her first session was awful. She was paired with Zoe, who really did try to go easy on her. She showed Nora how to build her core and arm strength with the different machines, and then they moved to the treadmills and jump ropes for cardio. Nora looked longingly at the stationary bikes, but Zoe firmly kept her away from them, telling her she had to learn to use *all* the equipment. Zoe had obviously been a gym rat long before Ganymede; the girl had muscles even the boys were jealous of, and she flexed them at every opportunity, her ebony skin gleaming.

At the end of their (very sweaty) workout, it was time for sparring. Nora really tried to get into the rhythm, but her hands were made for delicate work on ivory piano keys and computer screens, not for hitting things. This was also, incidentally—when Nora's hair was plastered to her face with sweat and she just *knew* her cheeks were blotchy and red from exertion—when Bastian and Olivia came into the gym, Olivia resting her hand lightly on his arm.

"*Bolivia*," Zoe muttered, seeing Nora's stare.

"Sucre!" Lara called from across the room, and—with a broad grin—flipped the boy she was sparring with flat on his back.

"What?" Nora asked, tearing her eyes away from what Raina had once called the First Couple of Ganymede.

"Bastian plus Olivia. Bolivia. Sounds better than, what, Olastian?" Zoe said. "Hands up. Olivia is a real pro. Don't let her know how tired you are."

"But I'm exhausted," Nora said, bringing her hands up as Zoe had showed her.

Olivia—though she smiled and tossed her hair whenever she caught Bastian looking at her—had missed her true calling as an army drill instructor. Despite her supermodel-worthy good looks, the girl was made of iron.

"Come on, ladies. Hey, Hypatia, this isn't naptime. Get those feet in line!"

"Why is she picking on me?" Nora grumbled. "Doesn't she realize I'm trying to catch up on months of what you guys have been doing?"

"Of course she does," Zoe said, throwing a series of slow punches toward Nora, which she, clumsily, blocked. "That's why she's so hard on you. You've got a long way to go."

"Can't she at least call me by my real name?" Nora panted. Olivia had been alternating between yelling at Nora and teaching the other girls, sometimes stepping in and dealing a few blows herself.

And then Olivia clapped her hands, apparently a signal that they were—finally—done for the day. Olivia sauntered over to Bastian, handing him a water bottle. Olivia, of course, didn't sweat. She wasn't even breathing hard. Nora decided she really didn't like the Swedish princess at all. Bastian, whose tanned skin seemed somehow golden under the fluorescent light, had been helping teach the boys—Greg, Ty, and the others. Seriously, how did Bastian have a tan in space? It wasn't fair.

"Yoohoo, Earth to Nora!" Zoe said, waving a hand in front of Nora's face. She sighed, rubbing her neck, and grabbed the water bottle Zoe was offering. Zoe looked over at "Bolivia."

"I heard her say that Bastian is going to be admiral someday," Zoe said. Nora looked over at him. Was there ever a more dedicated or disciplined person in the solar system? She doubted it.

"Oh?" Nora said, turning away from the couple.

"And Olivia said she's going to be his XO. Well, I think the phrase she used was 'First Lady of Ganymede,' actually," Zoe continued. Their other roommates joined them as they left the gym dome.

"Now there's a girl that lacks ambition," Raina said. "Why be his first lady when you could be admiral yourself?"

"Hey, is that my favorite angry little feminist I hear?" a voice called from behind. It was Ryan, a dark-haired Original boy in the year ahead of them. Raina's face screwed up as she opened her mouth to yell at him.

"Easy there, Raina," Zoe murmured, putting her hand on Raina's shoulder. "We don't want him to end up in the Medical Bay like the last one."

The boy stopped, alarmed. His gaze flickered between the two of them, and as he was figuring out what to say, he was bailed out when someone yelled for him. He turned to go, looking back once over his shoulder before leaving.

"Stupid Original," Raina muttered. Zoe kept her hand on Raina's shoulder—she dwarfed the petite Raina—and then put her arm around her, steering her from the dome.

"You *were* joking about sending someone to Medical, right?" Nora asked, looking askance at Raina. The girl just shrugged.

"She's feistier than she looks," Zoe said, hugging Raina to her. "We just gotta work on that temper."

◢◢ ◢◢ ◢◢

The next few sessions didn't go well, either. Nora ended up with bruises and aches in muscles she didn't even know she had. She thought she saw Bastian hiding a smirk more than once when she'd caught him watching her—no doubt worried she'd embarrass him—and tried her best to ignore it. Her muscles got gradually better at the weight machines and cardio, but at sparring she was, without a doubt, the worst in the group.

After a particularly grueling—and humiliating—match against Raina, who soundly knocked her on her butt at least a dozen times, Nora left the group to get a drink of water. She was heading back to the ring, stretching out her sore back, when Bastian caught up to her.

"Doing all right there, cadet?" he asked. She refused to look at him. She was sweaty and sticky, and Olivia was glaring daggers at her for dawdling by the water fountain. She was most certainly *not* in the mood for Bastian's commentary.

"Fine," she said, walking back toward the sparring matches. Even her toenails hurt.

"Liv says you're making good progress," he said. She couldn't *not* look at him now, so she glared.

"You're getting updates on my 'progress' from your girlfriend? You could have just asked me," Nora said.

"She is not my girlfriend," Bastian chuckled.

"Does *she* know that?" Nora said, nodding toward the blond girl. Bastian sighed, running a hand through his hair.

"Yes. And yes, I asked her how you were doing. The continued excellence of my reputation hinges on your ability to hold your own, ever since I went to the admiral for you."

"I'll try not to let you down," she mumbled. "Sorry I'm not some MMA rock star like you are."

"You want to know why I'm a good fighter?" he offered. She paused, looking up at him. He had barely even broken a sweat during his session. She, on the other hand, was what her mother would have referred to as a "hot mess." Life wasn't fair sometimes.

"It's because I practice. A lot. Even after everyone else has gone for the day. And I learned the rules. I studied them as much as anything else and discovered that once you learn the rules, you find how they can be bent and how some can be broken."

"Just like flying. And like jazz," Nora said, struck by the analogy. This elicited his infamous half smile, which relieved a little of her grumpiness.

"Just like jazz," he agreed. "Are you ready to go back?" He nodded toward Olivia, who was watching them, arms crossed, eyes narrowed.

"Bring it on," Nora said, rolling her shoulders.

The arrival of the J'nai cadets was a welcome distraction from classwork. What had initially seemed exciting and groundbreaking about it quickly became schoolwork like any other, complete with homework and exams and stress and a fair amount of procrastination. The only one who really seemed to become immersed in it—and stay there—was Cat. She was by far the most studious and the smartest of their year, and she would have been considered a teacher's pet if she weren't so shy. In fact, the strain of it all occasionally got to her, manifesting itself as terrible migraine headaches. She would miss a few classes a month due to them, and when they passed, they left her pale and shaky. Sophie had insisted that Cat get checked out in the infirmary after the first one, but all the tests said she was fine.

Zoe brought up the idea that maybe it was a genetic problem; perhaps something had gone wrong in the clone juice the mad scientists had concocted. After that comment, none of them slept at all. Every minor muscle pain became a sudden cause for alarm. Even the usually unflappable Lara got spooked.

By the third headache, Sophie was ready with Tylenol and a heating pad when Cat texted her through the shared virtual chat room on their tablets. Raina looked sideways at the bottle, her arched eyebrow forming her unspoken question.

"What? I got it from the infirmary for cramps," Sophie said, tucking Cat into her bunk.

"I didn't know they gave out bottles," Raina said.

"They don't," Sophie said simply. "I never said they *gave* it to me. Here, Cat." She dropped two of the white pills into Cat's trembling hand. Cat took them and then drew the curtain closed on her bunk to block the light.

"Maybe she should go back to the infirmary," Raina said, her lips pursed. Zoe shook her head.

"They ran their tests. They say there's nothing wrong."

"Maybe she just needs to relax," Nora said. "She works so hard." She was sitting on one of the long tables in the middle of the room, between towers of notepads and tablets.

"Hang on a tick," Lara said. "You think she's just working that big brain of hers too hard?"

"Maybe *she* should have a secret boyfriend she won't tell any of her roommates about, one she sneaks off to see at all hours of the night," Sophie said. "Maybe that'll help her relax."

Zoe landed a punch on Sophie's arm before she was even done talking. Lara stuck her tongue out at Sophie, but didn't disagree.

"I just think she puts a lot of pressure on herself to be the best here," Nora said. Cat curled herself up into a tighter ball in her bunk, moaning slightly.

"So you're saying she needs a distraction," Sophie said after a moment, her patented devious grin spreading across her face.

And that's how the six of them ended up front and center for the landing of the J'nai ships later that week. Sophie made them camp out all day to be sure they had the best spots in the dome to see the new arrivals. They'd dragged folding chairs into the dome to set up a kind of camp, and one of them would periodically make a run for coffee. They got some strange looks from the mechanics and engineers, but Nora had to admit it was kind of fun. Sophie refused to let Cat bring her tablet along, and the pale girl huddled in her chair, her fingers twitching every so often, as if they longed for the device. Sophie noted this, and shot Nora a knowing look, one eyebrow arched high. Nora shrugged. When Cat saw the shared glance, she sighed softly.

"Really, Soph, is this really necess..." Cat started.

"Absolutely," Sophie said. Her tone was firm, confident. "We'll let you get back to your books in a few hours. Look! There's the first one!"

A swarm of PJs soared into the dome, the overhead fluorescence glinting off their smooth black lines. Nora sighed at the sight of them – was it just cabin fever that made her yearn to be back on one of those ships, to get off-station for a little while?

It seemed like every deckhand and mechanic in the station was there, carrying all kinds of wrenches and tools in their navy overalls, ready to jump into action as soon as the shuttles landed. Usually the J'nai cadets would have arrived in September, at the start of the semester, but this year they had been unusually delayed. On Terra Prime, they needed every able-bodied J'nai at home to help rebuild for as long as possible. Not even Deltas could be spared, except for maybe the last few months of classes. Nora knew the details because it was one of the few things Bastian complained about: being stuck on the station for longer than he'd bargained for, until his ship returned.

With a soft *whoosh*, the first cargo ramps lowered, and soon the hydraulic systems on all the PJs were opening. The deck crew sprang into action; it was like a ballet, each running to his or her predetermined assignment. Nora couldn't figure out how they could tell the ships apart, but they knew, somehow.

The J'nai went back to Terra Prime during the summers for training and a holiday at home and usually returned each fall, like exchange students, to complete their coursework just as their human counterparts did. Other than J'hara and Dalton, there weren't a lot of them at the station year round.

But now, as the ships emptied, the deck was covered with one hundred J'nai crew and cadets of all shapes and colors. They were mostly tall and lean, and they all had the same silky white hair, either done up in various exotic styles or simply left down. Besides that, though, they were an assorted group. There were some with light pink skin, like J'hara, and some with blue skin and slightly pointed ears. Some were a dark gray that was almost black, some were yellow, and some were lilac or teal. Some had gills, some had fins, and some had tattooed gold marks down their necks. The shades leaned toward pastels, which made their sharp navy uniforms—identical to the ones the human cadets wore—all the more jarring.

"Aren't they *gorgeous*," Sophie breathed. Nora found herself nodding in agreement. It was like someone had upended a jewelry box all over the flight deck. If arriving at Ganymede Station was the most important event of Nora's life, this was a close second. The enormity of the mission struck her. Here was an alien race, whose Star Ports they'd be working to restore in a model of intergalactic cooperation. A warm feeling of Earthly pride grew in her chest.

"Stop gawking, girls, and let them pass. You'll have plenty of chances to meet them in class tomorrow," Aditi said, coming through the gathered crowd. She gave them a wink. "I know it's exciting. But would you appreciate being looked at like you were in a zoo? Go on now."

Sophie sighed, momentarily defeated, and they—along with the rest of those assembled to see the new cadets, which was practically their whole class—followed Aditi from the dome.

There were close to sixty new J'nai cadets, of all years. Nora's class size jumped from fifty to sixty-five. In Science 101, she got to meet her first young J'nai. A pair of them sat in the desks beside her, their skin a light sky blue. Sophie was talking to a group of them in the middle of the room, while Lara was talking with a gray-skinned J'nai boy in the corner.

"Your name is Jane," Nora said, not believing her ears. The blue-skinned J'nai looked up at her, a huge grin on her face. She wore her short white hair in, of all things, pigtails.

"Yep! And this is my brother, Mike," she said, nudging the taller J'nai next to her. He begrudgingly stuck out his hand for Nora to shake; the manner struck Nora as so utterly human, so like a disgruntled teenage boy back home, that for a second she was more stunned by his demeanor than his name.

"Really?" Nora got out eventually, raising an eyebrow.

"We were told that humans have a hard time pronouncing our native language. We thought it would be fun, as a class, you know, to come up with human nicknames to make it easier for you! And it was *so* fun! Of course, we tried to stick with single-syllable names. Oh, not to insult your intelligence or anything, of course," Jane apologized. "It was just, you know, we're trying to fit in. You know, be cool!" Her eyes were wide and earnest. Nora liked her immediately. She was like an overeager puppy.

"And how did you pick Jane?" Nora asked.

"I read this beautiful book by a human called…"

"Hey Nora, can I borrow you for a minute?" Greg was at her side and nodded for her to follow him.

"Nice to meet you guys," Nora called.

"Nice to meet you, too!" Jane called back. "Honestly, humans are just so friendly! They're not at all like I imagined," she confided to her brother in barely accented English.

The absolute normalcy of the situation was astounding. Here she was, meeting teenaged aliens like she was greeting foreign exchange students back on Earth! The idea made her giggle. What was just as astonishing was how easily the J'nai seemed to be assimilating with the rest of the students. It was one of the supreme evolutionary advantages given to their race, Nora knew. They could mold themselves to fit any situation, any environment. It was the reason the J'nai had spread across the galaxy like an unfurling flag, planting colonies on all kinds of planets.

"Hey, look," Greg said, as the rest of the room gradually settled in their seats for class. "I'm sorry about what I said the other day."

Nora sighed.

"It's okay," she said, but he interrupted her before she could continue.

"No, it's not. I was stupid, and I mean…I didn't even realize until later that you said maybe we *could* be dating if I wasn't such an ass, and I thought maybe if I apologized for being one then…"

"Mr. Allen?" Dr. Hooper called. "Is it okay with you if I proceed with class now?"

"By all means, professor," Greg said, leaning back in his chair. He shot Nora a wink. She tried not to grin.

Mike and Jane were in her next class, too, and by lunchtime Jane had decided that the three of them would be best friends for life, a term she had learned by watching all the downloaded MTV shows she could get her hands on. She was also very chatty, and as they sat down with their lunch trays—Nora couldn't bear to eat the fish sticks after her first trip to the greenhouse—Jane launched into the sort of rapid-fire description of her home planet that would have made an auctioneer jealous. Even Cat warmed up to her.

"So, is your skin blue due to methemoglobinemia, or is it more of a hemocyanin component in your blood?" Cat asked. It was one of the longer bursts of language Nora had ever heard her make to anyone besides her roommates. Even if Nora didn't understand half the words.

"God, Cat, you can't just ask people why they're *blue*!" Zoe exclaimed in a valley-girl accent, grinning. She was answered with blank stares. "What? No one here's seen *Mean Girls*?"

"Did you hack into Greg's movie database or something without telling me?" Sophie accused.

"Oh, I saw it!" Jane said, raising her hand. "I've seen every single movie in the database—some twice! And…"

"Actually, it's a combination of living near a dying star with orange light and high exposure to silver and iodine in the atmosphere from the vents. It's quite interesting, really, a sort of hybrid argyria…" Mike cut in, and soon he and Cat were discussing biology in terms that Nora could no longer follow. Cat was as animated as Nora had ever seen her, and Mike seemed to have lost some of his churlishness when discussing genetics.

"Good on ya, Soph," Lara said, sitting down with her tray. "I knew the J'nai would be good for Cat. Get her out of her shell a bit." The gray J'nai Lara had been talking to earlier was with her, a boy named Dan who was barely taller than Lara (who was almost six feet herself). He was polite but reserved, though he seemed to get on with Lara well.

"I literally have no idea what they're talking about," Nora said, watching Cat and Mike. She shook her head.

"You're a Hypatia. Aren't you supposed to be good at all that science-y crap?" Zoe said around a mouthful of kale.

"You're a Zenobia, an African queen, aren't you supposed to have some manners?" Sophie said, sticking out her tongue. Zoe grinned, her teeth shining very white and cat-like against her dark face, and threw a carrot stick at her.

By the end of lunch, it was hard to imagine the station without the young J'nai. They were, for the most part, eager to blend in with human society. Most of this generation had been born and raised on Terra Prime, or on large spaceships. By all accounts, Terra Prime was a truly beautiful place, with soaring architecture and a lush, temperate climate. Nora had learned more about the J'nai in just a few hours than she had in all of the previous months – for example, the J'nai were, as it turned out, very fond of peaches, so the station's chefs had done everything in their power to accommodate this and make them feel at home.

"Have you looked at the menu for this week? Peaches every day now. I never thought I'd say this, but I can already feel myself getting sick of it," Zoe said, dripping cobbler from her spoon.

"And peach-flavored coffee is just taking it one step too far," Sophie grumbled. "So, how's Greg?" she asked, innocently changing the subject.

"He's fine," Nora said. "He thinks if he apologizes enough for being an ass, I'll go out with him."

"And has he?"

"Not yet. But we're going to go watch the movie that that Edison fourth year downloaded from the mainframe. Greg thinks he can set up a big projection screen in the rec dome, like a drive-in movie but without the cars. Ty wants me to tell you that he wants you to go with him," Nora said. Sophie tossed her hair.

"Of course he does. Doesn't everyone?"

CHAPTER 19

"You mean I can go? Really?" Nora asked. She was in Aditi's office. Her friend and mentor had just told her she'd caught up enough—albeit barely—to qualify for her first off-station tour. The *Rapscallion* would be making a quick trip to Terra Prime to pick up supplies and then come right back. The entire flight would take about a week, during which time she'd actually get to experience what the hyperspace routes were all about.

"It took some convincing, but Benoit can be very...persuasive," Aditi said with a twitch of her lips. "The admiral didn't have a choice by the time he was done."

Nora's face heated.

"I've been working really hard," she mumbled.

"Nora," Aditi said. "I had no doubt you would pass."

A quiet pause lingered between them. Nora fidgeted, a thought tickling the tip of her tongue. Aditi waited, until Nora blurted out-

"I bet Hypatia never dreamed of piloting a space ship."

"This isn't because you're a Hypatia clone," Aditi said. "I know enough about you—and Thalia—and I've been on this station long enough to know that just because you have the genetics for greatness doesn't mean you'll achieve it. Half the people on this station are Originals, and they're some of the most brilliant, altruistic people I've ever known. What I'm saying, Nora, is that you have the potential to be anything you want to be, and not because of your DNA. If you put that big brain of yours to work, you can be a pilot, or a doctor, or an engineer, or whatever you want. You just have to *want* it bad enough."

"Thanks, Aditi," Nora said. She surprised them both by giving the woman a brief hug.

"Uh, sorry, I know that's not really the protocol here—no warm and fuzzy." Nora said.

"No. But thanks, Nora. I needed that." Aditi put her arm around the girl's shoulders. "Now. Let's go get you ready. I have to introduce you to Captain Soren."

Captain Soren was a J'nai. She was thin and graceful with pale yellow skin and large, piercing dark green eyes. She wore her white hair back in a severe bun and looked every inch the proper military commander she'd been trained to become since the J'nai first established contact with humans. Soren was one of the first captains for their inter-species crews—until her, most humans on J'nai ships had been merely passengers, observers. The *Rapscallion* had been built with both humans and J'nai in mind, and was Soren's pride and joy. They found her running some last-minute inspections on the supplies being loaded for their trip to Terra Prime.

"So, I see we're taking a cadet on board," she said in a crisp tone, looking Nora over. "Welcome. Make sure you're not late for takeoff. We won't wait until the sun turns green for you."

"That means something like 'we can't wait forever.' J'nai idiom," Aditi whispered with a wink, seeing Nora's confused expression. "You'll get used to them."

Nora grinned.

"The *Rap* is a great ship, cadet," Captain Soren said, laying a hand fondly on the hull. "I hope you'll have a good experience here."

"I can't wait," Nora said, and she meant it from the bottom of her heart.

▰▰ ▰▰ ▰▰

"Come on cadet, let's call it a night," Bastian said. Nora had just failed another sim; this time her subluminal engine had cut out, and no matter what she did, she couldn't get it back online before the Qaig ship took her out. She slammed the heels of her hands against the control panels.

"Ugh!" she cried. "I almost had it! One more time!"

"That's enough," Bastian said, opening the hatch to the sim pod. Nora blinked in the sudden brightness and rubbed her eyes hard.

"Just one more," she said, frowning. The switch-over should have worked, she thought. If she could have just re-routed the power... "Come *on,* Bastian. I think I've got it now."

"It's late, Nora. Tomorrow."

"It's not that late."

"It's past midnight."

Nora's jaw dropped, but Bastian was smirking.

"You're teasing me," she said, startled. He shook his head.

"I don't have a sense of humor. It *is* actually 12:04 a.m."

She thought about pushing again for one more run of the sim, looked at Bastian and his smirking face, and sighed, defeated.

"Okay, we can do it tomorrow then," she said and got up from the mockpit. Her back ached; she was bent almost double for a second as she fought to unkink the knotted muscles along her spine.

"Ow," she said as she stretched. Each muscle fiber tensed, relaxed, then settled into a low, dull ache. She could really use a massage after that. "Does it ever get easier?"

"No," he said, and she sighed. He watched her for a second before adding –"But you get stronger," he said. "You *are* getting stronger. *Pour estimer le doux, il faut goûter de l'amer.*"

Nora groaned and picked up her bag.

"So are you going to tell me what that means, or..."

"What, your fancy Fax brain hasn't mastered French yet?" he said. Nora shoved him lightly. He seemed to be in a good mood.

"You've got ... *comment dites-vous...* grit, I think is the word," he said. Nora rolled her eyes, but the comment warmed her, like a little glow inside her chest.

They were the last two in the sim room, the lights mostly dimmed for the night. As they left, Bastian turned off the lights and closed the door behind them. Her eyes blurred with fatigue. She could still see the swimming red outlines of enemy ships floating in the sim horizon before her. They walked in silence in the darkened hall for a few minutes, both lost in thought, and Nora could nearly feel Bastian's mood darken.

"She's just jealous, you know," he said suddenly.

"Who?" Nora asked, knowing full well who he was talking about. The suddenness of his words, though, had jarred her somewhat from her own thoughts.

"Thalia. That's why she waits out there every night." Bastian let out a long breath, and rubbed the back of his neck with one hand. She wondered if he'd only let her go so long in the sim room because he was an insomniac, or because he was hoping Thalia would be gone by the time they left.

"She's like a lion waiting to pounce," Nora agreed.

"You have to understand that Thalia is the kind of girl who isn't happy unless she has everyone's undivided attention. She had mine for a while. Now she feels like I'm spending too much time with you. It gets to her. Makes her feel unimportant. Weak. She has been pestering Olivia for weeks, and now it seems that she has turned her claws on you."

"That is…" Nora fought to find the words, her brain mushy with fatigue. "Just … so sad."

Bastian raised an eyebrow.

"That's probably why she works so hard in the lab. Like she doesn't think she's worth anything if she isn't the best, isn't the most popular, doesn't have the attention of the hottest guy on the station."

"Wait, what…"

"I mean, I get it. I'm not mad at her, even if she is obnoxious. I just wish people would stop judging me when they meet me, you know, thinking I'm another Thalia. I'm not. And doesn't it make you wonder what her life was like growing up? I bet her handlers were super hard on her. Lack of hugs in her childhood, something like that."

Bastian had stopped.

"What?" Nora asked, throwing her backpack over her shoulder. She'd been rambling—it happened when she was tired—but she didn't think she'd said anything offensive. She tried to remember the flood of words—just some psychological mumbo-jumbo about Thalia. Nothing too radical. But he had the strangest expression on his face, even with his eyes partly shadowed in the darkness of the hall.

"What?" she repeated. He shook his head.

"There are so many comments I want to make about your little tirade, I don't even know where to start."

"It was not a tirade."

"It was. But I think you are right about her - just maybe not that 'hottest guy on the station' part," he said with a smirk as they emerged from the hallway into the rec dome. Thalia was at the far end, showing off her electric-wheeled motorcycle to some wide-eyed cadets, the only other souls in the entire dome. The lights were dimmed here, too, making her motorcycle and blue hair gleam all the brighter.

"Of course I'm right about her. She's me," Nora said with a wry grin, pointedly ignoring the other matter and making a mental note to agonize over the fact she'd said it aloud later. "I'm granted a rather interesting insider look at what makes her tick."

Bastian shook his head.

"You are nothing like her," he muttered, watching Thalia. She revved the motorcycle, and when she caught him watching her, tossed her hair and waved. He nodded to her.

"Catch you later, Nora," he said and headed over to Thalia.

"Later," she called. Nora left as quickly as she could and without looking back this time. She didn't want to see what was going on behind her.

J'hara's next class was on the history of the Qaig. Jane and Mike seemed bored through the entire lecture—they'd been taught this stuff since infancy—but Jane found an opportunity to learn anyway. She sent Nora little messages throughout the class. Nora heard rapid-fire tapping from Jane in the seat behind her, and then a message popped up on her screen. She figured Jane was texting multiple people; there were way more taps than characters in her message alone:

Jane: I would like to ask you a question about your clone-sister, is that okay?

Clone-sister? She had to mean Thalia. Nora said yes.

Jane: I noticed that she has a lot of marks inked onto her skin.

Nora: We call them tattoos. Yes, she has a lot of them.

Jane: Do you have them?

Nora: No.

Jane: Good.

Nora: Why good?

She had to stop for a second—J'hara seemed to know something was up. Nora straightened herself and tried to pay attention, but the long-winded speech about the vague villainy of the Qaig was really over the top. At least J'hara had pictures of the Qaig up on the screen. They—like the J'nai—were vaguely humanoid, only much more reptilian in appearance, like a cross between a man, a lizard, and a toad, complete with warts. They were broad, grotesque creatures, with wide, lipless mouths and yellow eyes with vertical pupils. Their ships were just as clunky and awkward looking— boxy, olive-colored things that didn't look capable of flight at all, much less space travel. Just like any Grade-B science fiction movie back home, the villains were ugly and the heroes – the J'nai – were beautiful. Kept it neat and simple, Nora thought, then shook her head to clear it when her tablet buzzed again with another message.

Jane: Because I was worried you were a criminal too.

Nora: Thalia isn't a criminal. She isn't very nice, but I don't think she's ever been in jail or anything.

Jane: Then why does she have so many black marks on her skin?

Nora: They are just decorative. Humans put marks on their skin to signify things that are important to them, or sometimes just because they are pretty.

Jane: Oh. Only J'nai who have done bad things mark up their skin with black ink. It is to show the rest of the J'nai that they have done something wrong. We call them Omegas.

At that, Nora had to smile. She wondered if Thalia knew that the J'nai thought she was some sort of career criminal with her assortment of tattoos. She imagined Thalia would actually enjoy that.

"The Qaig lived in peace with the J'nai for centuries," J'hara continued to drone, though Nora only heard her vaguely. "Secretly amassing their weapons, until the day they turned against us, nearly twenty of your Earth years ago. We few are all that remains of an empire that once spanned the galaxy, our own technology, all but lost to us."

Jane: Do you know William Shatner?

Nora had to stifle a laugh; it came out as kind of a choked cough.

Nora: You know there are like six billion people on Earth.

Jane: That's a lot. So do you know him?

Nora: No, sorry.

Jane: I watched all of his programs. He must be a great man.

Nora grinned.

Jane: I don't think he actually ever traveled in space though, did he?

Nora: No, his programs are just stories, for entertainment.

Jane: Have you ever seen them?

Nora: Some of them.

Jane: I have them all on my tablet. I will send them to you.

Nora: I think J'hara is on to us—

Jane: It's okay. She likes William Shatner, too. She would want to see his programs with us.

Nora doubted a single cadet slept the night before the flight to Terra Prime. She certainly didn't. She'd repacked her bag twice, checked her alarm at least ten times to make sure it was set properly, polished her shoes to gleaming, and did every other little task she could think of until Lara blasted her with a pillow and told her to calm down and be quiet.

The next morning, she hugged her roommates goodbye and was surprised to find herself missing them almost immediately afterward. She'd never had sisters, hadn't even had all that many friends back on Earth, but these girls were different. They were like her. They were all here for a purpose. They knew what she was and accepted her—celebrated her, even. She and Lara waved goodbye for the hundredth time and made their way to the dome.

The hangar bay was a madhouse. Lara was immediately scooped up by a severe-looking Chinese woman. Nora threaded her way through the last-minute supply crates and crowds, looking around for her ship.

"Hey, Nora!" Greg called. "Hey!" He waved to her from a spot a dozen yards away, from under the protective wing of a PJ. He trotted over to her, his face practically shining, he was smiling so bright. His mismatched eyes were gleaming.

"You ready?" he asked. His voice was breathless with anticipation.

"Absolutely," she said, returning his smile. He reached for her free hand and squeezed it.

"Listen, when we get back…" he started. Nora looked up at him, his eyes nearly level with hers.

"Yeah," she said, agreeing with his unasked question.

Amped up on adrenaline, she was gifted with the sort of courage and spontaneity she rarely possessed. She reached up and kissed Greg on the cheek, but as she went to pull away, he wrapped a hand around her waist and pulled her in for a real kiss, one that made her feel warm all over, like some of his radiating giddiness was infusing her bloodstream.

"Well," she said, as he pulled back. She couldn't think of anything else to say. Her brain seemed to have completely shut down, and she couldn't keep the smile off of her face.

"Yeah," he said, still grinning. "Just didn't want you to forget about me."

"Yo, lover boy," a man called from Greg's ship. "We ain't got all day."

"When we get back!" Greg said before dashing to his ship. Nora had to suppress the grin on her face as she made her way to the *Rapscallion*. Time to be professional, Nora, she told herself—even if you just had your first real kiss.

But her brain replayed the moment over and over.

She wandered around in a meandering, happy daze until she nearly ran into Bastian.

"Hello, Earth to Nora," he said, waving a hand in front of her face. She beamed up at him. If Greg had been shining, Bastian was positively radioactive. He was finally getting his wish; he'd said if he had to spend any more time on the station he'd go mad. And for now, he was in such a good mood, Nora didn't think anything could tarnish his glow—not even knowing he'd have to spend the trip babysitting a cadet. And a Fax, to boot. Soren joined them after a minute, and made a beeline towards the far end of the dome. The landing dome was littered with identical PJs. How Bastian and Captain Soren could pick theirs out from the bunch, Nora had no idea. But they found it, and when they did, Captain Soren greeted the *Rapscallion* like an old friend, reaching up so she could run her hand along the rear-facing curve of the wing as they approached.

They boarded the ship and found a green-skinned J'nai waiting for them. He got right to business before saying hello.

"Right, so nice easy trip to the Terra Prime Star Port," he said. "Pick up some cargo with the rest of the fleet. Nice easy trip back."

"Good to see you, Asher," Bastian said, hoisting his pack over one shoulder so he could shake the man's hand. "This is Nora. She's our rookie for the flight."

"Asher, navigator," he said, shaking Nora's hand. "Welcome aboard. Hope you don't mind, we've put you in a bunk at the far back. Only one where you wouldn't have to share quarters."

Asher got up and led her to the space. It was tiny—hardly large enough for the cot crammed inside. The rest of it was filled by a narrow locker.

"Cozy," she commented, dropping off her pack.

"Doesn't matter. You'll be up on the Bridge most of the time anyway," Bastian said. "This way."

Bastian settled into the first mate's console to the front and left of the captain's chair and pulled up another rolling chair so Nora could watch him work, locking it into place in the floor so it wouldn't move when they started encountering G-forces. The console was like the sim pod's – yet entirely different. Here she was in an open space, not the enclosed simulator, and the wide window before them showed the hangar. Soon, it would be space. Her hands shook with adrenaline.

Bastian was efficient. He'd gotten right down to business as well, as impatient as Asher to be off, and had shown her the startup sequence before Captain Soren even arrived on the Bridge.

"Ready to go?" Soren asked, settling into her chair. She looked relaxed—a contented smile spread across her face.

"Flight is a go," Bastian said.

"Nav is a go," Asher said.

"Comms go," Donovan, the second mate, said.

"Engine is go," a voice said over the intercom.

"Who's that?" Nora whispered.

"Silas, the engineer. Kind of a hermit, you probably won't see him much," Bastian explained.

Soren nodded. "If you're lucky, anyway. Hold tight, cadet," she said, looking to Nora. "Take her out, Benoit. Let's lead the pack."

They rang the control tower that they were ready, and were the second PJ to take off from the hangar bay. Bastian ran the controls with a steady, focused hand, and Nora sat at his side, desperate to absorb anything she could about the way a PJ *really* handled.

A few breaths later and they'd cleared the dome. Bastian pulled them back into a smooth ascent. The mass of Jupiter loomed in front of them before dipping to the side as Bastian steered them around it. They were on the dark side of the planet now. A flicker of red danced along the horizon, the Aurora shimmering gently before flickering out. Nora grinned, taking it as a good omen.

"Ready for jump, Captain," Bastian said, adjusting the commands on the screen faster than she could follow. "We are in position."

Nora gripped the edges of her seat until her knuckles ached. Her stomach clenched, and she was glad she'd been too excited to eat this morning. She didn't want to throw up all over the *Rap*, not on the first time she'd been off-station since her arrival. She'd watched the PJs for months from the station, imagining what she would feel when she finally got to go again

– but all of the daydreams in the universe couldn't have prepared her for this. It felt like waking up and realizing it was Christmas morning, only a million times better.

"Nav?"

"Coordinates plotted, ready for jump," Asher said, his nimble fingers flying over his control screen.

"Hang on, Silas, we're jumping," Soren called over the comm.

"Roger," came the tinny response.

Bastian pulled in the coordinates for the jump and initiated the hyperdrive.

Nora held her breath.

Pop.

CHAPTER 20

Nora and Bastian had spent hours going over the finer points of the Star Ports. Each port acted like a stop on a subway; you could exit hyperspace at only one of those designated ports. Unlike a subway, though, you could jump on at any time and be sucked into the stream that was the massive hyperspace route the ancient J'nai had discovered, that Current where light moved faster. In this way, the J'nai had spread across the galaxy.

That is, until the Qaig blew up the Star Ports.

Now, like a string of Christmas lights with a blown bulb, the only ports the J'nai could travel to were ones where at least two were in sequence; for example, the port at Terra Prime and the port just outside Jupiter. Unfortunately, given the vast distance in between the ports, it was unreasonable to try to fly between them in the "usual" subluminal way. Even with the blue goo pods and the xenon ion engines, it had taken the J'nai years to reach this port, where they were working to rebuild a damaged port they'd had in storage. They'd never had any real reason to use the port near Jupiter before, except to mine the asteroid belt—a rich deposit of minerals, as it turned out—but once they'd been stranded, they'd reached out to Earth for help.

Hence the development of the Ganymede project.

No one knew how many J'nai were left in the galaxy. Some thought it was around ten thousand; others, perhaps less. Desperate to reach their stranded companions and relink the Star Ports, they'd traded their knowledge of space exploration for the manpower, brainpower, and resources that Earth had to offer.

But until now, the Star Ports were just something Nora had read about. Jumping onto the cosmic equivalent of the Gulf Stream was something no book or sim could have ever prepared her for. With a feeling like a popped champagne cork, they were thrust into the Current, a route that, Bastian said, would take them three days—mostly on autopilot—to reach Terra Prime, one day to load up, and then three days back. The sky was pitch black before them, other than the blinking light on the nose of their ship. Occasionally, a white streak would fly by outside the wide front window—a star they were passing at impossible speeds. Like viewing the night sky from underwater, the view was distorted, blurred.

But other than that, it felt, surprisingly, like they were barely moving at all.

That's not to say there wasn't plenty to keep them busy. Bastian showed Nora how to make sure the ship stayed within the hyperspace Current. Autopilot and Captain Soren could manage it for a few hours each night so Bastian and Nora could get some rest, but otherwise, it needed near-constant supervision. Getting blown off course could be catastrophic; if they dropped from the Current before the ports, which slowed the stream just long enough to let them off the track, the ship would be torn apart atom by atom, until it was nothing but a thousand-mile-long trail of glittering dust.

Still, they worked well together, Nora realized—like two pianists in a duet. After a few hours, she could predict what Bastian wanted to do before he asked her, what minute adjustments they had to make. She even got him talking—a major accomplishment in and of itself. Here, on his ship, he was more relaxed than he ever was back on station. He seemed to feel at home. He told her he planned on becoming a captain someday, but he liked Soren, and the admiral felt his talents were most valuable, for now, in this role. Good pilots were few and far between, and Bastian was the best.

When he wasn't quizzing her on the finer points of their course, she struggled to keep up with her studies. More than one professor had warned her that crossing thousands of light years of space was no excuse to fall behind on her coursework. It was a rather absurd thing to have to say, Nora realized, but all the same, she worked on her books while Bastian worked on his. He switched between a postgraduate course on engineering and a textbook on space craft, covering everything from the J'nai to the Qaig to the newest battle cruisers. Nora was dying to get a peek at it, and he teased her with it, like a prize to be won if she did a good job and didn't blow up the ship on their way back.

She also got to know the rest of the crew during their three-day jaunt to Terra Prime. Donovan was a linguist back on Earth, with limp brown hair and thick glasses that were perpetually falling down his nose. He was recruited as a communications officer. While most J'nai spoke a little English—some better than the humans back on Earth—not all did, and there were innumerable J'nai dialects, given the widespread nature of their race. Donovan spoke most of them better than native J'nai, Asher said of him with pride. Donovan had a penchant for bobble-head figures—which, to Soren's chagrin, he kept on his console dash—and faded T-shirts that featured obscure bands. Nora's favorite was one that said "Panda-monium" above a pair of panda bears in sunglasses.

Silas Dahl was the surly, block-faced engineer who pretty much kept to the engine room unless he was grabbing a protein bar from the kitchen. Bastian told her he'd even strung up a hammock in there, forsaking a bunk. He was terribly OCD, but that made him a great engineer. Nothing got by him, and he'd bite your head off if you tried to take a peek into his engine room, as Nora found out on her first day. He allowed Soren in, she found out, but only because the J'nai had an uncanny knack for engineering; in fact, the captain had been an engineer herself long ago and had admitted that she sometimes missed tinkering on machines.

Despite the long shifts, Nora found herself with plenty of free time, plenty of time to daydream as she lay awake on her little cot, trying to convince her mind to shut off and just go to sleep. Sometimes she wondered what Greg was doing, if he was maybe thinking about her as his own ship spun past the stars on a course paralleling her own.

She also thought about those back on Ganymede. If they'd stayed on Earth, what would have happened to them? Who would they be? Sophie would have eventually dominated something corporate, she was sure, with a closet full of stilettos. Cat would have ended up as a college professor somewhere, publishing papers only a half dozen people in the world could understand. And Bastian? He'd be the guy with long hair, ripped jeans, and aviators, cool and aloof; the guy who went rock climbing and skydiving on the weekends; the guy who never faltered, imbued with a *joie de vivre* and a fearsome curiosity.

Whereas Olivia, she thought, cringing, would be the jet-setting model who had handbags that cost more than Nora's parents' car. She'd get her hair done every other week and wear red lipstick that never smudged. And, of course, she'd live somewhere fashionable like Paris or New York.

Well, that wasn't really fair. Olivia could throw her on her ass if she wanted to, and had done just that numerous times since Nora had started going to Fight Club. One toss had left a nasty bruise on her left hip that made her limp for days; she'd caught Bastian laughing at her misery when he thought she wasn't looking. Eventually, though, the bruises were coming less often as her muscles became a little less rubbery. She wasn't Olivia, and she wasn't Thalia, either— but she was Eleanora Clementine Clark, and she was becoming a pretty good version of herself, too. What would the old Nora have been back on Earth? It was hard to say. She was starting to realize, though, there was no way any experience she'd ever be able to have on Earth could have prepared her and turned her into the person she was becoming. She was starting to feel—what was the word? Confident? That didn't really go far enough. How about empowered? She'd been thrown into this world, this incredible, strange world, and though she'd had a bit of a rocky start, she'd found something she was good at—really good at. She had made friends, and people respected her a little, and trusted her. She threw her shoulders back. She'd done something to be proud of. She might not be where she wanted to be yet, but she was on her way, and nothing was going to stop her. Not Thalia. Not Savaryn. Not anything.

On their third day, just after breakfast, a notice flashed that they were approaching the Terra Prime Star Port. Bastian showed her how to prepare the ship to break the jump and how to time it. She sat at rapt attention.

The ship exited hyperspace smoothly, and just ahead, Nora saw the giant ring of the Star Port more than two kilometers across. They soared through it before banking hard to the left, and then there it was: Terra Prime. The planet was spread before them like a mimicry of Earth, with its green land and cobalt seas. Nora was surprised to find her throat felt tight, and she had to swallow hard a few times to get rid of the feeling.

On this voyage, they weren't actually going to be landing on Terra Prime at all; rather, they'd be picking up their cargo in orbit. They saved a lot of fuel that way. A blocky J'nai ship, which looked to Nora like about four ocean freighters combined, was waiting with hundreds of containers constructed of the same white metal that made up about everything on Ganymede station. They could be filled with everything from fuel cells, to spare parts, to that delicious coffee, or any of the other foods grown on Terra Prime—and at least half of them, Nora thought wryly, would probably contain peaches, in all shapes and forms. Her stomach rolled at the thought of even *more* peaches.

Donovan communicated their location to the ship's operator in fluent J'nai, and they were directed toward their package. It was essentially a first come, first serve operation. The *Rapscallion* had a set of retractable claws on its underside and landed lightly on the first cylindrical container on the edge. Donovan coordinated the wireless link, and the container's ID flashed across their consoles. Like a hawk with a fish, the *Rapscallion* lifted off the container ship with the cargo carefully gripped below.

"When will I get to try that?" Nora whispered. Bastian grinned.

"Not for a while," he said.

"It's not as easy as he makes it look," Captain Soren said. "I tried it once."

"Captain, are you referring to the time you spilled the...."

"Yes, Asher, I am," Soren said, shaking her head. Nora giggled, the monumental nature of the moment making her feel giddy. "Do you mind? I thought we weren't going to bring that up again."

"Of course. I only…"

Wham.

The *Rapscallion* lurched heavily to its port side. Sirens blared overhead, and the Bridge went dark for a second. Then the emergency lights flashed on, in red, bathing the Bridge in a bloody glow.

"What the..." Donovan said, picking himself off the floor. His glasses had been bent wildly in the fall.

Bastian's fingers flew over the console, bringing up emergency power and rerouting the shields faster than Nora could process. He alone hadn't seemed to have budged from his chair. The overhead lights turned back on as the power was restored, she recognized hazily. She'd slammed against the console and had to scramble back into her chair. Her head stung—she must have hit it—but the feeling registered remotely, the pain dim through the muffled insulation of her coursing adrenaline.

"Silas, get us out of here!" Soren screamed over the comm. A swarm of blocky green ships poured from the Star Port in front of them, shooting laser fire as thick as rain. Nora's stomach felt like she'd been stabbed with something cold, like she'd been impaled by ice. Her hands were shaking so hard she could barely hold on to the console in front of her. Her vision blurred as something trickled into it – sweat, maybe – and she wiped her eyes, not quite able to believe what she was seeing.

Qaigs.

"Hold on," Bastian said, and the ship dove steeply. Nora rocked in her chair, the motion slamming her consciousness back into the ship.

"Status?" Soren shouted, strapping herself into her chair.

"Shields at 20 percent, weapons down. Hyperspace engine down. Subluminals at 35..."

Bang!

"Make that 15 percent." Asher's green skin looked positively gray as fear bleached him of his usual color. The console in front of Bastian flickered, the green lines wavering as the power failed for a second.

"Silas, what's going on down there?" Soren called over the comms. There was no answer. Bastian looked up from his controls briefly and caught Nora's eye. His own were steady, like a calm day at sea. The glance calmed her somewhat, and her hands stopped their shaking. He turned back and frantically dove the *Rapscallion* around green laser fire and storage containers that had drifted free from the J'nai ship. It was like the most vicious obstacle course ever invented, she thought – lasers and bits of ships and cargo came at them from all angles, at all speeds and trajectories. More PJ-type ships had started coming out of the J'nai container ship, and a fierce battle ensued. Nora gripped the edge of her seat. She was not prepared for this! That second wave of PJ's might be equipped for battle, but the *Rap* was not! Her guns were down – she was a sitting duck.

She felt like she was going to vomit.

"*Silas!*" Soren yelled. There was still no answer from the engine room. The warning lights still blazed red on Bastian's console. Soren spat something in J'nai, likely a curse, judging from the vehemence. Nora cringed.

"Benoit. You have the bridge," Soren said. She unstrapped herself from her chair and stood, resolute. "I'm going to the engine room."

"Captain, you can't, we need..." Asher said, visibly shaking.

"If Silas is injured, I'm the only one on this ship who can patch our engine and get us out of here. We can't fight back without our weapons, and our shields won't last long enough to get to Terra Prime. Too many Qaigs between us and there. Our only chance is to get to run," Soren said. Her mouth was a firm line.

"Let's make a run for the planet," Asher said, pointing to it. It looked like an oasis in the blackness around them.

"There are a hundred Qaig ships between us and there," Soren said. "We have a better chance of getting out of this in one piece if we jump. Benoit! Now, take the chair, that's an order." Soren straightened her jacket, then left the bridge as she spoke. There was no option but obedience.

Bastian paled.

"Nora," he said, his voice level despite his ashen appearance. "Take the controls."

He unbuckled his harness and moved to the captain's chair, from which he could monitor all the consoles and take over control as needed.

Nora took his place at the pilot's console. It felt wrong, sitting there without him. She felt detached from herself. Her hands took the controls, which felt slightly warm, a thought she again registered dimly, as if it were something happening to someone else.

"Bastian, where am I going?" she asked. Her voice sounded faint, even to her own ears. The ship groaned around them, and far away, something heavy thudded, echoing up through the hull. What was going on down there?

"Away from here, any way you can," Bastian said. "Just think of it like your first time in the sim and get us away. If Soren gets the hyperdrive working, then we can jump and get out. Donovan, are comms working?"

"Aye, Captain."

"Get a message to Ganymede. Tell them to get ready. If the Qaigs can reach this Star Port, they can reach the station."

Nora flinched. A piece of wreckage from the J'nai container ship narrowly missed them. She swerved around a persistent Qaig ship, dodging as best she could.

"Keep it up, Clark—just like practice. You just steer, okay? Asher, keep working on the shields. I think I can get the life support stabilized from here..."

"Ccc...cc.. captain?" Donovan stuttered, one shaking hand holding his comms headphones to his ears.

"What?"

"I can hear Ganymede... there's an emergency message going out through the Current. They're...ggg...ggoing to..."

Another blast rocked them from below, throwing them all from their chairs. Nora scrabbled back up. Her hands were gripping the controls so hard, she hadn't let go. Her knuckles were turning white from the strain.

"Shields at 5 percent!" Asher called.

"They're going to blow the Jupiter Star Port! We've got three days to make it back. After that, we'll be trapped!" Donovan shouted.

For a moment, no one on the Bridge spoke.

"Silas! Soren! If we can jump, we need to jump fast!" Bastian called over the ship's comms. A crackle of static returned, then came Soren's voice, small and full of static.

"Silas is dead. Something detached in the initial blast. Got him over the head. I think I can..."

Bam!

Something hit them from behind. The ship's engines slowed, sputtered, and then stalled. They were floating, no longer accelerating forward. Red alerts flashed across her screen, indicating near-catastrophic damage to most of the life support systems. Nora swiped them aside, focusing on the digital dials before her.

"Nora, can you get us out of here?" Bastian shouted. "I'm trying to get life support back online."

"One minute," she whispered, her fingers moving with a surety she did not feel. The muscle memory of her cerebellum was firing full force, thanks to their hours of simulations. Her fingers knew the hyperspace power was out, but the subluminal engine was out, too. The connections must have been fried in the blast. Wait, was the power supply to the subluminal engine still intact? If she could just…

She realized she didn't even *need* the subluminal engine. She rerouted power from it to the hyperspace engine, the one that would propel them back into the Current and to the Star Port. It might fry the fuses on the sublum, but that was a problem for another time. She saw now why the hyperspace drive wasn't working. It just needed a boost, a jump start…

"Nora, what are you doing? Get us moving!" Donovan cried.

"Hang on," she said, calculating the power in her head, multiplying by the increase in torque, dividing by the size of the…

Bang!

If she could just…

"We need to get moving, Cadet," Asher said. "Stop messing around and—"

"We're on!" Soren's voice crowed over the speakers, less than a nanosecond after Nora punched in her calculations. The hyperspace engine flared to life on Nora's screen, glowing the most beautiful shade of green she'd ever seen.

"Hold on!" Nora shouted, punching the hyperspace jump command.

Pop!

CHAPTER 21

And just like that, they were away from Terra Prime and the Qaigs. A flashing sign streamed across the consoles, warning them that the subluminal engine had been overheated and was no longer functioning. All other systems blinked critical—but stable —levels of damage.

For a moment, no one spoke. No one moved. Then they let out a collective, jagged breath. Nora pried her cramping fingers from the controls.

Bastian got up slowly from the captain's chair and made his way down to the console. For a moment, he just looked over what Nora had done, scrolling back through the commands. Then he looked up at her with the strangest expression on his face, a mix between confusion and something else—maybe admiration, she thought. Nora swallowed hard, not sure if she should be afraid of the consequences. After all, she sort of just blew up the subluminal engines.

"You did it," he said, after a long pause. Nora looked away, embarrassed by the look on his face and by the strangeness of his tone. It made her feel warm inside, at her core. Made her tingle. She breathed out, a long sound, and grinned up at him after a second.

"Guess I owe Hypatia for those logic and reasoning skills after all."

"No," he said, and when she looked back, she saw his signature half smile. "That move was all Eleanora Clark."

When he said it like that, drawing her first name out to a full five syllables with his accent, it didn't sound so bad in her ears. She almost liked it then, pronounced with such care.

Soren scrambled onto the Bridge, and Nora's thoughts were jerked back to the present crisis with abrupt force.

"What happened?" Soren asked. Her white hair was loose, her face smeared on one side with blood. It didn't seem to be coming from her, Nora noted. Her stomach clenched at the realization. Soren collapsed into the captain's chair, running the ship's diagnostics from the console with frantic speed.

"I was trying to get the hyperspace engine started. That first blast knocked out the power. Bastian, did you reroute the startup power from the subluminal to the hyperspace through the PPU?" Soren asked, scanning the console.

"No ma'am," Bastian said, his voice calm and cool. "That was Cadet Clark."

Soren looked up, her intense green eyes like twin laser beams.

"Is that so," she said. Nora paled. She wasn't sure why, but she felt like she'd done something terribly, horribly wrong. Well, she had destroyed a very, *very* expensive piece of machinery. She braced herself.

"Yes ma'am," she croaked. The J'nai woman looked at her for a moment.

"Cadet, get down to the head and get yourself cleaned up."

"Ma'am?" Nora asked, confused.

"Looks like you took a tumble," Soren said, pointing. Nora reached up and felt blood trickling down her scalp.

"Oh," she said. Her hand was shaking, fingertips red. So that's what she'd felt trickling down her face. In the heat of the moment, she'd thought it was sweat. Something stung at her hairline, a cut she hadn't noticed until now.

"Benoit, take the console," Soren ordered. Bastian sat, bringing the controls back from the review screen.

"Well done," he said, giving her a smile. This was a genuine smile, a thing of perfect symmetry, not the usual, ironic half smile. "Better get that taken care of, Nora. You know where the supplies are, no?"

Nora nodded.

"Good. come back up when you're done. I may need your help." He returned his attention to the console.

"Soren – Silas, he's really...?" Nora asked, turning back to the captain. Soren pursed her lips, and nodded.

"There'll be time enough to mourn him later, Clark. Right now we have to focus on making sure the rest of us make it back to Ganymede in one piece. Now go."

Nora sighed, the energy of the adrenaline rush starting to fade, and left the Bridge, tentatively reaching up every few seconds to check the cut on her face. Behind her, she could hear Soren trying to figure out what happened.

"Donovan, tell me everything the station's saying. I want to know where that attack came from and why. Was Terra Prime alerted? Did any J'nai ships get away? Is the fleet accounted for? Why..."

Then, suddenly, Nora was in the head. One second she was on the Bridge, and the next, she was staring at herself in the mirror, watching a glob of dark red blood slowly ooze down the side of her face. She reached a trembling hand to push the hair back and saw that the strands were matted with clots of blood. She looked at her hand and saw the amount of it, drops falling from her fingertips into the sink. The color spun against the metal bowl, spiraling as the drops coalesced with water and swirled down the drain. She looked into the mirror, into her own wide, wide eyes—and promptly fainted.

She came to gradually, like she was swimming up through a deep, dark pool of water. Everything was hazy at first, except the pain. Her head throbbed. That came through loud and clear.

"Hey there, cadet," Donovan's voice said through the fog. "Welcome back."

"What...?"

"We heard you take a tumble in the head. Asher went to check and found you down. You'll have quite the goose egg, but lucky you've got a thick skull. Nothing broken."

"Sorry," Nora mumbled, struggling to sit up.

"Oh no, not yet," Donovan said, pushing her back down. "I need to throw a couple of stitches in this."

"Oh no," Nora groaned. Donovan lay his instruments next to her on the fabric of her cot.

"It's okay. Benoit got you back to your room. And by the time I'm done, you'll be good as new," he said, preparing a syringe with a long, long needle.

"Can't you just knock me out?" She couldn't bear the thought of the crew finding her passed out, much less Bastian, whose grudging regard she may have finally earned—*and* he had to drag her back to her room.

"Sorry, we're gonna try to keep you sentient for a while," he said, turning her head. "Just a sting and a burn." The needle flashed in the light. A sharp pain shot through her scalp where he was injecting the numbing medicine.

"Ouch," she said.

"That's the worst of it. Hold still."

He was, at least, efficient. He cleaned the wound thoroughly with warm water and pungent orange soap. In a few more minutes, a neat row of stitches lay in her hairline near the temple.

"Scalp wounds bleed like nothing else," Donovan said, gathering his supplies and bundling the blood-soaked gauze in a bag.

"Hey, thanks," she said, laying a hand on his arm. "I appreciate it."

"Well, thanks to you for saving our asses back there," he said, cracking a smile. "Here, take this. Once the numbing agent wears off, that's going to be sore."

She accepted the pill and swallowed it.

"Can *we* go back…"

"Oh no. You're going to take a nap. Captain's orders. We'll wake you when it's time to relieve Bastian for a while."

"What?"

"Captain decided you can try some solo time on hyperspace. Don't worry, between autopilot and the captain watching, there's no way to mess it up too bad. Besides, Bastian's gonna need a break. He's been up almost twenty-four hours now. Even Iron Man needs a few hours of shut eye every now and then."

"Iron Man?"

"His call sign. Didn't he tell you?"

"No," she said, grinning as Donovan pulled the blanket up around her.

"Well, get some rest. And don't pick at the bandage. I'll take it off tomorrow. Sleep, cadet."

"Yes, sir," she mumbled. She had no intention of falling asleep, though. There was too much to think about: the Qaig attack, the limping engines of the *Rapscallion*, Silas's death, Bastian. But before she knew it, exhaustion wrapped her up, and she drifted off into a deep and dreamless sleep.

Five minutes later—or so it felt—a knock came on her door.

"Mmmph?" she mumbled, sitting up. Her head felt ten times its normal size, and when the door opened, the light from the hall was blinding. She threw a hand over her eyes.

"Hey," Bastian said, leaning on the doorframe, a slim dark silhouette backlit by hazy gold light. "How are you feeling?"

"Like my head's going to explode. You?"

"Captain is back on Bridge. She wants you to take a turn on controls for a while."

"How long have you been up?" Nora asked. He looked beyond tired—haggard, even—his usually tan face drawn and pale.

"A while," he admitted. He ran a hand through his hair, the long strands laying rakishly to one side. Her fingers itched from wanting to brush his hair back from his eyes. *What* was in that pill Donovan had given her? All sorts of strange thoughts were barreling through her neurons.

"Yeah, all right," she said after a moment and stood. For a second, she swayed, her equilibrium off balance. She put a hand out to steady herself on the wall.

"You okay?" Bastian asked. He had one hand on her elbow in an instant, steadying her. The room was so small, he'd barely needed to step inside to reach her. His eyebrows were furrowed, mouth downturned in an expression her too-large head couldn't wrap itself around at the minute.

"Just have to get my sea legs," she said, trying to smile. "It's fine, I'm fine. I got this."

"Sure," he said and backed out so she could exit her little room.

"I heard what you did," she said, pulling her hair into a ponytail to get the loose curls out of her face. "Sorry about that."

"I shouldn't have let you go take care of that cut alone. Sometimes it's easy to forget you're still a cadet, still just a teenager."

"Yeah, well," she said, feeling heat rise to her cheeks. Was it another compliment, or rather a reminder of her place in the crew—as an observer, a student, someone years younger than him. It was hard to tell, and there was no way her fuzzy brain could decipher his intent.

"Can I ask you a favor?" he asked, tugging her from her rambling thoughts.

"Sure," she said. She reached a hand to her bandage. Donovan had wrapped her skull with enough gauze for a turban. She was sure it made her look awesome. She hoped it made her look brave, but more than likely, she just looked ridiculous.

"We had to put Silas...um," he started, looking at his shoes for a moment. When he looked back up, his gray eyes were misty. "We put him in the crew bunk. Not a lot of room to, you know...And Donovan took his hammock in the engine room, so...." His voice trailed off.

"Go to sleep, Iron Man," she said, pushing him back into the room. "I'll come wake you when Soren's had enough of me."

"Thanks. I just need a few hours," he said. He lay down gingerly on her cot—they all were a bit banged up, she realized—and as she shut the door, she swore he was already asleep.

The Bridge was eerily quiet. Nora munched on a protein bar as she slid into Bastian's vacated console. It was just her, Asher, and Captain Soren.

"Autopilot's set, cadet. Just watch it for now," Captain Soren said. She didn't look tired at all—thanks, perhaps, to the steaming mug of coffee clutched in her hand. Her green eyes were alert and steady. She looked every inch a captain, and it steadied Nora's nerves to see it.

"Okay," Nora said.

Easing into the seat was an unnerving and yet oddly satisfying feeling. This was where she belonged, crisis or not. She was surprised at the feeling of pride swelling in her chest. She, Nora Clark, was an important part of this team, this ship. She had as much to contribute as any of them, maybe, even if she was still a cadet. It was a sense of belonging she'd never experienced back on Earth, except with her family. She thought of Soren and Asher and wondered briefly if *they* had family or friends on Terra Prime. Not many of the Deltas talked about their previous life, but surely they had friends on those other ships, just as she had. Her heart clenched as she thought of Greg and Lara and Ty and all the others. Were they okay? She couldn't even bear to *think* about anything bad happening to them.

"Any word from Terra Prime?" Nora asked instead, swiveling to take a look at her captain. Soren's jaw clenched.

"It's always hard to get any comms through when we're on the Current. Donovan thinks the Qaigs jumped on the hyperspace route somewhere nearby and used the Terra Prime station to exit. They must have gotten their fleet awfully close, snuck in right under our noses, and then jumped in through the port."

"Any idea how…I mean, did Terra Prime…"

"We don't know," Soren said, her lips in a hard line. "But I do know we would have been killed if not for your quick thinking. We have a saying back home that two kinds of things happen when carbon—such as yourself and us—is exposed to enormous pressure." She lapsed momentarily into native J'nai, conversing with Asher to make sure she got the translation right.

"Two things can happen," she continued after a moment. "Things get crushed, and diamonds get formed. You, little cadet, are our diamond, found in the rough, if I am getting my Earth phrases correct. If not for you, we would have all been killed. And I will never forget it."

Nora couldn't think of what to say. Her cheeks burned.

"Now, let's see how you handle the hyperspace route," Soren said, settling back into her chair. Nora turned and looked at her console.

Everything seemed to be running appropriately, the computer making minute adjustments as they coasted through the inky blackness of space.

They sat in almost-silence for hours. Asher and Soren chatted a bit in native J'nai. They seemed agitated. Nora kept her focus on the console, making minor course corrections when the autopilot suggested it. Asher and Soren periodically left the Bridge to make minor repairs to the life support systems and patch a few leaking pipes. Nothing critical was destroyed, but without prompt repairs, the ship would be torn apart on reentry near Jupiter.

After six or so hours, a rumpled Bastian came up to relieve Nora and Soren. The captain needed a break, and Nora was relieved to pass the controls back.

"Donovan wants to see you," he mumbled and took a long sip from a thermos of coffee in hand. Nora nodded, the movement making her gauze turban wobble, and went to find him.

Down below, Donovan removed the bandages from her head and took a look at his handiwork. The cut stung, but not as much as it had yesterday. Yesterday? Or was it longer ago than that? She realized abruptly she had no idea what time it was, or what day.

"Looks good," Donovan said. "You can shower if you want. Just don't scrub it, and when you're done, use this," he said, handing her a small tube of ointment. "Those stitches will need to come out next week. Just get yourself down to Medical, and they can do it."

"Okay," she said. After the trauma of yesterday, a shower sounded blissful.

Minutes later, she'd cranked the water to scalding; she was prepared to use *all* the hot water in the galaxy. She stepped in and could have cried, it felt so good. Globs of antibacterial ointment—and a few crusty bits of dried blood that she tried not to look at—fell from her hair as she washed. She took her time, and when she got out, the mirror was thoroughly fogged. *Perfect.* She didn't dare wipe it away. She knew she looked like hell; she felt like it, too. She pulled her hair into a loose bun, careful not to tug at the neat row of stitches in her hairline. Some of the curls escaped immediately, but that couldn't be helped. Tiny droplets ran down them and dripped onto her neck, and she rubbed at them as she finished dressing.

She grabbed another protein bar from the kitchen before heading down to the engine room, where Soren was going over the damaged parts with an exacting eye.

"Is there anything I can do to help, Captain?" Nora asked, chewing her snack from her perch on the grated steps that led into the engine room. The massive subluminal and hyperspace engines took up most of the room, dwarfing the slender J'nai with their steely gray bulk.

"Come on down, Cadet. If you're going to pilot one of these someday, you might as well see what makes them tick," she said, not turning around. She had her hands deep in the winding pipes of the subluminal engine, and her words were distorted by the small flashlight clenched between her teeth. Soren showed her how half the subluminal engine, the one that operated when the ship wasn't in the hyperspace Current, had been destroyed by a shot from a Qaig ship. The external combustion chamber was completely melted. She was trying to bypass the melted bit and see if she could reroute power to the other half of the engine. Once through the Star Port back home, they should be able to limp the rest of the way.

As it turned out, after hours of work that left them both covered in grease and sweat—which burned Nora's wound like acid—Soren concluded that the damage was irreparable. Once they exited the Star Port, they'd be floating, helpless. They'd have to hope there was another ship nearby that could essentially tow them home.

"Sorry," Nora mumbled. "If I hadn't switched the power supply over, the fuses wouldn't have shorted and the sublums would still be working..."

"And we'd be dead, Cadet," Soren reminded her. "They're just fuses."

"There was probably another way to do it. I just couldn't think of a way to save the sublum," Nora said. Soren shook her head.

"No more apologies, Clark. When we get back, I'll make you help install the new one. Will that ease your martyred pride?"

Nora flushed, but Soren was smiling, almost maternal. The J'nai put a hand on Nora's shoulder and led the way back to the Bridge.

Bastian was alone up there, watching the pilot's console like a hawk.

"Sublum's totaled," Soren said, sitting heavily in her chair. "We're going to have to call for a tow when we get home."

"That's fine. When we get back to Ganymede, I'll get it all overhauled."

"You think Ganymede will still be there?" Nora asked, her voice small. The Bridge quieted.

"Donovan heard bits of transmission from there a few hours ago," Bastian said, frowning. "Doesn't look like the Qaig are trying to hop through just yet. Besides, they'd have to be positioned somewhere between Terra Prime and Ganymede to even get to that Star Port—not a lot of ways for them to get there, most of the areas are patrolled by J'nai. We should have heard if they were in the vicinity."

"They couldn't have pulled this off without years of planning," Soren said, cupping her chin as she thought. "We'd hoped they were done antagonizing us, that our little pocket—our home world," her voice cracked on the word, "was small enough, and well protected enough, not to be a target. Not after so long…"

She shook her head and tried to steel herself. She took a long breath and stood with a groan.

"Right," she said, crisply. "I'm going to sleep. You two, call me on the comms if you need me."

"You can go, too. Get some rest," Bastian said to Nora.

"The captain asked *both* of us to keep watch. I'm not going anywhere," Nora said, pulling up her customary seat beside him.

"Okay then," he said with his half-smile. "What were you doing down in the engine room?"

"Soren was showing me how to trouble-shoot the sublum. Didn't make much difference though. Obviously. Why?"

"You have got a little grease… everywhere," he said, smirking as he pointed to her face. Nora felt her cheeks burning, and rubbed at her face with her sleeve. Sure enough, oily black marks were smeared across the fabric. Awesome.

"Is that better?" she asked. Her hands too, she realized, had bits of grime streaked across them.

"Not really," he said, and made a short sound which might have been a laugh. "Good enough, anyway. Now let me show you how to run diagnostics from here."

He showed her the finer points of checking the diagnostics on not just the engines but the other ship systems as well - Nora followed as best as she could, surreptitiously swiping at her cheeks with the cuff of her sleeve when he wasn't looking to see if any more gunk came off (which it did).

And then something happened that she did not expect - he plugged a small USB drive into the console, and flooded the room with the drifting melodies of Coltrane. The soft saxophones and trumpets fluttered through the Bridge, making it feel cozier, less stark, less industrial. She felt her heart rate slow substantially, eased by the sounds.

"It helps me focus," he explained. "There's no real melody to get stuck in your head. Like white noise, only better."

"It's nice," Nora agreed. She closed her eyes for a moment and savored it. "My mom always had music playing at home. She was a really good pianist. Chopin especially, for hours and hours…"

"Your handler?"

"No," Nora said, smiling a little. She treasured those memories. "I meant my mom. I know you think they were just my handlers—but they weren't. I don't expect you would understand it."

"I understand," he said, shrugging a little. "I guess it's no different from being adopted."

"Yeah," she agreed. "You know I used to play duets with her. She'd rather listen to me play, but I thought the duets were more fun."

"I bet you were good," he said. Nora looked up; it was a statement of fact, spoken in the same manner he would have commented on the location of the next star on their route.

"I was," she said, in the same manner. "I guess it doesn't matter much anymore, though. My dad actually sold the piano so I would focus more on my studies. Looking back, it makes sense. He wanted me to be more like Hypatia."

"It matters," he said. "You have a long way to go to be a pilot, but you have innate coordination, the hand-eye skill. I imagine a good pianist needs similar techniques—it's a different skillset than what you need to be a scientist in a lab."

"I imagine you're right," Nora said, considering.

"That's probably why you pick up on the patterns of flying so easily. Your brain is already wired to your fingers. Your muscles have memory that your brain can't understand. It's not something that can be taught."

"Sebastian Benoit, was that a compliment?"

"A fact," he said, but the corner of his mouth lifted a little as he said it.

They ran like this, sleeping a few hours in shifts, all the way back to Ganymede. Nora and Bastian alternated time at the helm so she could get some solo experience. These sessions were carefully timed to make sure Soren was available for supervision. Each time Nora collapsed onto her cot, which he always made up neatly, she had to try very hard not to focus on the faint smell of his soap on her pillow, or on the residual warmth in the sheets.

CHAPTER 22

By the time they jumped out through the Star Port, their exhaustion showed itself in every movement. Every word was taxing.

And as Soren had predicted, the subluminal engines failed to engage, and they floated, helpless, after leaving the Current.

However, there were plenty of options for a tow. The rest of the fleet was stationed at the port with weapons trained at the ring's opening. Luckily, the *Rap* wasn't blown to bits.

One of the PJ's attached a cable to their stern, and towed them all the way back. Though they'd been one of the first ships through the port, they were probably the last to make it back to the station. The process took hours. And being dragged didn't make things any easier when they got back to the landing dome. They'd dropped off their container on approach, letting it bounce along the craggy Ganymede surface, so Bastian could use what few controls were still functioning to try to cushion their landing. Even with his expertise, it was still rough. The *Rapscallion*'s wings clipped another container on the way in, knocking it over and swinging the PJ around. Nora was nearly bounced from her chair.

When they finally ground to a halt, the crew let out a collective sigh. They unfastened their harnesses and trudged down to the cargo bay.

"Hey Nora," Bastian said in a low voice as the ramp doors lowered. "You make sure to send me a line when you graduate, okay? I'll fly with you any day."

"Aye aye, Commander," she said. She tried to smile, but her face was as stiff as dried mud. She was exhausted all the way down to her toenails. Her feet felt as heavy as bricks as they walked out. As they disembarked, they were swarmed by a flurry of human and J'nai deck workers, officers, and cadets.

"You're the last ship back, you know," a man said, shaking Soren's hand. "Glad to see you're safe."

"Not all of us, Commander," Soren said, shaking her head. "We lost our engineer."

"NORA!" a voice screamed. Sophie tore through the pack and grabbed her in a bear hug.

"God, don't scare me like that," she said. Nora hugged her back, surprised by the tears prickling her eyes.

"Sorry," she mumbled into Sophie's hair. Something inside of her felt like it was cracking, and not just because Sophie was squeezing her so tightly.

"Are you okay? What's this? Ohmygod, what happened?" Sophie said, pushing aside her hair to look at the stitches. Nora brushed her hand away.

"It's nothing. I'm fine. Is everyone else...?"

"Oh, Nor," Sophie said. She clasped a hand to her mouth, tears running down her cheeks. She tried to get the words out, and couldn't. That scared Nora more than anything – never had Sophie been speechless in the time she'd known her. She swallowed, put a hand on Nora's arm, and said -

"Lara—she didn't make it back."

"Oh," Nora said. It was all she could muster. She stumbled the last few steps down the ramp, holding Sophie around the waist. Lara. Loud, brilliant Lara. It didn't feel real. Her ears strained to pick up that Australian accent, that crazy laugh from the hundreds of people around her. Surely it wasn't true. It couldn't be true. Sophie just hadn't been able to find her in this crowd, this mob of people and noise and engines.

"Nora, there's more..." Sophie said, but her words were cut off. Out of the crowd—and parting it a bit with his size—came Ty. The big man's eyes were puffy and red. Nora felt her stomach fall.

"Glad you're okay, Ty," Nora mumbled, hugging him.

"My ship did fine. We got here a few hours before you, and Greg too," he said, and Nora let out a breath she hadn't realized she was holding. Greg was safe. Thank all the stars – but where was he? Why wasn't he with Ty? And Ty, he was looking at her so strangely - "But…we kept waiting on more ships to come back. We kept waiting…"

"What happened, Ty?"

"It's Benny," he said, his voice cracking. Nora covered her mouth to keep from crying out.

"And Wingman," he continued. He put a hand on her shoulder.

She sunk to the floor, not noticing that people were streaming past her. Sophie crouched beside her. She was dimly aware of Sophie rubbing her back, mumbling something. Lara. Benny. Wingman. It was unreal.

"Nora?" She heard Bastian behind her. "On your feet, Cadet," he said. But his voice was not unkind.

He took her hand and helped her up.

"We lost a lot of good people out there, Nora," he said. "But we need people like you, now more than ever, to keep your head cool and help us figure this out. Okay?" He had one hand on her shoulder, the other lightly under her chin, forcing her to meet his gaze. His eyes were sparkling bright under the harsh dome lights, glittering with the tears he would not let fall.

"Okay," she whispered. Emotions flooded through her, relief for those who were safe, grief for those who has lost their lives, fatigue and fear, all at once. She hugged him fiercely, then, an overwhelming need for contact washing through her, and she pressed her face against the thick canvas of his flight suit. She could hear his heart beat a slow and steady tempo through the fabric, and she spoke into his chest, not wanting to raise her face. "I know you lost people, too. I'm sorry."

He returned the embrace after a moment, then pushed her away.

"Let's get back to work, Cadet," he said. He picked up his pack and was carried along in the stream of people rushing past, disappearing into the crowd as she watched.

"Ooookay, what was that all about?" Sophie asked. Nora shook her head, looking for him. As she did, she caught Greg's eye from across the dome. He stood still as a stone as people milled around him, a shocked look on his face. After a minute, he turned and walked away. Nora's heart sank. Had he seen her and Bastian? It was just a hug; it didn't mean anything.

"Hello? Nora?" Sophie said, waving a hand in front of her face. Nora blinked a few times, her eyes stinging, and sighed.

"Another time. We were the last ship back? Are they going to blow the port?"

"We don't have to," Sophie said, her face blanching. "The Qaigs blew up the one at Terra Prime. They're not coming here. And we can't go there to help the J'nai, either. They're trapped."

"Oh, man," Nora said. "That's bad."

"Yeah. Epically bad."

◢◢ ◢◢ ◢◢

Sophie linked her arm around Nora's waist, and they leaned on each other as they walked away from the dome. Nora didn't really think about where they were going, but somehow she and Sophie ended up back at Room 10013. They stood outside the door, silently contemplating opening it until Raina and Zoe walked up. After they hugged Nora tightly – seriously, Nora thought she heard a rib crack – and said how glad they were she was okay, the conversation died back down and they continued to just stare at the door. Raina's eyes were red and puffy from crying; Zoe was stoic, a human statue.

"Have to go in eventually, ladies," Raina said at last.

"Has anyone seen Cat?" Nora asked, as Zoe pushed the door open.

No one had to answer the question. Cat was squished back in her bunk, curled up with her knees to her chest. She was balled so tightly it seemed she was trying to make herself disappear.

"Cat?" Nora asked, going to her. "How…"

She couldn't finish her sentence. Cat was—for lack of a better word—catatonic. She rocked back and forth, back and forth, without saying a word. Her eyes were focused on some spot at the far end of her bunk. She stared unblinkingly as if her life depended on it. Her hair was coming out of its usual ponytail, creating a frizzy cloud around her drawn face.

Nora grabbed Cat's blanket and threw it over her, wrapping her like a child.

Sophie climbed a few rungs up the ladder to Lara's bunk and drew the curtain; the clanging of the curtain rings sounded like a coffin lid shutting. No one said anything for a long time. Raina and Zoe sat on Raina's bunk, not talking. Sophie—the ever-chatty Sophie—silently paced the room with her arms crossed. It was giving Nora a headache. It was all just too much. The flight. The battle. Finding out her friends were gone—even rude, stuffy Benny.

It hit her like a tidal wave. She got up from Cat's bunk and went to the bathroom. She had barely locked the door when the first wave of nausea hit, sending her to her knees. She clutched her stomach desperately. She knew this feeling. Tears streamed down her face, plopping unceremoniously like tiny glittering stars onto the cold tile of the floor. It felt the same when she learned her parents had died. The recognition of that loss—that a part of her would never be the same, that a piece of her soul had been ripped out and torn asunder—made the breath catch in her throat.

"Nora?" Sophie called, knocking on the door.

"I'm okay," Nora said. The strength in her voice surprised her. "I just need a shower after a week on that rust bucket."

She turned on the water in the little shower stall, and soon, steam filled the room in a warm, comforting haze. She peeled the sweaty uniform from her body and stepped in, letting the water hit her face and wash away the tears.

Her mind reeled.

Lara. Benny. Wingman. Lara. Benny. Wingman. The names echoed in her head like some horrible record.

Lara. Benny. Wingman.

She stayed under the water a long time, until her skin was red and burning and her mind was numb.

CHAPTER 23

The next morning, a high-priority message was sent to their tablets: the station was being called to a general assembly meeting in the amphitheater. Nora trickled in with her fellow cadets and noted that the station's officers were there, too. She caught sight of Bastian in the front row, the fluorescent lights glinting off his hair while he conversed quietly with Soren. Beside him, Asher and Donovan were in a heated debate. Nora watched as she filed into a row with her roommates. What could they be arguing about?

"Hey, little Hypatia," Thalia taunted from a few rows up. "Did you *actually* faint when you got a paper cut on your little trip? It's all over the station. So much for your promising career in aviation. I don't think they'll let sissies stay on board."

"Yeah, she did faint," Sophie called back, crossing her arms. "Right after she saved the entire crew of the *Rapscallion,* including your *ex-*boyfriend. So maybe you should be a little nicer to her. She's a hero."

"Hey, if she'd rather drive a bus than actually put that brain of hers to good use in the lab, that's on her. It's a real waste, if you ask me," Thalia said, inspecting her fingernails.

"We didn't!" Sophie said.

Thalia shrugged and walked off.

"*Bitch,*" Sophie muttered.

"God, I'm glad you're on my side," Nora said, sitting heavily. Her mind was still spinning.

Lara. Benny. Wingman.

"She's just jealous of you," Sophie spat. "For so many things." Sophie began to tick them off on her fingers. "Stealing the spotlight when you proved you were a flying ace, saving that ship, getting Bastian to fall for you…"

"Whoa, whoa," Nora hissed. "I'll have you know Greg kissed me before we left."

"It's about time!" Zoe called from a few seats over. Sophie shushed her.

"I mean, I agree with Zoe here, but did you *see* the way Bastian looked at you? God, I was getting goose bumps just watching you two."

"It's nothing," Nora grumbled. She caught sight of Greg sitting at the far side of the amphitheater with Ty. She needed to talk to him, to tell him that it wasn't what he thought.

Was it?

The theater was soon nearly full, the empty seats a blistering reminder of those they'd lost. Lara. Benny. Wingman. Nora swallowed a lump in her throat, but it stuck there, like a thick glob of peanut butter.

Jane sat by herself, her hair down in a short veil around her face. She was staring straight ahead, clearly in a daze. The seat beside her was conspicuously empty.

"What I wouldn't do for a coffee," Zoe moaned. She and Raina sat close, leaning on each other for comfort. Cat rocked back and forth in her chair, just as she'd rocked herself all night. She'd barely said a word since the news broke. She'd lost Lara, the closest friend she'd had, as well as Mike. She and the blue J'nai boy had quickly formed a bond. It seemed like if anyone had a chance to pull Cat out of her shell, it was him. But now he was gone, too. Nora was more worried about Cat than anyone else. It looked like a light breeze could shatter her entirely and carry off her pieces like dandelion fluff. The audience was wracked with people in similar states, either looking for comfort or else isolated and unsure how to respond. The shockwave of the situation was palpable.

Admiral Savaryn took the platform, silencing the quiet murmurs rolling through the auditorium.

"Good morning," he said. He had his hands clasped behind his back and prowled the stage as he'd done on the first day of class. This time, however, his short hair was unkempt, the top button of his jacket undone. It was nearly the full eclipse of Jupiter; just a sliver of the planet was visible through the highest window overhead. The sky was otherwise shrouded in black.

"To put to rest any rumors that may be circulating. Yes, the Qaig have attacked Terra Prime."

There was a brief burst of shouting from the audience. The admiral waited for it to subside, then continued.

"We managed to get a few communications through the Current before their Star Port was destroyed. The Qaig overtook a J'nai patrol ship near the *Cicero* system and used the coordinates for the ports and Current from that ship's mainframe to find an access point to our bit of Current. We estimate five dozen Qaig ships got in, based on the firsthand accounts." Here he nodded toward the PJ captains, including Soren, who were sitting bolt upright in the first row. "And through the transmissions from Terra Prime, we know these ships have advanced weaponry and superior maneuverability. It was an ambush."

He stopped for a moment, letting his mercury eyes wander across the room.

"The Star Port was destroyed," he continued. "We don't know the status of Terra Prime, the ten thousand souls living there, or the remainder of the J'nai fleet."

Out of the fifty J'nai cadets and the handful of graduates, less than two-thirds were present now. Nora looked around and saw that they all wore the same stony expression: straightforward look, blank eyes. Were they all that was left of the J'nai race now? She wondered if J'nai anatomy would even let them cry. There were plenty of sobs from the humans in the audience.

"What we do know is this." The admiral's voice rang out, a strong and resolute gong through the room. "We know the Qaig have come out of hiding after decades of quiet. We know they have attacked the last stronghold of the J'nai people. But we also know we have the best minds in the history of both our races in this room. And we know we have the courage and the fortitude to do what must be done. We also know…" He paused, fixing his steely gaze on those seated before him. "That we will not rest until we have rescued our friends.

"Cadets. Graduates. Officers of the Ganymede Station. Your resolve will be tested in the months ahead. Your spirit will be stretched until you think you cannot take another moment, but we will overcome. I have no doubt of that.

"Classes will be on hold until further notice. Each of you will be assigned a task in accordance with your abilities. You are all a piece of the puzzle in the effort to regain Terra Prime. I know you will each give your task 110 percent of your focus and energy. You will receive the necessary information as the tasks are divided. Dismissed."

The crowd exploded. What were these tasks and to what end? Why the compartmentalization? Some people immediately took out their tablets, already scanning for their assignments.

"What do you suppose that means?" Raina asked. Her eyes were dark with unshed tears.

"War," Zoe said, hugging her around the shoulders. "It means Ganymede Station is going to war."

Nora and her roommates trudged back to their room. On the way, they ran into Jane. Nora instinctively reached out to her, but she was unsure if J'nai grieved the way humans did. Jane looked miserable, her face drawn, her hair a mess, but she was not crying.

"Jane, I'm so sorry about Mike," Nora said. "Are you okay?"

Jane shook her head and walked off without a word.

"J'nai spend two days—well, like forty-seven hours really, it's two days on their home world—anyway, they don't speak during that time when someone dies," Cat explained softly. "It's a respect thing, like lowering the flag or wearing black."

"So you're saying I just offended an already grieving J'nai girl who is desperately missing her brother," Nora said. It was like pouring salt on an open wound. Well done, Earth girl.

"Pretty much, yeah," Zoe said, clapping her on the shoulder. "Come on. Let's get back to the room."

Sophie had drawn the curtain across Lara's bunk in a gesture of respect, but the gray curtain just reminded them of a shroud. It made the air in the room feel heavier. There was no banter that night, no teasing or complaining about homework. The gravity of their situation had come crashing down on them hard and fast.

The station had also implemented a curfew. All cadets had to be in their rooms by 9:00 p.m. and were not allowed out until 6:00 a.m. This was to make sure, the memo said, that each person had sufficient time off from his or her tasks to rest and recharge.

"Feels more like a prison," Zoe said, frowning as she read the bulletin. Cat sat on a window ledge in the corner, staring up at the sky. Jupiter had eclipsed the sun now. It was the full dark time, when the sky above was simply black and full of stars, faintly burning spots of light – but there would be no shenanigans, not on this night.

"Cat?" Nora asked, coming to sit by her. She put her hand on the girl's shoulder. Cat didn't move. "You okay?"

"No," Cat said simply, staring up at the stars. "Lara's gone. She wasn't…she wasn't even supposed to go on the trip. She begged them to let her, said that as a future officer she needed the experience…" Her voice trailed off into silence. Nora could feel her vibrating like a raw nerve.

"I hate to say it – but Savaryn's right."

The phrase came from Sophie's lips, but was so unlike anything she had ever said that no one at first knew how to respond.

"Um, Soph? Really?" Zoe asked at last.

"We do what they want," Sophie said. There was fire in her eyes, steel in her spine. Her eyes were flashing.

"Where did this sudden burst of patriotism to Ganymede come from?" Zoe said, folding her arms.

"When those Qaig bastards decided Lara had to die," she said, sitting at the table and pulling out her tablet, along with and a pen and notepad. "I don't care who started this whole stupid war anymore. The Qaigs killed our friends. It's time to get down to work. If playing by the admiral's rules for once means justice for Lara, then that's what we're going to do."

"Faxes forever," Raina said. She joined Sophie at the table. Soon, they all did.

"Guys?" Cat said, her voice shaking. Her tablet had just beeped. "I got my task. It looks like something to do with the propulsion systems."

Seconds later, everyone else's tablets began to chime with their assignments. Zoe and Raina would be with the mechanics, getting the fleet ready. Cat's work would take her into the lab, and Sophie would be in the communications room helping scan all known frequencies for stranded J'nai.

"I didn't get a memo," Nora said, looking down at her tablet. The chatter quieted.

"Are you sure?" Sophie said, taking the tablet. She shook it and checked again: no memo, no chime.

"I'm sure," Nora said. Seconds ticked by.

No memo, no chime.

"You're the hero of the *Rapscallion*. They're probably just still trying to figure out where best to put you," Sophie said encouragingly. She was already drawing a schematic, glancing at her memo from time to time.

More time passed. Nora's hands grew damp, and she chewed on her bottom lip – maybe Soren just expected her to help back on the *Rap*? Getting that new subluminal engine installed like she'd said?

Someone knocked on their door—two sharp raps. The girls exchanged glances.

They knocked again, harder. Nora got up and went to the door. She looked back over her shoulder to see her roommates watching her. Sophie gave her a thumbs up.

It was Bastian.

CHAPTER 24

He was wearing his formal uniform, not his flight suit, for the first time since Nora had known him. She took it as a bad sign—even if he did look very, very good. Something about the structured navy suit complemented his blue eyes and offset his dark bronzed hair, which remained rakishly askew. She'd never really appreciated just how handsome the formal uniform of the Ganymede Station was, with its bright brass buttons, its stark white braid, the way the *Benoit* nametag sat just-so. She swallowed hard.

"Uh," Nora said, trying very hard to focus on the nametag.

"Captain needs us. We are to report to the Bridge," he said. Her eyes snapped up to his.

"Uh," Nora said again, cocking her head, not sure she'd heard him properly.

"What's the problem, Cadet?" he said. Her brain seemed to have stopped working entirely. The Captain. Soren. She wanted to see her? On the bridge? The last time Nora had gone there, it hadn't been a pleasant experience. If Bastian could see the gears turning in her head, he made no outward sign of it. He turned and left, calling for her to hurry up.

"Don't forget your jacket, Nora," Sophie said sweetly, handing it to her with a wink. Nora shrugged it on and raced after Bastian, who was already halfway down the hall.

"How did you know where my room was?" Nora asked when she caught up to him. Her hands went to her hair, frantically trying to get her curls into some sort of decent bun before meeting with Captain Soren. He looked at her sideways but apparently didn't deem her question worth the energy of a response.

They joined the flow of men and women, human and J'nai, all in their impeccable dress uniforms, trickling into the Bridge in a murmur of voices. The room was packed, but Nora and Bastian soon found Soren, her yellow skin gleaming under the florescence. She was standing with her arms crossed, looking angry—almost like a golden monument, or a thoroughly pissed-off statue.

"What's this all about?" Nora asked. Soren motioned for her to be quiet as the admiral stepped into the center of the room, commanding the attention of all present. The murmuring voices hushed, awaiting his words. Nora's heart was pounding so hard, she felt sure everyone in the room could hear it.

"Thank you all for coming," he said. Nora exchanged a nervous glance with Bastian, but she caught another familiar face in her peripheral vision. Across the room, Thalia stood with another crew, looking like a model on a photo shoot in her perfectly neat uniform. Nora rolled her shoulders to straighten her jacket and fiddled with the buttons she'd forgotten to close. Thalia caught Nora staring before they both turned their attention to Admiral Savaryn.

"McGregor and I have found a way to get back to Terra Prime," he said. A ripple of whispers ran through the room, like a rock had been thrown in a still pond.

"But sir, the Star Port is down," a pale yellow J'nai said from the opposite side of the room. "There's no way for us to exit the hyperspace Current. It's suicide, even if we had the forces to make any sort of impact."

Rather than being annoyed by the interjection, the admiral simply nodded.

"Not if you bring the Star Port with you. Arthur?"

McGregor stepped up. He was an imposing man like Savaryn but had a dignity and grace of bearing that his superior did not. This was a man born to leadership. It was in his very DNA. And he'd stood up for Nora on more than one occasion. She couldn't help but admire the man.

208

"We've had the graduates, led by Thalia Jones, working on a portable Star Port for the past two years. It attaches to the wings of the PJs and can essentially open a hole in the hyperspace Current at any point along the track. We don't need to rebuild every single Star Port in the galaxy to get the J'nai back to their alienated colonies. We just need a way to get off the Current."

"Why didn't we know about this?" someone called out. This was met by shouts of agreement. McGregor shifted.

"Because it hasn't been tested yet."

"So…still suicide," the same man said. McGregor frowned.

"I'm not asking you to put yourselves at risk for a prototype. As it is, we only have one model now. Captain Soren has volunteered her team for the mission. Captain?" Savaryn said, gesturing for her to join him in the center of the room. Soren stepped down, head held high, back straight. Nora was simultaneously proud of being a part of her crew, but something deep inside of her was always twisting, as her mind tried to wrap around exactly what it was that Savaryn was telling them.

"Our mission is simple," Soren said. Her voice rang out clearly, and the rising din of the room quieted. "Ms. Jones and her team will join us on the *Rapscallion*. We will enter the hyperspace Current, and when we are in the vicinity of Terra Prime, we will use the device. We will spend as much time as possible gathering intel on the situation there before jumping back on the Current and returning to Ganymede."

"And if the device doesn't work?" Donovan called. His arms were crossed over his chest, his lips tight. Clearly, Soren hadn't run this by him before "volunteering" her crew for the mission. Nora was still wondering why Soren had wanted her here – would she need her help with the repairs before they left?

"Then we turn around and exit back at the Jupiter port."

"And when will this…device be ready?" Donovan said.

"About a week," Savaryn said. "I'm not saying it's without its risks. But if we pull this off, we'll have a weapon that the Qaig can't match. We can round up J'nai from all over the galaxy, and we can put an end to those slippery bastards once and for all."

A murmur of agreement ran through the room.

"All right, now get your crews moving. I don't have to remind you all that this is extremely classified. If I find out one of you leaked this, you'll be moonwalking without an EVA suit. Do I make myself clear?"

Nora swallowed hard. She looked up at Bastian, who returned her gaze. His eyes were steely, but he was silent. A second later, Soren joined them, along with Asher and Donovan.

"Look, I'm sorry I couldn't tell you sooner. It was…"

"Classified. We get it," Asher reassured her. "You're the captain, Captain. We go where you go."

This seemed to satisfy the J'nai. She put a hand on Asher's arm, grateful of his support. Donovan, still tight-lipped, said nothing, but finally nodded his assent. A thrill of excitement and also of coldness seemed to ripple through the crew of the *Rapscallion*.

"Anton?" Soren said, motioning for the admiral to join them as the man was about to leave the room. "I want Clark to come with us."

Nora froze.

"Absolutely not," he said without even looking at her. He spoke to Soren alone.

"She saved our lives on that last run. Hey flying is …. Unconventional, you might say, but I've never seen such potential in a human before, not even in Sebastian. If I'm going back, she's coming, too. She's one of the only pilots I've seen who can outfly them. You need me, you need my ship, and you need Benoit. Those are my terms. She comes, or we don't go."

Bastian crossed his arms behind Soren, but didn't disagree with her.

"You don't have room for another pilot. What you need is an engineer to replace Dahl."

"I can be the engineer," Soren said, unflinching. Savaryn sighed.

"You can't be both engineer and captain," he said in a clipped tone. "You can't be in two places at once."

The Bridge was still buzzing like a swarm of bees from Savaryn's announcement. He seemed to be having trouble keeping his voice to a harsh whisper. Bastian stood close behind Nora, and she was grateful for his presence – the catfight unfolding in front of her was making her acutely uncomfortable. She didn't like being near the center of this argument.

"So make Benoit the captain," Soren said.

The buzzing stopped. Time stopped. Everything stopped. Nora looked up at Bastian. His eyes were on Soren, his mouth a straight line, his dark brows furrowed down over his steely blue-gray eyes.

"You want me to remove our best pilot from the cockpit and replace him with a cadet? Have you gone mad?"

"You and I both know he deserves it," Soren said. "And he's wanted it for some time. Give him a chance for this run."

"And the cadet? You want *her* to fly this mission?" The incredulity in his tone brought heat to Nora's cheeks – but a small part of her agreed with him.

Soren shrugged.

"Clark will have Benoit and me backing her up. He can handle the trickier bits and let her handle the easy stuff...Sir." She added the formality as an afterthought. The room held its collective breath. Everyone was watching the exchange.

"Fine. But she has to choose if she wants to go. I won't be forcing a cadet into a mission like this without consent," he said, then walked off. People parted ways for him as he came through.

Soren turned to her. The J'nai woman was intimidating, but she was also one of the only people on the station who believed in her. Soren's support warmed her soul, even if the idea of a week on a tin can with Thalia—no, Thalia *and* Bastian, together—made her want to vomit. Not to mention the pressure of flying a PJ into God-knew-what at Terra Prime, not to mention they'd *also* be using a top secret piece of equipment that had never been tested. Piece of cake.

"Well, Cadet?" Soren asked.

Nora looked to her, into her green eyes as intense and bright as lasers, then to Bastian. She thought of the potential dangers – there were too many for her to count. Then she thought about Lara, and her crazy accent and her loud laugh. And she thought of Mike and Benny and Wingman and the countless others they'd lost at the attack on Terra Prime. She thought about what Soren said – that she *needed* her, wanted her with them, for this most dangerous mission. Soren trusted her to handle this.

"I'm in."

Donovan clapped her hard on the shoulder.

"Well, I feel better already," he said, though it was hard to tell if he was being completely sarcastic. Bastian pushed past her to talk to Soren.

"Captain, I…" Bastian began.

"You're captain now, Benoit," she interrupted. She put out her hand for him to shake, and he took it. "Congratulations."

"Thank you," he said. "I'm honored that you think I'm ready."

"Honor has nothing to do with it. It's a pain in the ass job, and I'm sick of it," Soren said with a smile. "Besides, the J'nai will have the big battle cruisers up and running within a year or two, and I plan on captaining one. We'll need as many experienced captains and pilots as we can get. Now I get to train both of you on the same run. Even if you will technically be my superior. But don't think for a second that I'll hesitate to let you know if you do something stupid."

"I'm counting on it," he said, flashing a grin. Soren nodded, then was pulled aside by Asher, who was chattering away in J'nai so fast Nora could barely see his lips moving. She turned instead to her mentor.

"Congratulations, Bastian," Nora said. She beamed up at him; no one deserved it more. If they pulled this off, it would be one for the history books, and Sebastian Benoit would have his name all over the tale. He had put his trust in her not to let him down, and now she put her trust in him. She had no doubt in her mind. Her heart swelled with pride.

"Thank you, Eleanora," he said. He opened his mouth to say something else, but -

"Well that's enough work for one day. How about we go celebrate, Captain?" a cool voice said.

Thalia had appeared out of nowhere and slipped her arm around Bastian's waist. He extricated himself gracefully.

"I have some things to do tonight. Lot of work. Some other time, yes?" he said. Thalia pouted but didn't argue. Bastian shot Nora a glance, then turned his back on them, moving toward Soren and the other captains, who were heatedly discussing this new hyperspace engine.

Thalia glared at Nora before heading from the bridge. Nora sighed. She wanted to join Bastian and Soren, but it seemed they were in a discussion way above her pay grade. She turned and left, too. As she made her into the white corridor, her head suddenly ached. She shook it, but that only agitated the stiches in her hairline. She put a hand to it, but it did nothing to stop the spinning in her brain – a portable star port. A top-secret mission. Her thoughts turned like clothes tumbling in a washing machine. How she was going to keep all of this from Sophie and her roommates, she had no idea. With a sigh and a final massage to her scalp, she left the Bridge and headed towards the hangar bay.

CHAPTER 25

She wanted to get a look at the *Rapscallion* before curfew to see how the repairs were coming. With only a week—and a blown sublum engine—it would take some serious grunt work to get it going again. It may need to be entirely replaced. Nora had no idea what something like that cost, but she was willing to bet there would be a lot of zeroes in it. She still felt vaguely guilty.

She was just about to turn the corridor to the landing dome when she heard, "Eleanora, wait up." It was Bastian. He seemed in a hurry, like he had something to say that was going to burst out of him.

"Hey, Captain," she said, smiling as he caught up to her. "You know, my friends call me Nora," she said.

This took him aback for a moment, halted his momentum. Then he smiled, that perfect expression with no hint of mockery in it. He had recognized his own earlier comment in her words.

"Nora," he repeated, and seemed more at ease than he had been.

"Looks like the station's lab rats have some work to do if we're going to be ready for the Qaigs," she said, nodding towards the *Rap*.

He frowned a little, gazing over the landing dome. Everywhere, humans and J'nai and scuttling little bots moved at a frantic pace. Welding torches fired sparks through the air, thick with the smell of metal and grease. When he looked back to her, his brow was furrowed, his eyes intense. Something was bothering him deeply—something more than just the stress of his new job.

"Don't you see, Nora?" he blurted. It was like he was asking her to read his mind. She searched his eyes, but found no further explanation there.

"See what?"

"Look around you. What do you see?" he said.

"Cadets...?"

"No. Look again. Tell me what you see."

"I see Originals and Clones."

"And what are they? Who are they, really?"

"Bastian, I don't know what you're talking about."

"Look," he said, pointing to a group of Originals in one corner. "They are being trained, not for piloting ships on supply runs, not for fixing a Star Port, but for war. They are training warriors. That Fight Club they have us in? It's not to keep us in shape. It's training."

"And the clones?"

"Ever wonder why they didn't clone a Ghandi? Or an Aristotle? Or a Thoreau?"

"It's crossed my mind," Nora whispered. "We're scientists." It was the reason that comment from the guy waxing the floor she'd messed up rattled with her so badly. Somehow, her subconscious had picked up on the theme Bastian was trying to get her to recognize. No Rembrandts here.

"And military strategists. Charlemagnes. Washingtons. Even some of your roommates—clones of warrior queens," he said, his eyes locked with hers. "Scientists put the Star Ports back together, and warriors defend them. Either the admiral knows something big is coming our way and hasn't let on to anyone or Ganymede was never designed to be a scientific utopia at all."

"So you're saying it's awfully convenient that we just so happened to have been working on a portable Star Port when the Qaigs show up 'out of nowhere' and attacked Terra Prime."

Bastian pulled her into a corridor and looked around to make sure no one was coming.

"There is nothing convenient about it," he said in a harsh whisper. His eyes bored into hers.

"There has been a rumor circulating in the station that Savaryn and the J'nai Queen made a pact to not just restore the Star Ports but to wipe out the Qaig."

"Why would they keep that a secret? Surely we'd want to help the J'nai retaliate against the race that committed genocide against them, wouldn't we?"

"Unless there's more to it," he said intensely. Nora's heart pounded. "The Qaig destroyed the port at Terra Prime, true. But they've made no move against us here. Why?"

"Maybe they're gathering their forces?"

"Maybe," he said, but he didn't look convinced. A pair of J'nai officers rounded the corner, heading straight for them.

"Look," he whispered. "I can't say more right now. Meet me in the sim room once curfew lifts tomorrow, okay? I'll set you up with some stuff to practice, and I'll tell you what I know. If you're coming with us, you should know what you're getting into."

"And what do I tell people when they see me in the sim room? It's not exactly private," she said. She crossed her arms. What was going on?

"You're right. I think I can rig up something to the *Rapscallion*'s Bridge. We'll do that, then. Meet me there. Tell your roommates nothing. Tell them... you are working on repairs."

"All right," she said.

He was staring off at something, some distant point far beyond the walls of the station. He was as tense as a coiled spring, ready to fly apart. It was a jarring departure from his usually calm façade. Then he turned to her, studying her face, before speaking again.

"I can count on you, no?" he said. It sounded like he needed the reassurance.

Nora smiled – as shaken as she'd been by the events of the past week, she now had a purpose and a compatriot on the journey. No matter how unlikely.

"Aye, aye, Captain," she said. This elicited one of his rare smiles, but it quickly faded.

"All right, get out of here, Cadet. If I keep you out after curfew, I'll be demoted before my first mission."

She started to go but saw that he was looking somewhere far off again, drumming his fingers against his arm in a rapid staccato.

"You okay?" she asked.

For a second he didn't respond, so she reached out and touched those fingers, gently stilling them with her own. He looked back to her sharply, reflexively taking a step away.

"I'm fine. Now get out of here, Cadet."

He crossed his arms crossed tightly, turned away from her, and paced down the side hall like a caged animal. She squared her shoulders, took a deep breath, and headed the other direction.

When she made it back to the room, she faced a veritable firing squad of questions from her roommates. What did Bastian want? Was she *really* going out on an asteroid-hauling mission now once her ship got fixed, like she told them she was? Wasn't that dangerous, flying out there in the belt? Nora swallowed hard, the lie falling uneasily from her lips. She thought Sophie was looking at her funny, but her ever-chatty roommate was, for once, thoughtfully silent. That unnerved her more than anything.

"And now you get to spend all week training with Captain Perfect-Cheekbones," Sophie said at last. She sighed dramatically and threw herself onto her bunk. Nora couldn't help but grin.

"I don't think I'm really his type. Besides," Nora said, "why would he even look at me when he could be with Thalia or Olivia?" Her heart clenched. Bastian was years her senior (how many though, three? Four?), and even if he could pry himself away from his ship or his studies for more than five minutes, he didn't need a nerdy little cadet. Still, the idea had set her stomach quivering with butterflies. Despite everything, the idea of spending time with him made her feel warm and funny all over – even though a small part of her ached uncomfortably when she thought about Greg, and how he'd been avoiding her since their return from Terra Prime.

"God, do you *want* him to be with Thalia?" Zoe said, shuddering. The idea seemed to have broken her out of her shrouded mood.

"Don't you get it?" Raina said, sharper than she meant to—or so Nora hoped. They all turned to look at her. "Thalia *is* you, you idiot. You think she's prettier than you? *Better* than you? You are all the things she is, except you're not a jerk. You can admire her strengths, but don't ever forget you have them, too."

Nora hugged Raina hard. The smaller girl squeaked in protest, but eventually gave in as Zoe, Sophie, and Cat joined them.

The next morning, a memorial service was held in the recreation dome, the one that adjoined the hangar bay. Nora and her roommates had all gotten up early and put on their dress uniforms – no jumpsuits permitted this day – and made their way with the other silent cadets, teachers, and staff, Human and J'nai alike. The lights in the dome were dimmed, and a series of caskets, about a dozen, each draped with a flag, were laid out in rows on the grass. Everyone assembled on the walkways, quiet except for the intermittent sniffling of those trying to hide their tears – and the occasional outburst from someone who couldn't. There was no eulogy, no one offered a prayer or reading, but they played a recording of 'Taps,' followed by a song Nora had only heard once before, the weirdly delicate J'nai anthem.

It was stupid, Nora thought, sniffling and wiping her nose on the thick wool of her sleeve. It left a silvery streak, but she didn't care. Most of those who died in the Qaig attack hadn't made it back. What had happened to them? Were they still floating around in space? The idea made her shiver.

"Look," Sophie said, pointing to the far side of the dome. There was a series of tables set up, with photos and flags for each of those lost. They made their way over. Sophie looped her arm through Nora's, her lips pressed tightly together. They stopped when they saw Lara's smiling face in front of them, with a little Australian flag in front of her picture. Sophie gripped her arm tighter. A few pictures back was Benny, and next to him was the giant blond Wingman, both with little American flags. They were smiling in their pictures too, proud in their uniforms, full of hope.

"I don't know what to say. We should say something, don't you think? Do you know how to say 'Goodbye' in Australian?" Sophie whispered.

"I'm pretty sure it's just 'goodbye,' right?" Nora said. Sophie smacked her arm.

"I know they speak English, thank you very much," she said. "But you know how she was always going on with her slang and calling us mates and drongos and all that?"

"God, it was annoying. I couldn't understand her half the time," Zoe said, coming out of nowhere. Raina was close behind, and a few others. Zoe gave Nora and Sophie a quick hug.

"Found someone for you," she said, gesturing to the side with her head. Ty was there, hanging back silently, as if he didn't know if he should approach. Sophie left Nora to go to him. She hugged him for an uncomfortably long period of time, though she had to stand on her tip-toes to do it.

"Geeze, you two, get a room," Zoe said. Sophie laughed, wiping her eyes. Nora smiled, which felt a little out of place given the occasion. She rubbed her arms, feeling like she didn't know what to quite do with them, without some to hold on to. Just as the thought entered her head, she saw a bright flash of bronze hair disappear through the airlock to the hangar bay, and she grinned.

"She wasn't supposed to be there," Cat said, and everyone swiveled to look at her. Nora's attention was brought abruptly back to the service, and to her friends. She thought that Car seemed to shrink, her arms wrapped around herself, but she didn't offer any further explanation to her words. Nora thought she knew what she meant though – Lara had begged to get onto that mission, and she wasn't even on the pilot track. Rumor had been that she'd had some strings pulled to make it happen.

"Did any of you ever figure out who what mystery boyfriend of hers was?" Zoe asked, clearly following the same line of thought. Sophie shook her head, sending her black ringlets dancing.

"Not even you? Sophie, I'm disappointed," Zoe said. Raina shoved her, and Zoe shoved her back. "What?" Zoe whispered to her.

"It's not for lack of trying," Sophie said with a shrug. "Guess we'll never know, now…"

The group was silent again. Ty moved to put a protective arm around Sophie, and she let him, leaning into him. Nora met her glance and raised an eyebrow, but said nothing.

Then someone announced over the intercom that the funeral (as informal and unorganized as it was) was officially over, and everyone could please return to their tasks immediately. The mass of people moved as one, funneling into the various corridors off of the dome, as intent on their tasks as bees in a hive.

Nora made her way to the *Rapscallion*, and though she could have barely gotten there any sooner after the funeral, the engineers and Thalia's crew were already hard at work. Thalia didn't so much as look up when Nora passed; her crewmates offered a curt hello. She wondered briefly if they'd even gone to the funeral. She hadn't remembered seeing Thalia there.

She found Bastian on the Bridge, going over a checklist with a man in grease-splattered overalls. How he'd found time to already change into his jumpsuit, she had no idea. The thought brought a brief smile to her face – he hated the formal uniforms, though he seemed to respect that certain occasions called for them.

"I brought coffee," she said, setting an extra cup near him. He gave her a grateful nod before returning to the checklist on the tablet. Nora took a look at the console; nothing had been rigged up yet. She booted up the controls in safety mode (designed for running diagnostics without the engines going online) and with some creative hacking—including rerouting some wires under the console, hopefully without damaging anything—she pulled in the flight practices from the sim room.

"Here," Bastian said, after about twenty minutes of conferring with various people on the Bridge. He pointed to a program he'd installed on the console. "Open this. It should run those sims you brought over. I've told the mechanics to ignore any red flashing lights from the Bridge. It'll simulate loss of power, life support, you know. I don't want them freaking out."

A mechanic left the Bridge murmuring, his eyes glued to his tablet screen.

"Bastian, about last night..."

"What about last night?" Thalia said cattily, one eyebrow raised. She sauntered onto the Bridge, wiping her hands on a rag. Nora flushed.

"Last night, Nora and I ran simulations, same as every other night," Bastian said in a bored tone. Nora looked up at him; they'd done nothing of the sort.

"Right," Thalia said archly. "Anyway, I'm going to disable the lateral gun turrets. Have to. You'll just have to hope your practice sessions have this little Hypatia up to par before we run into any Qaig ships."

Bastian shook his head.

"We need those turrets. Figure it out."

"I'm telling you, I can't install the P2 with them there."

"Fine. I will be there in a second, Thalia, and we can work on it together. Let me get Nora set up on the sim, okay?"

Thalia turned, flipping her hair over her shoulder, and left. Bastian let out a long breath.

"Okay, where were we?"

"You were showing me how to bring up the sim. And," she said, looking around the Bridge, "you were going to tell me why the Qaig aren't coming through the Jupiter port."

"We are going to have to blow that port," he said, shaking his head. "If this mission goes badly, that port will be the only way for us to get off the Current. But it will also be the only way the Qaig can get to us, maybe even get to Earth."

Nora's stomach clenched hard at that – she hadn't even considered the possibility that the Earth, too, might be under threat from the Qaigs.

"But they haven't come through yet," Bastian continued. "Maybe it's because the Qaig have nothing against us. Maybe *they* are retaliating against *their* genocide, from the J'nai."

"That's impossible," Nora whispered.

"Is it? We only know one side of the story, Nora, the side the J'nai *want* us to believe. Haven't you ever wondered why the Qaig attacked the

J'nai in the first place? I've seen the archives, bits of data that Savaryn thought were wiped from the station's mainframe. The relationship between the J'nai and the Qaig goes back much further than we were told, maybe even thousands of years. The J'nai enslaved the Qaig. They spent generations using them like beasts of burden, until a few hundred years ago, when they fought back and left the J'nai systems."

"Why weren't we told any of this in class?" Nora asked. There was an odd, queasy feeling just under her breastbone – hadn't she started to suspect as much, though? Between Sophie's discovery on the computers, the propaganda, the secrets Aditi kept?

"Come on, Nora. Isn't it easier to elicit pity for the J'nai when they're portrayed as victims of an ugly, villainous race? Would you be so willing to help them if you'd know their past?"

"But...what about Soren, and Asher, and Jane and Dan and the rest? I can't believe..."

"I don't know if all of the J'nai know about it," he said. "It's been years. The lies were told and retold until they became ingrained in the J'nai culture and were accepted as fact. And I don't know the answer for sure. None of us do. That's why this mission is so important. We have to see, firsthand, what the Qaig are up to and why."

"Does Soren know?"

"She suspects," Bastian acknowledged, after a few seconds pause. "We always thought she was more of an Alpha than a Beta or Delta. She's nobody's fool."

"That's why she volunteered..." Nora said. Bastian nodded.

"I didn't want you dragged into this," Bastian said. "You're just a cadet." Nora flushed. It was the second time he'd reminded her of her place—or reminded himself.

"Soren wanted you to come because she can count on you if we get into a tight spot," he said. "There aren't many people she trusts right now, and you're one of them. Whether it's because you're still new and naïve or because you were uncorrupted by your handlers, I'm not sure."

"There's a compliment in there somewhere, I think," Nora said, frowning. Her brain felt like it was inside a washing machine, whirling and spinning faster than she could consciously keep up with it.

"I think she also wants witnesses," Bastian said. "You'll be a neutral third party, more or less. She'll have a J'nai, an Original, and a Fax present to witness…whatever happens. And don't say Thalia counts as a witness because she doesn't. I'm not sure she can be counted on to ever tell the truth. She's brilliant, sure, but with a secret like this…"

"So all that talk about Soren wanting to train me…"

"I think she does mean it," Bastian said. "She wants to train both of us. She does not trust the J'nai council any more than she trusts Savaryn. She needs good people on her side."

"Okay," Nora said, swallowing hard. "So who else knows?"

"Just Soren, Donovan, Asher, and me. And now you. We need Thalia and her team to focus on the P2. I don't need to stress how important it is that this be kept secret, do I?"

"No," she said, her voice cracking a bit.

"I mean it," he said. "Not anyone, not your roommates, not your boyfriend…"

"He's not my boyfriend," she said sharply. A lump formed in her throat. She wasn't even sure Greg was her friend anymore. He hadn't spoken to her since they came back from Terra Prime – in fact, she hadn't seen him at the memorial service, either. Not that she'd been looking, she thought with a cringe of shame. Bastian looked startled.

"Oh," he said. "Sorry."

"Yeah," Nora said. She looked up at the lights. She'd read once that if you looked up, particularly at a bright light, it would keep tears from falling. It helped, anyway. Sort of.

"Look, I should go," he said.

"Go," Nora said, blinking hard. "Thalia is going to tear your ship apart if you don't stop her. I'm just going to practice for a while."

He nodded and left the bridge. Nora sighed, trying to let out the tension that had settled into her shoulders, and squared herself to look at the computer, blocking out all other thoughts.

She worked on the sims for the next several hours. It was harder to run them in the ship, and the overhead lights and sirens were distracting—for the mechanics as well—but she supposed that was the point. Every time she stopped, she thought about the last encounter she'd had with the Qaig. She'd gotten off lucky; one more shot and they probably wouldn't have made it. And each time that thought ran through her head, she decided to run just one more practice sim, then just one more.

It went on like that all day. She couldn't detach from the sim, and as a result, it was nearing curfew when she eventually left the bridge. Asher had brought her a sandwich at some point—and peach cobbler—but by the time she left, her stomach was growling, her neck cramped, and her vision blurred from so many hours sitting over the glowing green lights of the console.

She gathered her tablet and notes (copiously scribbled over the course of the day) and made her way to the rear ramp. She heard raised voices as she walked and paused to listen.

"Thalia told me the good news," a female voice with a trace of Scandinavian accent said.

"Liv, come on," Bastian said. Liv. Olivia. Nora knew she should keep walking and announce herself, but the next words kept her frozen in her tracks.

"So you expect me to just be okay with you spending the next week in close quarters with your ex-girlfriend and her doppelgänger? You're the captain. Make them leave!"

Oh. Nora hadn't really thought about it that way. She cringed.

"It's not like that," Bastian's measured voice said. "Be reasonable, Liv. I need them both on this mission. It's just a job."

"Sure," she sniffed. "Top secret. Right. So top secret you won't even tell your girlfriend."

"Olivia," Bastian said. "We have been over this. I never meant to lead you on. You are amazing, but whatever it is you think we have is just in your imagination."

Nora winced, and put her hand over her tired eyes. Bastian was never one to sugarcoat his words, but that was harsh, even for him. It sounded like he'd said it to her before, maybe more than once. She'd known Olivia was persistent, but Nora's heart ached for her all the same.

"Liv," he tried again, a little more gently. Nora thought she could hear stifled sobs echoing up the cargo bay.

"I want you to be happy. You know that, yes?"

"Oh, I am happy," Olivia said, her voice retreating. "Happy that I'm rid of you! Enjoy your little honeymoon, *mon cher.*"

Nora heard what she imagined was a booted foot striking one of the ship's landing gears. She swallowed hard, then squared her bag across her shoulders and headed out, moving briskly. She saw Bastian leaning against the wing of the ship. His back was turned toward her, and his posture sagged, held up by an outstretched arm on the wing.

"Hey Cap, I'm done for the day. Heading back before curfew," she called as cheerfully as she could. "Same time tomorrow?"

"Yeah," he said. He didn't turn around. Nora pursed her lips and left the dome. Olivia had been totally off base—unless there was still something between Thalia and Bastian? He hadn't made it seem like there was. But Thalia had been the one to break the news to Olivia; Nora could see the nasty little grin on her face when she told her. Surely, she'd thrown in the bit about both Hypatias being on board for good measure, an extra gleeful dig. She never wasted an opportunity to cause mischief.

CHAPTER 26

The next morning, Nora and Sophie grabbed a quick breakfast in the cafeteria prior to their daily tasks. Two Tesla boys immediately spotted Sophie and started following her around like ducklings. Sophie gave Nora a look that said, "You see what I have to put up with every day." Nora smothered a laugh.

"Don't you boys have something else to do?" Sophie said, after five nonstop minutes of their prattle.

"Nope," one of them said.

"You can't really blame us for wanting to spend time you with, Soph. There are all these chemicals racing through my bloodstream when I'm near you..."

Sophie rolled her eyes.

"You boys and your hormones."

"Hello, we're teenagers! We're practically *made* of hormones!" Tesla One said.

"Yeah, who decided it would be a good idea to put a bunch of hormonally charged kids at work designing things that could potentially blow up the biggest moon in the solar system?" said Tesla Two.

"Only if *you* do it wrong."

"I won't do it wrong, *you'll* do it wrong."

"A bunch of hormones controlled by underdeveloped pre-frontal cortexes," Sophie sighed. "We're doomed.

"So, Nora. Care to save me from my lab monkeys today?" Sophie begged.

"Can't. Training," Nora said, sipping her coffee.

"Right," Sophie said. "For the top secret mission with Captain Broody Brows."

"It's not top secret, Soph," Nora said, hating herself for what she was about to say. "I told you. It's just a supply run. The station needs all the pilots it can get. Other cadets are training, too."

"Other *Originals*," Sophie said. "But hey, I get it. If you won't tell your *best friend* what you're up to, if you'd rather pretend you're not a fax and hang out with *them*..."

"Soph, just drop it," Nora begged. "I know you. I know you're going to go down to the lab, fire up your computer, and hack into something until you figure it out. Just...leave it alone. Please?"

"Not a chance," Sophie said. She picked up her tray and left, the Teslas trailing behind her. Nora sighed and buried her face in her hands. Fighting with Sophie was not something she ever wanted. She'd been her best friend since day one. How could she possibly face the mission ahead without her?

She grabbed a pair of coffees and made her way to the landing dome. Thalia arrived mere *seconds* before her and shot Nora a nasty wink before approaching Bastian—with a cup of coffee, which she offered with a syrupy-sweet greeting.

"Thanks," he said. His face was tight, his usual dash of blond stubble longer than usual. Thalia waved a cute goodbye to Bastian, then looked to Nora with a triumphant smirk as she scurried past to her crew. Nora tried and failed to make it up the ship's ramp before Bastian saw her.

"Morning," he called. She nodded, trying to conceal the extra coffee she'd brought.

"You brought coffee, no?" he said, trotting up to her. Nora's face flushed, and she stammered.

"I didn't realize Thalia..."

"She always puts too much sugar in it," he confided in a whisper. Nora grinned and handed him her spare cup.

"You are a lifesaver," he said. He made sure Thalia wasn't looking and offered her coffee to one of the passing mechanics, who accepted it with a gruff thanks.

"So. How's it looking out there, Cap?" she asked. He took a sip of the coffee, savoring it, before replying.

"Not bad. Thalia was right about the lateral guns, though. They will have to go."

"So we'll just have the ventral cannons?"

"Pretty much," he said, sipping.

"Good to know," Nora said. "Well, if I can help, you know where to find me." She moved to leave. He nodded and turned back to the group of mechanics systematically destroying two-thirds of the ship's offensive systems.

▰ ▰ ▰

It was another long day. Nora finally made it back to the dorm with seconds to spare (the doors locked at precisely 9:00 p.m., a precaution, the higher-ups said). She dropped her bag by the door and looked up at her bunk; the seven-rung climb seemed as daunting as Mount Everest. Or Olympus Mons. Or something else really, really tall. She decided to sit on the window ledge instead, stretching out her legs with a groan. Even her butt hurt after so many hours in the cockpit. She supposed she'd have to get used to it—marathons of sitting, every nerve in her body poised and focused. She hadn't thought it could be so frustrating and exhausting.

"You look like hell," Zoe said. She and Raina were sitting on her bunk, watching something on a tablet screen.

"Just tired," Nora said, laying her head against the window. Despite everything, she was enjoying herself. The simulations on the ship were so much more real. It was starting to feel like the *Rap* was an extension of her own consciousness. "You guys hanging in there?"

"It's not so bad. They forward tasks to our tablets, and once we mark them complete, we get another. Most of them aren't terrible—although Raina had to clean the..."

"Yes, well," Raina interrupted, punching Zoe on the arm. "I took a shower, and now you can barely smell it anymore."

Cat had already drawn the curtain on her bunk; Raina whispered that she'd been working all day on some sort of fix for the Star Port. Nora could only assume she was working on the P2, although she couldn't say it out loud.

"Not talking to me now, Sophie?" Nora called. Sophie was sitting in her bunk, headphones on, ignoring them all. Sophie shrugged and continued typing. She'd gotten a portable keyboard for her tablet, and her fingers were furiously flying across it.

"Uh oh, lover's quarrel?" Zoe said, raising an eyebrow. Nora sighed.

"I think she's just upset because I get to spend all day working in the landing dome instead of down in the lab with Tweedle Dee and Tweedle Dum," she said.

"I am not," Sophie called. "I'm mad because…"

What was likely to be an epic Sophie-style tirade was cut short by a knock on the door.

"Uh," Raina said, shrinking back onto her bunk. "It's after curfew."

"Door's locked!" Zoe called. "Duh!"

The lock clicked. Nora exchanged a glance with her roommates, then got up —she was closest, after all—and opened it. It was the girl who'd escorted her to the admiral after her initial sim battle.

"Sophie Bauer?" she said.

"Uh oh," Raina croaked.

Across the room, Sophie slowly removed her headphones.

"Yes?" she said.

"Come with me."

"It's after curfew," Sophie argued.

"Admiral's orders."

Nora and Sophie exchanged a glance. Sophie's mouth was set in a firm line, her jaw clenched.

"Fine then," she said.

Sophie slipped on her shoes and left without a backward glance, the click of the door shutting behind her as loud as a gong in the silence of room 10013, the curfew-enforcing bolt locking with a final thud.

Sophie didn't return for hours. The other girls didn't know what to do. Sophie was, after all, their self-appointed leader. There was speculation, of course. Most of them assumed Sophie had been busted breaking a rule or two; after all, that was kind of her thing. Nora felt a pang when she realized their earlier conversation had probably initiated it—whatever "it" was. If she had been truthful with Sophie, her friend wouldn't be in who knows what kind of trouble now.

Eventually, they all went to bed, but Nora was still awake when Sophie crept back into the room in the middle of the night. She quietly closed the door, removed her shoes, and padded across the room to her bunk, careful not to disturb her roommates.

"Soph?" Nora called, hanging over the edge of her bunk. There was a pause.

"Yeah?"

"You okay?"

There was no answer. Nora bit her lip. She should let Sophie sleep.

No chance. Fear and concern got the best of her and she crept down the ladder of her bunk. Sophie was barely visible in the waxing light of Jupiter, curled up with her back to Nora.

"Hey," Nora said and sat on the edge of her bunk. Sophie sighed and turned over. The dim light made her look even paler than usual.

"They busted me," Sophie said. She actually managed to sound disappointed in herself. "I told them I was trying to hack the task app, see what everyone else was up to, try to piece it all together."

"But…that's not what you were doing?"

"Oh, at first," Sophie whispered. She pulled her legs up to her chest to make room for Nora to sit beside her. "But then I found a file in the mainframe with your name on it."

"Don't we all have files?"

"Not like this," Sophie said, shaking her head. "These were hidden. I found them on Cat, too."

Nora's pulse skyrocketed. Sophie licked her lips, for once hesitant to continue.

"I think we may have been right before, about your parents. And Cat's," she said. "It looks like yours had no intention of letting you come to Ganymede. They had a bunch of meetings with someone in Louisiana who gave them fake IDs, passports, currency—all to keep you away from here."

Nora fell back against the headboard, her breath emptying from her lungs in a long *whoosh*.

"I was trying to download the file when little Ms. Bossy Pants came and got me. I guess I wasn't as sneaky as I thought," Sophie said with a frown.

"Did they...I mean, are you in trouble?"

"A few extra shifts sifting compost for the greenhouse," Sophie said, wrinkling her nose. "Could have been worse. Dr. Prasad was great, though. She kind of took control of the meeting, said some stuff about 'kids being kids' and how I'm basically wired to be curious, like Hedy, and how that's such an asset. Stuff like that. I got off easy."

"Do you think she knows?" Nora asked. She'd always regarded Aditi as something like a kindly aunt, someone she could confide in. Was she involved in the subterfuge the entire time?

"Not sure," Sophie said.

"Soph, I'm sorry," Nora said, putting a hand on her friend's arm. Sophie sighed and leaned her head on Nora's shoulder.

"I'm sorry for being such a busybody," she said, sniffling. "I can't help it, you know."

"I know," Nora said. Guilt twisted her gut. "All these secrets are tearing this station apart, aren't they?"

"Yeah," Sophie agreed. "You going to be okay? I mean, what do we do with this now? Should I tell Cat?"

"Not yet," Nora said after a second. "Let me see what Aditi knows. Then we can tell her. She's just so worn out. I haven't seen her conscious since the tasks started."

"I know," Sophie said.

CHAPTER 27

The following morning, Nora went to the PJ dome as usual, but around noon, she couldn't take the anxiety anymore and left on a "lunch break." No one seemed to notice her, anyway. Bastian and Soren were nowhere to be seen, and Thalia didn't so much as glance in her direction.

She made her way past the cafeteria dome and down toward the academic wing, to Aditi's office. She stood in front of the door a second before knocking.

"Come in," came Aditi's muffled voice through the door.

Nora let herself in and found Aditi seated behind her desk, tablet in hand, her forehead creased as she read something.

"Nora," she said. She smiled, but her eyes remained flat and black. "What can I do for you? Would you like some tea?"

Nora stood on the other side of Aditi's desk, placed her hands flat on the surface, and leaned forward.

"Sophie told me about last night."

Aditi sighed.

"Yes, well, unfortunately Ms. Bauer broke the rules, and without rules, we are no better than…"

"She found out about my parents. You know she did. Why didn't you tell on her?" Nora whispered, her voice harsh with restrained tears.

Aditi eyes flickered across the room, then she pulled a piece of paper and pen from the top drawer of her desk as she spoke in calm, soothing tones.

"Nora, I know you and Ms. Bauer are friends, and it's truly admirable that you want to help her," she said, scribbling. Nora shook her head, confused. Aditi was usually straightforward with her.

"Now, I think you will come to realize that Ms. Bauer was dealt with fairly," she said with a smile. She turned the paper around for Nora to see, shielding it on the right with a strategically placed tea mug.

Not safe. Ganymede listening.
Rec dome, 8:00p.m.

Nora blinked, rereading the note. Before she could open her mouth, Aditi covered the paper with her mug. She gave Nora another broad smile.

"Run along and get some lunch now. I hear the kale is particularly good today."

Nora looked at her, trying to read the intention in the worry around her eyes, in the way her lips pinched at the corners. Whatever was going on here had Aditi Prasad scared.

Which meant that Nora should be absolutely terrified.

"Kale. Right," Nora said, shaking her head. "Thanks. You're right. Sorry for interrupting you."

"Quite all right, dear. You know you are welcome here any time," Aditi said, her head already bent back to the task on the tablet before her. Nora stepped from the room, the door hissing shut behind her, and let out a long breath.

What in the hell was going on? Nora spat out a J'nai curse – one Asher had taught her, inadvertently, after the Qaig attack – and headed back towards the hangar bay, twisting a curl around her finger as she walked.

▰ ▰ ▰

Promptly at 7:45 p.m., Nora shut down the PJ console and put her notes in her bag. She was getting up to leave, stretching out the kinks that had worked their way into her neck, when Bastian came on deck. He leaned against the wall near the door, his arms crossed over his chest.

"Need something, Cap?" she asked, shouldering her pack. The gears in her brain were turning wildly, anticipating her meeting with Aditi. What would the woman have to say to her?

"Is everything okay?" he blurted. "You don't seem like yourself today. You haven't said two words to anyone. Am I pushing you too hard? Do I expect too much from you?" It was not an accusation, she realized, but concern.

"No," she said, plastering a bright smile on her face, wanting to alleviate his worry. "Just…a lot on my mind."

"Yeah, I get it," he said. He ran a hand through his hair before speaking again.

"I was going to the café to grab a coffee. Want to come?"

"Oh God, the coffee!" She smacked her forehead with her palm. "I forgot to bring you coffee this morning. I'm so sorry."

"I'm perfectly capable of obtaining my own caffeine, Cadet," he said with a chuckle. "Though it is a nice thought."

She nodded, feeling kind of silly, and suddenly felt like looking at her shoes, at the scuffs across the once-spotless patent sheen. She should really take care of that at some point.

"Come on," he said, gesturing for her to follow. "Let's go."

"I can't. I have…this meeting thing, and…"

"Well, I'll walk you out, anyway," he said.

Thalia was still berating her crew as they left the cargo bay, though she did manage to replace her scowl with a brilliant smile for Bastian when she saw him. He sighed, stuffing his hands in the pockets of his flight suit. Even after a long day, even after everything, his suit was still perfectly pressed. His hair was perfectly rumpled. The only signs that anything was out of the ordinary with his usually tightly controlled self was the growing stubble on his chin and the shadows under his eyes.

"Are you okay, Cap?" Nora asked. He glanced at her sideways.

"The Captain is always okay," he grumbled. His accent was thicker when he was tired.

"Well, someone's gotta ask you, anyway," she said, dodging an oncoming line of mechanics and engineers.

"I'm fine, Cadet," he said with a smirk, but Nora saw how quickly it vanished. She couldn't imagine the mental strain he was under, a lot of it self-inflicted, his perfectionist nature at war with his sanity.

"Maybe you need a break. Go beat up that green guy or something," she said. He actually laughed at that.

"Dalton?" he said. "You know him?"

"I just…maybe saw you once, when I was in the gym. I only remember because he was the biggest J'nai I'd ever seen."

"Well, it's not a half-bad idea," he admitted. They came to a juncture, where the halls to the cafeteria and rec dome split off.

"This is my stop," Nora said, gesturing down the hall.

"All right," Bastian said, turning toward her. "See you tomorrow, then."

In the hall light, she could see just how dark the shadows under those blue-gray eyes had become. As scared and stressed as she was, she knew Bastian had it worse. He was responsible for the lives of the entire crew, which comprised two J'nai who might be involved in a conspiracy and one ex-girlfriend who was doing everything she could to cause drama. Nora bit her lip.

"Tomorrow," she promised. He looked at her a moment longer, like there was something he wanted to say, but he just nodded and turned away. She watched him for a second, hunched over as he retreated down the hall, before she released a breath she hadn't realized she'd been holding and turned toward the rec dome.

She found Aditi waiting, sitting on a bench with a bagel she hadn't touched. Nora joined her, and for a moment, they just sat and watched as a pair of da Vinci Faxes tossed a Frisbee the length of the field. She looked up at the dome overhead for a moment, the bright white ceiling a hundred feet overhead. She never knew she'd miss something as simple as the sky. Then one of the da Vinci's leapt into her field of view, performing an acrobatic catch of the Frisbee, and her brief reverie was broken.

"They're pretty good at that," Nora remarked. Aditi smiled and picked at her bagel.

"No one can hear us here, Nora," she said with a gentle smile. "There are cameras here but no mics. Just keep smiling and pretend like we're having a normal conversation."

"So there are bugs in your office," Nora said, accepting half the bagel from Aditi. She nodded.

"And you know what Sophie found in my file," Nora said.

"I know what she found, yes," Aditi said. "And I knew about the file before then."

Aditi crumbled part of the bagel, the bits falling to the ground. One of the cleaning droids would be along soon to pick them up; it's not like there were ants in space.

"You knew?" Nora had to fight to keep her face calm. She gazed around the dome, pretending to follow the flight of the Frisbee while looking for anything that might be a camera. She didn't see one.

"I knew," Aditi said. "Your parents—they were my friends, a long time ago. They didn't want you here, Nora."

Aditi's dark eyes flashed with barely suppressed emotion.

"But why?" Nora said. "They didn't want me to leave them?" She knew now that her parents loved her, that they always had—no matter what the other Faxes said, no matter all the talk about handlers.

"Because they knew secrets about Ganymede," Aditi hissed. "Secrets that could destroy the very façade that this station is built on, the illusion that we are here for peace and science, to help the J'nai and advance the human race." Her face was contorted in anger, but she quickly caught herself and smoothed her expression.

"What kind of secrets?" Nora breathed. She wasn't sure she wanted to know—but she *had* to know.

"That the admiral and J'nai queen have more at stake here than some broken Star Ports and a peaceful trade agreement," she said. "That the Qaig may not be the villains that they seem, but a ploy to get our races to work together. That the board of directors has done things to protect their investments, and when someone stands in its way…"

"Like my parents," Nora said. She and Aditi sat in silence for a few moments, watching the clock on the far wall tick down to curfew.

"I shouldn't be telling you this," Aditi said. "But please believe me when I say I've wanted to from the beginning. There are…some of us are trying to breach the inner sanctum of Savaryn's secrets…"

"I want in," Nora said. Aditi shook her head.

"Not yet," she said. "Go on this mission with the P2. Observe everything you can. When you get back, we'll talk again. A revolution is at hand, Nora. And we should all be prepared when it happens."

"They had my parents killed, Aditi," Nora said, fighting back tears. "I need to know more."

"When the time is right," Aditi said. "Know that your parents loved you like a daughter from the minute they brought you home. When they came to me, asking for help in keeping you, I…" her voice faltered. "It is up to me now to keep you safe, Nora. For them. Keep this to yourself for now, and when you return from your trip, be ready."

Aditi smiled and stretched. She was acting for the cameras. Anyone watching would think they were actually having a 'perfectly normal conversation.'

"Thank you," Nora said. The clock ticked closer to curfew. "I should be going then. Don't want to raise suspicions by lurking about after curfew."

"Go on," Aditi said, laying a hand on her arm. "I'll let you know if anything changes. Keep your tablet nearby, just in case."

"I will," Nora said.

She picked up her bag, waved a cheerful goodbye that took a surprising amount of effort to fake, and left the dome. Aditi was still sitting on the bench, the bagel forgotten, when Nora turned back to look at her.

Nora's mind raced the whole way back to her room. She knew she should be upset with Aditi for keeping her parents' fates a secret, but despite it all, she trusted the woman. She trusted that she was working to overthrow the corruption, to bring the station back in line with its original premise: one of peace, not one dedicated to wiping out a race of aliens that had, perhaps, done no wrong.

What if, Nora realized with a sinking heart, she had inadvertently sided with the bad guys?

CHAPTER 28

Nora woke up groggy and grouchy. A shower and two cups of coffee later, her eyelids were still barely propping themselves open. She made sure to grab an extra cup for Bastian and headed back to the *Rapscallion*.

Three days. Just three days until departure. Thalia assured them the P2 would be ready, and a team of engineers had already swapped out the damaged parts of the subluminal engines. Sparks were flying from welding devices as she approached—the sound and light grated on her fraying nerves.

"Morning," she said, handing Bastian his coffee. Thalia was—thankfully—nowhere to be seen.

"Good morning," he said, looking at some schematic on his tablet.

"Can you help me boot up the sim program?" she asked, nodding toward the Bridge. His brow creased.

"You can do it," he said. She'd done it herself every day, after all.

"No, I mean *can you help me* on the Bridge?" she repeated, accenting the phrase carefully. He looked up at her. Held her gaze. She swallowed hard, and nodded her head towards the ship. He stood up, leaving his tablet on the table.

"Okay," he said, and followed her onto the ship.

"What's this about?" he asked. She glanced around the Bridge. They were alone. She leaned in close to him, her voice barely above a whisper.

"Did you know that the station is bugged?"

After a second, he nodded.

"Is the ship?"

He shook his head. "Soren wouldn't stand for it. She found one once and sweeps the ship every few days to make sure they haven't planted more. How did you know?"

"A friend," she said, letting out a long breath. "The friend I met with last night."

"I see," he said. She was suddenly acutely aware of how close they were, and her cheeks heated. She stepped back, and he sank into his chair, the captain's chair, and leaned forward, his elbows on his knees, his chin on his clenched fingers. "Is there something else you wanted to tell me?"

Nora took a deep breath. Bastian had trusted her with the rumor of the J'nai manipulations, had vouched for her, believed in her when no one else had—and he was her captain. If anyone here could be trusted, it was him.

So she told him what she'd learned from Sophie and Aditi, leaving out nothing but their identities. Bastian listened, not interrupting. When she finished, he sat back, rubbing a hand over his chin.

"So the problems run deeper than I realized," he said. A bearded mechanic came onto the Bridge then, mumbling about something to do with the wiring for the P2 running through the side panel. He clanked about with his tools for a few minutes while Nora wasted time, booting up the sim program on the pilot's console. After a while, Bastian left without another word.

That afternoon, she took a break to go down to the Medical Bay. She hadn't actually been there before, but like the rest of the station, the hall was clean, sterile feeling. The only noticeable difference was an overabundance of those little cleaning bots running around, keeping the floor polished. She had to avoid stepping on them several times.

She made her way to a reception desk and placed her thumb on a touch screen identifier that prompted her with a series of questions related to her current complaints. In her case, it was just one: removal of stitches.

The machine spat out a receipt with a bold "14" and flashed a sign that told her to have a seat; the doctors would see her shortly.

The waiting room looked like what you'd find in any hospital, if smaller: simple plastic chairs, a flat screen showing the day's activities around the station. Apparently the third-year science classes were having a robot battle in the rec dome – that one looked interesting. The lecture series on pan-galactic politics did not. She took a seat—she was the only one there—and waited, watching the images on the flat screen flicker from the activities list to photos of smiling, cheerful cadets and J'nai happily at work around the station.

She didn't have to wait for long. She'd barely sat when a frosted glass door next to the reception desk opened, and a tall, dark-haired man stepped out. He looked around the room expectantly and finally caught sight of her in the corner.

"Hola," the man said, grinning at her.

"Wesley!" she said, relief welling up in her. It had been forever since she'd seen him—and a friendly face right now was just what the doctor ordered. She hugged him fiercely.

"Hey, are you okay, little Hypatia?" He was holding a tablet with her file pulled up in the hand that was not busy disentangling himself from her. She couldn't answer.

"Come on. I hear you hit your head on that last mission," he said. He led her through a stark, orderly room lined with stretchers on either side, all empty except for a man snoring in the last bed, an IV with what looked like blood running into his arm.

"Yeah," she admitted. Wesley led her to a bed close to the snoring man and sat her down.

"So how have you been otherwise? You like being a pilot?"

"I like it," Nora said. And she did—she really, truly did. The ship moved like it was a part of her, the way the piano responded to her touch back home. "How about you? You like the medical stuff?"

"When I'm not studying, I'm working," he said, flashing his handsome smile. "Now, come on. Let's see what we have here." He had her look down so he could inspect Donovan's handiwork.

"Looks good," he said. "Would have been better if he'd shaved this area, but the scar should be hidden in the hairline. The stitches are definitely ready to come out, though. Just let me get some supplies."

"No one is shaving my head," Nora mumbled. Her hair was pulled forward, obscuring her vision like a fluffy black cloud, so that Wesley could see the stitches above her temple.

He rifled through the drawers on a nearby cart, pulling out scissors and tweezers and antibacterial ointment and neatly lining them up on a tray. He was about to put on a pair of gloves when the frosted door burst open and two men pushing a stretcher hurtled in.

"Coming through!" one of them yelled. Nora pushed the hair back from her eyes. The boy on the stretcher was convulsing, froth flecked with red spewing from his mouth.

"Went down in the Cafeteria, status epilepticus," the other man said, trying to start an IV on the thrashing boy.

"Get me two milligrams of Ativan IM! Now!" another man yelled. A stream of men and women—human and J'nai—in white scrubs and armed with equipment came pouring from the back of the room. The boy's limbs whipped against the rails of his bed, rattling the whole thing. His back arched, his mouth open in a wordless scream, before he flopped back down and then tried to jackknife upright.

"He's still seizing! Why is he still seizing? Do you want him to fry his brain? Push another milligram!" someone yelled.

"Second time this week," a J'nai said, hooking up a bag of yellow fluid to the IV and pushing the boy back down on the stretcher. She shook her head.

Wesley, who'd been watching the spectacle thoughtfully, pursed his lips, and drew the curtain around the bed where Nora was sitting.

"Shouldn't we help?" she asked, trying to see through the small gap where two pieces of the curtain met. Wesley shook his head.

"They've got this," he said. "And I'm not even a real intern yet. I'm barely allowed to take out stitches, let alone help run a code. Look down again." She did so.

"Wesley?" she asked.

"Yeah? Hang on, this might sting…"

"Ouch." She winced as she heard the scissors bite.

"Just a few more bits," he coached, continuing his work. "You're doing fine."

"Wesley, that kid—I think that's Bati," she whispered. "He's in our class."

"He's a Clone," Wesley said. It wasn't a question, and she didn't know how it was relevant. She understood that not everyone viewed Originals and Faxes as the same—but Wesley? True, she hadn't seen him in a while, but he'd always been nice enough to her. Or was that just because he knew her before he knew about clones? Nora bit her lip.

"A Kublai Khan, I think," she said, staring at the scuff marks on her shoes.

"That explains it," he said, setting down the scissors. A moment later, she felt the cooling oiliness of the antibacterial ointment on her scalp.

"No hair washing until tomorrow. Then no scrubbing until the scab is gone. If it bleeds, come back and let me check it out, okay?" He stripped his gloves and turned his back to her, busying himself with clean up.

"Wesley," she prompted again. He stilled, then sighed. "You know something. What's wrong with Bati? What do you mean, 'that explains it'?"

"We've been monitoring him for a while," Wesley whispered. He came and sat on the bed next to her. "He's been getting sick."

"Is it…something genetic?" she asked. She didn't remember anything about Kublai Khan, but if he'd had some genetic illness, Bati clearly would have inherited it, too.

Wesley shook his head.

"It…happens sometimes, with the clones," he said, meeting her eyes. "Something about the process of … creating you. Something they added to the serum."

"Something who added? Does this happen to *all* the clones?" He hesitated, then shook his head—to her immense relief.

"Not everyone. But some of them. We're not sure why."

"Is he going to be okay?" Her fingertips were suddenly icy. Wesley shrugged.

"Sometimes they are," he said. "Other times…"

"Is the medical team watching other clones?"

"Yes," he said, then hurriedly added, "but just a few. Not you. They're not worried about you."

"Like Cat," Nora said, with sudden clarity. She was horrified, and could barely get the next words out. "With her headaches."

"We think her headaches are just headaches," Wesley said quickly. "Well, I'm probably not supposed to be discussing her with you, but…yes, we are keeping an eye on her, too."

"I see," Nora said. More secrets. The thrashing and groaning from the latest arrival had quieted somewhat. She wanted to see what was going on and didn't at the same time. What had been added to the cloning serum? She spat out Asher's curse again, getting a surprised look from Wesley in the process.

"I should get back to the hangar," she said, getting up from the cot. There was sudden quiet from the other side of the room. Bati had stopped moving. "Lots to do," she said absently, suddenly in a hurry to get out of there.

"Sure. But keep this quiet, okay? We don't want to start a panic. Everything's under control."

"Sure," she agreed, but she didn't believe him. Could Bati having a grand mal seizure be what he considered "under control"? Why was it that every time she turned around, some new and terrible secret came to the surface?

She made her way back to the hangar, finishing her sims for the day without talking to anyone. Her mind was still churning when she went back to her room.

CHAPTER 29

Nora opened the door to their room minutes before curfew and found Cat standing just inside, tears streaming down her cheeks.

"Is it true?" Cat sobbed. Her hands were clenched at her sides, her hair a wild mane around her pale face, which was now blotchy with anger.

"Uh," Nora said, closing the door, trying to figure out what had gotten her meek little roommate into such a state.

The rest of their roommates were seated at the table behind Cat. Sophie was leaning back, arms crossed, lips pursed.

Sophie. She told.

"You *knew*—don't try to deny it! You and Sophie found that file and decided to keep it a secret from me! Didn't think poor little Cat could handle knowing the truth!" She stomped her foot. The lights overhead flickered briefly, and everybody jumped.

Privately, Nora was a little relieved for the interruption in Cat's tirade. She had initially feared Cat was confronting her about the headaches, and she wasn't at all sure her roommates should know about that. After all, Nora certainly didn't feel any better or safer for knowing. If anything, she felt much, much worse.

"Well that was weird," Zoe started to say. Cat glared at her.

"Don't you *dare* try to change the subject!"

"I'm not," Zoe said soothingly. "It's probably nothing."

"Well, you see, technically *I* found the file…" Sophie started. Nora shook her head in warning. Not a good time to argue.

"Cat, we were going to tell you—once we had a little more information," Nora said, trying her best to sound calm.

"You thought you would protect me?" Cat said, her tone climbing several octaves. "You thought you would look out for me instead of letting me decide what I can and cannot handle! Do you realize what you've done?"

Nora shook her head. Behind Cat, Sophie shrugged.

"You're doing the *same thing* they're doing! You're as bad as they are!" She threw her hands in the air. Nora bit her lip.

"That's not—"

"Oh yes it is! They give us this curfew, they compartmentalize the tasks so no one knows we're not going to fix the port at all, that they've built a whole new kind of way to get off the Current, and..."

"Wait, wait," Raina said. She came over and wrapped her arms around Cat's shoulders. Cat stopped yelling and just started sobbing. Raina turned Cat and held her, rubbing her back, whispering reassurances until she calmed down. After a minute, Raina took her to her bunk and lay down with her.

"Did...everyone else hear Cat say there's *another way* to get off the Current?" Sophie said after a minute. They all exchanged worried glances. Nora swallowed hard.

Cat was right. Nora should have told her about her handlers' potential murder. She had a right to know. But was it really so wrong to keep the P2 a secret? Did that make her part of the station's conspiracy? She was following station orders, and violating them could have gotten her into serious trouble. The P2 was a prototype, a gamble. As much as she didn't particularly like the admiral, she couldn't fault his reasoning for wanting to keep this quiet. She didn't want to worry her roommates, despite what Cat had said about doing just that.

Nora sighed and pinched the bridge of her nose. Somehow that spot ached horribly – she hadn't known she could actually wear out the muscles of her forehead from frowning so much. This was all becoming so exhausting.

"Yeah," she said, shaking her head. "Is that what they've got her working on down in the lab?"

"Like you don't know everything about this, little miss 'top secret training sessions'?" Sophie said, glaring. Nora frowned again, her forehead aching.

"Hey guys," Zoe said, trying to break the tension, her perfect teeth very white against her dark skin as she smiled. "You could say, the *cat's out of the bag* with this, right? Am I right? Because Cat said it?"

"You're awful," Raina said from the bunk, but she was smiling a little, too.

"That's why you love me," Zoe said, crowding into the bunk with Cat and Raina. Raina pulled a blanket over Cat, who was lying motionless and staring at nothing now.

"Nora?" Sophie said. "I'm not letting this go. You know something."

"I don't know anything you don't," Nora snapped. "I told you. We're fixing up the *Rap* so we can go asteroid hunting with the rest of the fleet. We need the extra material to rebuild."

"I thought we were friends," Sophie said. She went to Cat's bunk and sat on the edge, taking up what little space was left. They all looked at Nora, and for the first time, she felt like an outsider there, like she was the bad guy.

It sucked.

"You chose this, Nora," Sophie said, crossing her arms.

Something inside Nora snapped, like a wire under too much tension that broke free and caught her with a slap across the face.

"Yes, I chose this!" Nora screamed. "I chose this, and I would choose it again! Because this is who I am. I'm not Thalia. I'm not Hypatia. I'm Nora, and I'm a pilot, a damn good one. But I'm also your friend. And if there's something I'm not telling you, I'd hope you'd trust me enough to believe me when I say I know what I'm doing."

The room was silent.

She wanted to try the door, but curfew had passed and it was locked, so she kicked it instead and went to her bunk. She thought back to all the times she'd been mocked at school back on Earth—the whispered

Alien-oras, the stares, the giggles when she caught them staring. This was way worse. She couldn't put her finger on it at first. Why did this hurt so much more? But then she realized it was because she cared so deeply for her roommates. They were the first real friends she'd had.

She drew the curtain and curled up in a ball. She could hear them whispering at the other end of the room but couldn't make out what they were saying. But she knew it was about her.

The next day, she got up earlier than her roommates—she wanted to avoid any awkward encounters—and scurried off to the landing dome. Her eyelids felt abnormally puffy, and she rubbed them with one hand as she turned a corner, running smack into another cadet.

"Oh, sorry!"

"No problem," Greg mumbled and pushed past her.

"Greg!" she called. He stopped but didn't turn around.

"Greg, come on. What's going on with you?" This was seriously the last thing she needed right now. Was everyone on this station mad at her today?

"What's going on with *me?*" he said, whirling, the words coming out in a torrent. "*I'm* not the one throwing myself at Sebastian Benoit."

"I am not," she said, lowering her voice to a whisper as a group of cadets passed and gave them curious stares. "I am *not* throwing myself at him. In case you didn't notice, we'd had a pretty rough few days. He's my captain. And my friend."

"Yeah, you *looked* pretty friendly," Greg said, stuffing his hands into his pockets.

"Greg," she tried again.

"No," he said. He put a hand up to stop her from saying anything more. "You know what? I don't care. It's not like I had any claim on you. Just don't come crawling back to me when he throws you off like everyone else—like Thalia and Olivia and the rest. That man's an emotional ice cube."

"But I..."

And he left, stalking down the hall. Nora furiously blinked back tears for the second time in the past twenty-four hours. How had she managed to offend almost everyone she cared about in such a short span?

Sniffling once, she then squared her shoulders, and headed to work.

Nora was about to run back to the landing dome from the room; she'd only come back to change her pants, upon which Thalia had "accidentally" dumped a container of grease. Cat was the only other one in the room. Her fingers were flying furiously over her tablet, cups of coffee and papers strewn across the table in front of her. She looked paler than usual, more frail, and didn't even acknowledge Nora at first.

But then she looked up. Nora suspected she actually *hadn't* heard or seen her enter the room, so engrossed was she in her task.

"Hey, Nora," she said.

Two words were enough. It broke the icy tension.

"Hey, Cat," Nora said, smiling. She sat next to her, eyeing the papers she'd amassed. "That's a lot."

"Yeah, but I'm getting pretty close to having it figured out. We really may be able to fix the port at Terra Prime from long distance."

"That's amazing, Cat. But look, about last night." Nora paused; it felt like a rubber band was squeezing her heart.

"I don't want to fight," Cat said. "It feels wrong. I don't like it."

"I don't like it either," Nora said. Tension left her body like a burst water balloon. "And I'm sorry I kept that from you. I…may have found out something else, something about clones, and I wanted to tell you, but you were just so mad at me."

"Just tell me," Cat said, pushing her tablet away. "No more secrets."

"Cat…when I went down to the Medical Bay to get my stitches out," Nora started, the words coming out haltingly. Cat nodded.

"While I was down there, they brought in Bati. He was having a seizure or something. I know this guy who works down there—Wesley. Do you remember him from the Halloween party? Well, he said they've been keeping an eye on Bati for a while, and that…something didn't go right during the cloning process. That it can happen to any of the clones, and they've been keeping an eye on the ones they're worried about. He didn't get into specifics, but it seems bad."

"I haven't seen Bati in days," Cat whispered, then her eyes widened in realization. "Are they…like my headaches?" Nora nodded after a second.

"I didn't mean to pry. It just kind of came up. But he told me they think your headaches are just headaches. He said they're going to keep an eye on you. If anything seems off while I'm gone—any change in your headaches, anything strange—go down to Medical and ask for Wesley Solomon, okay? He'll know what to do."

Cat was silent for a long moment. The lights in the room flickered again.

"Zoe thought that there might be something scrambled in my genetic makeup," she said at last. "I heard a rumor about some of the upper-level Faxes, some of them having nervous breakdowns. I wondered if that was the station's way of covering up the glitches in their clones…"

"Cat, you're going to be fine," Nora said, putting her hand on the younger girl's shoulder. "We all are."

Cat reached down then, picking something up from her bag.

"I was going to give these to you last night, but you and Sophie made me too mad," she said, handing Nora a small piece of crumpled paper. Inside was a pair of small stud earrings in some kind of grayish metal, made to look like a dainty cluster of stars.

"I used my printing allowance this month to make them for all of us, so they're really small," Cat said. Nora immediately put them on, turning her head so Cat could admire her handiwork.

"They're an alloy, just some metal we pulled from the last batch of asteroids. I just thought that, since you're going away and we're staying here," she mumbled, "it might be nice if we all had something that made us think of each other." Her pale cheeks flushed with pink as she pulled back her frizzy hair to show Nora her own matching pair.

"Thank you," Nora said, hugging her. She still felt a little guilty that she couldn't tell her about the P2, under penalty of whatever torture

Savaryn could come up with. She decided it was less of a "secret" and more of a "classified" sort of thing, though it still rankled her.

But what Aditi had told her?

That one was definitely a secret.

━━ ━━ ━━

That night, when Nora made it back to the room just before curfew, Cat, Zoe, and Raina were already in bed. Cat and Raina were reading. Zoe was tossing a ball against the bottom of Raina's bunk. But Sophie was conspicuously absent.

Zoe threw her the ball, which Nora caught and tossed back. At least her other roommates seemed to have forgiven her.

"Where's Sophie?" Nora said.

She glanced at the clock. Seconds passed, and so did the curfew time.

"Anyone know what the consequence is for breaking curfew?" Zoe said. She tossed Nora the ball again.

"Detention for a month," Cat said, flipping through pages on her screen.

The door opened.

The lock had never engaged.

"Only if you get caught, dear," Sophie said, closing the door behind her. She had a large brown bag in her arms.

"How did you…?" Nora asked.

"Puh-lease. Hacked that bit of code in about ten seconds. Sometimes the largest barriers are the ones in your mind." She tapped Zoe on the forehead as she passed.

"When were you going to let us know?" Zoe whined, chucking the ball at Sophie. She dodged, and the ball bounced harmlessly against the window behind her.

"When it became relevant. Like, for example, now—after a late-night raid on the ice cream freezer."

She pulled out several white pint containers, each with the vegan-friendly frozen dessert that passed for ice cream on Ganymede. Milk was hardly reasonable to import, but somehow, frozen almond milk, plenty of sugar, and fruit from the greenhouse combined to make a delicious frozen treat.

"I figure since Nora's leaving tomorrow, we deserve a bit of celebration, yeah?" she said, handing out spoons. The girls thawed somewhat as they dove into the ice cream, swapping pints to try the different flavors.

"Sophie, you are my favorite little kleptomaniac, you know that?" Zoe said around a spoonful of raspberry.

"I know," Sophie said with a self-satisfied little grin. "Consider it a peace offering. I want us all to be friends. No secrets. No bad blood. Agreed?"

"Agreed!" they cheered. Nora—despite the onset of brain freeze—was beginning to feel warmer on the inside than she had in days.

"You know something, don't you?" Nora accused. Sophie's spoon paused halfway to her mouth.

"Look," Sophie said, dropping her spoon with a sigh. "You're right. I know you're not going on the asteroid hunt with the rest of the fleet. I don't know why, but I trust you have a pretty good reason for keeping it from us. I just wanted you to know that I support you, and I know you have our backs, too."

"If this is some reverse-psychology babble, it's pretty sophisticated. Even for you," Raina said, swiping Zoe's sherbet.

"Ugh, what is this supposed to be?" she said after a taste. Zoe grinned and started whistling, *Oh my darling Clementine.*

"Orange. It's ORANGE," Nora said, glaring at Zoe. "I want to tell you. I really do. But I promised. Something big is coming—maybe something really big. When I get back, things will be set into motion. I don't know all the details, but I promise, I'll tell you everything."

"You better," Zoe said, kicking Nora's chair. "I can't handle it when you and Sophie are fighting. Makes it feel like absolute zero degrees in here."

"You have to be careful, guys. Did…," Nora lowered her voice. "Did you all know the station is bugged?" Of all of them, only Sophie was unsurprised – in fact, she nodded emphatically, crossing her arms.

"I've got a program now that's got all the bugs in the station mapped out, or at least most of them, I think," Sophie said. "I'll send it to your tablets. There's about a thousand of the little bastards."

"I say that when Nora gets back, we knock 'em all out. Think you can write us a virus like that, Soph?" Raina asked.

"Just promise that you *will* come back," Cat said quietly. The girls paused. Nora put a hand on Cat's shoulder.

"I'll try," Nora said. She had every faith in Bastian—and as much as she hated to admit it, she had faith in Thalia's scientific brain, too.

"After Lara and Mike," Cat said, her face slack and eyes glassy, "I'm not sure I could handle anything else. I think I know what you're doing out there. I think I may have had a hand in the design. If anything happens to you…"

"Nothing is going to happen to her. Or to any of us," Sophie said firmly, her mouth set in a line.

"Faxes forever, right?" Cat said, smiling a little.

Nora nodded. "Forever."

"Forever," they chimed, clinking their ice cream spoons together.

CHAPTER 30

They prepared the bridge for takeoff. Bastian was at the pilot's console, Nora sitting next to him, and Soren had momentarily assumed the captain's chair. It was just like last time – only a million years seemed to have passed since then. There were dozens of other PJs being prepped in the same way—ones that were actually going to the asteroid fields. She patted the console affectionately – the *Rap* had really grown on her. She was really starting to get to know the ship, from the bolts in her new engines to the delicate electronics on the bridge, she was one really remarkable piece of machinery.

"Okay, Cadet," Bastian said, pushing his chair back from the console. He gestured her towards the controls. "Take her out."

"*What?*" Nora squeaked. Everyone on the Bridge—including Thalia and three of her scientists—turned to look at her. Bastian gave her a patient smile.

"Just like we practiced. We'll take off last, so there'll be less chance of you hitting anything."

"Like with the Rover?" Thalia commented. Bastian shot her a glare.

"If you aren't going to help, Thalia, you are more than welcome to spend takeoff confined to the cargo bay."

She crossed her arms but shut up.

"Bastian," Nora whispered, adrenaline surging through her system. Taking off had *not* been part of their plan. "I really don't think now is the time to…"

"Here," Bastian said. He handed her a pair of what looked like small foam earplugs and a small metal square that fit easily within the palm of her hand. Nora looked up at him, confused.

"Earphones," he said. She put them in, and he pressed a button on top of the metal square. Immediately, the soothing sounds of Beethoven's *Moonlight Sonata* trickled into her ears. How particularly appropriate, she thought, grinning. It wasn't loud enough to block out his voice, but it was *just* loud enough to drown out her own racing heartbeat with the slow, melodic triplets. She felt her pulse conforming to the music, and her panic, abating.

"How did you...?" she asked. "I thought we couldn't download anything from Earth." She'd tried. Even Sophie hadn't been able to hack the barrier keeping them from downloading—or uploading—anything from Earth's Internet.

"That's my secret," he said. "There are some advantages to being me, even without a big Fax brain," he said, with a little smile. "Besides, I remember how nervous I was before my first takeoff. Jazz always calms me, but I thought you'd do better with the classics. You can do this. I didn't tell you about this before because I didn't want you having time to panic."

"Too late," she mumbled but moved into position in front of the console.

She took a deep breath. He'd already done most of the flight prep, the checklist all but completed. And over the next fifteen minutes, he made sure the other systems were ready to go, too. Classical music drifted into Nora's ears as she prepared, the songs as familiar to her as her own name. She caught herself smiling as the tracks changed, each time recognizing the new piece. Bastian knew her well—that was abundantly clear. She checked her pulse, placing two fingers over one wrist, feeling the slow, steady beat in time with the song. Sixty beats a minute, as steady as a metronome.

When they were the last PJ remaining, Bastian gave her a nod.

"Time to go," he said.

All she had to do was fire up the boosters and fly straight from the hangar.

She licked her lips and took the controls with trembling hands. She pushed the ignition switch. The shuttle lifted jerkily a few meters, and she retracted the landing gear. She took a deep breath and moved the controls forward. The ship lurched a little, jumping forward, and she pulled back, slowing them to a crawl.

"Easy," he said. He moved his chair in beside her and reached his right hand over hers on the controls, his grip warm and steadying, though a thrill seemed to shoot up her arm at the contact. The ship moved smoothly now, and as she became more confident, his grip on hers gradually loosened. She didn't even realize when it had gone completely - and then she was actually doing it—actually *taking off*—on her own.

"That's it," he coached. The ship breached the dome, and she pulled back to turn into a graceful upward arc, away from Ganymede.

It was glorious, made even more so by the loud sigh of discontentment she heard from Thalia behind her.

"Well done," Bastian said. He put an encouraging hand on her shoulder for a moment, then stood and took the captain's chair back from Soren.

"Steady, Cadet," he said. "Are you ready to engage the hyperspace engines?"

"Ready, Captain." She'd done this part at least a hundred times this week; there wasn't much to it. She just had to bring the engines online, make sure the shields were up. The start-up calculations she'd done a thousand times over, and were already plugged into the navigation.

"Whenever you're ready," Bastian said. He was leaning forward in his chair, carefully watching her motions over the console. Soren had come to stand behind her, but so far, she hadn't made any corrections.

"Jumping in three...two...one...," she said, and initiated the second set of engines.

Pop!

The engines were purring like contented little kittens. Outside the view screen, streaks of white passed, but otherwise the ship was still and silent. Nora grinned widely – she was doing it!

"Thalia, upload your coordinates to Asher," Bastian said.

Thalia didn't take well to orders. Nora was tempted to look to see if she was upset, but she didn't dare take her eyes off the console. After some time, Thalia's equations were uploaded, and Asher had made the necessary adjustments, setting the final course – the calculations flashed across her own computer screen. Nora directed the ship to their destination, and after about three days at this speed, according to the computer, they'd arrive.

"All right, everybody," Bastian said. Everyone swiveled toward him. He stood behind the captain's seat, his hand resting on the back, and under the gleam of the overhead lights, he looked every inch a captain: calm, collected, in control.

"You all know how important this mission is. I do not have to remind you how critical it is that we continue to function as a team," he said, subtly glancing at Thalia, who stood with her arms crossed. "If we pull this off, not only will we have retrieved valuable information on the Qaig situation at Terra Prime, but also we will have become the first ship ever to employ the P2. We have three days to get ready. Are there any questions?"

No one spoke, but Soren nodded approvingly.

"For this flight, Soren will be acting engineer. Any questions regarding the new sublum, you go to her. If anything else comes up—any concern, I do not care how small or unimportant you think it may be—please know that my door is always open. Now, all right," he said, clasping his hands together, "let's have a good flight."

The activity on the bridge soon reminded Nora of a beehive, the subtle hum of motion and murmured conversation a reflection of the crew's industriousness. Thalia and her scientists—two Faxes and one J'nai—monitored the P2 engines and continued running their simulations and safety checks.

At one point, Thalia came over to the pilot's console and had Nora run a few programs she'd installed that would link hers and Asher's consoles—navigation and steering—with the P2. Usually, they could count on the ancient J'nai Star Port technology to get them out of hyperspace; now, Thalia and her crew had to modify what they knew of the two-kilometer-wide Star Ports and package it into something the size of a Smart Car.

The J'nai in her crew was reportedly a leader in astrophysics. He was an emaciated-looking gray-skinned man who kept his white hair shaved—or maybe he just didn't have any hair. His name was Daven, and he almost never bothered to look up from his tablet, where his bony fingers played a constant staccato piece against the touch screen. He also almost never spoke, either, and that wasn't because he had nothing to say; he just deemed most interaction unnecessary. Which, Nora figured, was probably how he managed to tolerate Thalia.

The other two were Faxes named Sun, a clone of a Chinese physicist, and Harris, an Edwin Hubble. Sun was pretty much the same as Thalia, as far as personality went, but at least Harris was friendly enough—if awkward.

"Okay," Thalia said, hovering over Nora's console. "That should about do it. I'm going to head down to engineering to continue running diagnostics. If you see any of those alerts go off"—she pointed to the new icons on the console—"would you let me know over comms?"

"Sure," Nora said. Thalia nodded and left the bridge, her crew following like ducklings.

After a few hours, the icons started flashing.

"Uh, Thalia? Got an alert," Nora said, pressing the comms button that would broadcast down to engineering. A second later, the speaker at her console crackled to life.

"Got it. Damn PPU connections. Is it still on?"

"No, looks like whatever you did fixed the problem," Nora said.

"All right," Thalia's voice said. "Let me know if anything else changes."

That minor blip was the only hiccup on that first day. After several hours, Bastian sent her to get some rest while he took over the console for a while. And she was grateful for it; her neck hurt something fierce from the tension of hovering over the console all day, desperate not to screw anything up. She shot Bastian a smile and left the Bridge, rolling her shoulders as she left.

She headed to the kitchen and found Thalia, Sun, and Harris making coffee and discussing the P2—though "discussing" may have been too polite a term. They were arguing, and loudly. Thalia and Sun seemed to think there was a better way to route something called a hyperspace inertia regulator, and Harris was of the opinion that doing so would blow them all to smithereens.

Nora swiped a protein bar and tried to escape before they noticed her.

No such luck.

"Nora, wait up," Thalia said. She chased her down the hall, then turned to yell at her lab mates. "I'm not finished with you, Harris. You show me some data to back up that stupid idea and then we can talk."

"But anyhow," Thalia said, turning her attention back to Nora.

"Anyhow," Nora said.

They set off walking in silence for a moment, Thalia following Nora to the cargo bay where their cots where laid out. The crew had had to get creative to accommodate the extra personnel on board – which meant the female staff got to sleep in the cargo bay. Only Soren – like Silas before her – preferred a hammock in the engine room.

Nora didn't know what was going on and felt uncomfortable with Thalia, more so now that they were alone. She couldn't make herself uncross her arms from in front of her chest—it was all the protection she could get. She made sure Thalia didn't get between her and door, like she'd heard you should do when in a cage with a wild animal.

"Look, I know we got off to a bad start," Thalia said, running a hand through her hair. It stuck up like a lion's mane. Nora swallowed.

"Uh," Nora said. She cocked her head to the side. Wasn't *that* the understatement of the year?

"I'm not an easy person to be around," Thalia continued, sitting on her cot and motioning for Nora to sit next to her. Nora stood her ground, arms still crossed.

"I'm not going to disagree with you," she said.

"You know, I had a friend back on Earth," Thalia said. "When she turned twelve, her parents adopted a baby boy. She'd been an only child, and then that baby started getting all the attention her parents had once given her. She began acting out, sneaking out to parties, smoking—you know, all kinds of things."

Thalia leaned back on her hands.

"I think that's kind of how I felt when you came along. I was used to being the best," she said, and something like an apologetic smile crossed her usually downturned mouth.

"You *are* the best," Nora said. "I didn't understand any of what you and Harris were talking about."

"I know," Thalia said, beaming. "That's what made me think maybe I don't hate you after all. You're not a threat. I mean, you're basically a glorified bus driver."

"Um, thanks?" Nora said. She shifted her weight to her other foot, and shook her head a little, like the comment was rattling around inside.

"I mean, you're not a threat in the science program. I hear you're becoming a decent pilot." She tossed her hair. "Bastian brags about you all the time."

Nora looked down at her hands and began picking at the cuticles. She tried to hide the blush that Thalia's comment brought to her face. She didn't like that Bastian and Thalia talked about her "all the time" – and she didn't like to think of them spending any time together, actually. She'd never been good at concealing emotions; her mom always said she was an open book.

"Anyway. I guess I wanted to say sorry." Thalia stood and put out her hand—nails a flawlessly polished black—and said the most astonishing thing Nora had ever heard (and she'd heard a lot of astonishing things in the past few months).

"Can we be friends?"

Nora's jaw came unhinged and hung there, open in disbelief. Was she for real? Being uncomfortable around Thalia had always made her feel a little off, like she was uncomfortable with a part of herself, something she couldn't understand. Besides, it would be nice to have Thalia's acerbic nature allied with her rather than working against her, for a change. Stunned, she took Thalia's hand, her own slightly clammy in Thalia's firm grip.

"I'd like that," she said eventually, mind still reeling.

"Good. Now that we're friends, I need a favor."

Nora sighed. She tried really hard not to roll her eyes. Of course Thalia was up to something.

"Yes?" Nora said, irritated.

"Can I borrow your shampoo?"

"What?"

"I forgot mine back on the station. Would you mind? Working in the engine room all day has left my hair a mess," she said, twirling the blue strands around her fingers. Nora grinned, relieved.

"Is that all?" she said. She went to her locker and tossed Thalia the bottle.

"That's it," Thalia said, giving her a thumbs-up. "And thanks."

"No problem," Nora said. Thalia grabbed her towel and headed back up the stairs to the head, whistling as she went. Nora watched her go, then sat heavily on her bunk, her mind still spinning.

Thalia was actually being nice to her. Was it true, maybe, what she had said about being threatened by Nora? Could they actually become friends, these two Hypatias who were yet so different? Thalia was as Type A as they came, but since Nora wasn't in her way anymore, maybe, just maybe…

CHAPTER 31

She made her way back to the Bridge for her next shift—it was nearly 2:00 p.m.—and found Soren in the captain's chair with Thalia and Asher running scenarios on the pilot's console where Bastian usually sat.

Thalia's hair was a mass of black and blue curls—a cloud around her head, shot through with cobalt and teal lightning—that seemed to defy gravity. Nora had a lifetime of tricks up her sleeve from the constant battle that was curl maintenance. Thalia, it seemed, had no such luck. She struggled to conceal the snorting laugh that threatened to escape her.

"Hi guys," Nora said, slipping up beside them, pointedly not looking at Thalia. "Nice hair."

"Yeah, I forgot your primitive little Puddlejumpers don't have modern conveniences like hair dryers," Thalia said, running a hand through her hair, which just made it stand up more. "I don't know how you manage to keep it under control. It has a mind of its own."

"Practice," Nora said, grinning. "Maybe I can show you a few things later."

Thalia actually smiled at her. It was almost like looking in a mirror.

Nora was starting to wonder what alternate universe she'd been sucked into.

"Ladies, if we are done discussing hair products, can we please get back to the topic of *trying not to die*?" Asher said. "I don't know if you both are aware but the fate of *both* of our worlds are probably at stake here."

"Yeah, yeah, stop being dramatic," Thalia said and reached over his shoulder to grab her tablet. "All I'm saying is that we probably need to extend our hyperspace travel by a few nanoseconds, and…"

She and Asher went back to the nav console, still talking. Nora sat at her own station and took over the flight management from Soren. Despite his flare for the dramatic, Asher wasn't exactly wrong. A shiver ran down her spine at the thought, and she started focusing on the task in front of her, as busy as the bees back in the greenhouse.

It was another long day on the Bridge. Eventually, Bastian came to relieve Soren, and Nora let him go over her course adjustments for the day. He didn't find anything to correct, which made her nearly giddy. Thalia came up and joined her later, taking the side chair Nora usually sat in when Bastian was flying.

"So," Thalia said, crossing her arms behind her head, her fingers sinking into several inches of unruly curl. "You were talking about controlling this mess."

"I do know your hair pretty well," Nora started, grinning, and they launched into a discussion on the finer aspects of hair care, including the best way to dry curly hair. The rest of the crew on the bridge collectively sighed and rolled their eyes.

"Oh, you don't *ever* want to brush it," Nora said, shaking her head. Thalia threw her hands up in surrender.

"You think Hypatia ever cared about what her hair looked like?" Thalia asked. She put her feet up on the console, out of Nora's way, and leaned back in the chair.

"Well, we do," Nora said, pulling her feet up under her. "So I bet she did, too."

"Hey, I was wondering, do you have the same freckles as me? Like these five here that kinda look like…"

"The Cassiopeia constellation?" Nora finished for her with a grin, rolling back the sleeve on her flight suit to show Thalia the same cluster of dots. "Yep."

"Crazy," Thalia said, sitting back in her chair. They watched the white streaks outside the shuttle zip by, whole star systems passing them in less than the blink of an eye.

"So did you ever hear why there are only two of us?" Thalia asked after a moment. Nora shook her head. Honestly, she'd never thought about it – she'd just been grateful there hadn't been more people like Thalia running around, at least until lately.

"Not enough DNA. She was killed and then burned for being a heretic," Thalia said, sighing. "She was so far ahead of her time, and no one knew it. Anyway, someone saved a fingernail, I heard—like the relics they used to keep from saints."

"We come from a fingernail?" Nora said, and shivered. "Gross."

"Totally," Thalia agreed. "Anyway, there was only enough for two clones: me and you."

"You really admire her, don't you?" Nora said. Thalia nodded. "Don't you?"

"I don't know as much about her as you do," Nora confessed. "Just what I could find on the intraweb. I'm guessing that's why you have an astrolabe tattoo."

Thalia looked down at her forearm, at the golf ball–sized round mark with a second circle and a series of divisions inside it.

"That one was for Hypatia," Thalia agreed. As usual, she had her flight suit peeled down to her waist, the arms tied at her hips, and wore a tight tank that revealed her many tattoos. Nora had always wanted to ask about them, and now it seemed their new friendship would give her that chance.

"What about that one?" Nora said, nodding to a line of strange marks down the length of her other arm.

"Vulcan. *Live long and prosper.*" She leaned forward and pulled her hair up, revealing another round tattoo at the base of her neck. This one, like the others, was sketched in simple, graceful black lines.

"This is in circular Gallifreyan. This one," she said, lifting her shirt to reveal more tattoos around her ribcage, "is in Elvish."

"What do they say?"

"Always bring a banana to a party," Thalia said, grinning impishly, and looked down at the Elvish marks. "And this one says 'Home is behind, the World, ahead.'"

"And those?" Nora asked, pointing to one on her shoulder that looked like a chemical symbol.

"Dopamine," she said. "And this is a neuron." She was pointing to a spindly small one at the base of her thumb.

"Wow," Nora said. It must have taken hours to get all those done— long, painful hours. "Did you get them done on Earth?"

"There's a Leo who does tats on the station," Thalia said. "Can you imagine? Getting a tattoo from Leonardo da Vinci. What a crazy universe we live in."

She laughed, and Nora had to smile.

"What about that one? Is that for your lightning bike?" Nora asked, pointing to a circular tattoo on Thalia's shoulder that looked like a wheel from her bike. It practically glowed under the bridge lights. UV ink, maybe?

"Oh, you mean AGETHA?"

"You named your bike Agatha?" Nora asked. It seemed out of character for Thalia to give a name to an inanimate object.

"It stands for Anti-Gravity Elec-Tronic Hyperbolic Aerocycle," she said with a snort. "It's based off some of the J'nai tech. I hear some of the first years are making hover boards out of the stuff now."

Nora grinned, and Thalia offered to let her try it out when they got back. Nora hesitantly accepted.

"Come on, you're flying this crazy thing. AGETHA is just like riding a bike. Nothing to it."

Thalia stuck around for a bit longer, then said she'd been on break long enough and needed to get back to running equations.

"Well if you need another break, you know where to find me," Nora said, rubbing her eyes. She was starting to go cross-eyed from fatigue.

"Will do," Thalia called, waving over her shoulder as she left, pointedly ignoring their captain. Nora saw Bastian watch her leave the Bridge, then rubbed the back of his neck. It was just the two of them now.

"Why don't you go get some sleep, Nora," Bastian said, pulling the flight controls over to his console before she could protest.

"I'm fine," she said, frowning. *He* was the one who needed rest.

"Not a suggestion," he said, though he did give her that half smile. "Maybe I'm already asleep and dreaming—or was Thalia actually being nice to you?"

"Nothing like a crisis to bring people together," Nora said. She stood and stretched, reveling in the motion. It felt so good to stand after sitting so long. She rolled her shoulders and released her hair from its constraints, fluffing it out with her fingers. She turned and found Bastian watching her. After a second, he nodded his head, indicating that she should go.

"Don't stay up too late, Cap," she said as she left the bridge.

She was alone in the cargo bay. As exhausted as she was, she couldn't quite believe Thalia was still working. She must have some inner strength that Nora hadn't really seen before. Nora contemplated this as she got ready for bed. She couldn't have been in her cot more than two seconds before she was asleep.

Nora woke up early for her shift, and still no Thalia. Had she not gone to sleep? Sun, her Chien-Shiung Wu crewmate, was snoring softly, sprawled on her cot. Otherwise, the cargo bay was empty. Nora padded softly to the locker to grab a fresh flight suit and her shower supplies; the shampoo bottle was damp and slipped in her fingers. Thalia must have borrowed it again last night. She glanced back at Thalia's cot. It definitely didn't look like it had been disturbed at all since yesterday. She didn't make her cot, claiming she was just going to mess the sheets back up anyway, but the pillow was in the same place, halfway down the narrow mattress. In this way, Nora grinned, they were also alike.

Nora couldn't believe how rapidly her opinion of Thalia had changed. Despite her snarky attitude, Nora had come to realize how brilliant her clone was, how focused and determined. She was developing an admiration for her that she could have considered impossible just a day ago.

Nora yawned and made her way to the head for a quick shower, arms full of clothing and soap, nearly stumbling up the grated steps from the cargo bay. She nodded a mute good morning to a zombie-like Donovan as he passed on his way to the kitchen. Her tongue felt thick and tacky in her mouth, a result of the dry, recycled air. She licked her lips, trying to get some moisture into them. She was just turning the handle to the head when a soft creaking noise made her turn.

The head was just down the hall from the captain's quarters on the *Rapscallion*. She half expected to see Bastian coming out of his room. He rarely seemed to sleep anymore. She was glad that he'd been able to take a break for a few hours.

But it was Thalia emerging from the room, instead. Her hair was a mess of curls, her flight suit wrinkled. She caught Nora's eye and gave her a smirk and a wink before stretching, and passing a slack-jawed Donovan as she walked, humming, toward the cargo bay.

Nora nearly dropped her shampoo. A thousand thoughts went flying through her sleepy brain: Thalia not coming back to her bed last night. Thalia with messy hair sneaking out of Bastian's room at four o'clock in the morning. That self-satisfied look on her face.

Nora changed her mind in a flash. Thalia was nothing but trouble. What had all that friendly talk been about yesterday? Nora groaned. It had to have been for Bastian's benefit. Thalia must have known he'd be watching them on the Bridge, and she showed him she could be friendly with his little assistant. It was as though she were screaming, *See Bastian, I've changed.* And Bastian—Nora had thought better of him. It was immensely disappointing that, after all his protestations avowing that he and Thalia were through, that he couldn't even tolerate her anymore, it was all nothing more than a farce. But to what end?

Nora slammed the door open to the head and started up the shower. The cold water took her mind off the shock of seeing Thalia and numbed her skin until she could think of nothing else but the bitter cold.

A few minutes later, her wet hair back in a bun, a steaming cup of coffee in hand to ward off pneumonia after her frigid rinse, Nora made her way to the Bridge.

Bastian was there, watching over the pilot's console from the captain's chair.

She mumbled something that roughly sounded like "hey" and slid into her seat. The green button flashed to let her know he'd returned control of the flight to her console, and she started to work. She wasn't sure what she wanted to say to him. Maybe: "Good morning, Captain. You're looking particularly tired this morning. What's the matter, didn't sleep well? I wonder what might have kept you up all night?"

Donovan shot her a look when he came on deck, glancing at Bastian and then back to her, before settling himself at his workstation.

The entire day was intensely awkward. Bastian—despite whatever had transpired last night—was in a black mood. His dark brows remained furrowed all day, as if carved into stone. There was a phrase Soren had used at one point: a heavy burden leaves a mark. It seemed an appropriate J'nai aphorism for Bastian's mood today. He seemed in control, as always, but with an edge, a darkness that made her chest ache every time she looked at him.

At one point, Thalia and her crew came up to the Bridge to discuss the P2—most of their computers and such were in the engine room, which had kept them thankfully away most of the time—and Bastian had been curt, bordering on rude with them all, especially Thalia. It was a startling contrast from his typical, disciplined professionalism. Nora didn't know what to make of it. Even Asher and Soren were unusually subdued. She caught Donovan whispering to Asher around noon, then caught them both sneaking glances at Bastian. She tried to ignore it. Donovan wasn't the subtlest of people. She had no doubt that, by now, the entire ship knew what he and Nora had seen that morning.

Nora spent hours flipping between the flight manuals on her tablet and the numbers on her console. Soren watched, correcting her when necessary. Nora was thankful for something—anything—to occupy her mind, to distract it from what she'd seen that morning, and from the uncertainty of what lay ahead in their mission.

CHAPTER 32

It was late into the evening when Soren finally made her leave the Bridge to get some rest. Nora stretched, surprised again at how stiff her back was, and made her way to the kitchen. She grabbed a protein bar and some juice and stood pacing the little room. She couldn't bear to sit down, not after having her butt plastered to that chair again all day.

She tossed the wrapper in the trash, rinsed out her mug, and set it back on the cabinet shelf. She was just leaving the kitchen when she nearly ran into Bastian, who was storming down the hall.

"Sorry," she mumbled, stepping back. He'd nearly run her over. She didn't know what else to say to him. The vision of Thalia coming out of his room flashed through her mind, and she couldn't help cringing a little.

"Come here," he said. He took her arm—not roughly, but it surprised her anyway—and dragged her down the hall. They stopped about midway between the Bridge and the engine room, near the head and the Captain's room. If he had something to say, this was as good a place as any to avoid being overheard.

"What?" Nora said, snatching her arm away. He ran a hand through his hair. His eyes were ringed with darkness, the usual glitter in their gray-blue depths now flat with fatigue. His uniform, usually immaculate, was unbuttoned, the sleeves rolled back to his elbows.

"There's a rumor going around that…" he stopped. Donovan was clumping down the hall toward his bunk. He shot them a curious glance, pushing his thick glasses back up on his nose, before continuing on his way. Bastian waited until the man was out of ear-shot to continue.

"Look, I need to tell you…" he tried again. This time it was Thalia's crew that interrupted him, making their way up from the engine room to the kitchen, arguing loudly. Bastian rolled his eyes.

"*Mon Dieu…*" he said. He took Nora by the arm again and pulled her into his room, locking the door behind him.

She'd never seen the captain's quarters before. It was nothing special—just a small bed, a desk, a lamp—unique only in its privacy. The bed was neatly made, every bit of paper, each little mechanical device—for charting and calculating their trip—in order. Its stark orderliness—a reflection of the usually collected man who was now barely holding himself together—reminded her sharply of the first time she'd met him, when she'd bumbled into his room looking for the jazz music.

"Bastian, what's going on? Are you all right?" She tried to put a hand on his arm, but he pulled away, pacing the room. He was as agitated as she'd ever seen him, although at least this time it didn't seem to be directed at her.

"Thalia came into my room last night," he blurted. He stood staring at her, his hands hanging loose at his sides. Nora nodded.

"I know," she said, slowly. He let out a sigh. He looked deflated, like the rest of the air and strength in him went out with the sigh.

"Donovan told you?"

"No, I…kind of saw her coming out this morning," she said. Her face heated up at the memory. She'd been intruding on a private moment, and it left her insides feeling squirmy and uncomfortable. She didn't like it.

He started to talk, then turned and took a few steps, then turned and came back. He took a deep breath.

"It's not what you think," he said at last. Nora shrugged. She wanted out of that room, wanted to escape the tension and awkwardness, wanted to be far away from whatever explosion was lurking under his barely maintained façade of control.

"It's really none of my business," she said. She met his eyes briefly, then looked away, at the desk, at the little shaded lamp, at anything. He sighed again.

"You know Thalia and I...we were together for a while, yes?" he said. Nora nodded. There was a sort of oriental-scrolling pattern around the lampshade, in gold and green.

"At first I thought it was great, you know, she was great. She is witty and smart and driven and so, so fierce."

She had no idea where he was going with this, and she certainly didn't like to hear him compliment Thalia. She crossed her arms, rubbing her hands on them to calm the goose bumps that were starting to appear.

"After a while, those things just couldn't make up for the fact that she's also obsessive, jealous, and can be entirely cruel." He shook his head.

"I know Donovan—and probably Thalia—have been spreading a rumor that we...were together last night. That we are getting back together," he said, fumbling. Nora glanced at the door, then back at him. She wondered if he would stop her if she tried to leave.

"That's nice," she offered into the silence. He looked up, suddenly focused. A quiver of adrenaline sneaked up her spine like a slowly twisting knife.

"No, it's not," he said. His voice was clipped, harsh. "I was asleep last night. God, I must have been nearly comatose. And the lights were off when she came in."

"Bastian, really, you don't owe me an explanation. I get it," Nora said, trying to be comforting. And she really didn't want to hear any details about, well, anything. Her cheeks felt warm, then hot. "You've been under a lot of pressure, and I know you haven't been sleeping. So really, you don't have justify how you unwind to me. It's none of my business."

"I thought she was you," he blurted.

Nora stared at him, stunned, for a long time. Her throat felt constricted, her chest, tight. She couldn't have said anything even if her brain could have put the words together.

He finally broke eye contact and looked away, out the small port window above his bunk. She felt a slow creep of heat up her neck; it was anger toward Thalia and confusion about what Bastian was saying. And maybe something else, too. Something she couldn't put her finger on. Something tingly, that warmed her all the way through, that melted through all the coldness she'd been harboring moments before.

"I'm sorry," he said, still facing the window. "Like I said, I was asleep, and it was dark. She just crawled in beside me. She said she *was* you, said it with your voice. She had her hair down like yours. God, she even smelled like you."

"*What?*" Nora said. The word came out squeaky, several octaves above her normal range.

"Your hair, I mean," he said sheepishly, turning toward her.

"What about my hair?" She reached for the wayward curls that had already escaped her attempt to tame them in a bun. Her scalp wound still ached when her hair pulled on it too tight, so she'd taken to just lightly tying it back—which resulted in a number of escapee strands.

"It just…it is nice. You use a different shampoo than she does, or something," he mumbled, looking at the floor.

"She borrowed my shampoo last night," Nora said. She could kick herself for believing Thalia's stupid little deception. How could she have been so gullible? In what universe would Thalia ever have really wanted to be her friend? Bastian turned back to the window.

"I'm so sorry," he repeated. The sound barely reached her ears. Nora couldn't ever remember hearing him apologize—for anything—before, let alone twice. "She just…it was so nice, holding her. Comforting I guess. After everything that has happened, it just felt…" He trailed off and took a deep breath.

"The first time I met you, it was like I saw a ghost. I thought I knew what you were going to be like, another Hypatia, another thorn in my side. But all things that drove me crazy about Thalia—I realized last night that you are the opposite. Warm where she is cold, kind where she is cruel. Supportive where she is jealous."

Nora stumbled back until she was against the cool metal of the door. The cold was bracing, somehow. She closed her eyes. She didn't want to hear any more.

He let out a shuddering breath.

"And then she kissed me," he said. Nora's eyes flew open.

"And that's when I knew it was her," he said, and the words came out in a rush. "We fought, and eventually she left. I just... God, Nora, this is such a mess. I just wanted you to hear it from me, before she got to you, before she tried to cause even more drama on this damn mission."

Nora swallowed hard. He was looking at her with those beautiful blue eyes, now ashamed and vulnerable. It was so unlike him, and it hurt to see it. It pierced her sternum and left her stomach feeling like she'd been punched. She could strangle Thalia for what she was doing to him.

"It is kind of ironic," he said, shaking his head. "She's been jealous of the time you and I have spent together. She would never understand how we operate, that you and I have a good working relationship, that we are a team. She just sees attention and misinterpreted it as...well," he said, pausing for a moment. "Maybe her effort to get my attention just made me realize how much I admire the things about you that are nothing like her at all."

"I don't suppose we could shoot her out the airlock?" Nora said, trying to relieve the tension with some black humor. She was rewarded with a flicker of his half smile. There were a dozen feet between them, but she felt like it could have been miles. So why was it suddenly so hard to breathe?

"I thought about it," he admitted, sitting on his bed, then standing back up. "I almost didn't tell you. I want you to be focused, to only have to think about flying. *We* need to be focused. This mission is too important for stunts like this."

"The mission comes first," she agreed. He nodded. The statement cleared her own head, firmed her own resolve, at least a little.

"Nora. I respect you. You've worked hard to get here, and you deserve to be here. You are a good pilot—you may be great someday. I did not think it would be possible when I first met you."

"You always have a backhanded way of giving compliments," she said absently, then felt her resolve bubble up. "I can handle this."

She would not let Thalia get to her, but she would never forgive her for trying to get to Bastian. She put her hands on the door at her back, feeling the cold trickle into her palms. She still felt claustrophobic, despite the distance between them.

"I know you can," he said.

"So," Nora said, trying to avoid his gaze. "What do we do now?"

"We go on. We do our jobs. And when we get back, I'll make sure Thalia can never hurt either of us again. She'll never leave the station again. I promise you."

"Okay," she said, licking her lips, which had suddenly gone bone dry. She wasn't sure she could blame it on the lack of humidity this time "But maybe you should rethink your open-door policy and start locking up at night. Just in case."

He smiled, and for a second it was like the sun was rising again. She suddenly felt warm, to-the-core warm, like she'd never be cold again as long as he looked at her like that. With a few steps, was at her side, his hand on the door, ready to open it for her, but not yet ready to let her go. He was an inch away from her; she could feel his breath, warm on her cheek. Here was this man—this incredible, unobtainable man—right before her. She could see the lines starting to form at the corners of his eyes, the strength of him. She could feel the warmth radiating from him like a sun. She suddenly wanted, desperately, more than anything in the universe, to be the girl he held in his arms at night, to bask in that warm glow. She took a deep breath and closed her eyes, willing her heart rate to normalize like it had when she'd first taken off in the *Rap* a few days ago. He said he respected her. Even admired her. But that was it.

Or was it?

Hadn't he just said how good it felt to have her—or someone he thought was her—sneaking into his room, snuggling up to him? Was that what you said about someone with whom you had a "good working relationship"?

"Nora..." he started. The softness of her name on his lips sent a shudder down her spine. She shook her head, keeping her eyes closed. She was on the verge of crying for some reason she couldn't name.

"Can we talk about this when we get back?" she said, looking up at him, into his stormy eyes. She was flooded with emotions she didn't understand, nearly drowning in them. "I'm just not sure I can keep my focus if you say anything else."

He nodded but reached out and—hesitantly—pushed a curl from her face. The tip of his finger brushed her cheek, ever so slightly, and she felt the trail it left on her skin even after his hand was gone, scorched into every single nerve ending.

"Please," she said, though the word barely made it passed her lips. She reached up, then stopped, uncertain, before reaching again, and put her hand on his chest. She pushed him back. Even through the uniform, she could feel his heartbeat, pounding. Her throat constricted. He stepped back, but put his own hands, warm and strong, over hers, keeping it pressed against him, for a long moment. She could feel her arm start shaking, and pulled her hand back when his grip loosened, hoping he hadn't noticed. He did not stop her. She wondered briefly if this would make him angry with her, but he just smiled, that radiant smile, and she felt herself thaw somewhat in return.

"Okay," he said. "We will get through this. And when we get back, when things have settled down, maybe we can talk again, yes?"

"Yes," she agreed. His rigid posture relaxed slightly, the tenseness in his jaw fading a little. Part of her yearned to comfort him—and yet part of her was dying to be comforted. The feeling left her torn, paralyzed. She tried to speak, and her voice cracked. She rubbed her palm on the side of her pants – it tingled where she had touched him, like a thousand little sparks. She bit her lip, took a deep breath, then tried again.

"Will you be okay?"

He paused.

"Good night, Eleanora," he said after a moment and opened the door for her. She walked out in a daze, not wanting to look back to see if he was watching. She didn't hear him shut the door until she was almost to the cargo bay.

She did hear him turn the lock, though, which brought a smile to her face.

It was hard to sleep. She was exhausted, but like a toddler who refused to nap, she was almost *too* tired to sleep. Thalia was sound asleep on her cot, like nothing in the world was wrong, like she hadn't just toyed with the emotions of the man in charge of getting them all through this mission safely, a mission that could be the fulcrum of the entire J'nai war.

She wished, more than she'd ever wished for anything, that Sophie were here, that she could talk to her. She'd know exactly how to handle this situation, how to put Thalia in her place, how to talk to Bastian without sounding like an idiot. She wished she could kick Thalia down the entire length of the ship like Zoe would.

And she missed Greg. She missed his laugh and his ease, how comfortable it was to talk to him. She never felt tongue tied around him, not like with Bastian. So what did that mean? Did it mean what she felt for Greg wasn't real? Being with Greg had made her feel warm, like sitting in front of a roaring fire when it was cold outside. Comfortable, secure. She missed him with a dull, fierce ache that lodged in her throat.

But being with Bastian?

It was like staring into a supernova. It was witnessing something nearly beyond human comprehension and knowing she might just get blinded or consumed or vaporized in the process—and not even caring.

If she was honest with herself, she'd basically been one of Bastian's fawning fan girls from day one. But she always knew he was unobtainable. It was like having a crush on a movie star. He was something to think pleasantly about, but from the safety of knowing nothing would ever come of it.

She flipped onto her stomach and buried her face in the thin pillow. She was worried she was about to soak it in tears. He admired her. He respected her. That knowledge did bring a certain warmth to her soul. He was a hard man to impress; she still blushed when she thought about some of their early encounters, when he'd been so utterly disappointed in her.

She was half glad his door was locked tonight. It would keep both Hypatias at bay. A small, previously quiet part of her mind was screaming at her to go back to his room, to be the girl who...

She sighed, flopping back over, staring at the rivets in the ceiling. Her face felt hot, and her nose was running. She sniffled.

"Give it a rest, cadet, you're keeping me up," Sun grumbled. Nora hugged her blanket to her chest as she curled into a ball.

Please, don't cry, she thought. She couldn't bear Thalia, two beds over, hearing her cry and knowing she was the reason. She didn't want to give her that satisfaction.

Eventually, she pulled out the ear buds and small square drive Bastian had given her. She stuffed the buds into her ears and turned the music up until it drowned out the frenetic screaming of her thoughts. The strains of *Clair de Lune* washed over her, easing the strains of the day the way waves might wash away footprints in the sand, until—finally—she slept.

CHAPTER 33

The next morning, her alarm must have blared for a solid five minutes before she woke. Sun and Thalia were moaning, burying their heads under pillows and muttering what was probably a string of creative vulgarities in at least two languages. Nora gathered her things and headed to the shower. The water was soothing. She kept it cool, hoping it would decrease any trace of puffiness around her eyes. She wiped the steam from the mirror—puffiness was satisfactorily minimal—pulled her hair back into a loose braid, and put her earrings back on. Her eyes lingered over the stars for a moment, wondering what her friends were up to. She put her hands on the sink and looked at her reflection in the mirror, at the new determination she was seeing in herself.

There was no way she was letting Thalia get to her. She'd show her—and Bastian, too—that she was above the drama, above the stupid games. She was a pilot in the Ganymede armada, the clone of a revolutionary philosopher, but better than all of that, she was Eleanora Clementine Clark, and she would not back down.

But first, coffee.

Cup in hand, she plastered a bright smile on her face, took a deep breath, and walked onto the Bridge. Asher, Soren, and Donovan were already there. She took over the controls from Soren and set about perfecting their position in the Current. One more day; tomorrow, they'd reach the destination where Thalia said they'd be able to activate the P2 and jump out of hyperspace, hopefully near Terra Prime. In the meantime, Nora was going to go over every command in the console with a fine-toothed comb, leaving nothing to chance.

She used her lunch break to meet up with Soren in the engine room—pointedly ignoring the P2 crew—to make sure every nut and bolt in both engines was ready to go. Silas had kept the engine room in top-notch shape – until Nora blew up half of it. At the thought of the surly engineer, Nora's throat tightened. He hadn't exactly been warm and friendly towards her, but the ship just didn't seem the same without him. Still, the mechanics back on Ganymede had done a beautiful job with the new subluminal engine—though they'd reinforced the fuses, she noted sheepishly.

"Listen, Nora," Soren said, ducking behind one of the engines. Nora followed; back here, with the hum of the engines, the P2 crew wouldn't be able to hear them.

"Yes?"

"You're doing a wonderful job, you know," Soren said. Nora felt a rush of heat to her cheeks.

"We have a saying: a single instrument can play ten thousand songs. The *Rap* sings under you," she said. "But tomorrow, I want you to let Benoit take the console when the P2 is activated."

"Of course," Nora said. Had Soren actually thought that Nora *wanted* that job? It was a moderately terrifying proposition. "I thought that was the plan. I know I've come a long way, thanks to you and Bastian, but I'm not exactly comfortable with exiting hyperspace using an untested device into what is probably a war zone."

Soren swallowed hard, nodding.

"God, I'm sorry Soren. I mean, we'll be scoping out the situation. I'm sure the J'nai are fine. You guys are so strong, and ..."

"It's okay, Cadet," Soren said. "I know what you meant. And you're right. We have no idea what we might be flying into. I just didn't want it to come as a surprise tomorrow or make you feel offended."

"Totally not offended," Nora said. "But I can still watch from the Bridge, right? I'd like to be able to see how the P2 handles, in case it becomes the standard now."

Soren smiled, a little tiredly.

"Of course you can. Now go back to the Bridge," she said, waving toward the door. Nora nodded and turned to leave.

"Oh, and Cadet?" Soren called. Nora was almost at the door. The P2 crew was pretending not to listen in.

"I just want you to know that I think of you as a full member of this crew," she said, her voice clear and loud. She turned her glare on the P2 crew. "And anyone who wants to bother *any one* of my crew members will have me to answer to."

The only sound in the room was the subtle hum of the engines. Even Thalia had stopped. No one spoke. Nora caught Soren's gaze and grinned, thankful.

She went back to the Bridge with a lighter heart than she'd had all day.

The rest of the day passed without incident. Bastian didn't ignore her, exactly, but he certainly didn't go out of his way to talk to her again. She decided it was a good thing, really. Even if she really wanted him to come say hi and brush her hair out of her face like he had the night before. She would not embarrass herself by staring at him or by trying to get him to smile again. She just kept herself busy, her head low, running final checks and helping the crew with errands.

She was profoundly grateful for the business; it kept her mind off certain other things she'd rather be doing. She even managed to get an entire five minutes of sleep that night.

The following morning, tensions were running high. Thalia and her crew were on the Bridge. Soren had taken her seat back, and Bastian sat at the pilot's controls, with Thalia explaining how to activate the program she'd written into the usual exit protocols. Every time she leaned over him, or lay her hand on his arm, Nora wanted to scream. He needed to focus. This was not the time for her games.

Bastian, it seemed, was too absorbed, too focused, to let even Thalia's most desperate antics get to him. He was a razor blade, honed and ready.

Nora was proud of him for that. She took her seat next to him at the pilot's console and strapped herself in.

"Hey, little Hypatia, don't forget your sweet little mixed tape," Thalia said, tossing the ear buds at her. She must have taken them from Nora's cot. Bastian snatched them from mid-air before Nora could even react. There was a long moment where the Bastian and Thalia stared each other down, before Thalia looked away, throwing her long hair back over her shoulder.

"Ms. Jones, countdown to start on your mark," Soren said. She gripped the armrests of the captain's chair, the only clue that she, too, was nervous. Her face was calm, her dark green eyes focused, her voice in control.

"We will be approaching it in a minute," Thalia said, checking read-outs on her tablet. "Turning on the P2 now."

A loud buzz filled the air, and the ship shuddered, like a dog shaking off droplets of water.

"Is that normal?" Soren shouted over the buzz. Nora gripped the console. The shuddering increased. It became a vibration, like the entire ship was a plucked guitar string.

"None of this is normal," Thalia shouted, her fingers flying over her tablet. Nora snuck a glance at Bastian. His lips were a thin line, his knuckles white. Nora swallowed hard. She'd known this trip was dangerous. A thousand million things could go wrong, and yet, she trusted Soren and Bastian to see them through. And as much as she hated Thalia, she at least trusted her skills with electronics and the laws of physics. She had never really entertained the idea that they might not make it through this, that the P2 might fail them. What would they tell Sophie if she didn't return? Would they lie, make up some excuse, a stray asteroid impact maybe? She lamented not telling her roommates the truth. She swore if she ever made it back, she'd never, ever lie to them again.

"It's getting worse!" Donovan shouted, panic in his voice. The P2 crew was freaking out, poring over their tablets and talking in frantic voices. The vibrations increased, knocking a mug off Asher's station and rattling the bolts in the hull. Fear trickled through Nora, tendrils claiming her in grips of icy dread. She'd thought she'd known fear before—fear of failing her midterms last year, fear when she'd left Earth for the unknown infinity of space, fear when Aditi told her she wasn't who she thought she was. Those fears didn't really leave her down-to-her-bones afraid. Not like she was now.

This was what real fear felt like—ice where her stomach once was, her nerves electrified, her senses laser focused on survival, blocking out everything else. She could see every flashing light in the room individually pulsing as if in slow motion, could feel the stir of air where Bastian breathed beside her. Panic like nothing she'd ever experienced gripped her; there was no escaping this. Her heart hammered a *prestissimo* beat in her ears. Some animal instinct inside of her screamed, but it was no use. There was nothing she could do.

"She can't take much more of this," Asher warned. A split second later, a siren sounded over the buzzing, and red emergency lights flared overhead.

"Just a few more seconds!" Thalia shouted. "Bastian, on my mark!"

The rocking intensified. Red alerts popped up on the console faster than Nora could read them. Something somewhere started hissing, gas escaping as the ship tried to tear itself apart.

"In FIVE...FOUR..."

A teeth-rattling shake tore open the ceiling panels, exposing wires that popped and cracked overhead, sending little showers of sparks through the red-lit room.

"THREE...TWO..."

Bastian's hands were poised over the controls, his body coiled like a spring.

"ONE...NOW! NOW NOW NOW!" Thalia shouted. Bastian slammed on the P2 engines, the equivalent of throwing a parking brake while driving one hundred miles per hour as he tried to maintain control and keep the ship's engines and steering from pulling it in a million different directions. The ship groaned; something overhead popped with a sickening crunch. A scream erupted behind her. The ship lurched heavily to the side, throwing Nora hard against her restraining harness.

Then everything went dark.

But she was still breathing. She couldn't see anything, but she could breathe. Her chest hurt from the harness, and something heavy was laying over her, but she was breathing. That meant she couldn't be dead. Right?

The emergency lights flickered on, bathing the room in a soft red glow. Smoke was coming from the ceiling. Asher and Soren were talking loudly in J'nai.

Nora struggled to right herself in her chair. The straps were cutting into her chest and arms, and something—Bastian. He grabbed her harness and pulled, getting her upright. He'd been the weight on her. He had either fallen or thrown himself on top of her when they'd exited hyperspace.

They must be out of the Current. She couldn't hear the hyperspace engines. The ship had stopped shaking.

It had worked!

The realization brought a surprised grin to her face, and when she turned, she saw Bastian was smiling, too, his face an inch away from hers. His eyes glowed like stars in the dim light of the bridge. They'd made it.

Forget putting the mission first, forget waiting until they got home from this mess. He was going to kiss her. Now. The fear she'd felt just seconds ago melted away, nothing more than a distant memory. God, she wanted to kiss him so badly it throbbed in her chest like a pounding drum. She couldn't breathe.

"We fried the P2," she heard Thalia groan, as if from a great distance. Thalia slammed her tablet against the wall and screamed, a primal roar of frustration. Nora jumped at the sound, and Bastian looked up, the spell broken.

Nora sat back, sighing. She unstrapped her harness and rubbed her shoulder where the nylon had dug into her. So much for *carpe diem*. Bastian quickly looked her over and, certain she was in one piece, went back to his console to check the status of the engines.

"Where are we?" Soren said. "I don't see Terra Prime. I don't see the fleet."

"This isn't like driving a car, you know," Thalia said. "We figured as much as a 0.001 percent error would be acceptable, given our time constraints."

"Which could still put us light years from our destination," Donovan moaned. "And the sublum is all jacked up, thanks to your stupid port-a-port."

"Soren can take a look at the engine," Asher said, looking at his console. "If she can get us back to hyperspace, we can still use the Jupiter port to get home after I figure out where we are. All we have to do is…"

"Figure out how to get around *that*," Soren said.

Everyone looked up.

A hundred Qaig ships appeared before them out of thin air, hovering like vultures over a dying animal.

And each one had its guns pointed directly at the *Rapscallion*.

END